"Kristy Cambron has long delighted readers with her richly textured tales of epic historical episodes and the intimate, intricate workings of the human heart. In her latest work, *The British Booksellers*, Cambron delivers yet again, with her powerful punch of assiduous research and skillful, lush storytelling. Sweeping across generations and both World Wars, this is a luminous ode to the soul's deep and indelible yearning for love, hope, and truth."

—ALLISON PATAKI, *NEW YORK TIMES* BESTSELLING AUTHOR OF *FINDING MARGARET FULLER*

"With pitch-perfect prose and impeccable research, Kristy Cambron brings to life the Forgotten Blitz bombings of World War II—and shines a light on the ways in which we find hope in even the darkest moments. A testament to bravery, loss, and the power story has to unite us, *The British Booksellers* will steal readers' hearts. This stunning novel is a poignant reminder of the indomitable nature of the human spirit and the enduring power of true love. Five huge stars!"

—KRISTY WOODSON HARVEY, *NEW YORK TIMES* BESTSELLING AUTHOR OF *THE SUMMER OF SONGBIRDS*

"From page one, the dynamic, endearing characters in *The British Booksellers* stole my heart. Kristy Cambron is an assured storyteller, weaving together dual periods and complex family structures with ease. Fans of *Downton Abbey* will adore *The British Booksellers*."

—ERIKA ROBUCK, NATIONAL BESTSELLING AUTHOR OF *SISTERS OF NIGHT AND FOG*

"Set in the English countryside and spanning two wars, Kristy Cambron's latest, *The British Booksellers*, is a beautiful and enlightening novel that captures the lost love and youthful dreams of two unlikely soulmates, Charlotte and Amos. Full of longing and sprinkled with literary gems, I was completely swept away with this enchanting tale."

—NICOLA HARRISON, AUTHOR OF *HOTEL LAGUNA*

"Impeccably researched and highly inspirational, *The Italian Ballerina* shows the complex political and human plight of those fighting for freedom in World War II Italy and how personal sacrifice and daring can have an impact on generations to come. Cambron uses her considerable talents as a writer of historical fiction to bring to life a large cast of characters scattered across the globe in several different time periods, each of the 'good guys' someone we would be honoured to call a friend. An uplifting tale that educates, energizes, and comforts the reader. I was captivated from its enigmatic, action-packed beginning to its most wonderfully satisfying end."

—NATALIE JENNER, AUTHOR OF THE INTERNATIONAL BESTSELLER
THE JANE AUSTEN SOCIETY AND *THE BLOOMSBURY GIRLS*

"Incredibly researched and emotionally evocative, Cambron—once again—takes us into the depths of war as well as to the heights of love, bravery, sacrifice, and devotion. I thoroughly enjoyed every moment within this story and must warn readers—you'll completely lose your heart to young Calla. Enjoy!"

—KATHERINE REAY, BESTSELLING AUTHOR OF *THE PRINTED LETTER BOOKSHOP*
AND *THE LONDON HOUSE*, FOR *THE ITALIAN BALLERINA*

"With rare insight and remarkable finesse, Cambron excavates the forgotten fragments of history and crafts them into a sweeping masterpiece. Encompassing decades and inspired by a true story of extraordinary audacity, *The Italian Ballerina* explores how the ripples of the past merge with the present and reminds us of the capacity of ordinary individuals to rise against darkness and leave a legacy that outlasts their generation. Intricate and transportive, soaring and deeply resonant, this is Cambron at her finest."

—AMANDA BARRATT, CHRISTY AWARD–WINNING AUTHOR
OF *THE WHITE ROSE RESISTS*

"Gripping and atmospheric, *The Italian Ballerina* explores the collective, intercontinental strength and struggle of those brave men and women who stood up against injustice to end the horrors of World War II. Cambron centers her story on civilians transformed to heroes—the prima ballerina turned nurse, the farmer turned medic, the small child turned pillar of strength, the soccer star turned caretaker—and readers are reminded that there are no small parts in this life. Though Cambron shines a spotlight on the vileness of hatred and war, she equally illuminates and emphasizes the way an 'ordinary' gift, if used, can be a lifeline to hope for generations. Awash with vivid characters and exceptionally well-researched, *The Italian Ballerina* is an outstanding work of historical fiction."

—JOY CALLAWAY, INTERNATIONAL BESTSELLING
AUTHOR OF *THE GRAND DESIGN*

"Poignant and inspirational, *The Italian Ballerina* captured my heart and wouldn't let go. Told in a non-linear style, the stories of Court and Julia in the past and Delaney in the present are woven into the life of Calla, a little Jewish girl caught in the horrors of World War II. Cambron's extensive research is evident, but it is the individual journeys of the characters that make this book special."

—ROBIN LEE HATCHER, CHRISTY AWARD–WINNING
AUTHOR OF *I'LL BE SEEING YOU*

"Based on true events, this exquisite tale impresses with its historical and emotional authenticity. Historical fiction fans won't want to miss this."

—*PUBLISHERS WEEKLY*, STARRED REVIEW, FOR *THE PARIS DRESSMAKER*

"Told with precise details of the Nazi occupation of Paris, the story moves swiftly along, alternating between Lila's story and Sandrine's. The pacing is good, the characters entirely believable, and the revelations of the French underground's workings are fascinating."

—HISTORICAL NOVEL SOCIETY FOR *THE PARIS DRESSMAKER*

"In the timeless fashion of Chanel, Ricci, and Dior, Cambron delivers another masterpiece in *The Paris Dressmaker*. Penned with unimaginable heartache, unforgettable romance, and cheering defiance against the oppression the Nazis inflicted on Paris, readers will be swept away into a story where battle-scarred good at last rings victory over evil. *Tres magnifique.*"

—J'NELL CIESIELSKI, AUTHOR OF *THE SOCIALITE*

"Kristy Cambron's masterful skill at weaving historical detail into a compelling story graces every page of *The Paris Dressmaker*. A thoroughly satisfying blend of memorable characters, evocative writing, and wartime drama that seamlessly transports you to the City of Light at its most desperate hour. Well done!"

—SUSAN MEISSNER, BESTSELLING AUTHOR OF
THE NATURE OF FRAGILE THINGS

"Rich with evocative descriptions of Paris and harrowing details of life during the German occupation, *The Paris Dressmaker* satisfies on all levels. *Tres magnifique!*"

—SARAH SUNDIN, BESTSELLING AND AWARD-WINNING
AUTHOR OF *UNTIL LEAVES FALL IN PARIS*

"Destined to delight fans of Melanie Dobson and Natasha Lester, *The Paris Dressmaker* is a well-researched and beautifully interwoven treatise on courage and conviction in the midst of oppression."

—RACHEL MCMILLAN, AUTHOR OF *THE LONDON RESTORATION* AND *THE MOZART CODE*

"Cambron rises to a new level with this intriguing, well-written story of love and triumph."

—RACHEL HAUCK, *NEW YORK TIMES* BESTSELLING AUTHOR, FOR *THE PARIS DRESSMAKER*

"Stunning. With as much skill and care as the title's namesake possesses, *The Paris Dressmaker* weaves together the stories of two heroines who boldly defy the darkness that descends on the City of Light. This is Cambron at her very finest. A luminous must-read, and a timeless reminder that light conquers dark."

—JOCELYN GREEN, CHRISTY AWARD–WINNING AUTHOR OF *SHADOWS OF THE WHITE CITY*

"Another page-turner! Kristy Cambron will enthrall readers with this gripping tale."

—KATE BRESLIN, BESTSELLING AUTHOR OF *FAR SIDE OF THE SEA*, FOR *THE PAINTED CASTLE*

"Meticulously researched, intricately plotted, and elegantly written, Kristy Cambron weaves a haunting yet heartwarming tale that spans generations. Highly recommended!"

—SARAH E. LADD, BESTSELLING AUTHOR OF *THE LETTER FROM BRIARTON PARK*, FOR *THE PAINTED CASTLE*

"Enchanting and mesmerizing! *Castle on the Rise* enters an alluring land and time with a tale to be treasured."

—PATTI CALLAHAN, *NEW YORK TIMES* BESTSELLING AUTHOR OF *BECOMING MRS. LEWIS*

"Cambron's lithe prose pulls together past and present, and her attention to historical detail grounds the narrative to the last breathtaking moments."

—*PUBLISHERS WEEKLY*, STARRED REVIEW, FOR *THE ILLUSIONIST'S APPRENTICE*

"With rich descriptions, attention to detail, mesmerizing characters, and an understated current of faith, this work evokes writers such as Kim Vogel Sawyer, Francine Rivers, and Sara Gruen."

—*LIBRARY JOURNAL*, STARRED REVIEW, FOR *THE RINGMASTER'S WIFE*

The

BRITISH
BOOKSELLERS

The
BRITISH
BOOKSELLERS

A NOVEL OF THE FORGOTTEN BLITZ

KRISTY
CAMBRON

THOMAS NELSON
Since 1798

Published in Nashville, Tennessee, by Thomas Nelson. Thomas Nelson is a registered trademark of HarperCollins Christian Publishing, Inc.

Published in association with the Books & Such Literary Management, 52 Mission Circle, Suite 122, PMB 170, Santa Rosa, California 95409–5370, www.booksandsuch.com.

Thomas Nelson titles may be purchased in bulk for educational, business, fundraising, or sales promotional use. For information, please email SpecialMarkets@ThomasNelson.com.

Chapter opener art © Vector Tradition / Adobe Stock

Library of Congress Cataloging-in-Publication Data

Names: Cambron, Kristy, author.
Title: The British booksellers: a novel of the Forgotten Blitz / Kristy Cambron.
Description: Nashville, Tennessee: Thomas Nelson, 2024. | Summary: "Based on real accounts of Britain's Land Girls and the Forgotten Blitz, The British Booksellers highlights the courageous choices we must make to live, love, and - in the face of all that tests us - fight for what matters most"--Provided by publisher.
Identifiers: LCCN 2023043342 (print) | LCCN 2023043343 (ebook) | ISBN 9780785232247 (paperback) | ISBN 9780785232254 (epub)
Subjects: LCSH: Women's Land Army (Great Britain)--Fiction. | World War, 1939-1945--England--Fiction. | World War, 1939-1945--Aerial operations, German--Fiction. | Coventry (England)--Fiction. | LCGFT: War fiction. | Novels.
Classification: LCC PS3603.A4468 B75 2024 (print) | LCC PS3603.A4468 (ebook) | DDC 813/.6--dc23/eng/20231010
LC record available at https://lccn.loc.gov/2023043342
LC ebook record available at https://lccn.loc.gov/2023043343

Printed in the United States of America

24 25 26 27 28 LBC 6 5 4 3 2

For the booksellers—
readers, writers, waymakers, and friends.
A heartfelt thank-you for the stories we've shared.

GLOSSARY

AFS: Auxiliary Fire Service

ARP: Air Raid Precautions

BEF: British Expeditionary Force

Ha-ha wall: A low wall with a ditch just in front of it, keeping grazing animals out of more formal gardens while maintaining a view of the surrounding landscape

HE: High Explosive

RAF: Royal Air Force

SMLE: Short Magazine Lee-Enfield rifle

WLA: Women's Land Army

Time, consoler of affliction and softener of anger.
—Charles Dickens, *Dombey and Son*

PROLOGUE

17 October 1908
Broadgate
Coventry, England

*H*ow many times in life could a boy say he was risking his
neck, doing the very last thing he'd expected . . . for a girl?

It was a first for Amos Darby, pounding on a shopkeeper's door
to convince the old man to open up after dark. But to find himself standing in Coventry's most eccentric secondhand shop in the
market square to sell a lady's property from a steamer trunk? Unimaginable. He'd not have believed it, save for the curiosities on all
sides—a wall of clocks with mismatched chimes, towering book
stacks, ladies' hats teetering dangerously close to the edge of the
counter, and a moody raven chittering behind the brass bars of
his cage—and the old shopkeeper taking his sweet time to inspect
what Amos had brought in.

The plan to be in and out in ten minutes flat had been sorely
tested.

If only he'd known that making it out of the shop would be the
easy part. Now Amos very nearly regretted winning the cat-and-
mouse game of haggling over the gilded goods. By the time he'd
hauled the wooden cello case and a canvas bag full of books he'd
bartered down the length of the cobblestone street, he'd passed the
confectioner, tobacconist, and greengrocer shops back to Greyfriars
Lane with arms screaming all the way.

The carriage waited right where he'd left it, in the shadows of the alley untouched by the glow of gas streetlamps.

A quick peek over his shoulder—praise be no one was about to notice them in the twilight—and Amos rapped on the door. Charlotte poked her head around the curtain. And then, as if it had appeared by magic, her face brightened when she set eyes on the hefty brown instrument case leaning into his side.

The door flung wide on crying hinges. Charlotte pushed her riding cloak back off her arms to better reach for the cello. "Oh, I can't believe it actually worked! He bought it all?"

"Everything, including your trunk. Here." Amos eased the messenger bag strap from his aching shoulder and dropped the load onto the carriage floor. "You can thank me later. Just help me get this thing inside, and let's get out of here before we're spotted."

This friend of his—golden hair and eyes both, bright as her infectious smile—seemed completely undone by the mere presence of the instrument. Charlotte set about angling the case so she might open it right then and there. And while Amos would have enjoyed nothing more than to let her, those clocks on the shop wall were still ticking.

"We've no time, Charlie." Amos referenced the pet name he'd whittled down from "Lady Charlotte Terrington" some years prior. He climbed in and sat across from her, latched the door, and tapped his boot on the floor to signal the driver it was time to make tracks. "You're certain the coachman will keep this to himself?"

The carriage lurched, and they were on their way to the outskirts of the city, back toward her family's estate.

"Of course. He'd never betray us. I've been a pet of his since the day I was born."

Satisfied for the moment, Amos nodded and leaned deeper into the seat cushion, plush velvet allowing him to rest taxed limbs. And breathe. And try not to wonder what had just occurred to him as Charlotte inspected the rosewood case in her arms . . .

Was she a sort of pet to Amos? Or worse, was he a mere pet to her too?

How else could this little slip of a twelve-year-old heiress convince a farmer's son, only three years older than she, to barter designer gowns to buy back the beloved cello her mother had sold? And he to obtain books he'd never have been able to afford in his lifetime? Amos had no answers. All he knew was by some miracle, they'd not been discovered—neither for this mad excursion to the city nor for the secret friendship they'd kept up since childhood.

"If your mother finds out I sold your dresses . . ."

"She won't. And you didn't—*I* sold them."

"And if she sees them in the shop window tomorrow?"

"Mother never comes into Coventry. Besides, I've so many she'll never notice they're gone. Only my maid would, and she won't tell. Especially if I slip her a little something extra from our next London shopping excursion."

Charlotte waved the notion off, then went back to hugging the top of the case against her shoulder. She'd not soon let it go again.

"What did I tell you? Designer names like *Worth* and *Lucile* would be enough to convince the shopkeeper you knew more than he on the matter of their value. And here is my treasure, back in my arms. How can I ever thank you?"

"No need," Amos whispered, smiling to himself. "It was more your doing than mine anyway. I didn't know half of what I was saying about the cello, countering the shopkeeper with 'It's a Betts, but not a Stradivari model . . .'"

Charlotte was cleverer than her privileged upbringing gave her credit for. She had tracked down the shop her mother had sold the cello to, convinced their coachman to take them all the way into Coventry to fetch the valuable cello back, and feigned a headache so she and Amos could slip away while the earl and countess entertained manor guests for dinner. It was a plan worth appreciating, even if he'd have a crick in his neck and sore biceps the rest of the week.

"All I had to do was cast your lot's posh speech out and the shopkeeper bit. Pride convinced him he needed what Hanover's shop didn't have down the street, more than holding on to a used cello and some old books."

"Yes—the books! I'd nearly forgotten." She gazed down at the prize in the canvas lump at their feet. "What did you get us?"

"Everything you asked for: Jane Austen, Emily Dickinson, the Brontës, Keats, and Kipling, though your mother wouldn't approve."

"Indeed she would not approve of a young lady filling her head with frivolities from romance novels when she could be learning the noble art of how to marry well. She doesn't see that Austen could actually be an instruction manual toward that end." Charlotte shifted the cello to one side and pulled a volume free from the bag. "*Dombey and Son.*"

"Got a few I wanted too. For the risk, of course. If I'm going to own a shop one day—"

"*We're* going to own it." She tipped her brow. "Remember? An even split. That's what we said."

"Aye. If we're going to own a bookshop, we'd better read what we sell. Dickens seemed as good a place to start as any."

"I'd have advocated for Austen." She tried to look stern but gave up and softened her lips into a smile as she handed the book over. "But seeing as you've returned my treasure today, I cannot be cross. Though I won't sleep until I can slip away to the glasshouse and play all day tomorrow." She paused, then with a softer tone asked, "You will meet me?"

"I'll be there."

The glasshouse—their hideaway near Amos's farm on Holt Manor, in the garden bordering Charlotte's family estate. It would be the perfect hiding spot for the cello her mother claimed was unseemly for a young lady of breeding. And it would shelter the books Amos's da said a farmer's son had no business wasting time over. But what did parents know? They believed each child had a position in the hierarchy of life and ought to know what it was.

Yet despite this, Charlotte and Amos had always managed to find a certain freedom in each other's company—she playing the cello to her heart's content, and he reading their books aloud. And neither thinking of how those days were numbered as calendar dates rolled by. Or how contentment was simple, and neither a palace of plenty nor a humble farmhouse could define it.

Amos's gaze drifted to the calloused hands in his lap without realization. When he felt her eyes upon him, he looked up and crossed his arms over his chest to hide rough palms. Charlotte stared back with her index finger tapping a silent melody against the cello case, her gaze flat rather than delighted as she'd been mere moments before.

"What's wrong? I thought you'd be overjoyed right now."

"Do you wish to be a farmer?"

Sighing, he stretched long legs out on the bench, one over the other, the patch at his knee visible even in the shadows. "We don't need to talk about this now. Just be cheered by your prize."

His russet crown was already north of six feet; Amos knew he could pass for older. That—and the confidence of a steely glare— might have bought him bargaining power in the secondhand shop. But a permanent line of dirt under his fingernails and patched trousers didn't lie. Even inside a darkened carriage. A tenant farmer's son had no business dreaming beyond their childhood days, no matter how much he might have liked to with the earl's daughter, who wore Worth and Lucile and hatched harebrained schemes in her spare time.

"Do you?"

Easy to see she wouldn't back down. "Fine. No—I don't want to be a farmer."

"Yet you plan to take over your father's tenancy one day."

He shrugged. "Who else will do it?"

"I've borrowed nearly every book in my father's library for you. And you read more than any tutor I've ever had. Probably know more too. Why wouldn't you at least try to receive a formal education?"

"And with what living would I pay for it?" Amos laughed at the absurdity of her thinking such a thing could be possible for someone like him. "With a farmer from Newcastle as a da and a Coventry farmer's daughter for a mum? Some of us are destined to our lives before we're even born. I don't cry over it; it's just the way it is."

Charlotte leaned forward and, in her youthful way, could see none of the obstacles that required Amos to spend grueling hours in the fields day in, day out. She couldn't understand such things while walking a manor's gilded halls or enjoying London shopping trips with endless streams of coin from the family coffers.

Theirs was a chasm between worlds. She couldn't see so far to the other side.

"'Books are an escape that beckons the reader from the heavy burdens of this world.' Isn't that what you told me once? They can challenge as well as comfort. Entertain and educate. Even save us in ways we'd never expect. You've used the words *art, oxygen,* and *life* all to describe them. Anyone who can see such value in these pages ought to also see that they could take him away from a future he doesn't want. If anything, that is what Dickens wrote for his characters. Isn't that what you wish for yourself?"

"I said all that?" Though he knew he had. Amos cupped his hands behind his head, his casual gaze attempting to defy every word. "Sounds rather poetic for someone like me. Perhaps I should read the Keats first."

"I am perfectly serious, Amos."

"As am I." He gave her a shot of the same direct tone she'd handed him. "What would you have me do, Charlie? How could you possibly understand a future already planned out?"

Charlotte furrowed her brow a bit to register the jibe had hit its mark and lifted the edge of her skirt, questioning his choice of words.

Bad form, Amos.

"Right. My apologies." The last thing they needed was a quarrel over a girl's place in society when they each had constraints pressing on all sides. "You do understand. More than I could in your shoes, I suspect. But I have no trunks to sell. All I meant was we'll grow up one day and may be forced to accept things as they are. And that's why we'll meet at the glasshouse. I'll read my books. You'll play your cello. As long as we can until reality sobers those dreams."

She turned to the window, watching the landscape pass by under the shades of an ink sky and sprinkle of stars inhabiting it. "I still hope we never give up dreaming."

"Even if we both know where our roads take us?"

"And where is that?"

Amos smiled. Always did when he was with Charlie—the heiress who hadn't a clue of the things he didn't say. That their shared dream was what kept him going. And he'd already decided, deep down, if ever there was a boy who'd risk his neck for a girl more than once in his lifetime, even over and over again, it would be him for her.

All she had to do was ask.

"For now? Home—no matter what tomorrow brings."

CHAPTER ONE

24 December 1913
Brinklow Road
Coventry, England

*I*f the party had started . . . his goose was cooked.

It was a small consolation that Charlotte's family hadn't decided to hold a Christmas celebration at neighboring Terrington Hall, or Amos surely would have been spotted from the road. As it was, not a soul passed by as he led the packhorse to cut across the field on foot, toward the golden glow of Holt Manor, standing guard on the hill overlooking Brinklow Road.

Arriving late on the night of a Holt Manor party was never done. But to arrive at half past—frozen stiff with livery drenched in mud—was by all accounts unacceptable. Especially if Amos wanted to keep his position as footman for parties at the big house. The only plan now was to slip through the service door at the back of the manor and, by some miracle, do it unnoticed.

Amos checked around as he trudged into the yard, the horse stamping its hooves behind him. He patted the poor beast, led it to the cover of the larder awning, and stopped to blow his breath into curled fists.

Anything to warm up, even if the cloud turned to frozen fog.

"Oy! Where you been?"

Amos turned at the cockney shout to find snowflakes gathered on Tate Fitzgibbons's baker boy hat and jacket, tweed-covered arms weighted down with a crate of produce from the larder. Lemons and carrot stalks hung over the top of wooden slats, blowing in the wind as the junior footman balanced the load and curled his ankle around the door to kick it closed.

Tate gave them a once-over ending in a squinched face at Amos's presentation. "What happened then?"

"Cow was calving at Mum's. Thought I could get it sorted and be back in time for the party."

"No luck?"

Amos shook his head. "A broken axle sent us off the bridge into the bog. Had to leave the trap in the ditch and walk this poor chap the rest of the way over. I couldn't leave him out there to his death."

"Oh, mate." Tate rolled his eyes heavenward, understanding the working-class life all too well, even if he'd come from London's dockworker trade. "I knew that rubbish rig was goin' to be your downfall one day."

"Not today. I need this position."

Adjusting the load in his arms, the younger footman cast a fleeting glance to the service door. "I told 'em you were polishing a silver serving tray for the party. I knew you took care of that yesterday, so it'd give you a few more ticks on the clock to get here. And with rumor of some big announcement from His Lordship tonight, they wouldn't notice the kitchen burnin' down, let alone a tardy footman and his horse wanderin' into the yard."

"Praise be for that." Amos got the poor old horse settled in the shelter, tying him up in a stall, then swiped a carrot for the animal from Tate's load and gave the horse a right good rub of the nose for being such a sport about it all. "What announcement?"

"Heaven knows. Something to do with the toffs. Here." Tate adjusted the load long enough to dig in his pocket and pull a key ring from his pocket. "I swiped the key to the silver cabinet. Get what you need for the party, then get out again quick as scat. And don't show up in the dining room lookin' as you do, or we'll both be queuin' at Daimler's hiring line come morn."

Amos slipped the key ring into his pocket. "Thanks, mate. I

keep a spare livery put by, so here's hoping it's enough. I don't have the foggiest idea what to do about shoes, though."

"Shoes are the least of your worries. Come on," Tate countered, and he led Amos toward the glow of the kitchen windows. "I don't know where we can put you where staff won't see. The house is full up for the holidays, and lookie-loo valets and ladies' maids have taken up every spare corner of the servants' level."

"Then I'll change in the alcove of the downstairs library." Amos yanked the mud-caked bow tie from his neck with one hand as he followed. "Dark rugs and neglect ought to keep anyone from knowing I went that way. I've done it before."

"And if you're caught?"

"In an unused library? Not likely." Amos shrugged like it didn't matter, though they both knew it did. "But if I am, then you'll have to be promoted to first footman."

"You know I wouldn't take it. I'd rather make gum shoes in the factory than have to serve all these pompous nobs for the rest of me days. And certainly not without you to help endure it. Get on with you now." Tate tilted his head toward the service door and led the way back. "I'll distract Mrs. Cartwright until you show up in her kitchen with an extra platter in hand. Just be quick about it, yeah? And get that key back on its hook."

That should be the end of it.

Amos ought to find the library empty—it had only ever contained marble busts and the ghosts of past lords framed on the walls to witness what had become his would-be dressing room whenever he was in a pinch. He peeled off his wet shirt and stuffed it in the hiding place behind a row of books on a corner shelf. Then shook out the fresh one with a wave of crisp linen floating on air.

"Ah, Da." Amos sighed. Slipped arms in. And gave a hasty fasten to the cuffs. "What would you think of your son bowing and scraping to a bunch of toffee-nosed peers? Praise be you're not here to see it."

"*Oh*—I am sorry."

Amos froze. Swallowed hard. And, grateful he hadn't dropped trousers, turned toward the soft voice. Like a punch to the gut, he found Lady Charlotte Terrington by the window behind the grand piano, trussed up in some crystal gown illuminated by moonlight and a diamond-studded crown thing holding her hair back.

As soon as their eyes met, she turned away, her gaze reverting to the play of snowfall drifting beyond the glass. Propriety, it seemed, made her realize a half-clothed man and a woman alone in the same library would be fatal should anyone discover them. Even if their meeting was an innocent run-in between old friends.

He turned his back and began a hasty button down the front of his livery shirt. "What are you doing here, Charlie? Shouldn't you be dancing somewhere?"

"I didn't know anyone was in this room or I wouldn't have . . . ," she whispered, and then laughed. Actually laughed! Amos shot a glance over his shoulder as he fumbled with the livery buttons, hurrying only so he might protect her reputation. And all she could do was raise a gloved hand to her lips and try to cover that she found it terribly funny.

Rankled, Amos pulled the livery jacket free from the shelf, giving it a good shake to air out. "Something amusing?"

"No. I'm sorry. Truly. I just . . ." She cleared her throat and checked her composure, straightening her shoulders to start again. "I thought the trousers were going to make this a bit of an awkward moment. You know—even if it is an unexpected reunion between childhood friends."

"Not much of a reunion when you saw me across the fields last week." He shook his head, hoping she got the hint of hurry in his tone. "And you don't see me now, or I'm in a heap of trouble if I don't appear in the dining hall in the next few minutes."

"So . . . toffee-nosed, was it?"

"I didn't know anyone was here. I should have minded my tongue."

"But surely not your thoughts." Charlotte half turned. Peeked.

Found him clothed and turned the rest of the way again, looking back as the shadows of falling snow were cast over the side of her face. "Is that how you view me?"

"You know I don't. But this is . . ." He stared at her, all trussed up in ballroom attire for the Holts' grand Christmas to-do. And he, about to put on gloves to serve them. "Things are different. You're Lady Charlotte tonight. And I'm the help."

"I don't recall you using titles when we used to hide away at the glasshouse. Don't tell me you've forgotten."

"How could I?" He laughed, the memories of childhood still kind. "Da gave me a dressing down when he learned I was skipping out on chores to spend time with you. I never did find out if it was because he cared after the livestock, or more that I was daring to expose His Lordship's daughter to books that told her she could think for herself."

"Yes. And when my governess found me with the cello, Mother threatened me with being locked away in a tower for the rest of my days after such a breach in decorum. Even if my father relented and let me keep it, if I promised never to play in public again." Her smile faded. And even with the gaiety of party music lingering in the background, the air grew solemn. "I'm so sorry for your loss, Amos."

And she did—sound sorry, that is.

Everyone of a certain class knew his da. Brendan Darby had been a fixture at the Lion's Gate pub, in the fields he plowed for the Lord Holt at the estate adjoining hers, and in Coventry town long as anybody could remember. It wasn't fodder for talk in an upscale ladies' parlor, though, that a poor farmer had been laid in his grave months ago. How could she know?

"Thank you."

"Please, will you convey my condolences to your mother?"

"I will."

The mantel clock cut the air between them, its melodic chime filling the room.

Amos looked to the glow of light from the party at the bottom of the library's double doors. The string quartet still played, but it wouldn't be much longer before dinner was served. He'd have to make tracks if he was going to beat it.

"Oh yes. The time." Charlotte trailed a fingertip along the polished wood of the sofa back as she took hurried steps toward the door. "I'm afraid I needed some air from the party and found my way in here, looking for the book I'd misplaced. But seeing as I've now stumbled into a gentleman's . . . uh, solitude, I'll leave you to it."

Amos held firm. Stared back. "Which book?"

Charlotte let her fingertips drift from the doorknob and turned to face him. "*Dombey and Son*."

"I should have known."

"You remember our adventure to Coventry that time we came away with our first copy?" She smiled—that same genuine one that had always existed between them. Even as a young man, Amos had known it was an honor to receive a smile like that from her, because it was honest. And hard-won. And he'd believed once that a man could live from one blessed moment to the next, just on the hope she'd bestow it one more time.

"Aye." *Of course I do.*

The Dickens novel had become their favorite escape. And with it, their own private world reading volumes of Shakespeare. Milton, Kipling, and Keats. The Brontës. Emily Dickinson and Jane Austen—the latter which he could barely stomach, if truth be told. Save for that Charlotte doted on *Emma* and *Pride and Prejudice*, and that meant they were trifles he'd forced himself to endure.

Amos much preferred *Waverley*, being that Sir Walter Scott penned adventures a man could feel stirring down to his bones— even if Charlotte maintained the opening chapters were a snooze compared to the wit and high-stakes world of the Regency marriage market in Austen's novels.

It had remained the only disagreement between them.

They'd sit in the glasshouse by the rose garden, the old structure keeping them tucked away in the poplar grove, nestled behind the blackthorn wall that cut the Holts' and Terringtons' land. Their backs leaning against patina glass to hide from the prying eyes of governesses and well-to-do parents, they'd enjoy the satire and humor of their favorite author, who had always been Dickens.

Charlotte had never made Amos feel less-than for having seen the underbelly of Dickens's world. And even for the gritty reality in the pages, the novels were able to draw them together like equals through vivid stories and characters and brilliantly wrought words. She'd sit in silence as he read aloud, picking at wildflower petals from seed pots. And Amos would tend the mini garden they'd grown in the glasshouse while she practiced her favorite Bach arrangements on the cello, the fumbling of notes for only him and stray starlings to hear.

"Do you remember that day in the glasshouse, when we finished the book for the first time? You were holding it when you promised we wouldn't give up on our dream to—"

"Own a bookshop one day. I remember."

She nodded, keeping her smile, as if the memories were still warm. "Half the shop would have a reading room where we'd keep my books—the ones all the customers would wish to buy. And yours could be on the other side."

"You mean the side with the titles no one wants to read?"

She shook her head. "Perhaps they're the ones the rest of us *should* read, if we were brave enough to venture outside of Austen's wit."

"And you were going to play the cello for heads of state in the world's grandest concert halls. Have your name in electric lights and all that." Those eyes turned sad, and Charlotte looked down for a breath, like her gaze needed a place to land. "Well, it's a fine story. And all the more difficult to let go."

"Yes. It is. I'm sure I'll find the book somewhere." She turned away, opened the door, and peeked into the hall. "Shall I ask the quartet to play a song or two before we move into the dining room? Would that give you enough time to . . . do what you must?"

"I'd appreciate that. Thank you."

Light from the hall sparkled against the diamonds in her hair as she cracked the door but lingered with a gloved hand fused to the knob.

She looked back, that heart-stopping smile warming every inch of his insides as she whispered a final "Merry Christmas, Amos."

He stared at the closed oak door for long seconds after she'd slipped through.

Merry Christmas, Charlie.

To let go of a beautiful story like that? Yes. It had been difficult. More difficult than she could ever know.

→·←

11 October 1940
Bayley Lane
Coventry, England

The brass bell chimed over the shop door.

Amos looked up from the books in the back office of Waverley Novels and swiped his pocket watch from his waistcoat, jamming his thumb against the etched knob. The cover popped, revealing the engraved initials on the inside and storybook designs of sun, moon, and stars ticking up to the three o'clock hour in a colorful arc over its gold-rimmed face.

The headache of it all.

A customer at five minutes to close . . .

All of Coventry knew shops closed doors early to contend with the blackouts. Couldn't customers come in at a decent hour? Or was it only when a man wished to lock his doors and rest weary bones by a warm fireplace that they decided it was time to have the latest bestselling title in hand?

He shoved the timepiece in his waistcoat pocket and turned back to the page, trying to account for figures that refused to match up.

A blustery day with intermittent bouts of drenching rain meant the bookshop had seen precious few customers. And while Amos would rather have sent this one straight out the front door again for the grand annoyance of it all, something in him couldn't see fair enough to do it. Not when Eden Books across the way would certainly welcome a disgruntled customer from his shop. Charlotte would probably make the poor sod a cup of tea and set him up in that gilded reading room of hers for as long as he wished to linger.

Lose even one customer to the Holts?

Amos couldn't have that. Best let the customer look. Find their title. And trust them to read the posted sign to leave the money by the register so he could keep to the solitude of the back office.

"Hello?"

The customer's shout caused Amos to scratch a jagged line through the figures he'd been working. He growled against having to give the column an eraser, the numbers muddling into a smudge of graphite on the page.

The customer gave a cheery *knock-knock* against the front counter. "Anyone there?"

Amos gave up, tossing the pencil in the binding before draining the last trace of amber liquid from the tumbler on his desk. He corked the Glenlivet and, together with the glass and accounts book, tucked all in the hidden hollow of the bottom desk drawer. The Scotch bottle gave its usual sound of rolling back into place when he closed it up.

Dusting his palms against wool trousers as he stood, Amos tromped down the hall, the aged hardwoods groaning under the weight of each surly step.

"Aye," Amos called out, watching the young man from the edge of the shadows under the stairs, and pointed to the sign hooked to the register: *We Close at 3:00 Sharp.* "But we're about to close up. The blackouts, you see."

Amos eyed the stranger. Waiting. Annoyed. Then shifted to wondering after the fact that Coventry folk in their twenties didn't dress like they'd just come from dinner at Buckingham Palace. Even with the rain having doused the lad's trench and blond hair peeking out the back of a charcoal trilby, he'd obviously come from the gilded side of some palace gates.

"Oh—yes. Blackouts. Of course." The lad cleared his throat and gave a fleeting glance to the corners of the shop, as if checking they were alone. "I was told the bookshop on Bayley Lane is owned by the Holts. Is this true?"

"Aye. The Holts."

"Good. I wonder if I might speak with Miss Eden Holt then." A stranger wandering into a shop and tossing out one of Coventry's marquee-family names was decidedly *not good.*

Even if Amos's shop was at odds with the Holts', locals didn't take kindly to strangers during wartime. And the customer was exactly that—a posh young stranger in a part of the city where everybody knew everybody, down to the names of their great-grandparents and herding dogs on the family farm. Standing there with that suit, those sharp blue eyes scanning corners, and asking for Eden in particular meant the lad wasn't likely to be well received in any part of the city, let alone in a competing shop.

Amos stepped into the light—slowly, bringing the added layer of the defensive wall he owned as he waited for the lad to quit digging through his briefcase. Aye, and notice what now stood before him.

"Ah—here it is. I have official business to conduct with Miss Eden Holt and . . ." The lad pulled out a wax-sealed envelope before he trailed off, his voice dying once he'd finally taken in the full imposing view of Amos Darby.

Go ahead. Take a long look.

Get it out of your system . . . then get out of my shop.

It was the usual flow of his interactions with the public.

Amos knew the combination of his height and a beastly profile could intimidate anyone who came poking around. And they would on occasion—the schoolchildren tiptoeing outside to peek through the windows and steal a glimpse of the local recluse. And why not? There was a certain fascination with the macabre sight of a boorish middle-aged man with a mane of unkempt hair, deep russet-and-pepper beard, and angry scars screaming up the right side of his neck and face.

Though this lad didn't flinch or try to hide his horror in the face of a monster as most did. Instead he stood firm. Near equal height. And strange, but he looked Amos square in the eye and simply waited. Like he had all day to stare down Amos if he so chose. And something told him if there'd been that battle between them, this lad could win.

Not afraid? Alright.

"You are Mr. Holt, I take it?"

"Who's asking?"

"I am. Forgive me," the lad said, all polite-like as he removed his hat and set it on the counter next to the briefcase. "Jacob Cole, Esquire. Legal representative of Cole Jewelry Company Limited. By way of Detroit."

He tripped over adding the clarification of "in the United States" and then winced, it seemed, for judging Coventry as uneducated. He was, after all, in a bookshop with framed maps on the wall and scores of books in sections marked *Philosophy*, *Fine Arts*, and *Literature*.

"Sorry. I only meant that—"

"A long trip to make, especially during wartime." Amos moved closer, leaning his good palm on the countertop so he could casually drum fingertips against the worn English oak. "You couldn't have sent a wire?"

"No. Not for this, I'm afraid. It's a legal matter of a somewhat sensitive nature."

Amos's chest tightened.

He and Charlotte might have been at odds, for years now. But something in him couldn't ignore when the Holts were pulled into any ill dealings. Bookshop wars were one thing; legal matters with children were a whole other category of low he wasn't prepared to entertain.

"And if you're wondering, sir," he said, noting Amos's silence, "I'm obliged to state that I have reported my presence to Grosvenor Square, and the London consulate is aware of why I'm in the UK. I can't say your government trusts me completely, even if I am a full-fledged American citizen with nothing to hide."

"I can't say as I blame them, times being what they are. But you won't find the Holts here. Wrong shop, lad." Amos tipped his head the direction of the street and the Bayley Lane shop fronts painted in cardinal red, sunshine yellow, and French blue. "Over there. Blue shop with gold trim, posies, and pretention dressing the front window. Catty-corner, across the way."

"There are two bookshops." The lad looked over his shoulder to the street through the window before slipping the envelope back into the briefcase.

"We have a library and cinema too, if you can believe that."

"Yes, of course. I'll just head across the street then." The young Mr. Cole replaced his trilby but paused to check his wristwatch. "Is there a hotel near here by chance? If your train timetables are correct, it's looking less likely I'll make the last one to London tonight."

Amos eyed the lad, finding a little flicker in the return stare that said a shade of vulnerability existed in him. And no doubt, they both knew why.

It was autumn 1940; London was embroiled in a hellfire of bombs from the sky nearly every night.

England had already seen Blitz bombs and buried some dead. Their fair country had already endured Dunkirk and the ongoing battle for England's skies. Even Coventry was preparing for the worst, with factories that shifted production from residential iceboxes to Spitfire wheels and engines, and now manufactured gas masks for near the whole of the king's country. Amos himself had helped dig the trenches in Primrose Hill Park that summer.

They'd already sustained bombing damage in the city center in August and September both. Barrage balloons flew over the parks and factories. And they'd installed larger shelters—like the ones at Greyfriars Green and the local cricket pitch—only to turn around and repack plank and earth-lined ceilings with concrete when they'd learned the first ones wouldn't prevent rogue bullets from hitting bodies.

This Yank couldn't know the number of local boys who'd signed up and shipped off to war. Nor that a steady stream of farmers-turned-soldiers took flight from Coventry's train station, leaving the farms all but empty. The children soon followed, with tags tied to jumpers as they were packed on trains and sent away to be looked after by relatives—or even strangers—in the countryside. All that was left were crying sweethearts and bewildered mothers to amble through the fog of train platforms and trod past his bookshop windows on their way back to empty farms and city flats.

That was a highlight reel of all Hitler had stirred up since '38. And if Amos could judge anything about the city and the land and the good people of the Midlands he'd known all his life, it was that not one establishment in all of Coventry would offer a room to a man too fainthearted to stay in London. Nor to one asking too many questions about the Holts.

Amos shook his head. "Not much to be speaking of."

"No rooms. In a city this size? With two bookshops *and* a cinema to its credit?"

Bully for that. This one is a solicitor after all.

"You could try Queen's Hotel on Hertford Street. But they're more than sure to be booked. Tipton's Rooming House is over on Bishop. Down a ways." Amos waved his hand in the vague direction of the ill-fated rooming house, knowing the owner and his paranoid wife might report this lad as a German spy the moment his blond-haired, blue-eyed mug and questions waltzed through their door.

"Bishop Street, you say?"

"Aye. But . . . the scones are bricks. And the mutton stew's enough to send a man to hospital. I wouldn't recommend it unless you've got an iron stomach and a death wish to go with it. Best make tracks back to London. Or else be forced to eat the mutton and never live to tell the tale."

Mr. Cole did smile then and patted the counter as if that was that. "I see. Well, perhaps you're right, Mr. . . ."

"Darby."

"Yes, Mr. Darby. It might be wise to go on to London tonight, even with the blackouts and night raids." He extended his hand, offering a handshake. "You know what they say: 'Hospitality to the exile, and broken bones to the tyrant.' Wouldn't want to overstay my welcome."

Amos gave an unconscious tic of the brow at recognition of the quote from *Waverley* but kept his hand buried in his trouser pocket. The lad would, no doubt, misinterpret the refusal. But that couldn't be helped.

"Which are you—the exile or the tyrant?"

The lad took his hand back in a soft-curled fist, tipped his hat, and offered a knowing smile. "I hardly know these days. But I thank you for your time just the same. Cheers." He turned to leave.

"Wait. The Holts. They're, uh . . . good people." Amos kicked the toe of his shoe against the baseboard behind the counter, where Mr. Cole couldn't see. Defending the enemy again? Why could he not let anything go when there was the possibility it might impact Charlotte or her family? "Whatever business you have, just be kind to them. But don't say anyone put you up to it."

"Lawyers are the soul of discretion, Mr. Darby. I assure you. They'll hear naught on the subject from me."

As if on cue, thunder rattled the roof. And Lord knows, Amos should have let the lad go out into the rain and brave it. After the paces Charlotte had put his shop through over the years, it was fitting to send a solicitor her way. But before the lad could make it to the door, Amos felt his insides tug with a notion he couldn't silence. The same notion that had gotten him in trouble too many times before.

"You could come back here," he heard himself say. "If you don't fancy mutton."

There. I've said enough to regret the day I was born.

Again.

As a member of the Home Guard, maybe he ought to keep this Mr. Cole close. See what he was really after.

"What?" The lad stopped, his brow questioning. "But I thought you just said—"

"I've a spare room." Amos sighed and pointed to the ceiling. "Rent it out when the rooming houses are full. Usually with the Coventry Stakes and all that, but sometimes on regular days too. Just don't be spreading it about."

"You'd rent me a room? Here in this shop?"

"Well, it's my home too, but if you need one. I've no telephone, mind. You have to breakfast at the pub. And the closest shelter's a few blocks down, so you'll have to hoof it if the sirens cry."

The lad raised an eyebrow. "And do the sirens cry on the regular?"

"Nearly every night since summer. The American newspapers should have told you that's your lot in England. But I can offer clean sheets and a roof, if you're still brave enough to stay on."

"And you'd trust an exile just like that, would you?"

"In my experience, anyone who can quote Sir Walter Scott can't be all bad." Amos flicked a glance over to the shop's name on the sign hanging high on the wall, the thick Roman letters reading *Waverley Novels* in stark black paint. "Seems I'm willing to take my chances."

The lad eyed him. "Thank you then, Mr. Darby. I accept." He nodded and moved back toward the shop door, pausing to replace his hat against the deluge of a crying sky. "I'll be back. Just as soon as business is taken care of."

He stepped out then, the bell ringing loudly as Amos slipped around the counter and hurried through the shop to the door. The pocket watch chimed through his vest, warning that time had ticked past three o'clock. He clamped a palm down on it as he stared out the front window, dulling the melody from filling his ears as he watched the suit walk away.

"Just as soon as business is taken care of . . ."

Whatever that means for the Holts, I'm not sure I want to find out.

Amos gave a hard flick of the door bolt and knotted the blackout curtains tight against the brass wall hook. Had he just sent more problems to Charlotte's shop, or had he invited them to reinvade his own in due time?

CHAPTER TWO

11 October 1940
Bayley Lane
Coventry, England

*H*e's coming over."

Ginny Brewster peeked through the rounded display window at Eden Books, her gaze glued to the Georgian shop front of Waverley Novels across the way. She circled her fist over the glass, rubbing away condensation fogged there.

"Who is?" Eden gave a quick glance up from the manifest of their latest book shipment. "Let's hope a customer."

"You know who—the *suit*." Ginny tucked an unruly wisp of hair from her chocolate bob behind her ear and readjusted rose-gold spectacles over a pert nose. "That gent who marched into Mr. Darby's shop." She flipped her wrist to check her watch. "Not five minutes ago."

"Did he now? Imagine that. A customer went inside a bookshop. That ought to make tomorrow's front page."

It was Eden's part to wink at Ginny's cheek yet still play the incurious manager bent on nudging her back to the new titles awaiting uncrating in the fiction section. If only she could discourage their fourteen-year-old apprentice's preoccupation with goings-on at Darby's shop. But in truth, Eden couldn't ignore the curiosity of it either. Her long ebony waves were pinned back tight at the nape so she could scan the first page of their new shipment receipt unobstructed. And she did—three times already—only with no clue as to what titles she'd just read over. Perhaps it was time to give it up and enter Ginny's world of subterfuge; neither shop was looking to have a banner day with sales, raining as it was.

"He went in, sure enough."

"There you have it, Ginny. Espionage in its purest form." Eden ticked another mark on her list. Pity—no copies of *Twilight in Delhi* this month either. And they had customers clamoring for it. "You know, it's a sad state of affairs Hogarth Press has had to contend with in Bloomsbury. Imagine Virginia Woolf's house being hit with bombs. Twice! It's a mercy no one was hurt when the building finally did collapse."

"Looks like the suit's been tossed out of the shop like his tailored trousers are afire!"

"What?" That did garner Eden's attention.

In their experience a gentleman in a tailored suit only happened to their end of the cobblestone street for one of three reasons: he was a solicitor, a banker, or lost on the road to London. Though Coventry's industrial sector had been booming with automobile production for a decade, most of the shopkeepers had weathered a rough patch these last years, and many were clinging to a shoestring just to keep their doors open. A suit meant trouble. And if Mr. Darby had thrown the gentleman out, there must be a reason. Eden could only pray there wasn't unrest with any of their friends' shops along the street.

"He's coming this way. With no umbrella, mind. That's frightfully determined, marching through a downpour like this." Ginny rubbed the glass again and waved Eden over to the display window. "Come see."

Eden gave up, abandoning her clipboard on the front counter so she might squeeze in next to Ginny and peer out from behind tied-back blackout curtains. And there he was—the suit. With his trilby bent under the briefcase he held over his head, dodging puddles in the street. A tall, broad-shouldered man was indeed crossing catty-corner to their side of Bayley Lane. And looked as determined as Ginny had said.

"What on earth do you suppose he's doing?" Ginny remarked when his shoe plunged into a puddle against the low curb, and he stopped, both hands holding the briefcase over his head as he danced in full view of their window.

"Um . . . I'm not exactly sure." Eden stifled a chuckle. And tried not to find humor in the poor chap shaking off a sopping trouser cuff. He looked lost. And sorry as could be in such a dreadful downpour, with leaves whisking by the window and his trench getting caught up on a furious gust.

"He must really want a book," Eden offered. Though Ginny didn't bite. All she did was give an exacting glare through her spectacles.

"And I still say the gentleman is lucky to be alive. We ought to warn him never to step through that man's door again. Her Ladyship would."

"That's enough cheek from you, miss." Eden flipped the ends of the girl's hair. "I know Mr. Darby and Mama don't exactly see eye to eye where book sales are concerned. But it's more the talk of the town that keeps this rift alive than it is either of our shops. And I should think you'd show a little more charity, given Mr. Darby's circumstances."

"Charity we have. In spades. But that man? Never." Always adding punctuation to her opinions, Ginny crossed her arms over her chest and huffed as they continued staring down the street at the redbrick façade with slim Georgian windows and an oversized door of leaded glass. "All the world is at war in Mr. Darby's eyes—and that was before we had a real one to contend with."

"Then I'd wager he's seen enough of it. He fought in one and we haven't."

The girl sighed, only hers was a coltish girls-aren't-allowed-to-fight kind of bluster that said she'd have joined the Home Guard in a thrice were she allowed. But in Mr. Darby's case . . . all Eden could think was that in war—even that which engaged bookshop owners—perhaps the world had not been particularly kind to *him*.

For a steadfast foe, the oddest of contradictions seemed to follow the man.

There was a rumor that Mr. Darby wouldn't hear of an ungenerous word spoken against the Holts. Yet his method of battling her mother was far subtler. And equally as shrewd. In a wave of brackishness that swept across the street, the bookseller managed to anticipate their every sales push or author visit with maddening accuracy.

If Eden Books secured a visit from an author in September, Waverley Novels had already entertained them by August. To advertise bigger and better was his strategy, and he did—even in wartime—by besting the ad space her mother bought in every newspaper's ad section within one hundred kilometers. And all the while, Mr. Darby held a boorish air that said though he'd advertised for them to come, if patrons actually did show at his door, they might find it slammed in their faces.

It was a wonder the man managed to stay in business at all.

And so it went. For years.

Hop and scotch. Tick and tack. The back-and-forth continued until every stool at the famed Lion's Gate pub circulated the blather of the bookshop wars each night. And though Eden hastened to admit it, Mr. Darby seemed the oddest contradiction of shielding them from the tittle-tattle yet keeping it going at the very same time.

"What if 'the Beast' sent him to act as a spy?" Ginny whispered and pulled back from the window, giving the drapes a good shimmy back into place.

"Please do not call Mr. Darby that name. It's cruel." Eden placed a palm to the shoulder of Ginny's homespun sweater and squeezed.

"I didn't say it. It's what my brothers say they call him at the schoolhouse, because of his—"

"I know why they say it."

"But I still don't understand why you take up for the man. He's nothing to us."

Eden sighed. No—Mr. Darby was nothing official to them, especially given the strife between shops. But unofficially, there was something about Mr. Darby that Eden couldn't discount. He seemed a grump without much to do or anyone in particular to grump at. The man lived alone, kept tucked away with his books and his airs. Maybe that was enough that they ought to show the man some measure of kindness.

"Everyone is something to someone. Remember that. The scars we bear should make us more worthy of understanding, not less."

The brass bell chimed loudly as the man in the suit blustered through the front door, shaking rain from his trench.

"Off with you now," Eden whispered, and she slipped behind the register. "Look smart."

Ginny skirted back to the fiction section, pretending to give attention to uncrating their new releases, though her investigative eye was employed in flitting back and forth to the entry, like a stray hummingbird had gotten lost there.

The man removed his hat as he approached the counter. "I'm sorry for the mess."

"It's quite alright." Eden beamed friendliness in return as she arranged customers' orders along the back counter. "We're used to the weather's shifting moods around here."

"Shifting moods . . . indeed."

Ginny shot Eden a simper that said every bit of "I told you! Mr. Darby threw him out . . ."

Eden shook her head in a silent "hush," telling Miss Brewster to be about stacking while she engaged their customer.

"May I?" he said, asking to set his hat on the counter. A smile from him—even a small one—was a good sign.

"Of course."

"I wonder if you might help me, miss? I'm looking for the shop owners—the Holts."

Ginny popped up to stand on the far side of her book table. And eyed him with a little too stout a measure of Scotland Yard about her.

"You're in luck. I am one such owner."

He swept a folded docket of papers and envelope from the briefcase and set them on the counter. Followed by a small ox-blood leather-bound book, which he opened and scanned a page marked with a ribbon in the binding.

"Are you from the bank?" Ginny chimed in. As if Eden could stop her. Curiosity had pulled the girl to hover by the counter like a ghost, a stack of books still cradled in her arms.

The man's eyes—the lightest blue, clear, and . . . kind?—sparkled in response to Ginny's forthright query. Thank goodness he wasn't offended.

He turned to Ginny. "The bank, miss?"

She set the books on the counter and rested her elbows on the stack, as if intending to stay until she got answers. She added with a splash of vinegar, "Yes. We don't get a lot of strangers around here. And you look like every banker I've ever seen."

"Uh, don't mind us." Eden tried to cover the girl's blunt edges with a quick step forward, drawing his attention back. "Coventry is a 'small-town city.' We don't often entertain customers save for the regulars we've known for a long time."

"Right. Well, I'm not from a bank. I'm from Detroit, actually. It's Cole," he said to Eden as he opened the briefcase and began sorting through its insides. "Jacob Cole, Esquire—legal representative of the Cole Jewelry Company Limited. I can provide identification."

"Thank you, Mr. Cole. But I don't think we'll be needing all that. You've obviously come quite a long way just to speak with us. How can I help you?"

He glanced to the back of the shop, past the long row of two-story shelves and the impressive rolling ladder system that stretched back to disappearing against the stairs, and the peacock-walled reading room where her mother's famed collection of rare books were kept safe from the damaging rays of the sun.

"Are you Miss Eden Holt, only child to the estate of William Holt III?"

"I'm the one," she said, with Ginny correcting, "Lady Eden Holt," in the background—emphasis on *Lady*.

He glanced up to the sign above the counter, its cheery French blue matched to the paneling on the outside of the shop, as if to say, "Eden Books?"

"My mother was rather romantic in her younger years. Always wanted a bookshop of her own, apparently. And what do you do when you're young and idealistic but name a dream after your only child?" Her cheeks warmed. Heavens knew why. Everyone in Coventry knew how the shop got its moniker. Eden had no idea why the notion struck her as humbling now.

"Yes, well." He exhaled a weighty sigh. "I wish that could put a different color on it."

"A different color on what?"

"I'm sorry to do this, miss, but . . ." He slid the envelope across the counter, then presented a leather-bound book with its center part and lined paper lying spread-eagle. He pointed to a line half-way down the page, beneath a host of scrawled names. "These belong to you. Sign here."

"I don't understand. Sign what? What is this?"

He shifted his stance in obvious discomfort. "Your legal rights in the United States, and in the state of Michigan. In the sealed envelope is the official docket for the case pending against you."

"What case against us? The bookshop?"

Ginny slipped in beside Eden and opened the crease of the folded papers to begin nosing her way through. "Not us. *You*, Eden."

Mr. Cole cleared his throat and tapped the blank line in his little book. "Sign here, please. It's required for our records."

Was that why Mr. Darby had sent him over this way?

Oh no. When her mother found out about this . . . it would toss a truckload of paraffin on the flames between shops. Eden turned to the window and gazed out at the bookshop across the street. The edge of the blackout curtains shimmied behind the man's front window, then swept back into place.

"Why, that double-crossing tyrant!" Ginny refolded the papers, slammed the book shut on them, and slid the lot back across the counter to the saboteur. "Her Ladyship was right when she said we oughtn't trust that man."

"I'm sorry?"

"Oh, you needn't be sorry, Mr. Cole." Eden attempted to smile. Awkwardly, she knew. Because Ginny was fighting mad as her mother would have been. Though with effort Eden had been trying to mitigate between shops, any headway seemed all for naught now. "Our young employee here has just read too many Sherlock Holmes novels in her spare time. Sets her on the hunt for intrigue whether it's warranted or not."

"Intrigue my eye," Ginny cut in. "You can tell Mr. Darby that the Holts won't sign—not even in our blood. If it is a war he wants, he'll have it!"

Mr. Cole cleared his throat. Adjusted his stance. And truth be told, it looked as though he was battling back an unexpected grin at the girl's moxie. "And are you a Holt, miss?"

"An honorary one," she insisted, arms crossed tight over her chest again.

"I think I know what this is about." Eden tested her ability to cool tempers before things spiraled completely out of control. "You see, when the incident occurred at Waverley Novels this summer, I was the one who walked across the street to make peace with Mr. Darby. Even when the mix-up wasn't entirely our fault. I apologized for flooding his shop—"

His eyes widened. "You flooded his shop?"

"Not intentionally, of course. It seems some crates of books we'd ordered were mistakenly delivered to his shop. I had them carried back across the street—trying to be a good neighbor. And though it wasn't our fault, I still offered twenty pounds to cover the water damage."

"Water damage . . ." He didn't bother to cover the chuckle under his breath this time.

"That's right. Something fell and blocked the back door from closing properly, and the next day's rain flooded the back of Mr. Darby's shop. Improper drainage in the alley. It really was an honest mistake."

"Yes, but we take it all back," Ginny cut in. "On behalf of Lady Harcourt, we demand . . ."

"Who is Lady Harcourt?" he whispered to Eden, as Ginny kept steamrolling.

"My mother," she answered back, in time to catch the end of Ginny's declaration.

". . . and we will not give *that* man the satisfaction. If Mr. Darby wishes to take this to the next level, then you tell him the Holts shall see him in court."

"Ginny!" Eden blasted back.

"Yes—and he ought to be ready for the war he's started!" she sparked back with a fist pumped in the air, emboldened that the time for talking was quite over.

"Ladies, I assure you . . . I haven't the faintest idea what you're talking about. I don't represent Mr. Darby."

Eden blinked, deadpanning, "You don't."

"No. But begging your pardon, I'd be reconsidering if it meant crossing anyone in this shop." He offered a wide grin this time, in perfectly annoying amusement that chose that instant to appear unfettered upon his face. "In fact, I just met the gentleman. And while Mr. Darby can be a little . . . intimidating, he actually seemed a decent fellow."

"I'm sorry. I don't understand. If it's not Mr. Darby, then who is suing us?"

Suits meant trouble. Eden should have marked Ginny's words on that. And had her mother been here, no doubt Charlotte Terrington-Holt would have echoed the sentiment full throttle.

As it was, the stranger sighed, and the kindness that had been in those eyes fled as he offered nothing but the brutal truth. "I am."

CHAPTER THREE

24 December 1913
Brinklow Road
Coventry, England

Look for fluttering fans and batting eyelashes . . .
Charlotte had thought only to buy Amos more time when she'd left the library and made quick work of scanning the Holt Manor ballroom. But the heir to the Holts' vast holdings was the one who could delay dinner if Charlotte could pull William from his latest conquest of the night.

Pears danced on the ends of crimson ribbons, and brilliant baubles of glass and gold frosted the great Nordmann's fir at the end of the ballroom. The rich scents of juniper, cinnamon, and mulled wine spiced the air. A string quartet played. Couples danced. And candlelight illuminated the holly-decked mantel where she finally found Will—and his enviable good looks—positioned by the hearth.

He'd wrangled an ebony crown into submission with a tight part off his brow, and with long, lean lines filling his white-tie dress, mischief in a dimpled and far too dashing smile, and that spark in deep emerald eyes, his air was certain to leave many a young lady hoping to be chosen for the next dance.

With a break in the dresses, Charlotte caught Will's eye and tilted her head to draw him over. He shrugged dismissively, as if he couldn't get away from the sea of satin and smiles.

How in character.

Since their childhood days, Will had accepted that his place in life was to charm the whole of England. More than that, he meant to have a jolly good time doing it. One might have thought he aspired to hold a seat in Parliament for the way he massaged public opinion. Yet it was watching the gaggle of ladies who invariably closed in on him, Will transfixing the lot, and the quartet slowing their playing for the dinner hour that bolstered Charlotte enough to make the split-second decision . . .

This would work if anything could.

Charlotte wove her way through the crowd to the quartet. It took some convincing for the cellist to comprehend why a lady of breeding should need to borrow his instrument. But to the shock of the musicians—and to the never-ending horror of her mother—she swept the hem of her ball gown out of the way, pressed the elegant long lines of the cello against her body, and readied herself to play before anyone could stop her.

Playing the cello again proved to be magic—on Christmas Eve or any other day. Once Charlotte had removed her gloves and the bow touched skin, all games were lost. She didn't require sheet music, not when muscle memory sent her fingers flying across the fingerboard and the bow to caress the strings with ease. She just played, the chords of music sinking low within her where nothing existed but the tool and its master and the magic they could create together.

The crowd hushed as notes carried across the room—first from the deep-chested tones of the instrument itself and then as the melody careened with the height of the coffered ceilings—and fell into a stupor when they realized who was playing.

Yet with heart swelling and the exquisite tension of the strings beneath her touch, Charlotte managed to blot out the images of where she was. It was everything to fall back into the rhythm of playing, reveling in the nearness of a beloved friend.

To Will, the shocking display seemed a private intrigue. And that, more than anything, was the brand of amusement he had always favored. He'd drifted to the edge of the dance floor and seemed to delight not at the ladies near him but at their seething envy that the prize of the night had turned his attention Charlotte's way.

Entering the arena of competition for Will's glances was no lure to her. But to play the cello again? To have an opportunity to do what she'd loved most in all the world? That was another matter entirely. And if it would help Amos—and feed her heart at the same time—Charlotte could not deny herself.

"Go on," Will goaded, as shouts of "Encore!" filtered around the room. And in a surprising show of support, he winked, leaned down to the cellist's chair, and whispered against Charlotte's ear, "Show those ladies what true accomplishment looks like."

After she played through to the final note of the second arrangement, the guests paused, then offered polite applause enough to draw her back. And with a pang of guilt, Charlotte realized she'd fallen so far into herself that she'd forgotten all else. Her father was waving a fan in front of her mother's ashen face. Will appeared delighted and thundered his applause seemingly without care for the air of shock rebounding across the room. Dinner had indeed been halted, as even the service staff had stopped and gaped at the Terrington heiress's ghastly breach of propriety.

Yet Will grinned like a victor and took her hand to claim her for the dance floor as some unspoken prize. "So how does it feel?"

Snapped back from counting her dance steps, Charlotte looked up to Will. "Hmm?"

"I said, how does it feel to have single-handedly commanded the attention of an entire ballroom? You'd think a young lady would bask in such adoration."

"I'm not so certain it's adoration. I can't believe I just did that. My mother . . ."

"Your mother will be pleased all eyes have turned in our direction. And yet of all the young ladies in this ballroom, I find I'm dancing with the only one who looks everywhere but at the man who's holding her in his arms. Should I take that personally?"

"Of course not." *Think fast.* She painted a sweet smile on her lips and shrugged instead of searching the background for Amos. "It's just that the room is enchanting. Truly. Your mother has made everyone feel so at home. And I was overcome with wanting to play at Christmas, like I did once as a young girl."

"Enchanting?" He stared down at her with that little measure of play in his eyes—so characteristic of the veteran playboy from down the lane. "I agree. The view is that."

Will's words were silky, as always, well-chosen, and practiced. He knew what to say and when to say it. But Will's attention had always been focused elsewhere. And because she knew him so well, Charlotte could dance with the understanding that in the end, it wouldn't mean anything.

He'd flit to the next young lady in line—a line she'd never join.

"Charlotte?"

"Yes?"

"Could you at least try to look like it's not painful to be in my arms?" Will's brilliant smile greeted her, and he gave her waist a playful squeeze. "I was only joking."

"I know. I just haven't played in public. *Ever.* I think it's left me flustered."

"Oh, I knew you could play. Just not like that. I thought you'd given it up." The beaming faded, and he scanned the breadth and depth of the crowd instead. "Did you see their faces? Green with envy, I tell you. Every last female in here. And some of the men too, that you had the backbone to show everyone up. I don't know whether to scold or congratulate you for such a row."

"Your flattery is noted." She tried to find the right words that would keep her on safe and solid ground, with the backhanded compliment and whispering guests having pricked her awareness.

"So what's captured your notice tonight? Because we both know it isn't me."

"Nothing. It's just hot on the dance floor."

He slowed their pace. "You're ready to go through then?"

"Of course. If it's time."

"Good. I'll alert Mother. She's been holding dinner for you."

"For me?"

Charlotte looked over to the Christmas tree where the Earl of Harcourt stood, and with him the queen of the palatial Holt Manor looked on, preening at the sight of her son twirling Charlotte across the floor.

"Why would your mother do such a thing? She is hostess."

He shrugged, like the answer was obvious. "I wanted a dance. And I always collect what I set my mind upon."

"But I'm a guest."

The hand at the small of her back squeezed—a little too tight this time, with his thumb brushing in a caress that nearly burned through the fabric of her dress. Then he leaned in. Closer. A little *too* close for his intentions to be masked. And with a gaze that melted from playful to something it had never dared before.

"A very important guest," Will whispered, and he moved so the inches left between their postures were snuffed out. "Do you think I care a fig about a shocking display like that? As long as I'm the one who gets to dance with you now."

Confidence fled, leaving only warning bells to ring in her head. Charlotte leaned back, trying to put space between them even as Will pressed the side of his face to brush the soft wisps of hair at her temple.

"What do you mean?"

With the heat of his breath against her neck, he whispered, "Don't you see? Everyone is here tonight for us."

"Us," she whispered, only just connecting dots among the whispers that seemed to follow them around the room, making her body go rigid in his arms.

"Yes, Charlotte. *Us.*" He laughed. As if it were a joke. And yet he didn't deny it.

Will gave her arms a little squeeze. "Roast goose is on the menu, when the Holts have a Christmas tradition of orange duck and mousseline. We've Lady Charlotte Terrington's favorite peaches in brandy and hazelnut cake for dessert, when Mother sorely dislikes both. My place card sits next to yours. And umpteen boxes from Harrods are nestled under the tree with your name in gold leaf on the tags."

"But you already gave me a gift." *The book.* Which . . . she'd promptly left somewhere, checked the library for, and had the unexpected encounter with Amos instead.

"And there are so many more things I could give if you'd let me. Why do you think that is?"

"I couldn't guess."

Only she could. And didn't dare wish to.

No, no, no . . . Not me.

Not now. Not ever.

"It's to be announced at dinner." Will tipped his brow, like she ought to have been cleverer. She ought to have expected it. And have no qualms with what that announcement would be. "Are you honestly saying . . . Charlotte? I thought you knew."

"How could I?"

"But you can't say you're surprised."

"Of course I am. I was under the impression that our family had been invited to Holt Manor as in years past, for holiday cheer with friends and family. Nothing more."

"Family. As you are. As I wish you to be."

"You can't think that this could be decided . . . *Marriage.*" She swallowed, lest she choke on the word. "Not without at least consulting both parties who would stand before God to pledge their lives to one another?"

"My dear, look over there." Will nodded in the direction of the earls nursing their tumblers of port by the tree, their quiet discourse seemingly focused upon the dance floor. "Our fathers share the belief that they do not need consent to arrange the futures of their children. When it was posed to me in this manner, I said that I shouldn't have to go as far as London—or heaven knows, to New

York—to find a suitable wife. I've no need for an heiress. Not when the best option is right here in Coventry." Will gave her waist a little shake of encouragement as his grip drifted a shade lower. "The very angel in my arms."

"Will . . . please."

"What is it? We've known this would happen since we were children."

"We're not children anymore. And . . . you don't love me."

Will had a heart. She knew it. Perhaps deep down, it was concealed under layers of levity and white-tie dress. And appealing to it now was the only way Charlotte could see to break through his words. She searched his eyes, because—shouldn't he listen? Oughtn't they feel some measure of love if they were expected to do this?

"Do you? Love me?"

"How could you ask such a question?"

Evasion tactic. Classic Will.

"You're a friend, Will. A brother. And a very dear one, as you always should be." Charlotte moved her hand to rest on his shoulder, pressing in punctuation. "That will not change. But I could never presume to take the position of your wife—"

"You may presume, Charlotte. All you like. And for as long as you wish. Just say you'll marry me in the end."

The strings faded to a soft, melodic close. And Charlotte exhaled when he took her hand and pressed a kiss to it, keeping his lips in an intentional graze over her knuckles as the room fell silent. She battled to reconcile this—as if he hadn't just asked a woman to share the rest of his life, nor waited for her answer.

The walk from the ballroom to dinner was a blur of guests' smiles and holiday splendor. The flicker of candlelight shone against gold-rimmed chinaware, spotless crystal, and candelabras laced with ivory poinsettias. As guests found their seats, Charlotte looked to the livery uniforms hovering on the fringes of the room—desperate for a lifeline.

The sight of her must have said too much too fast; Amos furrowed his brow as Will led her by on his arm. And she caught the tiniest flinch from him as Will made a grand show of pulling out her chair. Charlotte moved to sit—and would have—until she saw the copy of *Dombey and Son* lying on the seat.

Will looked to her, and for one split second, all color drained from his face. Only one other person would know the significance of the book. And now, clearing his throat, he refused to acknowledge the sting of wounded pride that there was a secret understanding between Amos and her.

With an annoyed shimmy of the brown leather binding in the air, Will gave a silent bid for the service staff to respond.

The butler snapped to attention. "I'll take it for you, sir. With my sincere apologies on behalf of whoever left it there."

"No apology is necessary." Silky words made their appearance again, though Will's manners weren't as good-humored as they'd been on the dance floor. He waited for Charlotte to sit and, when she did, gave a rough push to the chairback until she was up against the table so tight, the fluted wood pressed a sharp edge to her bodice.

"Far be it from us to deny the working class their lofty aspirations, even if they are futile in the end." Will's words were light and cheery and loud, obviously for the benefit of the room, though his eyes were girded with steel as his glance shot to Amos's place in the service staff line. "It seems Dickens inspires their lot better than we ever could. Am I right, Lady Charlotte?"

Laughter cooled the room. And Will refused to acknowledge her after, putting all effort into charming the table and treating her like an impetuous child caught with her hand in the biscuit jar. And when it came time for Lord Harcourt to clink a fork to a crystal flute and declare that the gift their family was happiest to receive in the new year would be a new daughter-in-law, Will leaned forward to shake congratulatory hands while Charlotte sat offering silent smiles around the table. And all the while, she hadn't meant for her gaze to drift to the service staff line again.

Their eyes locked through the candlelight.

Amos stared back for a few steady . . . long . . . and dreaded breaths.

They lingered there, suspended together, until the party raised glasses of bubbly and toasted the happy couple. Charlotte was left with only two things she knew to be sure: Will had chosen her that night. But her heart had made its choice long ago.

And it could never be the man she was now pledged to marry.

→·←

11 October 1940
Bayley Lane
Coventry, England

The Philco sang from the reading room down the hall—Bach's Cello Suite no. 1 in G Major that Charlotte could still pick out by ear.

She clicked the bookshop's back door closed and pressed her forehead to the wood. Rain tapped a melody against the row of leaded glass windows at the rear of the shop, where book club ladies had just hurried out under umbrellas bobbing along the path that snaked to the exit gate on Bayley Lane. And with the last guest having gone, the façade Charlotte had kept up could crumble behind the safe haven of the bookshop door.

With invasion fears looming and sirens crying every blessed night, book club was supposed to be a frolic of distraction. Even though *Cold Comfort Farm* had been published several years prior, the ladies were keen for discussion of a lighthearted comedy clash between a Londoner's metropolitan ideals and the rural sensibilities of folk in a Sussex village. In their literary circle, the ladies saw themselves with a foot in both worlds like heroine Flora Poste and were aflutter to exchange their own interpretations of the bestselling story.

And what had begun innocently enough sparked like petrol to a flame within Charlotte. That, and the fact the Earl Grey was stale, and rationed flour and sugar meant the tea biscuits that Mrs. Farley had brought from their family's bakery down the lane dropped like lead in the stomach.

Leave it to author Stella Gibbons to tilt their world even farther off its axis.

The novel had flung open Charlotte's own woodshed doors she'd thought long since locked, dredging up memories of that Christmas Eve when all in her world had changed. So that by the end of the hour, she'd taken to crossing and uncrossing her legs, shifting in her chair, and twirling fingertips around the string of pearls at her collar as she begged the mantel clock to tick time at double speed.

Thunder rumbled—*blessed be*—and the ladies agreed they ought to adjourn early this month. Charlotte was left to see them out with a serene smile, only to dig her fingernails into the wood of the closed door as she battled back tears the instant they'd gone.

Push the memories away . . .

Charlotte turned back to the reading room.

It greeted her with the usual solitude: peacock walls and velvet curtains surrounded by built-in bookshelves, an iron ladder system flanking a great stone fireplace, and a soft glow from the lamps on tables spaced on either side of a cerulean sofa. Her cello case stood alone, hidden away in a dark corner where no one noticed it now. Nor remembered the county gossip of an unscrupulous display one Christmas Eve so long ago.

Charlotte collected stray teacups and flicked off lamps to conserve electricity. And fell into the ritual of refilling the robin's egg–blue bakery box with leftovers she always sent home with Ginny at the end of her shift—which, if the clock on the mantel had any say about it, was now.

The Philco sang from its post against the wall with usual symphonies that the ladies insisted added the "cultured ambience" of their literary gatherings, but all it did now was prick Charlotte's heart with cruel remembrances. She glared at it, stalked over, and flicked the knob with a sharp turn to kill the music. The silence revealed raised voices in the shop.

"Ginny?" Charlotte muttered. "Is that you?"

Not like their young apprentice at all. And unlike Eden not to have an orderly peace out front.

Eden was determined in anything she undertook—a carbon copy of her late father not just in looks but in that respect as well. In interactions with their neighbors, Eden was an unfailing model of kindness. From spending an inordinate amount of time to match a reader with the perfect title for them to gifting a free *Farmers' Almanac* to the penny-pinched farmers who ambled into the shop. The customers came first, full stop.

As for her dedication to Holt Manor and her late father's legacy . . . in that her passionate nature was unmatched. No heiress could have been more fervent or humbler at the same time. Eden Holt could be found in a milking pen by day and at a thé dansant by night—and refused to put on airs with either. It was a mash-up of the things Charlotte loved most about her girl, a tempest spirit if ever there was one. But something must have gone terribly wrong to have sparked a blowup in the shop under her watch.

"Milady?" Ginny rapped on the reading room door and, not waiting, bounded into the room.

"What's all the bluster? Are we in a bookshop or a barnyard?"

Ginny waved Charlotte over, urging her through the door. "You'd best come quick, milady. Or else I think we may finally have to do it."

Charlotte set the last teacup on the tray and hurried over to the arched doorway that led out to the shop. "Do what?"

"Murder that tyrant at Waverley Novels, that's what."

Amos?

Oh dear. What in the world have you done now?

Charlotte whisked out of the reading room to the long rows of polished oak shelves bordering the stairs, Ginny tracking alongside. Customers dotted the aisles, opening covers and making their selections before closing, but also remaining just discreet enough to toss furtive glances to the voices growing in decibel at the front.

This would feed the beast of gossip between shops if anything would.

"Whatever's happened?"

"Mr. Darby sent a solicitor, Your Ladyship. And the man says he's come with a legal summons for Lady Eden."

"He wouldn't dare . . ." Charlotte eased them out to the hall, taking furtive steps.

"The solicitor claims not to represent Mr. Darby, but he has mentioned Lady Eden's inheritance. Seems he's brought some sort of claim against Holt Manor. Lady Eden was cordial to the gentleman until she heard that. And then it set fire to her tongue and temper both."

Set fire indeed.

The poor gentleman hadn't a clue what he'd just done if he'd threatened to take away the one thing her daughter loved in all the world more than their bookshop. It would be no small feat to douse the flames he'd sparked if he'd threatened Eden's beloved Holt Manor.

"Who is this solicitor? Do we know him?"

They rounded the corner of the poetry section to where the shop opened up and Eden's voice echoed through the aisles. And as for the few customers she could see making a quick exit from the shop, Charlotte surmised the reason was the spirited exchange coming from the front counter.

"He's not from Coventry. He claims to be a Mr. Cole—Esquire. From America," Ginny whispered, as the front of the shop came into view.

"Is that so?"

"Yes. He started across the street at Mr. Darby's shop, then trekked over here through the gale outside. Sounds as if he's been asking questions about the shop owners on Bayley Lane. I should think someone will report him as a spy to the Home Guard if he's not careful."

"Well, I shouldn't worry about that. I'll speak with the local authorities if I must."

"And Mr. Darby?" Ginny's brow was furrowed. "What will we do to him?"

"*We* will do nothing, dear." Charlotte slowed them at the edge of the action with a gentle hand to Ginny's shoulder. Sure enough, there was her Eden, standing cross-armed and pink-cheeked as she glared at a man in a sharp suit and frozen posture. "I'll see it's sorted. Now, scoot."

"Are you sure, milady?"

"Quite." Charlotte patted the spot where her hand lay, nudging the girl back toward the hall. "Go on now. Your biscuits are waiting in the reading room. I'll send Eden to join you in a moment. You two can go out the back door today."

"Yes, milady." Ginny's shoulders drooped, disappointment weighing them.

Charlotte stepped out with what she hoped was a sparkling smile. "Eden, dear. May I be of help?"

"Mama. Hello." Her face softened as Charlotte stepped into the foreground. "I'm sorry if we disturbed the book club meeting."

"Not at all. We ended on time today on account of the weather." She tapped the watch brooch pinned to her breast pocket. "But oughtn't you be on your way? Your appointment . . ."

"Oh yes." Eden glanced at the wall clock and grimaced to find it ticked past three o'clock. "And now I'm late."

Stepping around the front counter until she was shoulder to shoulder with Eden, Charlotte caught her first look at the gentleman. For his part, the man didn't appear threatening. He was young—couldn't be much more than Eden's own twenty-five years. Quite handsome. Tall, and if her instinct was correct, with something akin to forbearance in his clear blue eyes. And with a candor in his silence that said he'd taken no pleasure in whatever legal summons he'd relayed.

"Mr. Cole, this is Lady Charlotte Terrington-Holt, the Dowager Countess of Harcourt—my mother. Owner of this shop." Eden paused to issue a last glare at the man before she shoved books and the shop's paperwork in her leather satchel. "And the other person who will fight you tooth and nail to preserve my father's estate, if need be."

He cleared his throat and tipped an invisible hat, his still on the counter. "Your Ladyship."

"Hello, Mr. Cole. Eden—you and Ginny can be off, out the back." Charlotte spotted the Waldybag strung over a chair, hooked the strap in her palm, and held it out to her daughter. "Don't forget this. I'll close up and see you at home for dinner."

Thunder boomed and rain rattled the display window as Eden nodded, sparing one last pointed glance to Mr. Cole as she accepted the gas mask bag. The gentleman looked from them to the deluge beyond the front window.

"But should you go out now? Perhaps if you wait for the bus . . . ?"

"If you can endure the weather, Mr. Cole, then I assure you we can as well. But we thank you for the concern just the same." Eden pulled her trench off the coatrack hook and slid her arms in. "I believe we would much prefer our bicycles than to trouble you any further."

Tipping her brow to her daughter, Charlotte asked silently, *Bicycles?*

It wasn't a curiosity the bus hadn't kept to its time. Train and bus schedules were near nonexistent now that petrol had been rationed, and sirens sang in the streets day in and day out. But sure enough, her daughter seemed determined not to wait for the wheeled savior to appear on the corner of Bayley Lane.

"Good day, Mr. Cole." Eden looked to her mother, the silent charge of understanding passing between them before she turned and disappeared down the hall.

Yes—regret was a formidable foe.

"Mr. Cole. It seems you've come a dreadfully long way to Coventry." Charlotte offered a smile to the young man. But instead of disclosing her real intention—to find out if Amos Darby had in fact started a new battle between their shops—she did what one would expect and played her part as the hospitable lady of Coventry's famed reading room. "Might I offer you a cup of tea?"

CHAPTER FOUR

11 *October 1940*
Brinklow Road
Coventry, England

A journey from Coventry city to the countryside revealed a most inconvenient truth: Eden Holt was too stubborn for her own good.

Or anyone else's.

To stand on principle where Mr. Cole was concerned meant that within moments of bicycling out of the city and slowing at the rise for the long walk up Brinklow Road, she and Ginny were soaked to the skin. And while the gothic figure of Holt Manor guarded mist-laden hills in the distance, willful mortals were punished down below.

A biting wind tangled silver birches and chestnut trees lining the road. The wretchedness was enough to convince Eden that the *Farmers' Almanac* had, in fact, been peddling lies that a dry spring and fair summer should forecast a pleasant autumn.

Eden balanced the umbrella over Ginny's shoulders for a second stop, so the girl might tend to a blister that wet stockings had chafed into her heel.

"Saints preserve us, Lady Eden." Ginny leaned her bicycle against a mossy rock wall and bent to unlace her boot. "Remind me, why did we refuse the bus again?"

"Because I would not give Mr. Cole the satisfaction of having suggested it." Eden bristled. Hard to be right, though, when they were at the mercy of the worst of autumn's petulant moods, and it was her bullheadedness that had brought them here.

"Oh, that'll show him. Mr. Cole and his suit are warm and dry in your mother's shop whilst we're out here about to catch our death from beastly wet stockings. And my mum always says a person will live or die by the state of their socks." Ginny looked up, those wise-beyond-their-years eyes managing to show pragmatism even in that instant.

"I am sorry. Truly. It's just that . . ."

"Whenever something dares threaten Holt Manor, it is a declaration of war by proxy. I know. Everyone knows, Eden."

"He didn't." Eden held her hand out to check the cadence of raindrops catching in her palm. It had slacked off some, thank heaven. "Come on. We're almost there." She held an arm out to balance the bike at Ginny's side. "I'll help you the rest of the way."

Ginny gave a nod and yanked her soppy sock higher on the ankle for good measure. "I suppose if you're not complaining, I shouldn't either. It's your estate that's on the hook."

A trek through a downpour was a small enough consequence, but Eden had begun to wonder if there was some truth at the heart of it. Those employed on the estate worked fingers to the bone to keep it all going in years that had been more famine than feast. Through poor crop yields, dwindling staff, and the increasing attraction of longtime estate workers to steady work in factories or shops in the city. And now a tired manor needed a new roof and more tending than the bank account might allow. Prodding unease over Eden's greatest fear: whether this was the end.

If something didn't change in their financial footing—and soon—the estate would break. They'd have to sell off land piecemeal just to keep a leaky roof over their heads. And in the end it might only serve to bandage a mortal wound, and Eden could lose the lot for good.

A lawsuit now could finish them.

"This isn't about negotiating the price of wheat or taking livestock to the fat show, Ginny. If that man is suing the estate, then he sues all of us—the very same land that employs half the county. And the home my father gave his life to defend." Eden sighed, pushing back the emotion that came with living life as a fatherless child only able to defend his legacy through estate land. "I'd just hate for one man to come along and, with a single blow, tear down what it took generations to build. And I won't allow that to happen."

Ginny looked up, revealing a face that had softened. "Right. And remember what you said? Taking in the Land Girls on the estate will help."

Yes, she prayed it would. If the Land Girls could help bolster their production levels, then Holt Manor could keep its contracts with the government. And they just might squeak through to another year.

"I just hope this wrinkle of Mr. Cole's arrival doesn't complicate our plans."

"I wouldn't fret about that. A spy would give up his secrets in a thrice under Her Ladyship's powers of persuasion. I'd wager your mother will have it sorted by teatime. Until then, you might want to—" Ginny ran an index finger under her eye, then pointed to Eden's face. "You've got tracks. Both cheeks."

Had she? Ginny took the umbrella and Eden balanced her bicycle on her hip so she could open her satchel and search through.

Passing over her fountain pen case, then the mass of paperwork she'd tossed in her haste to leave the shop, Eden dug deeper. There was the dreaded *Farmers' Almanac* she was still bitter toward. And Eden grimaced at the latest edition of *Vogue* magazine, with its rubbish advertisement for the new cream mascara the cheery model had promised would stay all day.

With no flash of gold from the Helena Rubenstein compact in the bottom of the bag, Eden realized she must have left it on her dressing table.

Again.

Wetting fingertips with raindrops teetering on the bicycle's handlebar, Eden rubbed at the ghoulish dark marks under her bottom lashes.

She turned back to Ginny, tilting her chin up to give a better view under the brim of her hat. "Better?"

"I suppose." The girl gave a squint-eye, then used her thumb to press the apple of Eden's cheek, grounding out a shadow that had seeped into the dimple she owned there. "That's as good as I can make it. What is this stuff anyway? Tar?"

"I'm beginning to wonder myself. Cream mascara, of which I have a mind to write Max Factor a letter of complaint after this. They'll simply have to issue a refund."

"Why did you try it anyway? I thought you loathed this type of thing. It's for posh girls. That's not you."

"Oh, thank you very much."

"You know what I mean. It's just that it's not your usual *you*, that's all. You've never needed any of that rubbish. And it looks like you might need paint stripper to take the rest off anyway."

"Marvelous. I'm not a posh girl and I have racoon eyes to prove it." Eden gave up trying to explain and checked her wristwatch— past four o'clock. What should have taken twenty minutes on a sunny day had taken a rain-soaked hour instead. Trying to make a good impression looked farther in the rearview than ever.

"Why don't we break here? I can head to the farm along the ha-ha wall and you can go up to the manor through the gate. It's much faster. And if you don't have to take me, you might still make it in time."

Oh no. That was not an option. Not when vigilance had hung over the countryside like a veil these last many months.

When war had been declared the previous autumn, it was a faraway notion that Hitler's conflict would reach England's shores. Or that it would turn into a real conflict at all. But the precautionary removal of stained glass from Coventry's famed cathedral had shocked them all into realization that real war loomed—and not the kind that was dubbed a "Phoney War" in *The Times*. As blackout curtains and ration books invaded English households, buildings were washed in fresh camouflage paint, and autos with doused headlamps became the norm . . . So did a growing spirit of angst.

Eden and Charlotte had taken all this quite to heart and made a declaration that any staff leaving the bookshop or estate were to do so in pairs. Even Mama followed her own edict, often waiting for the factories' night shifts to end so she might offer rides to working wives of their tenants. And the slimmer staff that remained in employ at Holt Manor were privy to air-raid sirens at all hours of the day, and that meant none could be left out alone—not even a young sleuth who could look after herself better than most adults.

"Mama would have my hide mounted over the hearth if I were to leave you, Ginny. And I wouldn't blame her. I couldn't live with myself if I left a friend to fend for herself. Times being what they are."

"The Germans aren't going to look for us out here. They've bigger fish to fry."

"That may be true. But I'm not of a mind to tempt them just the same." Eden tipped her head toward the stone gate, its curled iron lattice left open to the long span of gravel drive. "Come on then. We haven't far to go. And I've still time to wash up if we move fast."

They hurried through the gate, wheeling around puddles and choosing careful footing where the drive curved in a slow rise to the manor.

Here, field grass swayed on misty hills. Birdsong returned as the thunder drifted off, leaving starlings to fluff their wings and dart from tree to tree. The scents of earth and fallen leaves came alive on the crisp air, along with the blend of autumn spices and sweetness from the rudbeckias that peeked out from beds along the hedgerow.

This was beauty to Eden, where the land and sky melded together over Holt Manor—not some photo of a fashion plate in a cosmetics ad. She was about to remark on just that when Ginny perked up at a noise behind them, dropped her bike to the gravel, and bolted out to the middle of the drive, flapping her arms like a vulture fending off an attack. Round headlamps on a green Bedford truck grill cut over the rise.

"Thanks be to Providence!" Ginny shouted, flagging down the drop-side lorry as it lumbered closer. "It's Mr. Cox."

Eden sighed too. *Jolly-good timing.*

Their gardener's arrival meant she still might have enough time to drop Ginny at home, slip into the manor, and make herself presentable before she had to appear to her guests in the parlor.

The truck lumbered to a stop on squeaking brakes, the wipers swishing side to side as last errant raindrops caught on the windshield. Crates of soppy hens fluttered their wings in the truck bed and clucked their disagreement at the weather that had doused them.

Eden walked up to the driver's side. "Mr. Cox," she said, grateful to see the gardener's smiling face as he opened the door and stepped down, "are we relieved to see you."

"Why, Lady Eden!" Mr. Cox took the umbrella and held it over her, though the rain had all but faded. "What finds you out here like this?"

Ginny appeared at her side, wringing water from the tips of her hair. "A solicitor had the nerve to come into the bookshop and run us off."

"Uh . . . we rode bicycles from the shop today," Eden corrected. "When it appears we should have taken the bus home instead. Even if it was late."

He raised a bushy silver eyebrow at the state of them. "The bus, eh?"

"We know. It wasn't our brightest plan to date." Ginny offered an "I told you so" smirk to Eden. "But might you drive me home? Lady Eden wishes to tidy up before her guests arrive, and I've a notion Mum is fit to be tied with my tardiness already."

"Aye. Of course we can, miss. Come on then."

Mr. Cox ushered them to the passenger side and opened the

door to what could only be described as a fashion explosion into the forms of three brilliant, posh, and poppy-lipped young ladies sardined inside.

One pert blonde owned a sleek kelly-green ensemble, in the military styling that was fast gaining popularity in the new decade. Next to her, a fresh-faced brunette in a slender suit of pristine white with thick ebony blocking at the shoulders—every bit in the vein of a Hollywood starlet. And the last was a modest but no less pretty peach, in a suit and matching trench that were brightened only by the smile she offered behind baby-blue resin spectacles.

"Oh—I didn't realize you're quite full already. We couldn't trouble you, Mr. Cox. Or you, ladies," Eden said, even as the group watched from their place wedged in the old gardener's truck cab like a Mayfair's dress shop had been stuffed inside.

"Don't be silly." The blonde miss in Kelly green smiled back, then nudged the starlet to squeeze in tighter. "Shove over, Flo. These gals need a ride."

"Just me." Ginny pointed to the truck bed where Mr. Cox was loading her bicycle. "And I'm fine to sit back there. We haven't far to go."

"You're staying at the castle then as well?" the blonde fluttered, her enchantment over the manor unmasked. "We can't believe this place. We heard tell from some of the other WLA recruits that their post turned out to be stuffed in a Yorkshire hayloft. Can you imagine? With no heat or hot water—even if baths are rationed down to five inches in the porcelain. Did you know Buckingham Palace has drawn lines on the inside of their tubs?"

Eden shook her head as the glam kept going.

"And all we had to do was agree to work in some quaint bookshop and our accommodations are covered in full. Just wait until the other recruits find out we get to sleep in a manor fit for a queen! If you tell me Mr. Rochester is hiding secrets in that attic, I'd believe you."

"My family's farm is just down the way. But Lady Eden here is going to the, uh . . . castle." Ginny grinned and elbowed Eden. "In fact, she owns it."

"You don't say." The blonde leaned out, stretching a long, elegant leg to rest a T-strap heel on the truck's running board. She opened the pearl clasp on a satin satchel and retrieved a crinkled telegram. "Are we to understand you are . . ." Glancing down to the paper, she read, "Mrs. Holt?"

With a mascara-tracked face and bowler hat unable to save its soppy soul, Eden smiled and tried to present some semblance of pride.

"I'm her daughter."

"It's Her Ladyship. And this is *Lady* Eden Holt," Ginny interjected, making Eden's cheeks burn at always having to be addressed like royalty.

I know . . . I'm supposed to be a titled something, but instead I look like someone just scraped me off their field shoes.

"Oh, what luck, Lady Eden!" The blonde had no trouble echoing Ginny's penchant for formality as she tucked the telegram back in her satchel. "We've found you in the midst of this boorish country weather."

The Hollywood starlet leaned in. "We're from London. But even with that, not one of us has seen a gale kick up quite that fast. We're lucky we still own our hats."

"Yes. And if your Mr. Cox hadn't been such a hero to find us stranded in the storm at the train station . . ." The blonde gave a flirty pat to perfectly coiffed curls gathered under her hat. "But we're here now. And we should be introduced."

The blonde leader pointed to the posh-suited Hollywood starlet. "This is Miss Florence Abbott—Flo. Our little Chelsea-bred version of Joan Fontaine." Turning to the peach, she added, "This is Miss Ainsley Chapman, our expert seamstress. She can whip up a frock faster than a Royal Air Force pilot can pull you to the dance floor. Remember that, dearie, and both you and the RAF gents will be thanking her later."

She winked. Ginny choked over a laugh. And Eden felt her insides going green if this cheery lot was who she thought they were.

"And I'm Dale Kramer. Not nearly as interesting as these dolls, but I try." The leader thrust out a gloved hand—even that fashionable, with a delicate row of tiny pearl buttons locked at the wrist. "Isn't that fortunate that we should meet on the road to your home, Lady Eden?"

"You can just call me Eden." She offered what she hoped was her best smile. "But the telegram . . . ?"

"Oh, the weather almost held up the train. But in any case, thanks to Mr. Cox here, we made it for our appointment. And not a moment too soon."

Dread washed over. Leave it to the Women's Land Army to send them fashion plates instead of farmhands.

"You mean to say that you're our new . . . ?"

"Yes!" Dale quipped with an enthusiastic salute and smile bright as the returning sun. "We're your Land Girls, reporting for duty. And we can't wait to see those sparkling new uniforms."

CHAPTER FIVE

3 January 1914
Brinklow Road
Coventry, England

Snow, like affection, showed mercy to no man.

Amos trekked through bitter cold on the way to the barn, muscling the bucket of water he'd warmed on the kitchen stove from one hand to the other so he could shove the free one into the protection of his pocket.

Confounded wind. Creeping its icy fingers all the way down to squeeze a man's bones. And curse snowflakes that had the nerve to look peaceful. They weren't. Not when it had been this way since Christmas—drifts of nothing but white.

The post had been delayed for weeks. Roads and railways leading out of Coventry were blocked with snowdrifts taller than a man. The greengrocers carried an even thinner supply than usual with the weather, even if the Darbys were out of credit there. The bakeries and butchers had queues of sorry-looking souls shivering on sidewalks, hoping there'd be something left when they reached the front of the line. And while Amos couldn't complain about winter nights that sent him to bed with a book and a warm fire on the hearth, the weather did give a man time to think. To brood. And to stew over what to do next since being dismissed from the Holts' employ.

Aye, snow allowed far too much time to be thinking on what was done. Just as well in the end—Amos couldn't have worked for the future lord of Holt Manor any more than he could have stood by and watched Charlotte marry into that thankless brood.

Standing on principle was difficult to do, though, when it left Amos's family in a right fix in the bankbooks. As with Tate—who'd been dismissed, too, over the silver closet key the night of the Holts' Christmas party—each day nudged Amos closer to the long hours and low wage at one of the factories in the city. After low grass and a hot, dry summer the previous year, the herd had been stressed, and by the time the snows of winter came, the bad luck of sickness had spread like wildfire. They'd lost Da last year. And the lion's share of the herd to clostridial illness the year after.

Bad luck. That's what it is . . .

Just bad luck.

Amos coughed, his breath catching in a fog on the sharp morning air. He opened the barn door to tired hinges that cried out and cows that stirred as bitter wind whipped circles of snowflakes inside.

"Ah, Bess. Morning, old girl." Amos set the bucket down and patted their fawn Guernsey in the first stall, giving her a good scratch behind the ear. "How are you today?"

She was their best milker. A little churlish in the mornings but dependable. And if anything, they needed something they could rely on just then.

"You might be the last bit of luck we've got." Amos set the empty milk pail down and used his heel to scoot the wooden stool into position. "Let's get moving, eh? You'll provide breakfast for the Darbys, and the rest a jingle in the master's pockets."

He cleaned Bess with the warmed water and aimed the first few squirts of milk to hit the ground. The rhythm of milking started in, the metal singing with a light curl of steam rising as each warm spray hit the bottom.

"Hello?"

Amos glanced under Bess's body to the barn doors.

Empty.

Just more snow blowing across the blessed yard. And his mind playing tricks as wind shook the barn walls. Couldn't be this again. Not the same memory of the voice he'd heard in the Holts' library . . . nor in his mind through the long winter nights . . .

"Hello? Amos?"

At the sound of the *knock-knock* against the doorjamb, he froze, half holding in the shadows behind old Bess's back and watching in disbelief as a crown of blonde dotted with snowflakes came into view. Charlotte stood in an ivory dress with a lace hem and some fancy pink coat like she was bound for the opera—pretty, but fabric near thin as air. And ready to be marked by soil in a poor man's outbuilding.

"Lady Charlotte." Amos stood tall. Cleared his throat. And addressed her with more surprise in his voice than he'd intended. "What brings you out on a day like this?"

"I seem to have a habit of catching you at the most inopportune moments."

Bess chose her moment too, moaning and giving a right good kick that'd send a man to his behind in the dirt had Amos not been paying close enough attention. He was used to the old cow's fire by now. If she wasn't milked on the regular—and on her terms too—she'd let him know.

"If you'll forgive me"—he motioned back to the stool—"Bess here will kick up a fuss if I don't keep . . ."

"Oh yes. Of course."

Amos sat. Started milking again to distract himself. And Charlotte drifted in, uncaring that her lace train would be dragged through hay and the soil of leftover cow muck that had spilled out the edges of the pens.

Charlotte could be charmed by the humble in the same way gentry ladies were taken in by gilded bonnets and bows. The normalcy of morning chores seemed to interest her, if he read her smile right, and never did a lady not fit the surroundings more than just then as she stood inside the stone walls of his dilapidated barn.

"Your mother told me I'd find you out here when I knocked on your door. Is it too early?"

He shrugged. "Been up for a while."

Amos stole glances—just enough to see her notice the starlings that had bedded in the eaves and lean down to stroke the traitor tabby that had padded up and curled against her hem. Seemed a mite safer to keep to the rhythm of milk pulsing into a pail instead of getting caught looking, so Amos turned away. Pretended he wasn't thinking too much as the seconds ticked by. Why in heaven's name did Providence keep pushing her across his path?

Charlotte stepped away from Bess. And circled wide around the cow until she'd stopped behind him. Lord, what was that scent she brought with her? Something soft—like spring flowers cutting through the dead, frozen air of January. Probably from Paris, knowing her mother. And so distracting, Amos didn't dare stop what he was doing to look up again.

"But why would you be knocking upon our door, Lady Charlotte?"

"I have an appointment in London. With the break in the snow, I was hoping a train could make it out this morning. I'm headed there now. To the Coventry station, I mean. Your farm was on the way."

He glanced out to the yard with its specks of white flying by on the wind, now trying to fall with more aggression.

So much for the lull.

"You've a drive ahead of you then."

"Yes, but I have something—a Christmas gift. When I found out you'd been dismissed, I didn't know how else to get it to you. So I thought . . ."

A small, rectangle-shaped box appeared from her side, wrapped in olive paper with gold foil crisscrossing the sides and a gold pinecone bauble shining on top. Must have been something the Holts were doing for their tenants. Wasn't out of the ordinary for the master and mistress to offer a gift at the holidays, though it was usually a basket of Williams pears or, if it had been a fair yield in an abundant year, a small goose for Christmas dinner.

"I'll just leave it for you." Charlotte stepped up to the worn stall post nearest him and balanced the paper-wrapped package on top.

"Thank you." Amos nodded so she'd know he saw it. But kept to milking just the same. Things were different now that she was betrothed and about to become one of them. "Please tell Lord Harcourt the Darbys appreciate the gesture."

"I'm sure I would if it was from the Holts."

"It's not?"

"No. This one happens to be from me."

Something had changed in her voice. A little razor's edge of sharpness that said Charlotte Terrington could give back as good as he gave, just like when they were kids. And while the cello-playing heiress might have grown up, something in her tone said he ought to remember she hadn't changed all that much.

"Amos Darby. You are going to look at me eventually, aren't you?"

Not if I can help it.

"I'm sorry. Got to stay on task. Chores, you see." He flitted a glance beyond the barn doors. "And the snow."

Amos stared at the bucket—the last safe place he knew with her hovering so close behind. The hem of that pretty dress flashed a wave of lace before his eyes, too fast for him to respond as the toe of her shoe clipped the side of the pail and sent milk sloshing up over the rim.

"Oy!" He shot up from the stool, kicking a wet trouser leg. "What was that for?"

"To see if you're still alive." Charlotte posted fists at her hips and stared back at him. "Nice to know you are."

Those golden eyes, open and honest, held him in reproach for ignoring her as he stooped to wring out the wet herringbone of his trouser leg, until that pretty face melted into an unexpected smile.

Amos rolled his eyes because even warm milk turned freezing in bitter air. His only good pair of socks was now soiled. And Bess was fixing to make a royal ruckus if she didn't get relief soon.

"I didn't come to make trouble. And . . . I'll pay for that. The spilt milk, I mean."

"You think I'm charging our mistress for milk now?" He righted the bucket to save the trace left in the bottom, trying his darndest to appear indifferent.

"I am *not* your mistress."

"You will be soon enough."

"And I thought we were friends."

"We are. But things are different now." Amos challenged her with a gaze that held firm. "Why are you really here? Save for to punish me through my chores?"

"Well, if you wouldn't be such a stubborn . . . I only wanted to . . ." Back to vulnerable. She dropped her hands from their posts. Her arms and shoulders lost their tenseness too. And her eyes softened, then brightened as she looked back at him. "I wanted to make sure you were alright. You were dismissed because of me, after all. With what happened at Christmas dinner."

"I was dismissed because of me."

"But if Will hadn't seen the book—"

"It was my doing." He cut her off, but not with sharpness. "And I wasn't long for that position anyway. His Lordship would much prefer these rough hands working as a tenant farmer than serving in state livery in his dining room."

Amos didn't mean to, heaven help him, but his gaze drifted to her ring finger. Then he tore it away just as fast. If a diamond winked there, it was hidden under her glove. And he wasn't even sure he wanted to see the evidence of Will's having won the marriage game they'd been playing since all three of them were kids.

Knowing she'd seen, he offered a mumbled, "You're to be married."

"I am. And I'll accept your well-wishes, but only if you accept the gift in return. I'd consider it a truce between friends if you would."

How was he supposed to pretend a few kind words from her didn't feel like a cannonball to his gut?

Amos pointed through the barn doors, where the snow-speckled motorcar was parked by the road. "You'll miss the train. And your chauffeur's probably freezing to death out there."

"I'd say not, as he's still at home having his morning tea."

He should have known, and found himself almost smiling outright because of it. "When did you learn to drive?"

"A while back. I asked Father's chauffeur and he taught me."

"You asked."

She tipped a brow a shade higher. "Alright, I insisted. And that it should remain secret. Does that surprise you?"

"Not in the least, for an heiress who plays the cello in secret and coaxes carriage rides to part with her designer dresses."

"I suppose I've just never been good at standing back and letting others do for me. To every governess's chagrin and my mother's everlasting horror, I'm afraid." Charlotte did that thing when she was thinking out loud—trailed her gloved finger along something close by, this time choosing a slat of aged wood framing the stall. "But with that . . . there's the matter of the gift. This should be an even exchange, should it not?"

"I don't have anything to give. No trunks to sell, remember?"

"I should be the judge of that." Charlotte stepped up. Started stripping off her gloves, one dove-gray finger at a time. "Teach me."

"You want to . . . milk my cows?"

"Why not? I know how to drive. To play the cello even though my mother forbids it. And to appreciate the likes of Dickens and your Sir Walter Scott—though I'm still wary over the latter if truth be known. But if I will be mistress of this estate one day, then I should like to have my wits about me to prove I know more than how to entertain and redecorate parlors. I'd consider it a fair exchange if you'd teach me how to manage an estate."

"And would your fiancé approve of such an arrangement?"

The wind kicked up then, rattling the barn walls like an angry beast locked outside. They looked at each other as winter warred—he waiting for her answer, and she stalling in giving it.

"I hadn't thought to ask him." Charlotte squared her shoulders and tucked her soft leather gloves in the belted waist of her coat, then eased in beside him, matter-of-fact in pushing in. "So what do I do first? I mean, I know what to do—we've always had livestock. But I want to learn to do things properly. And Father would never allow it."

Amos stood behind. Frozen in more ways than one. Hating to see Will's ring mocking him, sparkling from her finger each time the canary diamond caught the light.

"You need to, uh, warm your hands first."

"Alright." Charlotte cupped her hands together and blew air in. "What next?"

"If you're just starting out, you wash her. But I've done that already, so you can . . ." Amos leaned in. Knelt at her side, trying to show Charlotte how without the pain of his hands touching hers. Forming his palm in the loose curl of a fist, Amos held his fingertips a shade away, his worn skin leather against her porcelain.

He cleared his throat. "Hold at the top—light. A soft grip but firm."

"Like this?"

"Aye. Then squeeze down. The first few sprays you put into the hay."

"Why is that?"

"Keeps sickness away to let the bad milk first. I've already done that, though, so you can, uh . . ." Amos eased back on a spark, his hand burning for having grazed the skin of hers. "Just keep going. And shoot straight, or that fancy hem will end up in a sad state like my trousers."

She laughed, and delight lit up her face to watch milk streams creating foam as they collected in the bucket.

A few stolen minutes became a gifted many.

It was all he'd wanted once, those many years ago, to stop time like this. To stay together. Talking. Doing something as simple as milking on a snowy morn. And if Amos were a braver man, he'd admit it was all he wanted now. If the world were different and they had the power to write their own stories.

His was to be with *her*.

Time melted until Charlotte's auto was covered in a blanket of white, and Amos's footprints across the farmyard were lost under a fresh layer of snow. And the pail was near full when she leaned back on the stool.

"That was fun." Charlotte smiled, flexing the cramp out of tired hands but still proud as a peacock with the bounty before her. "Is it like riding a bicycle then? You know, you won't forget once you learn?"

"With time and practice, you could do it in your sleep. But more likely it's the bitter cold mornings that'll do the remembering for you. I wouldn't call it enjoyable when you have weather like this and a couple dozen more head to go. But it is handy to know how to roll along before you freeze to death."

Her laugh was soft, just under her breath. "Right. What's next?"

"Haven't you had enough?"

"One doesn't stop until the work is done. Isn't that the way of it on a farm? The gift I brought cost a pretty penny."

"I can't accept it then."

"Oh yes you can, Amos Darby. You're going to teach me everything. Seems a few lessons on farming would be only fair." Charlotte stood. *Close.* Too close for either of them, it seemed, seeing as she turned on a dime and her nose nearly careened into his shoulder. "To, um . . . to . . ."

"Even things out?"

Edging back, she nodded and retreated until she bumped the stall slats behind her. Amos reached around her to retrieve the gift from the post. Something hard shifted about inside as he tilted the box in his hands.

"It's heavy. Must be telling the truth." Amos paused, then tipped his chin toward the flurries outside. "And it appears you've missed the train."

"Aye. I have." She half smiled, borrowing his word. "That's too bad."

"Want to come inside? Warm up by the fire?"

Charlotte gazed at the stone house beyond the falling snow, its chimney coughing smoke and promising a warm respite inside.

"I brought my cello, on the off chance I could play here. You know, if the gift worked out." She blushed, stealing some of his breath. "I can't play at home."

He smiled. Nodded. "We'll bring it in then."

"You're certain your mother won't mind?"

"Every farmhand gets a proper breakfast at the Darby table— her words, not mine." Amos stooped, grasping the handle to lift the heavy pail. "And if a lady worked for it, she's earned fresh milk in her tea."

→·←

12 October 1940
Bayley Lane
Coventry, England

Amos lay in bed, trying to count cracks in the ceiling as he stared through the dark.

With one arm draped over his forehead and the other turning the pocket watch in absentminded circles against the quilt at his chest, he battled to do what the tumblerful of single malt ought to have—block out images of so many yesterdays ago.

On a kind night, it was a pink opera coat waltzing into his barn with that gold-wrapped gift. The simple memory of a sweet smile as Charlotte milked her first cow was torture enough. But on the worst of nights, the barn fizzled, to be replaced by the anguish of a blood-bathed No Man's Land, where boys in uniform screamed before being picked off by sniper fire, or horse and rider were mowed down by a line of merciless machine guns. It was a never-ending tangle of blood and bombs and guttural screams as soldiers were blown to bits before his eyes.

Those nights Amos woke in a cold sweat. Breathing so fast he thought his lungs would explode. And wishing for nothing more than to find himself amid the safety of a Coventry farm—even if he was haunted by the ghost of Lady Charlotte—instead of the woeful trenches of France.

Would that it could be so easy to forget.

In a man's younger years, he didn't have ghosts lining up to torment him through the long hours. With the clock ticking like a snare drum in the night. And a man listening to the cadence of his own breaths. It was an aged man who knew that the hours grew in silence. The specters would persist. And all Amos could do was pray the burning swallows of Scotch would deaden his senses enough to welcome oblivion, enough to sleep and make it through the next day.

Until sirens cried out—middle of the blessed night—and twisted a man's gut like few things could.

Amos shot up out of bed. Dropped the pocket watch on the quilt in exchange for the trousers he'd hung on the footrail. He grabbed them up, yanking each leg through and buttoning up in haste. Then pocketed the watch. Tugged suspenders over the shoulders of his Henley and rushed to untie blackout curtains from the brass spoke to give a quick scan of the sky over Coventry.

Bombs had first fallen in June, killing three in the nearby village of Pailton. In the months that followed, searchlights flicked on over Brinley and Radford Roads with regularity. Plane engines hummed in the sky over Stoke Green. And the odd high-explosive bomb had hit in random places, like those that fell on Canley, Cannon Hill, and one night in Hillfields. Rumor had it planes were looking for the Daimler Works and had miscalculated, hitting the residential area of Cambridge Street and, for the first time, killing dozens of Coventrians. And come September, the terrifying sound of machine-gun fire could be heard echoing through the night, in one case ending when a German plane's bomb load had left a torpedo crater to split Wallace Road in two.

It could be another drill . . .

Searchlight beams blinked on, cutting sharp paths from roof to sky over St. Michael's Cathedral. Followed by the CB unit crackling to life in the corner of his bedchamber, echoing off the walls with an urgent summons to the St. Mary's post.

Amos yanked open the drawer of his bedside table, giving a few blinks to the copy of the Dickens book Charlotte had gifted him all those Christmases ago. He swallowed hard. Allowed only a split second to decide as his fingertip traced the gold-embossed letters on the cover, then snatched it up. It would just fit in his inside jacket pocket. Taking the loaded service pistol he kept next to it, Amos moved to the bench at the end of the bed to tug on his boots. He stood, tucked the pistol in his waistband, and yanked up his field jacket from the coatrack on the way out the door.

Until . . . his hand froze on the doorknob.

The half-sung bottle of Glenlivet stood quiet as a bookend to the row of spines on the mantel. He stared at it as the CB sparked with static again, a man's voice in the background crackling with warning. Even so, the Scotch called louder. Drawing Amos back to the shadows. Reminding that he needn't suffer through the night ahead if relief lay within reach.

It was easy enough to reason over the amber liquid, with its familiar promises and whispers of rationalization. It could be a long night. Amos's men needed a leader with his wits sharpened. And it would do no good to have the head of the Home Guard issue orders with shaking hands and bloodshot eyes.

Amos didn't think—just reacted.

A trance of habit took over and he filled the hip flask he kept on him, screwed the lid tight, and tucked the secret savior in his boot. One second he'd fled down the hall. In the next he nearly collided with an alarmed Mr. Cole, who'd stopped in the alcove at the top of the stairs.

That's right—the lad came back. Even as Amos had retired early, his eagle ears had known the instant the back door opened and had followed the sound of the lad climbing the back stairs.

"Good, mate. You're up." Amos nodded as Jacob mussed hair over his forehead with a sluggish palm. Though he had obviously been asleep, his eyes were sharp.

"All of Coventry is up by the sound of it." Jacob gave a hasty tuck to his linen shirt as he hooked a finger around the blackout curtains and looked out.

"I warned you."

"You did that. So this is real then?"

"Looks like it. But we still hope not in the end."

Always aware of the scars upon mangled fingers, Amos used his good hand to snatch the striped box of Pearl matches from the grab-and-go station he'd set up in the wall cutout by the stairs. He pocketed one box, offering the other to Jacob without looking up.

"Forgive me for being blunt, Mr. Darby, but I seemed to think you were warning me of air raids as a sort of joke." Jacob took the box. "You know—test the exile and all that? Hoping to send the enemy barrister out of town on a rail."

"We do enjoy a bit of a tale in Coventry, but never about this." Amos grabbed up a tin hat and held it out. "Here—compliments of the Darby Hotel."

Jacob covered his mop of blond with the helmet and reached for the metal torch nearby. "So we're making a run for it?"

"Aye. But an orderly one. Can't afford to have panic in the streets."

Amos picked up the Enfield service rifle leaning in the corner, trying not to think how fast the moment had come when he'd have to trust a stranger with more than just an unlocked back door and a room for the night.

"Think you can handle this?"

If he was surprised, Jacob didn't show. The lad just pocketed the torch and took the barrel in both hands, giving an expert's check to see it was loaded.

"Right then. Let's go." Amos led them down dark stairs to the hall at the back of the shop.

The ground floor, too, had been rearranged from home defense-force training. Bookshelves were cleared from aisles where they'd sat for ages, widening the path to the door. A set of keys hung on the nail at the bottom of the stairs, which Amos kept on his person during the day and returned each night. The extra service rifle was kept hidden under the counter, the strap of which he strung over his shoulder as they whisked through to the front of the shop. And a can of kerosene sat next to worn Wellingtons in the metal boot tray by the door. Amos fumbled through the haze of drink that still owned him, teetering first and then covering as he hooked the can's handle and lifted with his damaged hand.

If Jacob noticed, he said nothing. Just paused as Amos took a last look around, memorizing the still, shadowed face of the bookshop. They'd had some good years, the old shop and he. Seemed surreal now if he'd have to say goodbye.

The air was oddly thick for autumn. The moon peeked behind rickrack clouds and the city streets lay under a humid haze. Sirens screamed as doors opened and shut in the dark. A breeze tricked the mind into thinking wind was a plane engine soaring overhead. Coventrians looked up, even as shoes shuffled down sidewalks and wind toyed with stray newspapers twirling by. They watched, their vigil of the skies triggered with every few steps.

The trek down Bayley Lane proved an orderly one, with citizens stepping out of doors from flats above the shops and joining in the hurried calm of a Pied Piper's trek to nearby shelters. The largest was at Drapers' Hall, but even then it would house only two hundred. How many more were venturing down basement stairs beneath factory floors or hurrying to street shelters lined up along the sidewalk? It all happened behind blacked-out windows and doors and alleyways, where lamps had gone cold and citizens marched like ants through arteries of an underground world.

Amos had seen men crumble at the first signs of battle. It was bewildering then to find the Yank was quite steady. For an outsider with his first taste of a Blitz bombing, Jacob didn't seem inclined to run anywhere—certainly not like Amos had thought when nudging the lad back to London earlier in the day. He glanced over his shoulder to find Jacob had taken off the tin hat and given it to old Mr. Ansley, then kept eyes peeled to the sky with rifle in hand as he aided the man in helping his wife down the stairs of their paint shop stoop.

Once on the sidewalk, Jacob handed off the torch to the old man too. But, odd, Amos could have sworn Jacob was talking to Mrs. Ansley. Almost speaking in comfort? She nodded more than once to him, though her native tongue was German and her English spotty on the best day. It wasn't anything of note for Bayley Lane, as the couple had set up shop there long as anyone could remember, and they'd never be suspected of sympathies for a country that their own boy had lately shipped off to fight.

Amos shrugged it off—his own suspicious nature at play. He watched as Jacob sent the couple to safety. And instead of following on to safety himself, he slid the strap of the rifle over his shoulder and joined Amos in directing citizens forth. Watching the sky. Keeping the calm though nerves took over, so that citizens' start-and-stop trekking along the sidewalk became a hurried game of the Fairy Footsteps in the dark. And waving a hand in the direction of the shelters—asking Amos which ones would likely fill first and informing citizens which ones they might go to next.

"Go on now." Amos offered the triangle tin jerry can and pointed Jacob toward Drapers' Hall. "Get under cover."

Jacob accepted the can. Curiously, though, he didn't move. Just stood shoulder to shoulder with Amos before turning to watch the sky with him. "What about you?"

"I go to my post. The Air Raid Report and Control Centre, St. Mary's Street station."

"What's that? Command center?"

"Aye." Amos used his good hand to point in the direction of the searchlights from the roof of Drapers' Hall. "The Home Guard post. I'm section commander for the areas around Bayley Lane."

Jacob held firm on the street corner, watching as people hurried by in the dark. Looking over them one by one. Women with scarves covering hair crimpers . . . Men with serious eyes and shirts hastily tucked into trousers . . . Young children white-knuckling their bears or toy trains . . . And older siblings carrying them. Until his gaze drifted up the street the direction of the bookshop with the blue façade and rounded glass display window shrouded in shadows.

"What about the Holts? Shouldn't we see if anyone's at the shop? Just to make sure, you know."

"The Holts live outside the city—the manor on the hill over-looking Brinklow Road." Amos watched as Jacob shook his head and stared up the street, distant like, as sirens kept on with their wails. "You didn't know?"

"Lady Harcourt told me about their house in the country, just not where it was."

"A 'house in the country'?" He laughed, taken in by the lad's innocence. "It's the largest estate in this part of the king's land. And Her Ladyship the unelected queen of Coventry. She may live just outside the city, but she's much beloved in it. Lady Eden captains the ship now, determined as she is to pass on her late father's legacy with the estate. But if anyone is thinking to check the Holts' shop, I assure you it's been done. Thrice over by now. And will be looked after through the night by me."

"So that's why . . ."

As the few breaths ticked by, something shifted in Jacob's profile, like he was calculating in that solicitor's mind of his as he stared at the closed-up Eden Books.

"That's why what?"

"Nothing." Jacob nodded and gripped the jerry can handle tight like a weapon in his hand. "Alright. Let's go then. Which way?"

"Which way?"

"St. Mary's Street. We have a job to do, right? We should go."

Amos eyed him. Wondering what he hadn't said. And why he was willing to put up his life for the crowd of strangers marching past.

"We?"

"That's right. Unless you think Coventry folk prefer a stranger not step in their command centers or their rooming houses either."

"As section commander for Bayley Lane, it's my judgment to accept any pair of hands willing to hold a rifle. As long as I know the man behind the trigger is sure." And as long as he could keep an eye on the lad.

"What do you think then? Am I sure?" Jacob held firm, watching the flood of people filing past.

"Tell me—are all Yanks as eager as you?"

"I don't know about that, Mr. Darby, but I'd wager by the sound of those sirens, the Germans are. And that's more than enough to contend with right now."

CHAPTER SIX

*T*he glasshouse stood hushed and alone and hemmed in by poplars, as if trying to hide from all the world.

Charlotte stepped through the opening in the blackthorn wall to find the glasshouse with the same aged wrought iron and patina glass she'd remembered, and the high-pitched roof and a central turret fashioned after London's famed Crystal Palace. But now climbing roses twisted through iron pillars with peachy-pink blooms framing an archway over the worn cobblestone path. And curious, but the iron gate that used to be rusted over had been replaced and was now in good repair.

Approaching the glasshouse, Charlotte pressed her palm to the brass handle of the palladium doors—the metal dewy and cold in her grip—and pushed them wide.

They parted on a creaky hinge, then lay still in invitation.

This was not the abandoned place she'd remembered from childhood. Now, a fragrant mix of earth and florals greeted her, the scents having been awakened by the rain. In the first row of plants: potted geraniums, phlox seedlings, and roses in various states of bud. In the far ones: the starts of French beans, green tomato plants, and cucumbers that stretched to the ceiling on a lattice frame.

Fresh pots were stacked on an iron shelf, waiting their turn to be useful. Nearby, broken terra-cotta shards lay in a neat pile. Time spent at the Darby farm had taught her that one never wasted what could be used; these bits were perfect for pot drainage. Work gloves and a spade had been discarded in a seagrass basket on the workbench, with a half-full pot of peat moss nearby.

And . . . books? A lone stack on a high shelf. Just like they used to be all those years ago.

"Lady Charlotte?"

She raked in a breath—not at hearing her name spoken but at the sound of the familiar voice, rough and warm against the pattering of rain on glass. With a hasty swipe to catch tears under her bottom lashes, Charlotte turned with a painted smile. "Amos. Hello."

"It is you." Amos leaned over to the doors and clicked the glass to kiss at the center. "We have to keep these closed or even with the rain, there'll be a mess of starlings I'll have to chase out by day's end."

"Yes. Of course. I'd forgotten."

Charlotte hadn't seen him for weeks, since she'd stopped visiting the Darby farm. In the oddest way, standing before her now Amos seemed older—even in that short time. With a striped work shirt and canvas jacket rain-speckled at the shoulders and wool trousers that looked to have seen better days. Rain had soaked his hair, too, revealing the hidden sheen of russet Charlotte remembered from their childhood days. The locks hung low over his forehead now, dark and long, but not enough to hide curiosity playing in hazel eyes.

"Seems we have a habit of finding each other unawares. What are you doing this far out from the manor?"

"I was walking in the gardens and . . ." She rolled her eyes toward the wiry streams of water running down the glass and smiled at being caught. "The rain."

"Me too." Amos offered a hint of a return smile, though he tipped his head to the side, maybe doubting that was all there was to say about it. And if he knew her that well, he'd have been right.

The customary invitation for tea had set Charlotte and Mother off to Holt Manor again. Will sometimes appeared in the grand marble entry—and had that day—greeting them with a kiss to his mother's cheek and a wink to Charlotte. It was always the same, Will offering a quip: *"It's best to leave well-bred ladies to the secret delights of their parlors."* Then he'd scoot off to give attention to some other favorite haunt on the estate.

It was, as Charlotte was fast learning, Will's intention to shrug off these visits in order to spend time with his other great loves— horses and hunting—and avoid talk of their upcoming nuptials altogether.

That duty was left to the ladies in a ballet-pink parlor, with damask wallpaper and eggshell wainscoting, and tea set before a palatial stretch of manicured gardens beyond floor-to-ceiling windows. And whilst the mothers fell into spirited chatter of wedding preparations, Charlotte would smile and nod and stir honey in her tea, then clink her delicate silver spoon against the porcelain cup so the conversation drifted in and out:

". . . something with dill and something mousseline . . . something in white wine cream sauce . . . a seasonal something parfait and something torte . . ."

It worked—for a while. Until Charlotte's toes took to tapping under the hem of her tea gown and she stared out the window with longing, as if the Holt Manor gardens could save her from her matrimonial fate.

Understanding or caring very little, Mother had agreed to allow her a walk, even though storm clouds hung low in the sky and the air was heavy with the scent of rain. Each party slipped away into their own corners—the mothers into their usual rhythm of conversation and Charlotte to find solace in escaping through the estate fields.

"I'd wager they haven't noticed my absence." Charlotte shrugged, summing all up as an afterthought instead of the set of worries it was. "You know. Mothers and weddings being what they are."

Amos gazed through the glass, out to the fields. He took a few steps then, tracking fresh earth from the soles of his boots on the tile, until he joined her in the flower row.

"Was out pushing the herd through the south gate. Would be hard not to notice you fleeing like a banshee through my fields, like you were running from something that had scared the living daylights out of you. But that was before the rain, mind."

"Oh. You saw that . . ."

"Aye. *That*."

Trying not to think on the frothy layers of her salmon gown being sprayed with mud, Charlotte picked up the spade and began filling a pot, the distraction of peat moss rich and earthy as she dug in. "I didn't realize anyone had taken this place in hand again. It's so lovingly tended."

"It's not far from Foxhollow Farm."

His farm now.

"You don't mean . . ." She looked up, bewildered. "You?"

"We all take turns, the tenants whose land borders the manor. To keep it going for His Lordship. Seemed a pity it stood alone all those years. Now it'll be useful again."

"But how have you had the time, with looking after your farm and your mother and Caroline?"

"Just the farm now." He slipped his hands in his trouser pockets. "Ma's married again. Took Caroline up to Edinburgh to her new husband's land weeks back. I said I'd stay on. Look after things."

"Oh, I hadn't heard. Congratulations."

"Thank you. But for a few extra bob per week?" He glanced around; the rows were teeming with life. And if she judged the character of the man he'd become, she'd wager Amos did the lion's share of the work for a pebble's worth of notice. "Can't afford not to do all I can to keep the farm going, if it's to be my own."

Charlotte searched his face, waiting for a denial that the very thing he'd once said he didn't want, he still didn't want now. She caught sight of the spines stacked on the top shelf—the books they'd once pilfered together—and pointed. "They're still here?"

Amos rubbed a palm to the base of his neck, the ghost of a sheepish smile returning in answer.

"All those times I visited the farm, it was only livestock and chores. And me playing the cello for the cows in your barn. I just assumed you'd given up on books."

"Is that what we were doing? Chores?" Amos laughed, but it seemed not for any real humor in what she'd said.

"What I meant was, why keep them a secret out here?"

"Everyone has secrets."

Amos turned to her, and the friendly calm she was so used to seeing in him had been replaced by something far more deliberate. He was, at best, challenging her. At worst, what was he implying?

"Whatever do you mean?"

"What were you running from?" he whispered, again tipping his head to the fog-laden hills beyond the glass walls.

Charlotte swallowed hard, her hand stilling on the spade. Her cheeks flushed. This conversation was far too candid and her heart a little too lured by the earnestness in his words. "You shouldn't say such things."

"What? The truth?"

"A gentleman knows when it's appropriate to—"

He scoffed. "Good. I never claimed to be one."

"Nevertheless, I will be mistress of this estate one day. And you in my husband's employ. I'd wager Will knows when it's proper to speak and . . ." Charlotte slowed, hating the clumsiness of such a comparison to trip out her mouth. Her voice lowered to a barely there whisper, ending with "And when not."

"Is that so?" Amos sighed. Softer this time as he slid his hands deep in his trouser pockets. "Well, *Charlie*, I'd wager Will Holt will know how to play his every part with precision. When it suits him."

The implication of a loveless marriage bit.

And bit *hard*.

"I am not Charlie. Not anymore." Charlotte stiffened her shoulders at the childhood name, the scorn in her voice having surprised even her.

"Really? When I think I saw her recently? I believe she favored milking cows and playing her cello in my barn. And offering expensive gifts she has no business giving."

"Had I known books were such an affront to a man's sensibilities, I'd have thought better of it. All the way back to that carriage ride. You had every right to refuse them. And as for my personal affairs . . ." She lifted her chin higher. "You haven't the liberty to judge. And you should know more than anyone that I cannot just walk away from the responsibilities of my station, nor this estate."

"But you can run from them, hmm?"

Charlotte shoved the spade into the pot and whirled around, facing him. "Why must we continue to play this game?"

"What game?"

"Of you attempting to catch me out every time we meet." She fixed her glare, pinning him down with a steel-for-steel challenge of defiance. "Do you take pleasure in making me look a fool for my choices?"

"No. I—"

"Then how do you explain your anger toward the master who offers you a living?"

"I've no quarrel with Lord Harcourt. But Will is not his father."

"And that is not what I meant," she shot back.

The gaze that met hers was entirely open. And vulnerable. And heaven help her, but the same she recognized from across the Holts' dining hall that Christmas Eve. It was everything the tall, quiet, calloused-hands workman in him should have denied, but didn't.

Amos swallowed hard. "I apologize. I just thought we'd . . . offended you in some way."

Not at all what she'd expected him to say. "Offended me?"

"You came to the farm for months. Playing Bach in my barn. Fetching guinea eggs nested in the hedgerow and keeping me company while I repaired the fencing. You even baked bread and canned fig jam with my little sister while I read aloud in the kitchen. And then just stopped. With no word as to why."

Charlotte broke their connection and stared down at her hands. If only they could save her.

"I know. And I am sorry."

She'd told herself the visits had stopped out of respect for her betrothed. For her parents and for Amos's family. For her reputation, because if anyone talked, it started from the bottom up and spread like wildfire from there. And for a thousand tiny reasons that didn't seem to amount to much now. Not when Charlotte had run like a scared child, and they both knew it.

"Caroline and my mother had grown accustomed to having their mistress around. They felt her absence up to the day they left."

"Caroline and your mother did . . ."

"Aye." Amos tapped a loose fist against the workbench. "I suppose we all knew before long things would have to change."

"Not all things. When a woman—heiress or not—is her husband's property once she weds. My parents believe it. As do Will's. And as my closest male cousin is to inherit my family estate, there is no option for me but to marry into one. All are happy with such a tidy arrangement." She paused, disheartened to even utter the truth. "As I pay calls to society matrons who offer little more than witless gossip behind my back and manufactured smiles to my face, it is everyone else who decides my future. And don't think I am ignorant to the truth; they pass judgment, believing I ought to be grateful the prince of this county has chosen me as his wife."

Charlotte dared test him with her words, waiting to see whether he'd show her pity. Or worse, scorn. All for doing what she'd been bred to.

Amos braced his hands at his waist and parted his lips as if to say something, only to stop short. And that one decision—with the genuine look of concern in eyes that almost appeared hurt *for* her—told her it was safe to continue.

"How do I pretend to understand? I may not read the books we always loved. Nor play the cello. Nor entertain the dreams we had as children. No matter how dear they may be—" Her voice tripped on emotion but Charlotte caught it, drawing her arms in as a shiver overtook her. She rubbed her hands over her arms to chase the chill away. "Even if they are all I once wanted. Even if I should want them now, right this very moment."

Amos stood still. Sighed deep. And then slipped out of his jacket, careful and slow in how he draped it over her shoulders. With a voice raked over gravel, he finally whispered, "What can I do?"

"Grant me one small favor, for an old friend?"

His jaw clenched. "Milady."

"Let me visit the farm again? I never should have left as I did."

"Charlie," Amos whispered, his features pained with uttering the pet name. "It wouldn't be right. Not now that I live there alone. You know that."

Gripping the lapels, Charlotte squeezed the jacket together until she could almost feel Amos's warmth radiating through her skin. And waited, gazing back through tears she didn't try to hide now. "And if I said that I believe a few weeks of real beauty might sustain a lifetime without it?"

He searched her face, stirring tiny pinpricks inside that said they might both wish things were different.

"Every time I think of you marrying him, I am scared. For *you.*"

She blinked back tears, the rain trilling against the glass ceiling. "What choice do I have?"

To do what the "headstrong heroines" Mother always complained about from Charlotte's novels was to abandon reason. To turn her back on all that she'd been reared to believe as truth. It didn't matter. Not when Charlotte's hands begged to let go and instead reach for Amos. Or allow him to reach for her. And not just with the heat of his jacket to her skin, but to crash in the beautiful middle somewhere, where titles and land and the rules of marriage could not diminish a truth finally spoken over roses and rain.

Everything might have been different if not for the shadow on horseback that burst through the opening in the blackthorn wall, dismounted, and stormed up the cobblestone path.

The air split as Will swung the doors open, the sudden intrusion blasting them apart too.

Charlotte stumbled back, bumping the workbench with the small of her back as Will rushed in from the rain. He gave no impression at the compromise of finding his fiancée alone with one of the tenants. Especially *that* tenant. Instead, he eased Amos's jacket from her shoulders. Handed it back with a firm hand. And replaced it with the rain-dampened wool of his own as he delivered the news that Lord Harcourt had fallen from his horse in the glen. The physician had been called. And Charlotte's was an urgent summons to the manor to await news with the rest of the family.

All that was left was to issue a desperate glance back as Will lifted Charlotte into his saddle and swung up behind her. Amos stood in the frame of the glasshouse doors, holding his jacket in a clenched fist. She met the eyes she knew so well, begging them— begging *him*—to understand.

Though stolen moments had dared to whisper a different choice might exist, they both knew the rain would end. The sun would shine again. And starlings would find their way beyond the stolen moments in a glasshouse, through doors left open wide when Amos walked away.

They both knew the reality of their world was king.

And it would always win.

❖

12 October 1940
Brinklow Road
Coventry, England

Charlotte stood at the back of Holt Manor, staring out where sun bled through the poplars and the glasshouse met with smoke plumes rising in the sky over Coventry.

When the previous night's bombing raid had begun, Charlotte and Eden, the estate staff, and their WLA recruits had taken shelter in the root cellar, all packing between the dirt walls tighter than tinned fish. It wasn't until hours after dawn that the pulse of bombs stilled. The sirens quieted. And they could finally stretch out stiff limbs as the countryside calmed. All that was left now was a late start to the day and starlings to dance about the poplar trees, unaware they'd been spared the Luftwaffe's bombs.

This time.

It had felt much the same that spring of 1914, when all in Charlotte's world seemed teetering upon the edge of a cliff. Overnight, the talk in Lady Harcourt's parlor had shifted from planning the wedding of the county to lamenting a world fast decaying into the reality of war. No one—save for the fanciful, the desperate, or the truly foolhardy—dared plan a future under that yoke. Little did they know what was to come.

An engine rumble caught Charlotte's attention and she turned, scooting the memories off again.

Mr. Cox's green Bedford truck chugged up to the servants' entrance with corrugated steel rising from the bed—the first of several Anderson shelters to be delivered and dispersed among estate tenants in the weeks to come. It would prove an eyesore in the rose garden, but there was little choice in the matter to ensure the safety of those on the estate. Charlotte had agreed without hesitation with Mr. Cox and Eden's plans to transfer the roses to the manor's solarium before digging steel into their place.

As for the rest of the fields—all the way up to the glasshouse and its blackthorn border and the family plot nestled in the trees—those hills would be churned fresh with the harvest. And come spring, it would be the charge of Eden, their Land Girls, and anyone with able hands to help plow and plant the vast acreage for Holt Manor's contribution to the war effort.

Another cog in the machine of war, grinding ever closer.

"Good day, Mr. Cox." Charlotte slipped on oxblood leather driving gloves as she approached the side of the truck. "But given the state of affairs, I feel as though I should say I am dreadfully sorry instead."

"Milady." He stepped out and tipped his woolen cap to give a bow of the head in greeting. He followed her to the back of the truck, looking over the steel beast in its bed.

"It appears quite stout, doesn't it?" Charlotte ran a gloved hand over the edge of the roof, corrugated steel ridges bumping along her gloved palm.

"Sir John Anderson knows what he's about, I'd say. We've two more to come here, and one each at the tenant farms. 'Twas a fine idea of Lady Eden's to bury them on the hill instead of in the garden behind the manor—clever to give us the best chance of not flooding with runoff rains."

"That, and it seems my daughter read somewhere we could grow vegetables in the earth piled on the roof. Waste not, want not with her. Perhaps nearest the glasshouse is the best place for it."

"Aye, milady. You've come to supervise the dig then?"

"Oh no. I'm quite able to trust you in all that." Charlotte smiled and pointed to her Rolls-Royce Silver Ghost the chauffeur was just bringing around—the 1923 model Will's mother had insisted on purchasing after the war but that Charlotte hadn't the heart nor money to replace now. The auto was kept in fine tune nonetheless, gleaming as it rounded the far corner from the carriage house drive. It slowed to a stop and the chauffeur waited, standing by the open door. "I'm to town. Driving myself seemed easier for all concerned on a day such as this."

"The servants' hall was thick with it this morn, milady. We're all on tenterhooks to hear the city center took a direct hit." Dread squeezed in her chest as Mr. Cox continued. ". . . bombs fell on Queens, Warwick Road, Bishop Street . . ."

Charlotte had been plagued with ill nerves, too, since they stepped out of the cellar that morning and saw smoke rising in the sky. She looked over the span of Holt Manor land that turned to neighboring estates and then to the hills beyond that fed the roads leading to Coventry.

"I received much the same in the report from the Home Guard this morning," she confirmed, though the one thing Charlotte required to settle her heart she hadn't yet received information on.

"The row houses were not so fortunate along Leicester Row." He shook his head. "Along with the City Arcade having been decimated. All the shop fronts there are gone. I look at the smoke now and wonder what's afire. And who of our neighbors are suffering this day."

"I wonder much the same." It was why Charlotte had been shaking in her shoes upon hearing the bombing reports that had already come in. She knew what her heartbeat pulsed, to know the state of Bayley Lane. Would the bookshops still stand? And if they did, for how long?

"I'd wager we'll spend extra time in the pews at St. Michael's tomorrow."

"Yes, Mr. Cox. We will. And do our best to support our neighbors at this difficult time. It's why I'm to town. It seems prudent to check with the shop owners on Bayley Lane to see how we've fared."

"We all do our part, milady."

"I believe that is true. And yet it doesn't seem fair that you will labor in digging ditches whilst I boast in stacking books and making Earl Grey in a hot pot." Charlotte tipped an eyebrow in an exacting look at her attire—a coat and peplum suit in deep saffron, along with a pin-dot ivory blouse and pearls, set off by a smart tam and the ever-serviceable oxford heels. Not exactly garden-ready.

"Not at all, ma'am. I'd wager a cuppa and kind words are exactly what the shopkeepers need just now."

"Let us hope so. And Lady Eden is in the fields, I trust?"

"She is, milady." He tipped his chin the direction of the tractor and the ebony-haired lass in dungarees, a thick-weave fisherman's sweater, and a bright cherry kerchief holding her long braid back from her eyes as she steered the mechanical beast chewing its way across the fields. "Been out nigh on two hours now, checking the estate for damage. And already preparing us in case there's more to come."

"As is my daughter's way. You'll keep her from . . . any harm, I trust?"

"I will, milady. We've no mind to go poking around corners of the estate that don't need our help just now. I'll keep a watchful eye out. And report to you that all is secure."

A breeze whisked by, fluttering the wisps of ebony waves sneaking out of Eden's kerchief, and the mother's heart within her couldn't help but smile as she stopped the tractor to survey Holt Manor's rolling acreage before them. Eden noticed the truck with the Anderson and soon was heading in their direction.

"And it seems I will now have to remind my daughter that I am quite able to drive on my own, bomb craters marring city streets or not."

The troop of Land Girls thundered out of the manor's service entrance then, the little army bursting into the yard with fawn Peter Pan blouses, knit jumpers, and pressed khaki breeches, queuing like cherry-lipped soldiers ready for a posh photo shoot. They smiled and curtsied to Charlotte. And after greeting Mr. Cox, they began selection of Dutch hoes, drags, and picks from the shed to load into the gardener's wagonette.

They were cheery even though they'd spent their first Coventry night packed in a damp cellar and had emerged to a full English breakfast rationed down to tea with fresh milk, blood pudding without spice, canned beans, and rashers that were barely visible on the plate. Blessed be the estate still had milking cows and laying hens, or the lot would have rumbling stomachs to contend with. And as yet, they appeared completely unaware of what awaited them in the fields that day.

Aren't they marvelous . . .

"Our new recruits have been introduced to Your Ladyship, I trust?"

"They have. Thank you. I met them this morning. And I very much fear the enthusiasm my daughter has for protocol may be a bit . . . challenged in the near future? For a number of reasons."

"Lady Eden will have it sorted in short order."

"Indeed," Charlotte added, with a restrained smile. "Then I'll leave this in your capable hands, Mr. Cox. And my daughter to instruct our guests in their duties."

The sassy one by name of Dale stood out front of the Land Girls pack, spotted Eden cutting across the drive, and waved, then set her stance at attention and gave a cheeky little salute off the tip of her brown felt hat. Charlotte met Eden on the gravel drive, noting that she eyed the gaggle of girls and the gardener's wares and was putting it all together that the auto was without a chauffeur as she marched past.

"What's this, Mama? You're not leaving?"

"Yes, Eden dear." Charlotte pressed a kiss to her daughter's cheek. "I'm to the shop. To open up."

"You don't honestly believe anyone should be longing for a book on this day? Not with bombs blasting on our doorsteps all night. I'd eat my hat if there was even one customer to come through the door."

"Perhaps days like this are exactly why we have books in the world. To remember that not all is lost, even if we find ourselves in the unknown. I like to think we provide a haven for the wanderer. And help him remember he has a place to call home."

"Yes. I know. Philosophy of books and all that they bring to the world." Eden waved off the existentialism like a passing thought. "I don't disagree on a usual Saturday. But we've plans to tend here. Schedules to arrange. Ditches to dig. And your roses to move. Then there's the issue of Mr. Cole . . . You said we'd discuss it."

"And we will. When I return. In the meantime, trust me when I say all is well. Holt Manor is safe—from the handsome solicitor if not from Hitler."

Eden opened her mouth to reply, though her words died as the chirping ladies at the wagonette came into view. And her daughter turned a particularly pale shade of green.

"*Oh no* . . . Have you seen them?"

"I have. And I'd say the WLA sent us girls with genuine spirit."

"Spirit!" Eden stopped, aghast. "Then you don't see the problem?"

"Problem . . ."

Charlotte bit her bottom lip behind her glove at the sight of the Land Girls, posing in their duds for the invisible firing of flash-bulbs. It was as if they were Rita Hayworth on a red carpet, not farmhands who'd be knee-deep in English dirt within a few ticks of the clock.

"You know I couldn't care less for rules and regulations, as long as we bolster the estate. But none of them are wearing arm badges. We haven't a manual for the Land Girls just yet, but I took notes at the estate owner's meeting." Eden pulled a collection of papers from her dungarees' patch pocket, unfolded them, and scanned the contents of the first page. She pointed. "Yes. Here it is: 'Volunteers are asked to wear hats correctly; a good volunteer is a good advertisement.' How is this a good advertisement?"

Charlotte covered a smile. "I'd say a group of bright young things sent to shake us up could be exactly what we need."

"But these are the first assignments in the county. And the chairwoman for Warwickshire warned me, in the strongest possible language, that the WLA is to adhere to strict protocol or the post could be revoked. The Land Girls' uniform is to be precise, and look—they've tipped their hats off the back of their heads to accommodate pin curls. They're wearing earbobs. And rouge, for heaven's sake!"

"Well, we needn't toss these London girls into the deep end of the pool straightaway. We can ease them into country life by degrees. Besides, propriety could use a little"—she brushed up against Eden's shoulder with her own—"nudge now and then, eh?"

"Yes, and we'll nudge ourselves right out of what I need to keep this estate running. If the chairwoman sees them in the fields like that . . ." Eden gazed down the lane as an auto curled round the front gate and rolled down their long drive. "Please, no! Tell me that's not her now. We're not ready."

"I'd wager this chairwoman—"

"Mrs. Fielden. Of Kineton House. But it's one of the secretaries who's managing the day-to-day. A Miss Hildreth of Old Square in Warwick?"

"Ah yes. I am acquainted with Miss Hildreth. She's been quite involved with efforts to plant vegetable gardens in the city parks, and both the county library and organization of the ration book program in Coventry. But I'd wager she spent the night in an air-raid shelter just as we have, and now has far better things to do than dust about terrorizing estate owners."

"But Miss Hildreth is a pit bull for protocol. And I'd say the worst Hitler's planes did last night was throw off her schedule, and she's likely fighting mad as a result."

"That may be. But do try to remember that these girls have volunteered to work on this estate and in the bookshop, all for king and country. Might I suggest you choose your battles accordingly? Do not let their enthusiasm suffer on the very first day out of the gate."

Charlotte patted the rosy apple of Eden's cheek with her gloved palm and moved to take ownership of her auto, nodding to the chauffeur as she slipped into the driver's seat and he closed the door behind. She cranked the window down, offering a smile as the other auto rolled not to the front of the manor but around the back behind them.

"And I'd wager it is not Mrs. Fielden's secretary who's come to pay call to the estate today."

"How can you tell that?" Eden stared back, watching as the auto slowed to a stop behind Charlotte's. And out stepped the lithe figure of a solicitor in tailored trousers and shirt, his suit jacket slung over his shoulder as he flashed a quick wave in their direction.

How very American of him.

"Mr. Cole!" Eden whispered through gritted teeth. "Why on earth would he show his face here? And burning through petrol like rationing is a suggestion?"

"Oh dear. I'm afraid I may have invited him. And he must have talked his way into hitching a ride from Coventry."

"What? Why?"

"While I didn't expect him to be so prompt as to show up the very next day, I did give my blessing for him to come and learn more about us whilst he's in Coventry. I didn't see what it could hurt if at the same time, we could learn more about him. And at the very least, he appears quite capable of handling a shovel."

To Eden's chagrin, she glanced from the Yank strolling through the midmorning sun and then to the once-twittering Land Girls who'd gone dead silent as Mr. Cole and his dashing profile came into full view.

And groaned.

"Oh, *Mama* . . . How could you? How am I ever to get work out of that raggle-taggle wagon of lonely hearts with *him* around?"

Charlotte coughed into her glove. "My dear, I think Mr. Cole is not the enemy you imagine him to be. And had I the opportunity to share this with you last night, I'd have told you as much. But don't fret; Mr. Cox will be here to assist you, and Mr. Fitzgibbons from Foxhollow Farm has agreed to meet you in the grove at the top of the hill. So you needn't put up with our guest alone." Charlotte flicked her wrist. Checked her watch. "Oh dear. Petrol rationing being what it is, I've promised to fetch a list of wives for their factory shifts. And now I'm tardy."

"You're right. We all must do what we can. I suppose I can tolerate Mr. Cole for one day." Resigned, Eden nodded. "But you do plan to stop in at Mr. Darby's shop?"

The recoiling within Charlotte was too swift, as if she were caught out for her private worries. "Why would I do that?"

"I don't know. Just to be neighborly?"

She tightened her posture. Though it was a fair question pinging against the corners of her insides, how a certain shop on Bayley Lane had made out. "You'd like us to be friends with the enemy then?"

"Not friends exactly. I merely wondered how many christenings have been canceled if the city center is as bad as the rumors, that's all. Farley's Bakery may have leftover Godcakes in epic supply, being standard christening fare. I'd wager the Home Guard will have some scheme to assist those whose lives have been turned upside down. Perhaps Eden Books could help?"

Clever girl.

Eden edged back from the auto to let Charlotte be off, with a characteristic smile to boot. Surely her daughter thought she was bringing their shops together under the guise of charity. Yes, and believed Charlotte had no idea her daughter was scheming to draw a curtain of peace between the shops without either owner noticing.

All animosity aside, Eden knew nothing of the stormy history between booksellers. And why Amos's shop and Charlotte's hadn't built a bridge between them in all these years.

"Perhaps you're right. The city center was hit, after all. And we ought to help where we can. If you can entertain that notion here, then so can I at Eden Books. I'll fetch Ginny on my way and then I'll see you at the bookshop this afternoon. Hmm?" Charlotte blew a kiss from gloved fingertips. "You can bring the first of our Land Girls to learn how to run things during the afternoon shift."

Eden trotted alongside the open window. "So you will stop at Mr. Darby's to—?"

"Not to worry. I have every faith in you to manage here while I do there," Charlotte called out, allowing the auto to roll forward. "Making do is what we Holts do best."

Charlotte glanced in the rearview as she drove off, watching as Eden met the rest of the group and Mr. Cole joined in loading gardening sundries in the back of the wagonette.

It was never an easy pill to swallow, this act of doing what was best for your child though it felt beastly in the moment you must play it out. But when that child proved cleverer than the parent, Charlotte was ill-equipped to weather this uncharted territory. Of course she prayed Holt Manor would survive once again. But this time, regardless of drawn battle lines that split Bayley Lane between them, she'd do everything in her power to ensure Eden didn't make the same mistakes she had once upon a time.

A dashing smile could be the death of dreams, in more ways than one.

CHAPTER SEVEN

12 October 1940
Brinklow Road
Coventry, England

The haze of smoke diminished by midday.

Eden stood with a gum shoe anchored on wood slats at the back of the wagonette, surveying the horizon as their party lumbered uphill. Pity that the perch gave her the perfect angle to witness more than she'd wanted. After no more than five minutes in the company of the mysterious Mr. Cole, she was forced to concede that nothing could have quite the hypnotic effect on city girls as a man with a posh suit and a dashing smile.

Toss a bare ring finger in the mix and all bets were off.

The real-life playing out of one of her mama's favorite Austen novels unfolded with Land Girls lined up on hay bales, doing their artful best to survey the estate instead of sneaking glances at their Mr. Darcy in residence. And it seemed enough for them to move from twittering among themselves about the fair weather for working outdoors to batting eyelashes under the brims of cock-eyed uniform hats.

Mr. Cole, meanwhile, had opened a leather-bound notepad and put pencil to paper at ticker-tape speed, oblivious to the charms of the young ladies as Eden pointed out aspects of the estate they'd hope to engage Land Girls in over the next year or two. From timber measuring—which required specialized training none of the girls had yet—to gardening, regular milk rounding, glasshouse work, upkeep to the long stretch of rock walls and hedgerows across the estate, and even the anti-vermin squads' loathsome job of rat catching . . . the list was long. And without able-bodied men left to work, it was growing longer by the day.

"All of this belongs to the estate?" Mr. Cole waved his hand toward the curve of rock wall stretching to a farmhouse behind.

"Well, it belongs to *us*." Eden glanced down from her perch. "But yes. It is part of the estate."

He flipped back a few pages. Tapped the pencil against the pad. "That would be Foxhollow Farm—second-generation Fitzgibbons lease. Yes?"

How in the world had Mr. Cole managed to glean that information with fewer than twenty-four hours spent in their county? He must have been talking. And doing a lot of it if he'd spent the night in a shelter like everyone else. Eden wasn't sure she'd take kindly to planes crisscrossing overhead whilst he sat in a shelter, pressing terrified citizens for information on Coventry's largest landowner.

"It is . . . and the Fitzgibbons are quite dependable tenants."

"I'm sure they are." He ticked off something on the page, only half listening. "And who owned the lease before that?"

In truth Eden had never thought to ask. "I'd have to ask Mama."

"But it's the largest estate in the county. How many acres?"

The little furrow to his brow said he appeared to know, just as Eden did, the exact figures of every parcel of land assigned to the estate. And Mr. Cole referencing the land's lineage did the job of crawling under Eden's skin with ease.

Eden sighed. "To put it in American terms, a thousand. Give or take."

"With the tenant farms, manor house, gardens, and timber land . . . that is substantial. There would have to be records of when the estate passed into your father's hands." He paused for a breath, continuing to tick the pencil to the page like a mathematician calculating dates and figures in his head. "When did he marry Her Ladyship again?"

"Mr. Cole."

"Hmm?" He kept scribbling notes while Eden waited for him to catch up. And when it seemed the silence became too loud, he looked up. "Yes?"

It wasn't until those ice blues locked on hers—and in the same genuine way as they had in the bookshop—that Eden had any hesitation in her duty. Still, she crossed arms over her dungarees with the authority of a commander posted on the quarterdeck and stared down at him. Because wasn't that the way of it? The estate was her ship. And according to English law that allowed females to inherit, she was its next captain. Full stop. And if Eden didn't take the gentleman to task, who would?

"While we can appreciate your interest in our affairs, I hardly see how any of this is relevant to your volunteering to help us. That is why you're here, yes? To dig ditches for the Andersons?"

"Yes, Lady Eden. Of course." Curiosity curtailed by her directness, he popped the notepad closed and tucked it away in his suit jacket pocket. "That is exactly why I'm here. To volunteer with the rest of these happy recruits."

"Oh, we're not volunteers. We're getting paid." Dale flashed a smile, a perfect row of white sparkling in his direction.

He paused in rolling his shirtsleeves at the forearms and, with too good a shade of humor to be believed, added, "All of you?"

They nodded down the row. Even Ainsley, who'd sparked out of her quiet state enough to smile and join in.

"A tidy sum of 38 shillings per week. Above the standard rate. Plus overtime, to carry shifts in the bookshop." Dale tipped the brim of her hat. "Sorry, mate. Women's Land Army uniforms make it all official-like."

"Is that so? It seems I've been outfoxed then. I'll have to remember to negotiate a higher wage in the next recruitment meeting." He reached over, palmed a shovel with a sure grip, but looked it over like it was the first time he'd seen such a foreign object. "I wonder if I can figure out how to use one of these in the meantime."

The giggles came in waves. Followed by Eden's silent exasperation as she turned to face the fields again. She pinched finger and thumb to the bridge of her nose and drew in a steadying breath.

What in heaven's name could Mama have been thinking to allow this man anywhere near their estate? Events in the last twenty-four hours were playing hopscotch with Eden's patience, and the burdens that came with estate maintenance whittled down by rationing and a shoestring budget further threatened to irritate already frayed nerves. And now to have to entertain shameless flirting when she needed an honest day's work out of the lot of them?

She didn't know what was worse.

No matter how Eden might have wished it, nor how hard she worked to the contrary, financials didn't lie. Nor were the bankbooks particularly kind. And the very real threat of having to parcel off her father's land piece by piece looked more like their reality. To realize this jolly party could be all that stood between her and an estate crumbling to pieces made Eden want to offer him out for a fight. Even if she might have to cry into her pillow later.

"Pardon me, Mr. Cole." Flo broke the silence with velvet dripping off her tongue. "You do ask the most intriguing questions for a businessman. What is it you said you do again?"

The question left no veil. This was a kraken released on a full-blown reconnaissance mission of the marriage-minded ladies. The girls leaned forward, captivated in waiting for the answer.

"I'm a servant of the law, miss."

"A solicitor?" Flo released a sweet chuckle. "My, but you must be terribly clever."

"And you can drop the 'miss,'" Dale cut in. "The usual rules of country living need not apply to us city girls." She shoulder-nudged the starlet. "This is Flo. That's Ainsley over there. I'm Dale. And you are?"

"Jacob."

"We're all fresh off the train from Charing Cross Station, Jacob.

And let me tell you, that was a journey. You never know where you'll end up traveling by rail these days." She gave Flo a tiny wink, then smiled wider. "Did you hail from London? Though I'm certain I'd have remembered the pleasure of passing you in the streets of Piccadilly."

Oh, the trifling. Anyone with ears could tell he was a Yank, just by the accent.

Jacob seemed to pick up on this too, flitting his glance to Eden for a breath before he answered, "No. Uh—Detroit, miss."

At least he didn't bite at the inquisition, clearly having deliberately repeated the "miss" instead of using any of the ladies' names. And for that one mercy, Eden had to concede that perhaps this Mr. Cole wasn't completely devoid of character.

"A Yank?" Dale crossed one lithe leg over the other, leaning back against the wagonette slats in casual repose. "My, my. Do tell what would cause you to travel all the way to England just to dig ditches with us—in the middle of a war, no less. Should we expect more handsome Yanks to join up the Brits' fight as you've done? You'd look smart in an RAF uniform."

"I've no stomach for fighting. Outside of a courtroom, that is."

"No?" Unable to stomach another word of the banter herself, Eden turned to blast him face-to-face. "And how is that, Mr. Cole? Do enlighten us as to why our estate in particular should hold such interest for you."

"I'm sorry to disappoint. I'd wager similar circumstances that brought these ladies from the city have also brought me here today."

"And what are those circumstances exactly? If, as you say, you've not come to pick a fight? Why else would you set foot on this estate but with ulterior motive?"

Perhaps the glacial edge could have been left off her tongue. But once voiced, Eden's words couldn't be retracted. And by the looks of the ladies who stood silent, gaping, and with the jolt evident upon Mr. Cole's face, she knew the blow had landed.

"I've come to help and not harm, Lady Eden." The wagon came to a stop and he hopped down to the road to offer a hand as the ladies followed behind. "I'd wager with a war to face, we're all here with naught but the simple kindness of looking after our neighbors in mind."

The rest of their party hadn't a clue as to the undercurrent of their exchange. But Dale's widening of perfect mascara-rimmed eyes and Flo's honeyed "Thank you, Jacob" when he'd offered his hand to help her down said quite enough. He might have owned a sharp edge to his sword, and even sharper wit to his words, but the man suing her now looked like a hero. And Eden? An ungrateful master lording over them all.

"All out now!"

Mr. Cox's shout broke the ice with his usual congenial manner, and the gardener stepped down to begin unloading spade and hoe in a line against the hedgerow. He introduced the ladies to Alec Fitzgibbons from Foxhollow Farm, whom they appeared far too happy to greet as he dispensed leather garden gloves for each pair of hands.

Eden turned back to the wagonette, busying herself with sorting burlap and hand tools from the old wooden gardening caddy nearby. Trying to center her thoughts. And forget having been put in her place. Brushing a rogue tear from her bottom lashes, Eden drew in a steadying breath and straightened her spine.

"Can I help?" Jacob's offer was quiet from behind, with no triumph laced in his tone.

Eden shrugged. "As you like."

"What do I do?"

"Each parcel gets a stack of burlap, twine, and hand tools—a spade and hoe each. The burlap will allow us to transfer the rosebushes in the wagonette. And we'll pot them at the manor before we place them in the solarium. They're quite dear to my mother, so we're taking extra care."

"Good." He tucked in alongside her and reached for one of the crates secured to the side slats with twine and a gingham table-cloth covering the top. "And this?"

"Bedfordshire clangers."

His brow questioned what in the world that was.

"Traditional farmworkers' lunch." She lifted the tablecloth to release a heavenly scent and reveal a horde of rectangle pastries wrapped in wax paper. "Beef, potato, and leek on one side. Plum and apple on the other. It's not fancy. And less desirable with a mix of suet and barley instead of butter and flour. But it keeps stomachs full when we've shared most of the butter stores with our tenants."

"And suet is . . . ?" He waved his hands on air. "You know what? Maybe don't tell me. Ignorance is bliss and all that, yes?"

She tucked the gingham back. "In this case it is."

Jacob smiled, soft and honest, and Eden wished he wasn't trying so hard to appear amenable. And then wished even more he wasn't succeeding at it.

"Forgive the timing, Lady Eden, but I'd thought Lady Harcourt would have explained the affairs to you by now. About the legal situation, that is."

From lunch to smiles to legal in a snap.

Eden's insides hardened again, and she turned back to the crates. "And Mama would have done. But we hadn't time. I went straight from farmwork to spending the night in the cellar surrounded by staff. And once the air-raid sirens stopped this morning, it was all hands to the pump. Then you showed up. All Mama said was we'd discuss it later, but in the meantime perhaps it would be better coming from you—whatever this ill wind is that's blown over our estate."

"Lady Harcourt said that?"

"Well, not the ill-wind part. Those are my choice words." Eden thought she caught the ghost of a smile in his profile as he nodded but didn't comment. "But in the face of it, I have to wonder if you meant what you said. Do you wish to help and not harm by coming here today? Or did you mean that by coming to Coventry at all, your aim is not to harm us?"

"Can't it be both?"

"Is it, then?" She now looked back at him. "Both?"

"I have no right to ask you to believe me. But when I say I'm here to check on the estate, it's given the events of last night. When I heard bombs had fallen in the outlying countryside . . ." Jacob ran a hand through his hair and rested his palm at his nape, like he was caught out. He shrugged. "I just wanted to make sure everyone was alright here."

"Oh." Curse his solicitor's tongue. If he was playing her, the gentleman was as stealthy as a Spitfire in maneuvering it. "Then why all the questions about the estate—dates and land deeds?"

"Would you believe me if I said filling the gaps of my curiosity?"

Eden looked him square in the eyes. Waiting. Because it was so much easier to manage expectations of a tyrant like Mr. Darby. At least you knew where you stood with such a character. But this man carried an odd combination of opaque speech coupled with a forthright nature, so by the end of a few sentences from him, Eden had no idea which way was up.

"I'm afraid I actually do believe you, Mr. Cole. About why you came here today, anyway. I'll hold judgment on the rest."

"Jacob. Please."

"Fine. *Jacob*," she emphasized, even though saying his name felt like a familiarity Eden might not be ready for. "Curiosity doesn't explain why you've stayed when you could have had your questions answered in the gravel drive back there. Our manor stands. No bombs touched us. So why offer to shovel dirt in a suit that costs upward of a farmer's yearly salary?" She narrowed her eyes at him. "Be honest with me. Are you here to try to win us over before you pull the rug out from under our feet? Assuage your guilt for what's to come?"

"Hadn't thought of that. Though the idea does have merit," he joked, tapping a finger to his chin while the tiny hint of a grin he'd offered the Land Girls returned. And then just as quick, he dropped the jesting and grew serious again. "Look. What if I said there was a grain of truth in it? That there is a reason for my coming to Coventry. But it's not to see you shuttled into an American courtroom at the end of all this. I'd like to come to an agreement outside of court."

"Is that so. Then what's it to do with?"

"My father's passing."

"Oh," she whispered, and looked over to find that for a man who'd seemed content to be the life of the party only moments before, his profile had darkened considerably. "I'm so sorry for your loss. I didn't know."

"How could you? But thank you." Jacob gazed around at the activity of the Land Girls finding their footing in the rose garden. "And it's not the loss I'm here to discuss. Frankly, I need answers."

"Answers to what?"

"As to why amendments were made to my father's will—amendments that were unknown but to him and his private lawyer, up until the reading of that will just two weeks past. And as it names you co-heiress to the Cole estate, it means I am here in the interests of my family—principally, for my mother and the trust for my younger sisters, as well as their future endeavors."

"I don't understand. Did you just say co-heiress?"

He sighed. "I did. It appears the title suits you twice over."

"So you're not here to take Holt Manor from me?"

"No." Jacob chuckled, staring out at the vast view of green hills, poplar trees, and the old glasshouse with broken panes and patina warmed by the sun. "I'd be quite content to leave this slice of heaven in what appear to be very capable hands. On the contrary, that you have your own estate to inherit may actually embolden our case against you."

"The case against me . . . Forgive me, but for a solicitor you seem to enjoy talking in circles."

"Then allow me to be direct. I need to know why William Holt's only child is set to inherit exactly half of the value of the Cole Jewelry Company, the equivalent of roughly one million pounds. And I'm here to do everything in my power, Lady Eden, to ensure you don't receive a penny of it."

CHAPTER EIGHT

28 May 1914
Foxhollow Farm
Coventry, England

*A*ny farmer worth his salt knew a pounding fist upon his door in the wee hours was one of three things: a birth, a death, or both.

On what should have been a peaceful spring night, Amos stumbled into the farmhouse kitchen to the sounds of sheepdogs making a royal ruckus in the yard. Wouldn't be long before they'd stir up the livestock if he didn't get out to the barn and get it sorted.

Rubbing a hand over his face, Amos adjusted tired eyes as he stirred embers burning low on the hearth. He tossed another log on the fire and checked the old mantel clock just as a series of urgent *pound, pound, pound* thumps persisted against the mudroom door.

Not yet midnight. He groaned. Pity a poor farmer, for the precious hours of sleep left to him were now gone.

"*Oy!* Flaxon—I'm awake!" Amos yelled at his neighbor and dropped down to the mudroom bench lining the wall to tug on the work boots he'd tossed beneath. The crusty old sheepherder from the next farm over had said the day before he might need help birthing a ewe nearing her time. Must be that.

He yanked the plaid woolen coat down from the wall peg in a huff, muttering toward the door, "And why wake the whole of the countryside while you're at it?"

"Amos? Are you there?"

That voice. Amos dropped his coat and lifted the bolt to swing the door open in one breathless move.

"What in heaven's name—Charlotte?" Amos gave a quick check behind her, pulled her into the shadows of the mudroom, and closed the door.

The sight of her standing in his house in the middle of the blessed night was about the last thing Amos had expected. But there she was, in a simple blue frock and much-too-thin coat for the bite in the night air. Diamond earbobs winked at him in the faint glimmer of firelight as she shivered subtly, giving away that she was indeed cold and battling not to show it.

"Come here by the fire. Warm up." He led her around the kitchen table to the hearth and pulled a chair out, patting the back for her to sit. He lit a candle and covered the flame with a glass hurricane, only then noticing she hadn't moved.

"I'm so sorry for the hour." Charlotte still stood instead of taking the chair.

Family manners must have taught her to try to remain composed on the outside, no matter what was stirring on the inside. But her eyes were rimmed in red. Her cheeks were flushed. And he'd noticed her auto had left tire cuts in the mud of the yard and a door hanging on a hinge, as if she'd slammed it to a stop and run like her life depended on it.

He gave in—stepped forward into the firelight to search Charlotte's face, but in truth, he needed to search all of her to make sure she wasn't harmed. With eyes that intense, a chin trying not to quiver, and hands wringing in front of her waist, Amos's mind was running wild with every possible speculation—all of them bad.

"What's happened?"

"It's Lord Harcourt." Charlotte paused for a breath, like the words would pain her to speak them. "He's . . . dead. An hour ago."

Amos nodded. Braced his hands at his waist while he stared down at his boots for a weary breath. And for the life of him, he didn't know what to think.

"The doctor confirmed it: a head wound from a fall while riding in the glen. So bad that he could not recover." Charlotte sniffed, emotion trying to mist her eyes. "The bishop has been notified. And the funeral truck will be here at dawn to prepare for the burial."

A funeral to plan now instead of a wedding. The Holts must be reeling.

It was supposed to be years before the torch was passed from the Earl of Harcourt to his pretentious son. Years left for Will to learn proper estate management. To mature. To humble himself down from the lofty ambitions of his birthright and truly learn to lead men. And for the benefit of all employed by the estate, to take his place as he took a wife. But a tragedy like this? It shouldn't have happened, especially not mere hours after he'd found Amos and Charlotte inches apart and locked in some undisclosed precipice in his father's glasshouse.

If Amos had been a betting man, he'd have staked all he had on the fact Will wasn't about to let that go. Especially now.

"I'm sorry of it. Lord Harcourt was . . . he was a good man." Amos sighed with weariness that had nothing to do with the hour ticking on the clock. "And a kind master of his estate lands and tenants, to be sure."

"He was. And that is precisely why I'm here." Charlotte flitted her glance over her shoulder, toward the mudroom's tiny window where her auto was parked outside. "Do you still have the book?"

A thousand tiny pinpricks hit Amos at once, sinking in his gut with the flurry of memories. The sight of her in the Holt Manor library on Christmas Eve . . . laying the copy of *Dombey and Son* on her chair . . . the regret in her eyes when Lord Holt made the engagement announcement . . . and the steel vise squeezing his chest when he'd unwrapped the gold-embossed gift she'd given him after Christmas to find the copy of the Dickens classic tucked inside.

It owned a secret between them, that book.

His, if not hers. And it stayed where they'd left it. Unspoken. Known only to his innermost being. And now the book was tucked in Amos's nightstand drawer and answered to no one, along with the volumes from the secondhand shop all those years ago that still lined the mantel in his bedchamber. The books represented those stolen moments with Charlotte—all they'd read, discussed, and shared—and meant infinitely more to him than they ever could to her. At least that's what Amos had told himself.

Until now.

"Aye. I have it." He nodded. Best to act unaffected. Shove futile thoughts away.

"Good. Go and get it, please."

Amos didn't move. "Why?"

"I need it before they come."

"Before who comes?"

Charlotte widened her eyes in a little "you know who" kind of way, and something sparked inside. How quick blood pumping in a man's veins could make him ball up his fists and feel the need to punch through a wall. Or a certain someone, if the sod had dared been the one to cause Charlotte's current distress.

"Did he hurt you? Tell me he didn't dare raise a hand to you, because if he did—"

"No," she breathed out, that one syllable able to calm him instantly.

Amos's palms found Charlotte's face before he could stop himself, his thumbs brushing away tears slipping from her eyes. It meant the world that her hands met the warmth of his, her palms holding on in the first genuine skin-to-skin touch they'd had since those long-ago childhood memories.

"It's nothing like that," Charlotte whispered, shaking her head under his hold. "Will would never. But if I don't do something now, he'll try to hurt us in another way. You know the Holt family crest—the shield with a fox chasing through the poplars?"

"Aye."

"I'd never thought to look, but the crest is stamped in the front cover of the book I gave you. Had I known it came from His Lordship's library, I never would have . . ."

He sighed roughly. "Right. You wouldn't have gifted it to me."

Amos had just assumed about the book. Like a fool, he'd never checked the front cover either. Thinking she'd found her own copy somewhere. With those trips to London Charlotte always seemed to be making, it would have been easy enough to pop into a bookshop and pick up an extra copy. And if true, maybe that meant in some small measure, Charlotte had thought of him like he thought of her.

"I didn't think Will would care that the book was gone. It was only ever special to you and me. But because of it, I believe he means to wound me by hurting you."

He scoffed, crossing his arms over his chest. "Will Holt can't do anything to me."

"No—listen." Charlotte eased a hand to reach out and hold his forearm. "It's different this time. Will has appealed to the local magistrate to investigate the circumstances of his father's death. Constable Abbott arrived at the manor this eve, and in listening to Will's demands, he means at least to have you arrested for theft. And I believe if he could . . . Will would have the magistrate open a full inquisition as to where you were at the time of his father's accident."

"He knows where I was!"

"Yes. He does." Charlotte looked down for a breath and shook her head, like she ardently wished it were all untrue. "But he also knows you and I were in the library on Christmas Eve."

"How?"

"I thought I'd left the book, remember? And told him later I'd gone there to fetch it. I didn't think anything of it at the time. But when he saw it on my chair in the dining hall, he knew you'd put it there. And it must have been because we met in the library—*alone.*"

"That was innocent."

"Of course it was. But now that his father is gone and he is the Earl of Harcourt, Will has a position. And a title. And he will use them both to bring charges against you. Even if you and I know those claims to be baseless." Charlotte swallowed hard. And for the life of him, she looked like she was summoning courage for her next words. "But now, his family and mine know they are baseless too."

Dread washed over him. "Please tell me you're not saying what I think you are."

Though her brow softened, surety faded from her eyes as she stared up at him. "I told them you could not have been in the glen anywhere near Lord Harcourt's accident, because you were in the glasshouse . . . with me. Where Will found us."

"Charlotte . . ." Amos raked a palm through his hair as the ramifications of her words coursed through him. "What have you done?"

There was no taking this back; she'd be ruined.

"Don't you understand? If I take the book, then Will has no card left to play. You may lose the lease on this farm and I what is left of my reputation, but at least you'll go free. Isn't that all that matters now, to clear your name?"

"Did you want me to have it?"

Charlotte stopped. Crinkled the space between her brows, that little thing she always did when something didn't sit well with her, and fumbled out softly, "Of course I did, but—"

"Then I won't give it up. You know this is not about a book. Will would have put me out of the tenancy anyway. First chance he had. This is about a boy who caught us at the glasshouse all those years ago and turned our secret over to our parents. When a friendship never should have to be kept secret anyway. He wants *you*, Charlotte. Not revenge against me. And he'll do anything to win."

"But this isn't a game. I came to save you from arrest. Why must you be so stubborn?"

"Am I?"

"You know you are. If I only had time to talk to Will, to plead your case for the tenancy . . . I believe I could change his mind. But if you do this, as soon as Will arrives you will be arrested. Are you really willing to risk all of that?"

"*Yes!*"

Amos surprised even himself in reaching for her on the shout, his arms encircling her like they'd ached to do a thousand times before. Emboldened by the feel of her in his arms, he leaned down until their foreheads grazed in gentle meeting.

"What could Will do to me, Charlie, when all I have ever cared about is you?"

If one confession meant Amos was a man possessed, so be it. He could believe in the undercurrent that could bind two souls, one to the other, charging all the decisions a man made in his life. And that stirred a fight within him that had been dormant for too long. For what lay in his core—hidden, unrequited for years—wouldn't have to be held back any longer. If Amos could only speak his truth and have her receive it, then there was something left to hope for.

"I told him I can't marry him," she blurted out, the words burning between them.

Amos leaned back, enough to stare into her eyes. Searching her face. Daring to hope she'd truly said those words out loud.

"What did you say?"

"Well, actually I told Will I *won't* marry him. In front of everyone. I think my mother had swooned by the time I'd thrown open the library doors and stolen our auto from the chauffeur outside. I know it was foolish, but I just started driving . . . and ended up here."

He couldn't think. Couldn't breathe. Let alone speak. And heaven help him, he tried to. And as the seconds ticked by between them, Amos prayed he was brave enough. To ask again. Aye, to say what he must and wait to hear her answer.

"You broke your engagement?"

She swallowed hard. "Yes . . ."

"Why?"

"Because as his father's body lay cold upstairs and all were stricken with shock and grief, Will's first words were to me—in a fury as he demanded the book. He forced me to look into my heart. To listen to what it said. And to decide where I will stand. In my heart I've known that I wish to stand upon my own two feet." Gentle hands palmed his shirt, and she rose on her toes until her lips stopped a breath from his. "But that place has always been beside . . . *you*."

The last word, barely spoken—more mouthed between them—was the eclipse Amos had waited for.

They crashed together. Like two lost halves of a whole meeting in a kiss that was every bit of what Amos had imagined. And, as a man now, had hoped for. Charlotte's palms curled into fists that tugged his shirt in desperation while his hands held tight, palming the small of her back. Reveling in every breath, every precious tick of the clock. And drawing her so close there was no room for time, nor the past, nor even air to exist between them.

A clatter sounded outside, wrenching them back.

Charlotte tensed in his arms, her lips stopping against his as brakes screeched outside. Chugging engines stopped. And she stared back, terror-stricken, frozen as her breath warmed his bottom lip.

"Please don't go."

"It's alright." He squeezed and released her. "Stay back."

Amos rounded the table back to the mudroom window, parting the curtains. Three autos were outlined by moonlight, with Will at the front to lead the charge. Followed by one he didn't recognize. And then a police truck caught up at the end of the line, with doors open and uniforms flooding out the back.

Car doors slammed. Men's voices echoed through the yard, so even when Amos had dropped the curtains back into place and turned to her, Charlotte didn't need to question how serious it was.

"This is not worth your future, Amos."

"Isn't it? When I've waited years to hear what you just said? To hold you like that? I'd do it all again, even if only for that moment," Amos protested, though a tear that slipped down to catch on her lip was near enough to make him want to put up a fight against the whole world if he had to, just to fix this mess. "What if I sent for you, soon as I'm free? Would you come to me?"

"Amos . . ."

Curse the forces that demanded a man give a half-baked proposal and a woman sacrifice her whole world to accept it, even if it was the truth. Even if Amos had played it over in his mind too many times. It sounded feeble now—the antithesis of romance with a police truck screeching to a halt and sheepdogs barking in the yard and men poised to cart him off in shackles. But desperation won so that something snapped inside. It was now, or it was never.

"Would you marry me?"

"We can't." Her gaze fell down to her shoes. "I'm not yet of age."

After crossing the space between them, Amos pressed his hand to the side of her face, coaxing her to look up at him. "We can go to Gretna Green. There's an inn close by, in Durham. I'll get word to you and meet you there. And I'll queue up at every factory in Coventry and take shifts from dawn 'til dusk for the rest of my days if I have to. All I know is, you make me a better man. And if only to have a chance at living the vow you just spoke to me, I'd risk everything to walk through life at your side."

Amos hoped beyond hope, watching as she flitted her glance from him to the noise outside the mudroom door. He placed a palm to her cheek again, turning her back to him. "Please say you'll marry me. Say it and I'd give my life to be wherever you are."

Charlotte glanced back and forth from the door to him, then jumped back as a fist pounded with an authoritative demand of, "Magistrate. Open up, Darby!"

Amos stood before Charlotte, palms open at his sides. Waiting.

And holding firm as the bolt finally broke free, splintering the wood to pieces on the mudroom floor as uniforms flooded in.

The magistrate followed—Constable Abbott, who looked sorry behind that bushy-mustached smile of his for how many times Amos and he had shared pints at the local pub. And whose eyes widened when he spotted Charlotte in the kitchen with Amos. Didn't seem that outlandish to Amos, given that her car was outside. But Abbott eyed them with nervous energy just the same.

"Evening, Amos." Abbott tipped his hat as he stepped in, walked around the wood. And then nodded. "Apologies for the intrusion." He cleared his throat and gave an awkward tip of the hat to Charlotte, obviously having both expected and yet dreaded to find her standing in the center of the room. "Lady Charlotte."

"Albert. Can we help you with something?"

"Well, yes, Amos. Sorry I am . . . but it's this business of Lord Harcourt."

"We have heard of it." Amos held steady, eyeing Will as he'd strolled in behind the lot. "I'm terribly sorry for the loss. The Holts have my condolences, of course. But this is quite a crowd, just to bring a tenant solemn news."

Will remained silent. He gave no signals as to his thoughts, just kept to the usual coolness as he surveyed the humble space. And refused to acknowledge the rage that Amos knew must be coursing beneath his skin when he saw Charlotte standing with him.

The sounds of a hungry fire crackled on the hearth as Will stared at Amos, the two locked in unspoken challenge.

Will addressed the constable while keeping his eyes locked on his adversary. "Constable Abbott?"

"Milord?"

"Have your men escort Lady Charlotte outside. Her parents are waiting for her there."

"No." Charlotte took a step up to Amos's side, shoulder to shoulder, so that his every nerve ending wanted to smile for how she didn't hesitate to say what she wanted. "I'm staying."

"Charlotte, stop this. It isn't acceptable for my wife to—"

"I am *not* your wife. And you do not own me."

"You heard her, *Holt.*" Amos stepped up, adding a little vinegar to the way he spat the new master's name sans his title. "Charlotte is free to go or stay. But in the end, it's her decision. And if she wanted to go anywhere with you, she wouldn't be standing with me."

Both men charged—Will first, with restrained fury that drew him forward with a harsh step and reddened face. Amos blasted forward too, knocking a kitchen chair out of the way so it clattered to the floor, causing Charlotte to yelp, and stood before Will like a wall of stone fixed inches from his face.

"That's enough now!" The constable started on a shout, then ended on a heavy sigh as he turned to Amos. He pressed Amos's shoulder in a stand-down hold, easing him steps backward. "Look, lad. No one wants to see this turn ugly. We're simply here for property that's gone missing up at the big house. We'll just give it a once-over and that'll clear things up so—"

"Is it a book, by chance?"

Amos had interrupted on purpose, of course. Knowing he'd hit a mark when Will raised his chin and stretched his neck a bit, as if trying to crack stiffness out. The new earl composed himself again, running his hands along the bottom of his waistcoat to straighten the silk as his glare scoured Amos.

"It is," the constable said. "Something you'd like to tell us about that?"

"No. Save that you'll find nothing on this farm that doesn't rightfully belong to me."

"Except the farm itself. And tell us, Darby. Is it not true that you were dismissed from our employ on Christmas Eve after the key to our silver closet was found in your pocket?" Will countered. Waiting.

After a few long seconds, Amos gave a curt nod. It didn't matter what Charlotte had tried to say in defense of him.

In this, Will would always win.

"There you have it, gentlemen," Will snapped at the uniforms, with a point toward Amos's bedchamber. "Start in there. I've no doubt you'll find my stolen property. And then we can put this messy business behind us and leave a thief to the mercy of the courts."

A series of crashes resounded from his bedchamber while Amos stood firm, eyeing his rival as silent fury combusted between them. If this trumped-up lord was asking for a fight, so be it. Will could have the uniforms upturn every piece of furniture in his bedchamber, but Amos would make sure he did the same out there, starting with his fist rearranging Will's perfectly upturned nose.

Until . . . the butterfly's touch of fingertips warmed his own.

Charlotte's thumb eased the tension in his balled fist, opening his hand to brush the inside of his palm and softly, slowly, lace fingers with his own. It didn't matter when the uniforms emerged triumphant, handing the book over to the new Earl of Harcourt. Nor when Will checked the front cover and nodded to the constable, who sighed. Nodded back. And took shackles from his belt.

"I'm sorry about this, Amos. But given the evidence, I've got to take you. I trust you won't make this any harder than it has to be?"

"No, sir."

Amos gave Charlotte's hand a little squeeze, hoping a little too much that Will saw before letting go. He held his wrists out, accepting cold steel to encircle them.

"You remember what I asked?" Amos whispered, pinning everything on her answer.

"I remember." Charlotte swallowed hard, then offered a promise—one word through tears and strength and resolve that looked ready to take on the world with him: *Yes.*

He nodded. And kept his eyes locked on hers as he mouthed back, *I'll meet you there,* as uniforms muscled him out the door.

Amos had been right; it was a pounding fist upon his door that brought ill news that night. But with the night air outside blasting his skin, wrists shackled, and sheepdogs raising Cain around the edges of it all, he was forced to consider a different truth: a fist pounding on your door in the wee hours could also bring hope. At least now Amos knew there was a date penciled on the calendar, and the future they'd dreamed of would start the day he was released.

All he could do in that moment was be carted off to the county gaol with a smile.

➻﹒✦

12 October 1940
Bayley Lane
Coventry, England

"Mr. Darby."

Amos glanced up from the steaming pot of stoved tatties to find young Ginny darkening the doorway of Waverley Novels' stockroom-turned-soup-kitchen.

"Miss Brewster. Something in particular Eden Books has need of today?"

She drifted in, slow and cautious-like, hiding her usual skeptical glare behind the tower of bakery boxes in her arms. "I've Godcakes, sir."

"I can see that."

"They're for you. Given the bombings, christenings were canceled and Mr. Farley didn't want all this mince to go to waste. He brought some over from the bakery. To Eden Books, that is."

"And you've brought them as what—a peace offering? The gossips in this city might say I should check for pastry laced with arsenic."

"I'm not aware of arsenic in them . . . this time," she zinged back, finding a spot on the counter to slide the boxes into the chaos. "But we haven't any customers today. They'll just go to waste at our shop, so Her Ladyship suggested they be brought here."

Checking over his shoulder, Amos watched as Ginny peered out the open door, stretching to view the queue of people extending deep into the alley.

"Who's out there?"

"A couple of volunteers from the Home Guard are tending to the outside."

Her attention piqued, the girl lingered. "From the Home Guard, you say?"

"Aye. And I'm keeping things going in the back of the shop here. As you said—not a one's buying books today."

"You need help."

"We'll manage," Amos tossed over his shoulder as he disappeared through the kitchenette to grab the kettle singing on the stovetop.

Now you can go.

The Beast will wait in here until you do.

Though in truth, the slip of a girl was right.

Amos had been filling teacups, stacking used ones in the bin for a washout, and ladling bowls of high-heelers so fast he wasn't sure he'd be able to keep up. Joining the Home Guard efforts with the Bayley Lane shopkeepers meant they were hopping to distribute hot tea and stew, and now add Godcakes to the mix. Even without the rationed butter or sugar for Coventry's classic pasties, it looked like Farley's Bakery had managed to make a feast of kings for the weary Coventrians queued up behind the shop.

A steady stream of workers trickled in, weary from clearing debris-covered streets and directing foot traffic. Members of the Home Guard hadn't slept, let alone eaten—himself included. And with workers having stayed at their posts on rooftops all night, sixty sites across the city had Air Raid Precautions units all wanting for chow. Not to mention the citizens who were shaken after sustaining damage to their own homes still ventured up to St. Michael's to lend a hand clearing debris from the churchyard.

Amos paused. Listened. And expected the worst.

He could feel it coming, the girl haunting his back room, hanging around to gape at him and his scars. But maybe she'd left? All had gone quiet, save for the subdued chatter of people queued in the alley. Until porcelain clinked—loud enough to stir alarm that she was still here. Yes, and about to break a whole lot of something she had no business nosing into.

Rushing out from the kitchenette, Amos found Ginny with an apron tied round her waist. And now rolling the sleeves on her heathered-moss jumper to begin sorting through the mess before her.

"What do you think you're doing? Go home."

"Face it, Mr. Darby. You need help. And I'm as good as any member of the Home Guard. Better, even. I'll have you shipshape in no time." She pushed spectacles up higher on her nose and turned away from him. "Besides, you've a visitor out front."

"If it's a customer, they'll come back. And if it's my boarder, I'll settle up with him later."

"It's not a customer. This one's from Holt Manor."

Amos froze. "Lady Harcourt's here?"

"Yes. And Her Ladyship says that your Mr. Cole arrived at the estate this morn. A mite curious, he pushed his way into Lady Eden's plan to bury Andersons in the rose garden. And on her first day on task with the new Land Girls recruits."

"You don't say."

Ginny nodded, wrapping a tea towel around the handle of the steaming kettle to head outside and warm up patrons' brews.

So that was his business—pestering the Holts again?

On a day like this?

"Everyone gets one brew, one Godcake." Amos wiped his hands on a towel and tossed it to hang on the back of a chair. "And try not to set my shop on fire while I'm gone."

"I can't make any promises."

Amos smiled inside at the slip of a girl and her steel backbone—which he begrudgingly liked—and dashed down the hall. Trying to think with each step what in the world he'd say to Charlotte now. They hadn't spoken for months. Before that, not for years. At least not until the incident that flooded the back of his shop. Like a fool, he'd stomped across the street and had a row with Charlotte, when really it was the last thing he would have wanted.

Now it seemed they'd little need to speak again. Unless, of course, a new war decided to stir up everything. As it was now.

He slowed up at the end of the hall, spotting Charlotte standing by the shelf nearest the counter. She tapped a gloved index finger along the spines to inspect the fiction titles he'd put out.

How was it she didn't look a day older than his memories?

Charlotte had changed her hair—wore it in one of those sculpted bobs at her shoulders now. She favored brighter colors more than she used to and wore that bright yellow suit from time to time. And the corners of her eyes gave away the presence of laughter that she'd bestowed on others over the years. Yet if he dared look long enough, Amos could still see the young woman in Coventry's bookselling matriarch who stood before him. Those eyes, holding fast to the same depth of kindness. And the glow that lit up her every feature meant Charlotte was still able to waltz in, offer a single smile, and enchant an entire room.

Didn't matter how many years had passed; it still very nearly undid Amos each blasted time he looked at her. The same thought tortured in the back of his mind, that she should have been his. And might have been, had Amos owned the guts to be the man she'd needed all those years ago.

When the hardwoods gave him away by creaking beneath his boots, she looked up. "Ah—you are here."

"Milady." He slipped his hands in his trouser pockets and hung behind the counter, keeping the side of his face just turned away. "How can I help?"

"The Godcakes we brought from Farley's. But I also found your card by our register." Charlotte walked over to the counter, clicking the hardwoods in that hollow sound of proper ladies' heels. She held up folded papers in front of him. "Along with a ten-pound note for the tea?"

"That's right."

"But isn't that a bit much for loose leaf, even with the war?"

"Drastic times, you know. With rationing down to two ounces per week, we went through what I had in a snap. It was either offer your tea or the people queuing up outside would have to choke down chicory. And I couldn't do that to them today."

"You have a key to Eden Books then?" she questioned, putting things together.

"Well, Lady Eden gave me one some months back. I thought you knew."

"I didn't."

"Right." He sighed, the air crackling between them like it could light on fire. "It won't happen again. I can assure you."

"You think I'm upset that you let yourself in at Eden Books and borrowed—" Charlotte paused. Slid the banknote across the counter to him with a gloved index finger. "Or should I say, bought my tea without asking?"

"Aren't you?"

"No." She smiled. Soft and unexpected, like mischief lingered behind it. "I'd have done the same to you. And it means I cannot accept such an exorbitant amount in return. Unless of course you send some chicory our way." She stopped to give a little look around, scanning the walls to the windows and the rows of shelves to the floor. "The shop looks well. Even if the titles on your prime shelves aren't the ones that will sell."

"Is that so?"

"I'd applaud placing *Kitty Foyle* on the shelf at eye level. It appears intriguing enough for Hollywood to be making a film of it. And readers are clamoring for stories about strong women, so you might do well to set it face out." She pulled the spine from a low shelf and stood it upright on the top to show off the cover art, then motioned to the open floor space beyond the counter. "Perhaps put a features table here, with *Mrs. Miniver* or *How Green Was My Valley?*

They've been particularly popular with our readers and draw them to the other titles they might not have heard of. It's the same strategy employed by Foyles."

"I see. Though a London bookshop won't have readers with the same tastes of a city like Coventry, or a reading room like Eden Books."

"Meaning?"

"That setup wouldn't leave much space for the *Farmers' Almanac* or the new Hemingway later this month, or Steinbeck's *The Grapes of Wrath*. And they've been popular here. For hardworking folk. Factory workers. Farmers and farmers' wives. People who have to labor for everything they have. But then, we've never exactly seen eye to eye on what defines great literature. Or how to sell it. Have we?"

"Only once, as a matter of fact."

Oh, he wanted to smile back.

Amos felt it. Bubbling up from his insides. Wanting to extend an olive branch and show her friendship instead of standing with scars that made him fall back into all-manners-aloof. And what kept the rumor mill running at full speed.

He swallowed hard, searching for something to say that wouldn't make him a fool but that wouldn't reveal too much of his inner workings at the same time.

"I was trying to say I'm cheered all is well here at Waverley Novels, including with your sales."

"My doors are still open. Though it looks like they may need to be open at all hours if we have another night like the last one. Just to keep up with the tea queue."

"As I see." Charlotte peered down the hall to the sound of clanks and clatters in the stockroom. "And the Home Guard chose Bayley Lane because it's central?"

"That, and we were spared in this part of the city center when others weren't. The churchyard was hit, but not bad. They've volunteers still cleaning up. Seems the worst of it was at Tungsten

Carbide—the factory there nearly flattened. And there's a bomb crater in Leicester Row the size of a highbridge bus."

"We saw. Several of the streets were blocked off when I went to drop some of the tenant wives for their factory shifts. There's damage along Bishop Street too."

"Aye. Left Tipton's Rooming House razed to the ground. All got out though, before the HE bomb hit."

"What a relief," she said.

Amos nodded, but was it a relief in trying not to weigh the cruel fates that deemed who would live and who died? Who would have to face tragedy on this first day of the Luftwaffe's "local blitz"—the term already being passed around the streets for what had happened the night before? Who would have to face the same decisions of fate tomorrow?

If Jacob had stayed at Tipton's Rooming House, or if a bomb had hit when they were still directing foot traffic on the streets, or if Charlotte and Eden had come back to their shop at the wrong moment . . . It wasn't unlike the trenches in France where for any reason—or sometimes for no apparent reason at all—a soldier met his death. In a blink. Any of them could have been another life on Amos's conscience if things had worked out a fraction of space either way. It was beyond understanding for a man to know what to do with burdens flying around like that, landing with their suffocating weight upon his shoulders.

Having forgotten Charlotte's presence until the silence brought him back, Amos looked up and, for good or bad, found her watching him. Again. Like she had that night in the carriage. Only this time, Charlotte tilted her head to the side. Just a shade. Like she was thinking and looking deeper. Not staring at the scars on the surface but following something in his eyes that led straight down to his soul. And lingered there far longer than he'd allowed anyone to stay before.

"I meant, what a relief . . . that Mr. Cole had a place here with you."

Amos cleared his throat to find his words. "He told you then?"

"Yes. He wandered into Eden Books yesterday evening after he left here. And after my daughter exchanged a few choice words with the gentleman, I tried to cool both our tempers with a cup of tea. That's when he mentioned you'd offered him a room for the night."

Amos swallowed hard, remembering the lad had said something about solicitors being the soul of discretion. The few he'd ever known had been money-sucking leeches. But he hoped that if there were honest ones from time to time, Jacob had kept his word not to say anything about Amos's offhand comment to be kind to the Holts. "You have an objection?"

"Not exactly. Under normal circumstances, I'd not have said a word about your private affairs. But in this case, I'm prompted to ask. Is it sensible to invite Mr. Cole to stay here, even for one night?"

"Who says it's one night?"

Charlotte's brow pinched. "Isn't it?"

Jacob and Amos hadn't exchanged details about it. The majority of the night was spent taking in bomb reports and sending out Auxiliary Fire Service crews—the AFS responsible to tamp pockets of fires, keeping them from blazing across the city. That meant casual conversation was nil. Save for one fact that had passed between them: Jacob had learned straightaway his business couldn't be concluded in one day. And he asked if he might rent the room above Waverley Novels for a bit longer—in truth, for an undetermined amount of time.

"It isn't up to me. But Jacob told you why he's in Coventry then?"

"He did, of a sort. It's a legal matter I haven't fully grasped yet. But, I fear, one that could impact Holt Manor and my late husband's legacy. And that makes it of utmost importance to me."

"Then if it's about Holt Manor, begging your pardon, milady, it's nowt to do with me."

Charlotte blinked back, cueing that the abrupt reply had hit its mark. And he hated himself for it—the back-and-forth of it all, the festering wounds of Will and Holt Manor and the history of what it had done to them all.

A mere mention of it turned Amos to a brute every time.

"Yes. Well, I'm sorry to have bothered you." She turned, flustered, and in haste caught the edge of the counter so her satchel dropped, scattering its contents on the floor. "I shouldn't have come on such a morning when everyone is already so on edge . . ." Charlotte's voice faded as she crouched below the counter to scoop up whatever it was.

Amos could have smacked palm to forehead for pride tripping him up again. He swept around the counter. Knelt beside her. And, without thinking, reached for the bits and bobs that had spilled out: a tube of lipstick. A square gold compact. A sewing kit. A glasses case—Charlotte wore glasses now?

She looked up then. Met his eyes. And Amos hated that he'd put himself in sunlight from the windows, smack-dab where Charlotte could behold every burn and scar and white-hot mark screaming off the side of his face. And the hands that hadn't a moment alone to tilt a Scotch bottle to his lips that day had gained a noticeable tremor, making the glasses case flutter as Amos held it out.

"This is yours . . ." He handed it back and stood quick as lightning. Turning the unseemly away as she rose with him. "I apologize. I spoke before thinking."

Looping the satchel's strap over her arm again, she stood straight before him. And didn't seem angry. Or concerned about his shaking hand, if she'd noticed at all. In truth, Charlotte almost looked like she wanted to laugh at their obvious awkwardness and caught her bottom lip with her teeth to suppress the embarrassment.

"No permanent damage done."

Amos crossed his arms over his chest. Anything to hide his hands from her without showing he was hiding them. And since the stance could be misinterpreted, he asked a little softer, "You wanted to know about Jacob?"

"It's only that he showed up at Holt Manor today—I was

offhanded in giving an invitation I didn't dream he'd accept. And I wondered if you could tell me, do you find him genuine? What I mean is, do you think he'll injure us?"

"You mean do I think he has aims to injure while he's suing you?"

"It does sound a silly question."

"I couldn't answer either way. Jacob is here for his own reasons—the business of some inheritance for his family. He didn't give details. But being in the Home Guard and knowing folks assume any blond-haired stranger is a German spy, I did my due diligence and checked in with the London consulate."

"And?"

"He is who he says he is. As for what sort of man? I only know him to be honorable."

"How so?" She tilted her head, waiting for him to continue.

"In these streets last night, Jacob gave no thought to his own safety as he helped our neighbors to the shelters." Amos left out the tidbit of hearing the lad's fluency in German. Best keep that under his hat for now. "He took up arms with me and the rest of the Home Guard without question. Or sleep. Or complaint. He even showed up to the churchyard this morn to carry broken tree limbs out, chopped wood with an axe in his own two hands while some gave the stranger a side-eye as they went. And I hear Jacob's gone to Holt Manor to help there. When this isn't even his war."

Amos looked back into her eyes. Thinking of that fateful night in his kitchen all over again. And the disastrous road that had followed it. "Does it make a man honorable, to stand firm in the face of a fight he didn't start?"

Charlotte parted her lips to reply but paused, as if she'd thought better. Instead, she glanced down the hall to the streams of sunlight coming from the alley at the end.

"I agree with you, Amos. In the face of a fight that truly matters, it is the brave who show up at the front of the line. So—where is the tea queue?"

"Uh, out back." Amos tipped his head toward the hall. "Ginny's forced her way into the alley, just until I return."

"That is all I needed to know." Charlotte removed her gloves as she passed by. "We are booksellers. But neither is going to sell any today—featured titles or not. So let us be about the real work that matters, shall we?"

"And that is?"

"We agree to be civil to one another this morning, at least until everyone is served or the tea runs out. Whichever comes first."

They might be the dynamite in a pair of competing bookshops, for as many years as the stony silence had lasted between them. But the dreamers they'd been in youth and the practical people they were now proved the old adage was true: for good and all, some books ought to be left on the shelf, never to be opened again.

CHAPTER NINE

29 June 1914
Gretna Green Village
Dumfries and Galloway, Scotland

The afternoon sun began its slow creep behind the trees, giving way to clouds and mist that wilted Charlotte's wildflower bouquet and turned her traveling suit a darker shade of blue.

Many a couple had come single and gone married while Charlotte stood in the smithy's doorway, watching the north road in hopes an auto would clear the rise. And then she'd checked and rechecked the pocket with the telegram that had been waiting when she'd arrived at the Morritt Arms Hotel in Durham the night before:

MONDAY NOON STOP
BLACKSMITH SHOP GRETNA GREEN VILLAGE STOP
WE'LL BOTH BE THERE STOP
LOVE-A STOP

Amos was simply delayed after serving a wretched fourteen-day sentence at the county goal for petty theft and setting affairs in order to head north; it was all Charlotte dared tell herself.

She'd set out on a long journey the day before, from Coventry to Leicester and to Leeds by train, where she'd rented an auto. From there, she traversed the rugged road all the way to Durham—thank heaven she knew how to drive herself—while trying to assuage her guilt of having left her parents in the dark. And telling herself if she could just get to Amos's side, then they'd weather the coming storm together. It wasn't until she'd arrived at the country inn off the main road and held the telegram in her hands that their plans felt solid enough to be real.

That being the last message from Amos, she clung to it now. It might as well have been a D. H. Lawrence novel in Coventry, for an earl's daughter to have jilted one of the most eligible bachelors in England for a lowly farmer on the gentleman's estate. The newspaper gossip columns were thick with it—slander and suppositions to sell papers over a scandal of their own making. But perhaps a country inn this far north was less likely to have caught wind of it, nor had the newspapers opportunity to pass around her photo.

With proximity to Gretna Green, it wouldn't raise eyebrows for a lady to arrive alone one day and depart with a husband the next. And though Mother believed Charlotte had gone to Mayfair to visit a family friend and hide away from the family scandal plaguing them the last month, she couldn't think two days away should concern her parents at all—that is, until Charlotte woke the next morning, on her wedding day.

Splashed across the front page of every newspaper in the land by morning was the dreadful news that the day prior, the heir to the Austro-Hungarian throne and his wife had been gunned down by a young Serbian nationalist in a Bosnian street. And newspaper editorials now made every supposition about what it would mean for Austria-Hungary and Serbia, for England, and, by extension, for the world.

Times being what they were, Mother was likely to have worked herself into a frenzy, fearing her daughter's travel by rail, and would wish Charlotte to return home without delay. One telegram to Mayfair was all it would take for Charlotte to be sought, the truth discovered, and she found waiting for her groom at a lovers' hideaway.

"Miss . . ." A man cleared his throat behind her, his brogue soft. "The missus would like to know if ye fancy another brew?"

The vicar.

Or not a vicar.

In this case the blacksmith who was to perform the handfast ceremony and his wife had taken Charlotte into their care and offered tea and clootie pudding to pass time. The man stood off behind now as Charlotte waited in the doorway to the Anvil Room—the infamous smithy's sanctuary with an anvil in the center and a timber ceiling, whitewashed stone walls, a single window looking out to the road, and a plain altar set with glowing candles that flickered against stone steps.

"Miss?" he asked again, louder this time.

Charlotte turned, seeing the man offered just enough politeness in his attempt at . . . what? Consolation? Pity? Kindness? Or surely his white crown was bowed to offer solace, acknowledging that if Charlotte's groom was more than half a day tardy, then he wasn't to arrive at all.

"I'm sorry. What?"

"I said, should ye like to come in out of the rain, miss?"

"What time is it, please?"

He must have already known, because he didn't check his watch. "'Tis nearin' six o'clock. I'm terribly sorry, but—"

"You have other weddings to perform. Of course." Charlotte gathered her skirt in her hand, bouquet drifting to her side in the other. She stepped out to the cobblestone path, misjudged the sturdiness of her heel, and nearly took a tumble into a hedgerow of bramble.

The man grasped her arm at the elbow, holding firm.

"I'm so sorry," she fumbled, fighting to put words to tongue instead of allowing tears to take over in full.

"Dinna fash. 'Tis alright," he whispered, picking up her bouquet from the cobblestones to hand back to her. And yes, it was kindness.

Both in his voice and, blessed be, in his face when Charlotte looked up at the old man. "We'll help ye now."

Years of weddings. Decades of couples. And countless smiles of kindness to have carved the sweet laugh lines at the corners of his eyes. No doubt he'd seen them all. But how many times had he been through this? When one was left broken at the altar, how often had he saved the jilted from tumbling out the door into the hedgerow whilst his wife kept a kettle hot for cups of pity tea?

He seemed to know what to do. And helped her stand upright again.

"Please, come in out of the rain." When he was certain she could stand on her own two feet, he let go. And when Charlotte lifted her chin in the air—strength being a virtue and all that her mother had always told her—he nodded.

The glow of headlamps cut over the rise, quickening her heart.

Charlotte rushed forward, fumbling down the cobblestone path as an auto chugged into view. Her heart hoping and believing all over again it would be Amos to step out when the engine stopped. But it was a young man in uniform who hopped out, opened the opposite door, and held an umbrella for the young lady in a violet suit to hook his arm and join him on the path.

"See? I told you we'd not be the only ones with this clever idea." The young bride beamed at Charlotte and then at her own groom, a soldier who couldn't be aged more than twenty years himself.

He tipped his head to the smithy. "You still taking hopefuls? That is, if we haven't stepped ahead in line."

Charlotte shook her head.

The smithy sighed. "That we are, son. Come in."

"Here . . ." Charlotte raised the bouquet, holding it out to the violet bride. "You'll need this."

"Oh, darling! Look!" she exclaimed to her soldier and brushed raindrops off the petals, smiling at the bundle of sweet yellow blooms. "How kind you are. The newspapers are brimming with it, so in the commotion, I hadn't time to think about bringing my own flowers. And you've given me yours!"

Charlotte felt the pang of dread in her middle; what if they spoke of the gossip that had spread like wildfire in Coventry? Then she looked from bride to groom, whose faces registered something entirely different than her own troubles.

"Brimming with it . . . ?"

The couple blinked, staring back as the soldier answered: "War."

"Yes, of course. Forgive me." Charlotte tried to hide her embarrassment for so many things, the least of which was that the world was bigger than her personal humiliation, and war would certainly march through any person's pain without a second thought. "If it's to be war, that is indeed terrible news."

"So many of us already signed up on the thought it might come. But it'll have to be war now. And none to worry—England is ready. We'll chuck all we've got at them and 'twill be over in a fortnight," he said, a note of bitter and sweet in his voice as he peered at his bride and pecked a confident kiss to her cheek.

"Best not wait to start living, eh?" The bride radiated amour with an innocent smile.

"That's right, darlin'. We don't get a second chance at love."

No, Charlotte thought. *No second chances there.*

"Are you certain you don't want them? My mother pressed flowers from her bridal bouquet in a book. She kept them always." The bride beamed again, unknowing that her kindness was a dagger to Charlotte's heart as the girl plucked a sunny silverweed blossom from the bunch and held it out by the stem. "Might you wish to do the same?"

"Thank you." Charlotte accepted the stem but could not hide the tears in her eyes and turned her gaze down to the bloom. "But no."

Perhaps the smithy had motioned them forth. Or it had dawned on the lovers that this bride was alone, and if all had gone to plan, she oughtn't be. Either way, the soldier tipped his uniform hat and the lovers were off, marching down the cobblestone path with Charlotte's bouquet toward the glow of the Anvil Room, with the open door and flickering candles that would mark their first steps as husband and wife.

Plucking the telegram from her pocket, Charlotte stared back at the words: *"We'll both be there . . ."* Then let go.

The paper fluttered to the ground, its edges crumpling in death when it met the surface of a puddle at her feet. She stepped over it and walked on. The telegram was the last witness to a dream that would not be. And regardless of what awaited her as she drove south through the night, Charlotte knew she would never again wait to live her own life.

➤‥◄

12 October 1940
Bayley Lane
Coventry, England

The scents of a bookshop: leather, paper, the hint of citrus furniture polish, and the sharp-and-sweet aroma of honey in Earl Grey tea. Was there any better combination in the world?

Charlotte found the same warm nostalgia at Waverley Novels that she appreciated at Eden Books—her tea had been borrowed for steeping and serving out Amos's back door. But to venture into the hidden depths of his shop was to find a different setup altogether.

It might as well have been turned over by a horde of thieves, with the Godcakes Ginny brought already falling out of bakery boxes, piles of books shoved aside to climb the walls, and mismatched cups and saucers stacked upon a counter like the Mad Hatter was expected for tea. And the hungry ones who had the misfortune of being queued in a narrow alleyway whilst volunteers marched in and out of the back door had turned the ordeal into near collisions with kettles and tea trays that might as well have been trains jumping tracks. With the current system—or lack of one—there was little doubt volunteers would crash into one another, books would be marked so they were unfit for sale, and owners would be left brokenhearted when heirloom teacups were returned with chipped porcelain rims.

Charlotte looked up at Amos as they hovered in the doorway, tipping her brow to question him.

"It's a little beneath basic, I know." Amos read her with accuracy. Almost like he used to. "But try to keep an open mind. A last-minute decision means you make do with what you've got. And this is what we've got."

"And yet, I was merely going to ask where you'd like me to begin?"

"Alright. Miss Brewster is running a tight ship outside, no doubt. So . . . tea?" He tilted a head toward the tins from her shop now on the counter. "As is Her Ladyship's specialty, I'm told."

"Tea it is."

"I'll set more water to boil." Amos nodded as if that was that and they had nothing further to say, then disappeared through the door to an adjoining room.

The crank of a turned faucet sounded. And then water filling metal as Charlotte slipped out of her suit jacket and exchanged it for a pinstripe apron on the wall peg. She hung her tam with it and slipped the apron loop over her head, then busied herself tying it at the back and unbuttoning pearl cuffs to roll up the sleeves on her blouse.

It was only the second time she'd been in Amos's shop. And never before in the rooms to the back.

Little matter now.

With her foray into the confines of the enemy's camp, curiosity won out and she couldn't resist a snoop. She dusted a stack of spines with an index finger as if she were trailing a row of piano keys and looked over the author names—not unlike titles they kept in stock at Eden Books. A window in the corner let in natural light, illuminating an open rolltop desk with a brass lamp, a jar of pencils, and a pewter frame on its top. She lifted the frame to find sepia smiles of Amos's sister, Caroline, with her husband and three sons, all standing in front of a country church for what must have been the youngest's christening. But the photo was from ages ago. In fact, Charlotte had received a letter from Caroline every now and then and knew the eldest of the sons to be married and starting a family of his own.

How the years owned wings . . . and used them.

The water stopped and Charlotte jumped, setting the frame down. Leaning around the doorjamb, she peeked back at Amos.

He stood before a stove in a small kitchenette, broad shoulders and back to her as he stirred a wooden spoon in a stewpot. A butcher's block dominated space in the center of the room. A dinette with two chairs was pushed against the far wall. A cast-iron tower sat in the corner—he cooked?—its largest pots missing on the bottom shelf, perhaps because they were in use. And a cozy fireplace nook sat in the opposite corner, with a mantel boasting a rainbow of book spines, and brick benches with cushions and space for gathering on cold winter nights.

A tenderness struck when she saw an indentation in a striped cobalt cushion and a tufted stool centered in front of it. A book was butterflied on the armrest, like an old friend left hanging mid-page. Did Amos have someone special to sit beside him? Or worse, did he read there alone each night?

Pushing the thoughts away, Charlotte turned to find the first thing that made sense to do. "Should we wash the cups then?"

"Aye," he called back. "On the floor at your feet."

A bin of spent teacups with the trace of amber liquid rings in their bottoms was just under the counter. Charlotte knelt and pulled it out, and as she misjudged the load's awkwardness, the first attempt to haul the crate faltered in her arms and she dropped it against another one behind. The crate rattled, paint-peeled wood slats clinking against a melody of glass. Thinking it could be more cups, she leaned into the shadows, hooked fingers against the slat, and pulled it into the light.

Bottles . . .

A half dozen of them or more. And all empty.

A glance showed rows of a Glenlivet label, with its lion logo and *George & J.G. Smith's* stamped across the front. But they weren't dusty; this wasn't a discarded lot of old rubbish, forgotten in a cobwebbed corner. These whiskey bottles were clean. And though tucked out of sight, they were lined up in a smart row as if waiting to be donated in the next glass collection drive.

Oh, Amos . . . What are you doing?

"Did you find them?"

"Um . . . yes." Snapped back to the present, Charlotte tucked the bottle back and pushed the crate into the darkness again. "Just now."

Charlotte carried the teacups to the sink by the stove. She stood beside Amos now, watching his shoulders tense as she drew near and noticing how he angled his face ever so subtly toward the wall as he lit a match to the gas burner.

Was it this way now, his face turned away from the world?

And away from her?

Except for the few moments in the front of the shop when Amos had rushed around the counter and knelt at her side, Charlotte hadn't seen him close up in years. His beard was more pepper than russet now. The scars on his face always attempting to hide from a distance. And the soft hazel eyes she'd once known so well owned a hollowed look, with circles beneath bottom lashes that said he probably hadn't slept. Nor eaten. And while she found him as handsome as ever, Amos was also spiritless. And Charlotte couldn't hope beyond the obvious, that the bottles were evidence of some private pain—pain of which she had no right to know, but it seemed even as they were supposed to be enemies, she now did.

Charlotte spread a tea towel on the counter and turned the faucet, yelping when ice water shocked her fingers.

"Here. You have to—" Amos leaned over, grazing her hand as he jiggled the hot faucet handle. Then backed away just as quick, letting the warm water ease in on its own after that. "Give it a minute. It's finicky."

"Thank you." She began washing and rinsing as the ice abated. And kept her gaze focused on busy hands washing rosebud sprays and delicate gold rims in front of her. "Bringing the Godcakes by was Eden's idea. And having given you a key to our shop—for emergencies, of course—I suppose she believes we ought to work together. For the good of all on Bayley Lane."

He sighed and gave a frustrated groan. "Of course she does. Brilliant."

"No." She laughed. "I only meant . . . have you eaten? I could fetch one of the Godcakes for you."

"Not hungry."

"Did you sleep at all?"

"No." Amos stirred stew on the back burner, not looking up. "You?"

He thought she was . . . making small talk? Just like that. After all these years?

"I tried. But cellars aren't exactly conducive to a proper night's sleep, especially not with the dirt shaking beneath your shoes until dawn."

Amos stilled the wooden spoon in his hand. "Holt Manor was hit?"

"No. We were fortunate. This time. But even with new Andersons in the rose garden and the sirens able to alert us, I wonder how long those tides will continue to move in our favor." She set cups on the towel to dry and only then chanced looking at him— just his profile. The same strong jaw and expressive eyes she remembered. Why did it hurt to look at him now? "I sometimes wonder if we'll ever be able to sleep through a full night again."

"Well, who needs it really—sleep?"

"I'd say the section commander of our Home Guard has earned that much."

He shook his head, moving around the stove like a chef with an army to feed. "I can't. Not with all that's to be done."

"But may I say, with all sincerity, I do not agree. We'll keep on with it all, just like everyone in England. But you are depended upon by a great many people on this row, just as I am at Holt Manor. And we cannot do our jobs if we are walking into walls. That's the truth of it."

Amos almost turned to her—on instinct, maybe? Because once upon a time, they could give and take and be honest to the core if need be. It had always been natural, the way they'd talked. Despite upbringing or the exhausting confines of their stations, their way was just . . . different. Like coming home when you didn't even realize you'd been away. And the challenge one brought to the other was never unkind but with respect.

But he stopped himself now, keeping his profile fixed and attention glued to the stove as if it were the most important duty in the world to watch a kettle boil.

"I won't argue. Not today at least."

"That is progress then, if we don't wish to kill each other after five minutes." Charlotte shook water drops off the last teacup to set it in line on the towel, then turned fully toward him. "Enough that I wonder if we might come to an agreement. I know there's history enough between our shops to fill ten volumes' worth of stories. But if these bombings are to continue, then we could join forces beyond this morning—Eden Books and Waverley Novels."

"Are you not worried the lookie-loos down at the pub won't have anything to talk about if our shops start acting civil to one another?"

"Do they . . . talk about us?" She smiled in spite of herself, thinking of the old chatterboxes on their stools, having some craic over a couple of bookshops' tiff. "Never mind that. I keep thinking of the wives and children of the estate men who've gone off to fight. And the factory workers keeping production up so the RAF may remain in the air. Fire-watchers and AFS brigades work to put out fires at all hours. And those who've suffered harm from the bombs that have already fallen. While we hope days like today won't happen again, we have to prepare as though they may. Perhaps we can find common ground to work from whilst all this is going on, even if it's only to serve tea to our neighbors."

"So you're saying we may be at war, but our shops needn't be?"

"I would be willing to set the past aside and . . ." Charlotte stopped when he turned sharply and chose to look more directly. And heaven help her, but she felt butterflies mixing in her middle. Did he, too, think of Gretna Green just then? "What I mean is, we could put our opinions to rest in order to fight the larger enemy between us."

He gave a slow nod and seemed to be considering what she'd said. Then he added, with the tiniest spark of humor in his eyes, "Does that make me . . . the smaller enemy?"

"Not an enemy at all." How she wanted to add "not to me" on the end. *And please, let it be true.*

"You want to serve tea here, out of Waverley Novels. Instead of your reading room? I thought it was set up for that kind of thing—a posh place for raised pinkies and elegant talk."

"True, only the reading room is open to whoever may wish to use it, pinkies up or down. But if we can get organized and keep our civility"—she paused, letting that sink in after the posh pinkies comment—"we should do it here instead. You're closer to Drapers' Hall and it is a central location to St. Michael's. The Eden Books tea closet could be at your disposal. And we've recently acquired a unit of Land Girls to work the estate, and they've agreed to take shifts in the bookshop too. Having seen the same aftermath in London, I've no doubt they'd take up a regular post to help us serve. We'll have enough help. And the rest of it? We just allow it to unfold as it comes."

The kettle sang, and Amos wrapped a towel around the handle and moved it to the butcher's block. It broke Charlotte's heart a little that he was so automatic in keeping his profile turned away.

"If you'll take an emergency key to my shop too, I suppose I could see fair to do that."

"Good. Us too. I'll put it to Eden and we'll draw up a schedule to see what you think. But in the end I know my daughter. If she believes we've left any inroads behind in favor of peace, she'll agree. Heartily."

"Hmm. And with Jacob in the mix? What then?"

Oh dear. That's right. For the slightest moment in time, Hitler's looming threats had completely drowned out the matter of Mr. Cole and his legal aspirations.

"I'll have to see to him later. But in the meantime, as long as we've agreed to a temporary truce, I do have one more request. And I'm afraid it is not up for negotiation if you want my tea."

"Alright." Amos waited.

Charlotte looked to the ceiling. "What is upstairs?"

"Rooms." He flinched a little. She'd surprised him? "Uh . . . bedchambers."

"Then choose one. And use it. I'll send someone to wake you in an hour's time. By then, I should have this sorted and more hands at the pump to help us keep it running."

"But you're going to need—"

"I'll see to it. We've Ginny to help and the other volunteers. You have nothing further to worry about here, Amos. Go." She flitted her glance to the doorway. "Please."

Charlotte didn't know whether Amos realized he was barely able to keep his eyes open, or that his hand was trembling against that wooden spoon. Perhaps he agreed for that point alone, or just so he wouldn't have to linger in awkward conversation. Either way, he pulled a watch and chain from the pocket of his waistcoat, tapped the knob to check its face, and sighed when he'd read it.

"One hour?" he asked.

"Just."

"And you won't allow the stew to boil dry?"

She risked giving a glare of mocking—what a question. He must have forgotten the times she'd visited the farm and stirred jam over a stove in his family's kitchen. "I know my way around a kitchen, thank you. We'll be fine."

Amos nodded then and turned down the hall. He disappeared up the stairs at the other end, heavy steps creaking tired wood as he went.

It was not lost on Charlotte that she'd waited for him once. Checking the clock too. And reluctant to leave, even when the sun had set on Gretna Green and she'd stood alone. But something inside whispered not to lord it over Amos now. If the crate in the stockroom held anything, it was humility and pain more than the shame of empty bottles. And the walk he made to the stairs— tired, trudging, and without looking back—said Amos could know more about the weight of that day at Gretna Green than she might have once realized.

"Is that you, milady? We're nearly out of pasties." Ginny had marched into the stockroom with hands balancing a tray some- time later. And then gaped when she saw Godcakes were sorted, clean teacups lined the counter, and a steaming teapot was ready to fill them.

"Oh, Ginny. Good, you're here." Charlotte handed her a note. "I'll need you to go back to Eden Books, please. Post this on the door so our customers know where we've gone. If they should like to buy books today, it will be from Waverley Novels. And I'll ask you to please telephone Holt Manor for reinforcements before you lock up."

"We can't do it from here?"

"It appears Mr. Darby hasn't a telephone." Charlotte flipped her wrist, checking her gold watch. "Right—I should think they could be here within the hour. And have you any friends here in the city?"

"Uh . . . a few, milady. My brothers' mates live near Radford Road." She narrowed her brow and tipped her glasses back against the bridge of her nose.

"Fine. Telephone them as well, please. We'll need the features table in the center of Eden Books—you know which one I mean. It will take a few strong backs to carry it over here. Only we want it up front; we're moving everything from the alley inside this shop. Two lines will move faster—one for stew, the other for tea and cakes. And those in queue can browse for books while they wait. You will work the register and keep the receipts for Mr. Darby to review later. And once we've set up, your brothers' friends can pop by Mason's Greengrocers to see what they can donate, and Luckett's for any cuts of meat the butcher may have left. We'll be out of stew in a thrice if we don't. And I should hate to have to turn people away simply because of that."

Ginny blinked behind her spectacles, glancing first to the empty kitchenette, then back at her. "Begging your pardon, milady, but Mr. Darby won't allow—" She stopped, backpedaling from her choice of words. "He won't want the queue inside the shop. I agree that people ought to be on the front sidewalk instead of that dodgy alleyway. But Mr. Darby will scare everyone away when he sees what we've done."

"I understand why you'd think that. But Mr. Darby is . . ."

She looked toward the hall, reimagining Amos's weary form disappearing from view. No, he never would wish to be in the front of the shop. And he certainly wouldn't want something as private as the existence of the bottles discussed with anyone who might be working in back. Though if Amos had even one more bottle upstairs, Charlotte feared it would close out the day for him.

"He's what, Your Ladyship?"

"Nothing. It's not important." Charlotte course-corrected and shook off the worry. Concern could wait until she had a better grasp of the situation, and then she'd decide on careful steps for dealing with it. "What I can say is that Mr. Darby will not be back downstairs today. It's up to us to carry on."

"He won't?"

"No. And he's left me in charge. So let's hop to it. We've much to do."

Charlotte would send someone up to check on Amos once the hour had passed, just as she'd promised. And though the shop would soon fill with grateful voices and cups clinking saucers as customers perused bookshop aisles before the blackout curfew came, she was certain Amos wouldn't wake anytime soon.

One last prayer to pin everything on?

May the sirens go quiet tonight. And let him rest.

CHAPTER TEN

12 October 1940
Brinklow Road
Coventry, England

One million pounds . . .
The sum clicked through Eden's mind over and over, like a ticker tape humming in the background. She thought of it as they unloaded rosebushes and gardening supplies from the wagonette and still as they headed back toward the manor's front doors at afternoon break. And it would no doubt be a task to focus on the clergyman's homily in services the following morning.

Eden had a time enough of it trying to work with the Land Girls all day. From the moment she'd dragged her first claw rake through dirt, one thought would inevitably give way to another, like dominoes being tipped over at the front of an exhausting line. And whilst all the rosebushes were prepped for moving and the Andersons sank deeper in the earth, the list of misfortunes the Cole money could turn around ticked off before she could stop it.

The roof needed more than just patches and water buckets to save the attic during a drowning rain; it would require full replating. The windows had needed replacing for ages. The outbuildings, fortifying. The stable and plumbing, modernizing. And the autos, refurbishing. Even the poor glasshouse on the hill was in dire straits, with several panes of patina glass cracked by time and stray starlings' flights. And if they didn't see to it soon, the glasshouse would be unusable through the cold months when they needed every square inch of growing space to fortify their food supply through winter.

Beyond the immediate needs around the estate, all Eden could think of was that this could be the deliverance to ensure Holt Manor's survival for the next decade. And then some. If what Jacob had said was true, from the moment the case was decided, the funds could be wired in ninety days if all worked in their favor and not his.

That was the big question looming over the lot: What exactly did "decided" mean?

"Pardon, Lady Eden?"

"Yes, Mrs. Mills?" Eden snapped back to the moment, addressing their housekeeper—a slim Irishwoman of fifty years, with freckled nose and kind eyes—who'd appeared out front of the manor. Eden hopped down from the wagonette and began off-loading the tools with Jacob. "I know we're late. Was Mama worried?"

"Not a whit. But I've been sent with an urgent telephone message from Miss Brewster, on behalf of Her Ladyship."

"Urgent?"

Thank heavens they'd had telephones installed some years prior in the butler's office, in the manor entry, and in the downstairs library. But if calls were to come in related to the bombings for the foreseeable future, they might need more.

"Yes, milady." Mrs. Mills handed over a note folded down the center.

Eden's pulse quickened, until she scanned the missive and relief cooled her nerves with each word read.

"Not bad news, is it?" Jacob eased in at her side.

It must be an American thing to lean over a lady's shoulder and read her messages without permission. And perhaps it was the standing close—and not the liberty of reading her correspondence—that made Eden feel skittish enough to stash the missive in the front pocket of her dungarees and sidestep him.

"No, thank heaven. But I'm needed in town. At the bookshop. Mama asks for a couple of the Land Girls too, if we might spare them."

"Didn't it say at Amos's shop? Why would Her Ladyship ask us to go there?"

He'd picked up on the oddity too. And after his reception at Eden Books the day before, he knew of the strife between shops.

"She doesn't say. But you'll learn fast that when my mother asks for something, there is always a good reason. And an entire estate of loyal workers ready to drop tools and run when she calls." Eden flipped her plait over her shoulder and out of the way to drag a pot of silvery-pink New Dawn roses to the end of the wagonette bed. "Wait—did you say *us*?"

Jacob swept a forearm across his brow, the sun keeping them heated even though the afternoon had turned cool. "I wouldn't mind a wash either."

"Pardon?"

"Waverley Novels. You know. The bookshop? I'm rooming at Mr. Darby's."

The surprises with this man came in spades.

A court case. A million pounds of financial blessing within her grasp. And now he was rooming at the home of the enemy from across Bayley Lane. Did he always give such whiplash with his pronouncements? What might it be like to ever have a normal conversation with the man?

"You are rooming . . . at Mr. Darby's shop."

"I am. Is that a problem?"

"A problem?" She scoffed. Of course it was, for Mama at least. Every bit. "Why did you stay with him? There are other rooming houses in town."

"Because he offered." Jacob shrugged. "Right. I'll just help with carrying the last of the roses to the solarium and we should be on our way."

He climbed back up to the wagonette bed then, not waiting for an answer and forgetting he hadn't been invited to attend to her mama's summons. Instead, Jacob lifted pots of blooms, handed them down to Alec and Mr. Cox, and looked a little too dreamy with sun-kissed skin and his jovial smile lavished on the Land Girls still fluttering around like lost butterflies.

Eden shook her head. The girls seemed unfazed—by the work, if not also the gentleman. Even Flo, who'd managed to look a fashion plate despite hours of dirt, sweat, and sun under their belts, hopped down from the wagonette to beam in Jacob's direction.

"We need volunteers," Eden offered her. "A couple at the bookshop this afternoon. Would you like to come?"

"I would, Lady Eden. But . . ."

Turned hands revealed Flo's porcelain-white palms roughened to bleeding and skin seared with blisters, so much so that Eden couldn't see how the girl had kept working as long as she had. If first impressions were wrong, then she had to admit that Flo's beauty had proved to be substance on top of style, as she'd worked as hard as anyone else for the lot of the day. But that substance had cost her dearly, and Eden hated to think of how Flo would suffer through the night with the searing pain of inflamed hands.

"Oh, Flo. I am sorry. I should have told you what working with the tools would be like."

She curled her hands together, hiding the roughened patches. "It's alright, Lady Eden. I ought to have worn the gloves. I don't know why I didn't."

"I know why she didn't." Dale shook her head. "The nail varnish. She didn't want to mark those cherry-red fingertips with gloves pressing the tips. I'm sure of it. And it was a worthy sacrifice, darling."

"Let's get you taken care of. I'll find some softer gloves for you to use in the future." Eden led the girls toward the front doors, not wanting to humble a worker on her first day. One didn't become a farmer overnight. "Ainsley? Could you join us at the bookshop? I've had a message from Her Ladyship, asking us to arrive as soon as we can."

She brightened. "I'd be happy to, Lady Eden."

Dale didn't seem to mind, giving a cheeky wink in Jacob's direction. "Sounds like a cozy party. Unless we're dressing for dinner, of course. Is that done here at Holt Manor? I have some rather posh friends in Mayfair who dine. Every night, as a matter of fact."

"We used to. But not much since the war. The first one, that is. We dress on occasion now when we have guests and such. But most nights . . . no."

"Whyever not?" Dale asked.

"It's not practical. I get in from the fields and Mama from the bookshop so late that it's often a tray in my room and to bed with a book. Unless the sirens blare. And then the only difference is you read the book in a shelter."

"Doll, you are armed to the teeth with such a pile of stones here. Look at this manor, just waiting to entertain! Any eligible bachelors would be entranced after walking through your door. You'd seal the deal by the time the second course was through. And dance the night away with a ring on your finger."

"I am not in the marriage market. And I don't plan to be anytime soon," Eden countered, though she'd lowered her voice so the men wouldn't overhear. Best get the Land Girls to a point of understanding straightaway—this was an endeavor to win the war first and save the estate at a very close second. And she wouldn't need a ring to do either.

"Well, that's no fun, is it? I was going to wear a frock Ainsley made for me, as it's fit for a queen's table. I did take a peek into your dining hall." Dale hooked her arm in Ainsley's elbow and looked in the direction of the gents hauling rose pots. "Quite the affair. I'd say if we think really hard, we could conjure up some guests for dinner and dancing. Don't you?"

"Miss Flo?" someone said, and cleared his throat behind them. A hush fell over them all. Eden stopped and the girls did too. Even Jacob and Mr. Cox had turned their attention to Alec Fitzgibbons standing there, hat in his hands, brown eyes and unshaven face looking on one particular Land Girl.

Flo eased her hands into the pockets of her breeches. "Yes?"

"Pardon, miss. Have Cook prepare a mixture—one ounce beeswax, one ounce olive oil. Melt it down in a jar. After you've washed and dried your hands, rub it on when it's cool enough to handle. That ought to take the sting out tonight."

An old farmer's remedy.

Eden could have told her the same, and would have, along with the use of oat flour on the palms so you didn't transfer greasy fingerprints all over your bedclothes. But Alec was a quiet sort, always focused on work, handy with the tractor, and more knowledgeable oftentimes than the veterinary surgeons who came to see to the livestock. Any remedy he offered would be just the ticket. But indeed, that he'd offered it at all was what the lot seemed to find most curious.

"Thank you, Mr. Fitzgibbons." Flo smiled in a soft and sweet way, with just a flash of vulnerability. "I'm sure that will do nicely."

"Miss." Alec replaced his hat, tipped it, and went back to work. Just like that. Leaving the Land Girls and Eden standing in the doorway like gaping fish without a sea to swim in.

Eden's gaze drifted. For a breath. Maybe two at most. And for how she'd have thought Jacob would set his eyes on one of the Chelsea-bred girls with their rouge and verve and ever-winning smiles, he didn't. Instead, he stood atop the wagonette and, with a look of authenticity like Flo's, had fixed his eyes upon *Eden*.

Farmers and females. Sweat and sun. And solicitors offering a fight over a million pounds that on an old estate could soothe a long list of woes . . . Eden was convinced one could never predict which way the day would go on a working estate. Nor where bombs would fall at night. Nor what colors would paint tomorrow's sunrise. But with Land Girls in the mix, an invitation to step into the enemy's camp, and the whole of their world turned topsy-turvy by war, it seemed they ought to get accustomed to expecting the most unexpected.

CHAPTER ELEVEN

8 August 1914
Brinklow Road
Coventry, England

*I*f approaching the glasshouse started tearing up Amos's insides, listening to Charlotte play the cello within it just about finished the job.

The only witnesses to her song now in the emptied space were a few potted seedlings left to bake in the summer sun, starlings in the poplar boughs, and the scared-stiff soldier in the doorway, waiting for her to notice him. Amos watched her play, noting how her eyes closed as she fell into the melody and how unearthly beautiful she was in an ivory dress of lace that draped her form and outlined the cello she'd cradled against her body.

Something in her left hand slipped, causing her palm to jar against the fingerboard.

Oh . . . A new ring.

Charlotte hung her head and dropped the bow, covering the diamond and joined band with her palm like she was pressing out more than just physical pain.

Amos tapped the glass door, the hollow sound echoing sharply into the empty glasshouse. She looked up. Found him standing there in a khaki serge uniform tunic with matching trousers and a woolen service dress cap. And the way she started at his service dress said it all: Charlotte hadn't known he'd signed up.

"I was told I might find you here." Amos took off his service cap, turned it over in his hands, and gestured to the backdrop of the fields behind him. "I went to bid farewell and fetch the last of my things from the farm. And learned Tate Fitzgibbons has been given the lease at Foxhollow?"

"Yes," she said quietly, as if still finding her voice. "He has."

"Was that you, to appeal to His Lordship on Tate's behalf?" When she didn't answer, just blinked back at him to show small talk wasn't nearly going to suffice, he continued. "I can't tell you what it means to him and his wife, Marni, to be settled in a place before we go. And when their little one arrives."

"You're leaving, too, then?"

"Aye. Tomorrow. Train's at six." Where he would be sent after basic training, Amos didn't have the foggiest idea, though optimism had run rampant at the recruitment center that the conflict would be over by Christmas. But if it were not true, he half turned like the fool he was, unable to stand the guilt of seeing her now and knowing it could be the last time for . . . who knew how long? "So I'll just be off then."

"Is that it?" she whispered behind him.

He turned back. "Is that what?"

"How we say goodbye?"

"Milady, I—"

"Don't you dare call me *milady*. I deserve more than the distant regard of a title."

"Alright."

"Why didn't you come?" Charlotte demanded, and she shot up from her chair so that the cello slid off her shoulder and gave a little death groan as it busted upon the tile at her feet.

He stopped, trying not to be stunned that she'd left it there, her beloved cello, lying on the ground with split wood like it deserved every bit of what it got. "Charlotte . . . we don't have to do this."

"If this is goodbye, then I would ask for the truth before we say it."

Don't ask me to do that.

Anything but that.

How could Amos tell her he had gone to Gretna Green that day? That he'd parked well off and trekked through the rain along the road? And stood there watching her from afar as she waited in the doorway to the smithy's? Looking so hopeful and ungodly beautiful in a new blue frock that Amos had almost changed his mind and gone to her right then and there.

"I wish I could say what happened that day."

"We said if we both felt the same, then we'd be there, one for the other. I was there. And I waited for you. All day."

"I know."

"Then is that why you didn't come—your feelings had changed? I was willing to give up my entire world for you, Amos. I thought you were too. Weren't we to make a new world together, you and I? Despite the gossip and the newspapers and a reputation damaged beyond repair? None of it matters when I couldn't care about them like I did for you. The dreams we talked of that day in the carriage so long ago, when you'd brought my cello back to me. They were not supposed to end here." She paused, then added, "I loved you," on a tragic, drawn-out whisper.

Loved.

The past tense of that word crashed into him like a gale.

Amos tried to speak. Stopped. Tried again. Wished he were dead where he stood, for hurting her as he had. And it seemed Charlotte recognized the look that must have been on his face, where emotion was clawing at his insides so fiercely. Amos had nothing left to say that could make up for what had happened.

"I know that too. But it seems, uh . . ." Amos cleared his throat. Straightened his shoulders. Felt emotion lump in his throat like a boulder. "Congratulations are in order."

She nodded and looked down at the wedding set on her ring finger, pressing it with her fingertips like she wished she could hide the yellow diamond nearly the size of a robin's egg.

Yes. That.

It had been in the society column: "New Earl Marries His Countess." Lady Charlotte Terrington was now a Holt. And the enormous ring on her finger said the scandal Amos had caused could simply fade away and, if necessary, die with him in the trenches of France. And with the ring, Charlotte had been given title and rank, and enough position that the past could be expunged and her future secured—regardless of what war might bring.

"Yes. You said congratulations before when we were in your barn that day after Christmas." She absentmindedly fiddled with the ring on her finger. "But congratulations are not why I asked Mr. Fitzgibbons to tell you I'd be here."

Charlotte stooped to her cello case and opened it, and with every ounce of courage he wished he had, she retrieved a book. Brushing her fingertips over the gold-embossed *Dombey and Son* on the cover, she paused on an indrawn breath. Then held it out.

"Here." She made no show that the book affected her at all; the gaze was cold. Bland. And so devoid of warmth. "This belongs to you."

"I can't take that."

"You will. Someone once told me it's a difficult story to let go," she said through angry tears, tossing their words from the library that night back at him now. "But it should travel well, along with the rest of your books. Wherever the road now takes you."

With her shimmying the book on air, Amos relented and took it. Hating the cold feel of the binding in his hand when she let go as the gift became his once more.

"It was my price, you see. To marry Will. The only point I negotiated in my favor was that I could return this to you. And before you ask, he knows I'm here today. And that you are as well. And I have my husband's blessing to now close this unfortunate chapter between us."

Charlotte turned, gathered up her wounded cello, and enclosed it back in its case. "I wish you luck, soldier." The words were all that was left between them as she turned to leave Amos in the glasshouse a second time. "And the protection of Providence to bring you home safe, wherever that home may be."

Amos placed his uniform cap back on his head, stiffened his spine as he watched her path toward the manor, and walked out in the opposite direction, toward the road beyond the sharp cuts of sun streaming through the trees.

Childhood dreams had no place in the real world.

He knew that now. Their music faded over time, and their kinship became a cord that snapped when illusions stretched too far. Charlotte's home was Holt Manor. And his? For the first time in his life, Amos didn't know. All he could hope was the book would fit with the wares a soldier could keep in his haversack and allow him to carry a piece of home wherever the line to the front should stop.

➤·◄

13 October 1940
St. Michael's Avenue
Coventry, England

The statue of St. Michael stood guard over ancient wood pews. Early morning light fractured through stained glass, casting a colored glow on the cathedral's groin-vault ceiling and walls of stone.

Praise be worshippers hadn't trickled in to St. Michael's just yet.

This early, Amos could slip in, evade notice, and disappear before the sun had risen in full and bombings from the day prior packed out the prayer kneelers. He sat alone. Suit and tie occupying the shadows of the back row as he kept his marred profile to the wall and stared up at the archangel statue affixed to the wall supporting the cathedral's grand tower. And tapped his foot with impatience.

Michael had donned armor, brandished his shield, and angled his wings with a powerful point to the heavens. The archangel had drawn his sword, too, with a fierceness ready to protect the souls who'd soon be squeezing into the sanctuary for morning services.

Maybe that was what the people needed just now? To know that all of creation was on alert? And every sword had been summoned to give assurance that despite bombs falling, fires erupting, and the enemy barrage shaking the ground beneath the whole world's feet, they were not forsaken.

Aye. I believed that once.

Not anymore.

It was a fighting man's duty to remember who and what he was fighting for first, and use it in battle second. But then Amos had beheld the face of war, in all its agents of agony that men inflicted upon one another. There was no glory to be found where bombs blackened earth. And in it, to fight became only to live from one day to the next. It wasn't the brave or principled man Amos had hoped to be when he'd signed up but the broken one he was who'd limped home. Not even Michael's sword could fend that off.

"Ah, Amos. You're here." Provost Dick Howard slipped his tall frame into the pew next to Amos. "Good day to you."

His dark hair was combed to a tight, respectable part as always. Kind eyes looked out from behind wire-rimmed spectacles. And the humility that shone from his face was every bit as genuine as any man Amos had known. It forced him to consider how this clergyman could be forgiving that Amos hadn't graced a pew in years—not unless he was summoned as he had been now—and not stand in judgment at the same time.

Amos tipped his head to the provost. "You called, Father. I came."

"Yes, I did. And I ought to apologize for the hour."

"Don't be worrying about that. The sirens were kind to let us sleep last night."

"Weren't they just. And so fewer people than normal are likely to sleep through my homily this morn, and for that the Lord knows I am truly grateful." He smiled as he stared forward at the view before them. Then after a few long breaths, he pointed to the archangel's edifice shining from the wall under the tower. "It is beautiful, isn't it? Michael. He's the patron saint of the military, you know."

Amos nodded. Aye. He'd known it well. Once. Before everything changed.

"Yes, patron of those in peril and seeking protection from our enemies. But did you know, he's summoned to fight for the fighters—the soldiers, police, doctors—anyone who is willing to resist in protection of another. And he goes on to protect them. Remarkable." The provost leaned forward just enough that the wooden row creaked and clasped his hands over the back of the pew in front of them. "Not unlike the Home Guard, I'd say."

Discomfort from ill-deserved praise was something Amos didn't relish showing a soul, especially not in a pew. And especially not with scars of his own for people to be looking at, and judging, and finding every bit as abhorrent as he expected them to. Worshippers had begun their slow trek inside, and that meant Amos had best make tracks before kneelers came down and furtive glances started their drift in his direction.

"I called you here for a reason, Amos. And I find it's not easy to say. But I must ask."

"Alright." Hesitant, he shifted in the pew. "What can I help you with? Please tell me it's more than conversation about the art on the walls."

"Yes, of course." The provost nodded and leaned back again. "I'll get to the point. News of the tea queue has spread, and people were bolstered by it on a morning when they oughtn't have been. Especially when two bookshops that were known to be in competition have set all that aside in the interest of helping others. It's made quite an impression. I had a queue of my own in here yesterday, of people waiting to express their gratitude for what our local booksellers have done. Though when I spoke with Lady Harcourt, she refused any claim on it. She said it was your idea and yours alone to care for the people of this city in this way. Is this true?"

"It's not exactly how it happened. We fell into it more than anything, when an AFS member who'd been fighting fires all night stumbled through my door, asking if I had any brew. I did. And it just kept going."

"More than that, Amos. It was as much care and fighting for others as Michael could do himself. I'm aware you may not wish to step into the public eye. But I'd like you to consider making this a permanent fixture on Bayley Lane. We all can use a reminder from time to time that what we see and hear each week inside this cathedral is what people are actually living outside these walls. Benevolence, compassion, and love—bombs will never silence them when we put those virtues into action. Ordinary people like us become extraordinary fighters when we first seek to serve and love others. And we'd like to fund you from the church to continue doing just that."

"Mr. Darby? Father? Good morning." Charlotte's voice carried from the aisle just over Amos's shoulder. He half rose to stand, but she stopped him with a wave of a gloved hand. "Don't get up. Please."

She slipped into the pew in front of him, then turned to look back. Old statues and stained glass be forgotten. If this was Charlotte's Sunday best, in a powder-blue suit that brightened her smile and made her eyes a truer shade of gold, then the Lord Himself hadn't made a prettier sight to grace the cathedral in all the centuries it had stood on that ground.

"Perfect timing, Lady Harcourt. I'm afraid I must be off. Duty calls. Perhaps you can take the conversation from here and fill Amos in on the scope of our idea?"

"I will." She offered a hand to shake the provost's. "Thank you again."

"If you'll excuse me. And, Amos?" Provost Howard placed a gentle hand to Amos's shoulder, gave a pat that lasted no longer than a breath, and let go. "It's good to see you."

With that the provost was off. Worshippers gathered. And Amos's breathing quickened. People and pews, and Charlotte sitting close enough to look him square in the eyes . . . It didn't fit the recluse's portrait of a fine Sunday morning. Though the shadows had been a welcome place to sit only moments before, the rapid rise of morning meant there were fewer places to retreat with sunlight streaking across stone.

"Sometimes it feels as though this city has known Provost Howard all our lives, doesn't it?" Charlotte flitted her glance to the clergyman, standing with the people across the way. She tipped her head to an acquaintance in the crowd, then turned back to him. "Did you sleep?"

Why are you so interested in my sleeping habits?

He nodded. "Aye. All night. And then some. That was a nasty trick, sending me up when you did. Knowing I'd wake to the aftermath of a circus in my shop this morn."

She smiled, it seemed, in spite of herself. Or maybe in spite of him. "Somehow I thought we would get away with all that. Well, it is why I'm here of a sort. Why we're both here, actually."

"And that is—the tea queue?"

"Yes, and no." Charlotte straightened her chin. "I'd like to hire you."

"Hire me?" Not at all what Amos had expected her to say. Nor wanted. Nor would consider in the least. "I'm not the hiring sort, milady. Not these days. When I have a business to run and duties with the Home Guard."

"Did I not ask you to stop all that 'milady' nonsense once?" Charlotte scolded, though there was play in her voice. "If we've agreed to be friends, your shop and mine, then we should speak like it."

"Aye. But years of a habit now . . . it's tough to break."

"Fine. Then I shall hear every protestation you feel comfortable giving, in this the Lord's holy sanctuary, after I've said my piece."

"Not fair." He laughed. Softly and under his breath, but it was there. Cursed was the man who couldn't find humor in Charlotte's evergreen wit.

"I know. But what's fair when we're at war? We come armed as we must for the task at hand. And here it is: Provost Howard would like to see our bookshops work together for more than the tea queue. We'll keep that up, of course, but he proposed to fund a more formal partnership between us."

Amos swallowed hard; they'd tried that before. And he didn't know if going headlong into a crash-and-burn partnership was a clever move now.

"Meaning?"

"I've already told you we've taken on Land Girls at the estate. Part of the arrangement is that they're willing to take shifts at Eden Books, and now they'll also help in the tea queue at Waverley Novels. When needed, of course. With your knowledge of farming and of books, we thought you could teach them in both places."

"What would I be teaching at Holt Manor?"

"Well, *we* would be teaching them. We have solid management through Eden. But that's not enough when the workers left at Holt Manor are few. Including farmers, we've only the Land Girls, Eden and myself, Mr. Cox, and Alec Fitzgibbons. But the latter has his own farm to run—Foxhollow." She paused, a memory triggered from all those years ago. "You know Alec, don't you?"

"His father and I were mates, uh, before the war. The first one."

"Yes. And his mother and I became close while our husbands were away. Especially that first year . . . when she received her telegram from the War Office." Charlotte looked down, maybe thinking about when she'd received her own War Office missive?

She'd been wringing gloved hands in her lap and seemed to notice, settled them, and stilled her palms again. "Yes, well. As Marni moved back to London some years back, Alec has taken over the farm completely. He will be of great help to us, and now we have Mr. Cole—as long as an American solicitor can stand the work. Or until he plays his hand about the inheritance."

"You think he will?"

She shook her head. "I'm sure I don't know. But regardless of whether I like the young man or not, he isn't telling us everything about why he's here."

"And that's why you've allowed him to tag along at the estate."

"For now, yes." As was her way, Charlotte must have been thinking far more than she was willing to say. And she knew he'd catch on to it without her having to explain much. "We also have Mr. Cox, but he's not a true farmer. At least not like you used to be. But you ran a large operation. And every scrap of land at Holt Manor needs to be churned up fresh and used for growing food. All told, if we could do that and organize this tea operation both, we might make it a regular easing of burdens for the people of this city. And I know that holds a great deal of importance for both of us."

Amos glanced around at women in their refurbished hats, men in patched Sunday suits, even some workers who looked to have happened by with dust from the streets still clinging to their ties and suit jackets. Didn't know why he was, but he found himself considering. "What of the bookshops?"

"Ah. Yes. Perhaps we can share resources. If there is a shortage of supplies or shipments of stock are delayed, one supports the other. We could partner for author events as needed and divide the profits in an even split."

"Selling books is my business, but I have a larger responsibility to the Home Guard on Bayley Lane. A spot in the rotation for the fire-watchers and scheduled times on the rooftop of Drapers' Hall with the antiaircraft crews. Even the provost himself is assigned to the fire brigade here at the cathedral. We all have roles to play."

"Of course. I'd thought of that. What if you were given the title of agent for the estate and could have full use of our resources?"

"Estate agent . . ."

"Yes. You could come to Holt Manor and oversee the Land Girls, and support Eden in the finer points of how to farm a large commercial venture. We'd come under your direction for all of it. And you'd be free to come and go as needed, especially so you're back in the city at night. Our auto and petrol allotment would be at your disposal so you're not out after the blackouts."

Never in all the years since the last day at the glasshouse would

Amos have believed he'd return. And not only return to Holt land but, this time, be in charge of it. Whoever thought of Amos Darby as agent for Holt Manor?

"It seems you've thought of near everything. But just what does Lady Eden say about all this?"

"She'll agree."

"You're certain of that, when that estate is her most cherished thing on this earth? She won't see this as a play for me to take it from her?"

"It is for the estate and the greater good we can do here that I believe she'll see the benefit in this arrangement. But we can only do it if we work together. So what I'm really asking for is your help, Amos."

For the greater good. *Together.*

How he wanted to believe that. How Amos wished he didn't feel the clawing inside to walk out as the pews filled up or stay miles away from the very land that had once left him with nothing but the clothes on his back. Was that what made a man brave? Not the stepping forward when you didn't know what you were up against, but the going back to the fray, time and time again, when you did?

He picked up his flat cap and cleared his throat as he rose, ready to leave. "What time?"

Charlotte's face brightened. She must have thought it a no when he'd stood.

"Would nine o'clock tomorrow morning suit? I know the city would like shopkeepers to continue to close by three in the afternoon so the workers can travel home before the blackouts start. That should give the Land Girls ample time to work from morning until afternoon, and you enough time to return to your post at St. Mary's Street."

"Aye. Nine o'clock then. I'll be there."

Charlotte never was one for doing things halfway; she'd sell her entire trunk of gowns before she'd stop at a few. Nor would Charlotte pretend when there was something she truly wanted. And if

Amos knew anything about farmers in the Midlands, it was that an iron-clad contract was sealed with one word and a handshake between equals.

She extended a gloved hand—her left, to meet his unscarred one—and something sparked inside that she knew him so well as to notice that tiny detail, even after all these years. "Agreed?"

Amos shook her hand with his left palm meeting hers. "Agreed."

It was the smallest of gestures, a handshake. Charlotte stood and parted from him in the nave to walk to the memorial on the wall for the local boys who'd been lost in the Great War. Pressing a tiny kiss to gloved fingertips, she brushed the plaque as she breezed by.

Amos didn't stay; he wasn't ready to be social. But he took it as a good sign that he felt the tiny nudge to look back at Charlotte as she stood amongst the people of Coventry—her neighbors and friends—before retreating into the churchyard with the sun at his back and a smile warming some small corner inside.

CHAPTER TWELVE

24 August 1914
Brinklow Road
Coventry, England

Daybreak boasted incomparable moments at Holt Manor, and Charlotte soon found her heartbeat among them.

Most mornings now, fog rose from the hills under overcast skies. A palette of slate blue and titian watercolors painted the horizon, the colors mingling with clouds behind stable spires and the tops of poplar trees. The starlings were awake with the sun. The horses in the stables, sheep and cows in the barn too. And it became a haven for Charlotte to wake with them, venture out the service doors at the back of the manor, and spend her first hours playing the cello in their company.

A crisp breeze swept by the open barn doors, toying with wisps of hair that had come unfurled from her headscarf to dance against her neck. She turned her face toward the hills, relishing the peace and solace of the sun warming her face through the cool snap of morning air.

"There you are." Will appeared in the barn's open doorway, winded as if he'd been racing around the estate, and now blocked the doorway with his shirt half-tucked, hair mussed, and hacking jacket held back by hands planted at his waist.

"Will?" She squinted up against the sun's glare. "Are you quite well?"

"Are you trying to catch your death?"

"I'll catch my death in a barn . . . in August?"

"You know what I meant." Will peered around the open door, his brow flinching in some sort of realization. He swept in, stopping in front of the old spindle chair where she sat with the cello cradled against trouser-clad legs. "What on earth are you doing out here?"

"You asked me not to play at the glasshouse."

He shook his head. "I *suggested* not. And I thought my position was clear in saying so at all. It's not proper to play that instrument. Not now."

"But you didn't mind last Christmas. And I played for all of the party guests then."

"That was different."

"How?" Charlotte's annoyance increased each time Will questioned her as though she were a child. "Mother may have attempted to sway me to play the piano when I was young—or even the violin as a proper substitute. She thought I'd give it up. But from the moment I attended a concert and heard a cello sing Bach from a stage, I fell in love. And I've not been able to silence the music within me since. Surely you can understand that? I support your passion for horses. This is no different."

Fell in love . . .

Poor choice of words, Charlotte. It was the last thing Will looked like he wanted reminding of—the things she'd loved once. The cello, books, childhood dreams, and a farmer's son who'd shared them. When she'd said those three little words, it seemed he'd missed everything she'd said after.

"You look like a farmhand, darling."

Instinct sent Charlotte's hand to palm the back of her paisley scarf from her trousseau, the pretty pattern in rust with yellow birds she'd woven around the plait pinned at her nape. And the farmer's wares she'd borrowed from Tate Fitzgibbons's wife— dungarees with suspenders, a woven jumper in deep plum, and a pair of gum shoes that for what they lacked in fashion would make up for in keeping her feet dry on damp mornings.

Perhaps Charlotte wasn't the picture perfect image of a Gibson girl, but it wasn't as if she'd shown up at a ball wearing the latest style of potato sack. She judged herself quite respectable, being covered from high-neck collar to the tips of her toes. "The clothes—I borrowed them, thinking I didn't want to soil expensive gowns."

"Borrowed this. From whom?"

"One of the farmer's wives; Mrs. Fitzgibbons has been kind to me. And even though I'm the new mistress, she didn't expect I'd wish to wear a tea gown to play in a barn." It was a lighthearted statement, meant in jest and offered with a smile. Pity that Will's mood wasn't one to find humor in it. Then more serious, she added, "You know I cannot play in the manor. Your mother forbids it. And there is nowhere else where the house staff would not see or hear."

"I wouldn't have you out here at all." He sighed deep. "I woke to the housekeeper's voice in our chamber instead of my wife's. And found when the curtains were drawn back and the light let in, I was in bed alone. Again."

"Will, please," she mumbled, her cheeks burning as she glanced over to the stable boy out of the corner of her eye.

The poor lad seemed a mite dumbfounded to find the estate master and mistress engaged in conversation of such a private nature. Charlotte couldn't blame him. Was it a regular occurrence to discuss these matters as if they hadn't any delicacy at all? Married life was proving a lesson in abruptness even weeks into the arrangement—her husband's moods the most puzzling part of the equation. And her cheeks were now burning for it.

The lad chose to exit and close the door behind him.

"I missed you, Charlotte."

"I know. And I am sorry you woke alone, but—" She turned the bow over in her hand, wishing it were singing against strings instead of serving as a distraction so she wouldn't have to look him in the face over such a mortifying discussion. "I was already awake. And I didn't expect you'd want to breakfast together, being that you were out late last night."

Again. He ignored the tiny insinuation, choosing not to comment that he enjoyed many late nights at his gentleman's club, both in Coventry and in London. And never once bothered to explain or acknowledge that it was more severe than playing cello in the barn in the mornings.

"This is my time to play, Will. To hold on to something for myself, no matter how small. Do you understand?" The sun was up in full now, dawn rolling into morning behind his shoulders. And what a pang she felt to think of losing it. "Dawn is all I have."

"Breakfast or not, my wife was gone. Without a word to her husband. Nor with any care that Mother may have set appointments for calls today. Did you know? She's poised to miss them now because of your thoughtlessness."

"Oh dear." Charlotte leaned back and slid the cello into its case. She tried not to notice the little crack—the only sign it had once been broken and repaired—nor to think of the reason why. "I'm afraid I had forgotten that. We hadn't time to discuss our diaries yet for the week, but I just assumed that meant she'd proceed without me and pay her calls alone."

"You might have realized that is no longer possible. *You* are the Countess of Harcourt now. And she, the dowager. Day to day, this title will be your responsibility to uphold. It can't be any different than living in your father's house. The expectations of your station have not changed."

"No. They have not." She sighed because she'd hoped somehow that they would be different, and perhaps that she'd been a fool to think so was the greatest awakening of married life.

"Then you ought to consider Mother's feelings from now on. Learn from her. And take your rightful place in this family and in society."

A little flame of rebellion raced up her spine. She snapped the cello case closed, then stood tall, straightening her back before him.

"So this is to be a marriage guided by the dictations of a mother-in-law, instead of one that sees a man and wife able to discuss things together and make our own decisions?"

"Man and wife, Charlotte. I put a ring on your finger. So?" He stared down at her hand. "Where is it?"

"Oh. That." Charlotte pressed her fingers over the bare ring finger, thinking of the diamond and wedding band sitting smartly on the Egyptian jewelry tray on her vanity. "The setting is so beautiful, I didn't want the rings damaged. And I'm not able to play with them. The diamond is heavy and rolls around until it pinches my palm. And I'd risk further damage to the cello, and you know what that did to me last time it occurred."

"Yes. You were near inconsolable. But didn't I arrange to have that repaired too? I can contact our jeweler to have your rings sized. It's nothing a wife of mine wouldn't deserve."

"What I mean is, it's easier to play without finery. What good would a diamond do me out here? Or a dress, for that matter? Such things may be the way of it for an heiress, but I want more than that. I'd hoped we could enjoy our passions and work the estate too . . . together."

"That is precisely my point. Why would you need to? I have the means to hire workers. And you have access to every inch of the manor to do with as you please. To spend as you will. To decorate or plan dinners or support any of Coventry's charitable causes you so choose. You are to represent me in this county as my wife—countess and mother to my children. And yes, guidance in those things ought to come from the woman who's worn that crown with honor since she, too, married into this estate. Yet I've learned from Mother that you've already dishonored that by inquiring after the estate financials from my estate agent."

Her mouth fell open. "I did, but I didn't realize it would be a dishonor to speak with *our* agent. And Mr. Hall was quite accommodating."

"For what purpose do you feel it's your place to speak to the staff outside the manor?"

"I'd read a newspaper article this week that prompted a question. It estimated at present, some 80 percent of our wheat is imported to England. And the vast majority of our food supply as well."

Will crossed his arms over his chest. "What does that matter to us?"

"Our access to provisions will dwindle if this conflict continues, which the newspapers say we have every reason to believe it will. I simply inquired when we ought to plant the winter wheat. Mr. Hall advised that we wait until at least September, given the impact of insects and the potential for disease in wet weather. So we'll have time to discuss it and prepare the south fields—that is, if we wish to move forward. I believe we should."

"And who says we're planting the south fields? That's grazing land."

"I know it is. But . . . war will change everything. And we must meet its challenges head-on. I'd been hearing about Mr. Fitzgibbons's plans for Foxhollow Farm before he shipped off to the front. And his wife has put forth some interesting ideas about how we might better use that land. Marni's recommended a book to me—*A Pilgrimage of British Farming* by Sir Daniel Hall. It should support some of the theory behind it. I found a copy in the library, and I've already read the first chapter. I've marked pages. Perhaps you and I could discuss it and then decide?"

"What is it with you and books from my father's library?"

The barb landed a tiny cut but still proved effective to his point. Charlotte lowered her voice. "Will. That's not what I meant."

"Of course. Forgive me." He stopped. Sighed heavily. Then ran a hand through uncombed ebony hair, as if the real reason for his displeasure was not her misstep at all. More that she presented a

host of problems. Or perhaps she was the problem to be solved—
his problem now.

Will knelt beside her, meeting her glance for glance with a
tenderness that had been absent until that moment. It restored
a glimmer of hope. They might build a life together, and he could
respond in kind when she'd shown vulnerability to him. Surely he
would meet her in it?

"You do have purpose here, my love. But it is not playing the
cello for my cows or debating agricultural theory from the library.
I need a son. Or at least, I need to know I have one on the way
before I go."

And the razor's edge kept cutting.

Her gaze snapped to his. "What do you mean, go?"

"Charlotte, you know I cannot stand by and watch able-bodied
men ship out around me. I won't wait to be told to put on a uniform." Will clenched his jaw and reached out. Slow. And took one
of her palms in his own, fingertips just grazing in a caress across
the top of her hand. "I've signed up. And I ship out in a week."

"What?" She yanked her hand away and shot to her feet. "This
isn't like taking a morning walk. We're supposed to decide these
things together! You and I. Husband and wife. Isn't that what we
vowed to one another? How could you make such a decision and
not even think to consult me?"

"It wouldn't have changed my mind."

"And I wouldn't try to."

"Perhaps, unless . . ." He sighed again, looking to the straw at
his boots before he stood along with her. "Are you with child?"

Charlotte's cheeks burned with a mix of embarrassment and
fury. To toss out family planning on the cusp of a soldier's com-
mission . . . Was that truly all she was to him?

She crossed her arms over her middle. "No. Or I don't know.
How could I? We've only been married a short time."

"Then perhaps you ought to spend mornings in your husband's
chamber, instead of his barn. Hmm?"

The words were spoken with softness—his ill-formed attempt at affection. But for Charlotte, they landed like a shot of cold water to the face.

She stared back at him, blinking through the silence. Desperate to find something genuine in his eyes. Yet the county's most handsome face and chiseled jaw, which looked even more potent in the early morning light, remained ignorant of the inner workings of her heart. And resigned. And without any of the understanding she'd always hoped for in a husband.

"Come on, darling." He held out his hand. And if there was to be any civility between them—forget the childish dreams of romance—she must accept.

Though reluctant, Charlotte placed her palm in his to allow him to lead her out.

"But what about my—?" She reached out on instinct as he tugged her away, looking back to the cello case.

"I'll see to it. I am not without compassion. Perhaps we can find a space to put it in the attic where Mother won't see. I don't think she's been up there for ages. Now go." He winked at her in his way of trying to compromise and stopped in the doorway, tipping his head the direction of the manor looming beyond. "Get rid of those rags and into a morning frock before you set your diary with Mother. And I'll have a conversation with Mr. Hall this morning so my agent knows that my wife is not to be put upon to worry over menial farmwork again. And if she is, it will be his position that is eliminated. Do you understand me?"

Fully.

Charlotte was to conduct herself as a lady.

It would be a long walk to the downstairs library to return the book to its shelf. And an even longer one across the fields to return the work clothes lent by Marni Fitzgibbons. But if this was the life Will envisioned, Charlotte feared he wouldn't like that she'd plan more walks in her future. One to the church to pray when Will shipped off to war. And another to visit the shops in Coventry after he'd gone, where she'd buy work clothes and a *Farmers' Almanac* and stop by the jewelers to arrange to have her rings sized. And out to the barn every morning if it was her pleasure, to play Bach for her husband's cows and stray starlings in the morning sky.

War had come.

Their world would change with it. And though the tension between what was right, what was expected, and what was accepted of her station kept battling within her, Charlotte vowed she'd rise each morning to meet whatever challenges lay ahead. Even if in the span of one week, it meant she must do it alone.

→··←

14 October 1940
Brinklow Road
Coventry, England

For how the Land Girls chatted about London milliners' shops with their endless array of fashions making waves from Oxford and Bond Streets—namely the Six O'Clock Hat, dubbed for the hour one punched the clock and shifted to night play—it impressed Charlotte that they kept sharp to their times and worked tirelessly at their labors in between.

Though the sun was rising high in the sky, the air was still crisp with morning's bite and laden with the scents of autumn. Charlotte had sent Ainsley and Ginny off to the bookshops, and Flo and Dale had already breakfasted and were waiting in the wagonette with Eden by the time Charlotte joined them outside.

There she was as the lady of Holt Manor from the early days, dressed in dungarees and a Peter Pan–collar blouse borrowed from her daughter, with a sunny silk scarf holding her hair back. Almost like she was headed to the barn with a cello. She couldn't match the Land Girls' uniform—breeches and stockings, hats smart and at attention, and jumpers layered under khaki overall coats, all worn strictly to code. But they appeared pleased to see the estate mistress ready to work with them. And in seeing her dress, they brandished smiles of approval.

"It's nearly nine o'clock. Are we set then?" Charlotte slipped on leather garden gloves as she approached, Eden at the helm of the wagonette, bracing a palm to her forehead to block the sun's sting from her eyes.

"Just." Eden drew in a deep breath and tipped her head to the auto rumbling up the drive, then lowered her voice to a whisper. "Are you quite sure, Mama? It's not too late to cancel this mad scheme if you think either one of you cannot be civil to the other."

"I shouldn't worry about that, my dear. However much we choose not to admit it, we need Mr. Darby's help. And I'm not too proud to admit such."

"Ginny said she had to wonder why he'd agree to come out of his hobbit hole now. While I don't care for her choice of words, I can't disagree. Mr. Darby has enough to do in town with the Home Guard. Why should he ever want to come here to work with us?"

"Because I asked him to be our agent."

Eden was quiet for a moment. Then she nodded, finding sudden fascination with the worn wood slat on the wagonette, and ran her fingertip along its peeling paint. "Is this because I gave Mr. Darby a key to the shop?"

"Of course not. You told me why—after. It's quite smart with everything going on, to ensure someone can step in and help where it's warranted."

"And it doesn't matter that I've been working this estate for the last many years, and yet I wasn't considered for the agent role?"

"Mr. Darby may well be the last able farmer in this part of the country. I know you don't understand all that is happening here, but I beg of you to please keep an open mind. And do not feel your efforts are in any way overlooked or underappreciated. Especially not because you are a woman. Do try to remember who your mama is and who she's raised you to be."

Charlotte couldn't help adding a soft smile. Those early days at

Holt Manor hadn't been easy; she'd cried into her pillow at night more often than not. And soon lost the luxury of those mornings playing the cello against the sunrise. War took over all worries, and the instrument gathered dust after that. But once she'd had a daughter, Charlotte pledged Eden would be raised self-sufficient and emboldened to make her own choices, no matter what society might try to dictate. Her daughter could play every cello in England if she had a mind to.

"We've already learned that war is an unpredictable foe. And now, I believe Mr. Darby is our best chance to make this estate useful for the people who depend on us. If that matters to you at all—and I know it does—we'll listen to what he has to say, and we'll do as he asks."

With such an impassioned speech, Charlotte had near convinced herself.

As it was, she'd awoken on this particular morning with butterflies flitting through her insides such that she'd been able to stomach only half a cup of tea. Her palms were clammy enough to chafe her hands in her work gloves. And as Charlotte watched now, the sight of Amos's tall form stepping out of an auto created a hitch in her middle, and she began to feel pinpricks of indecision as the gentleman drew near.

Would this work? Could she trust him again . . . with all that she must now?

"Lady Harcourt. And Lady Eden. Good morning." Amos turned his unmarked profile to the wagonette, tipped his hat to the girls sitting on the bench in the bed. "Ladies." And he swept off to shake the hands of the men he knew in the crowd.

The Land Girls chimed their greetings, and Charlotte stepped up before the lot—ready but oh so out of her element after the many years spent apart from garden gloves and barns and the far more comfortable farmer's duds.

"Right. Let's get to it then. Everyone, this is Mr. Amos Darby, our new estate agent. He'll need to see our operation before he can advise us. We've milk rounding for the tenant farms—though all milking and cooling is done for today." She tossed a wink at Eden as she motioned toward the dairy barns. "Mr. Cox has managed to find replacements for the broken panes at the glasshouse; he'll begin mending them straightaway. And we've the starts of kale and cabbage, lentils, rhubarb, root vegetables, and oyster mushrooms to begin growing for winter stores. I will give Mr. Darby a tour of the grounds, and we'll join at the glasshouse for further instruction after. Does that suit?"

"Aye." Amos nodded. "That'll work."

Charlotte clapped gloved hands together. "Good. Mr. Cox—if you will?"

The gardener tipped his hat, and with a "milady," they were away.

The wagonette lumbered off, Charlotte trying not to smile at Eden's attempt to ignore Jacob's obvious congeniality. And the Land Girls seemed to notice that Alec, too, was cheerier among their number. They looked a jolly party setting off for a picnic by the river instead of farmhands facing a day of hard labor. Poor Mr. Cox, having to manage flirting alongside shovels and drags. Charlotte would have to see that they increased his pay at the end of it. And she was certain he'd earn every shilling.

"Let me guess. You're picturing a party on Box Hill right about now?" Amos slipped in at her side, never failing to miss a trick where her love of literature was concerned.

Why was it so easy for Charlotte to cross her arms over her front in mock defiance? "It remains my opinion that there is a Jane Austen reference to fit nearly any situation in life. And Emma, being the wittiest of the lot, would have the most to say."

"Let's hope we don't have to make the apologies as she did after it then."

"You read it?"

He sighed, as if wounded. "You made me."

Though she tried not to laugh—as always when with him—Charlotte couldn't hold back as they stood in the sun and the wagonette faded from view. "I suppose I did. Once."

Splitting the group had seemed a natural requirement for the morning, especially given what Charlotte needed Amos to see. But it had to be away from the others. And it must be on foot. Meaning it could set them off marching around Holt Manor on their own for much of the day, and now that they watched the wagonette disappear over the rise, it seemed she hadn't exactly thought things through.

When was the last time they were alone together? Or heavens, when had they last shared a laugh at anything? The last she'd seen him before the war had been that day at the glasshouse when they'd said goodbye. Her poor cello had taken the brunt of her hurt. Was it so long ago now that the pain could be swept away and she could actually laugh with him?

He cleared his throat. "Where to first?"

Back to pretending she wasn't feigning composure. "We'll start at the old stable buildings. Beyond the gardens, at the back of the manor."

"Lead the way." He extended an arm for her to step out first, though it was no secret Amos knew his way around the estate. They started off behind the manor, taking the gravel drive that led past the gardens and down the hill.

"It's been a long time, hasn't it?"

"Since we've worn clothes fit for farmwork, milady?" He didn't smile, but the tone said he might have wanted to.

"I meant since you've been on the estate."

"I know. It was an attempt at lightening the air. Seems I don't manage it as well as Austen."

"But the fact you've held your good humor makes me believe I can be direct as to why you're here today. I know you don't need to see our milking operation. Nor tour the rest of the grounds. I'm well aware that you'd remember everything you need to know about the estate. And what's changed you can see for yourself."

"Aye."

"I was forthright when I asked for help with farming the estate, but . . . that's not the only reason you're here."

"Does Provost Howard know why I'm here too?"

"No. This part of it he does not. But I assure you, it's honorable. And I believe were I able to tell him, he would heartily agree with my decision." She looked over at Amos's profile—the side of his face unmarked by scars. Was there a hint of a smile there? "How did you know I was holding back?"

He shrugged. "You never did talk that much as you did back there. Or that fast. Not to rattle off a grocer's list of veg to a bunch of young folks who couldn't care less. Unless something else has stirred your worry. And if I'm honest, that stirs mine." He nodded, the gravel crunching beneath their boots with each step. "So what is it you really want to show me? Andersons hidden in horse stalls? Black-market goods tucked in the cellar?"

"Not exactly."

The stone stables and barn were in use, but more for storage now—the odd tractor parts and gardening whatnots from the old days. They'd built new stables in the postwar years, and those would suffice for the remaining stock they had. And with cracked windows blocked by blackout fabric, rusted hinges on weathered-wood doors, and birds having packed straw nests in the eaves until the roof might fly away on its own, the buildings were a sorry sight as they came upon them. And hadn't served any real purpose in decades.

Until now.

"We used to keep the milking cows in the barn here, many years ago." She pulled a key from her dungarees pocket and turned it in a fresh lock that kept the doors chained.

Amos stopped before the doors and ran a hand along the post-and-lintel construction, testing its strength.

"Looks like they've seen better days."

"They have. But I recently had them checked for safety. They're stout, and I'm told they'll stand. Unless they take a direct hit, of course."

He flashed a glance in her direction, his brow questioning why she'd say it that way. "Right. What have you gotten yourself into then?"

"Do you remember when invasion fears were highest last month?" Charlotte shook her head as she pulled the chain through the door handles, metal clinking metal until they were freed. "Forgive me. Of course you do. Everyone in England was on edge over Invasion Weekend."

"Aye. The Home Guard was on alert round the clock for five days."

"We all were. I remember we had to close our shops for the first time. And it finally felt real and horrible after those first bombs fell on London. And so many people flooded the pews in St. Michael's here that a line extended out the door and the candles ran out of wax. But it seems that after touring an RAF airfield outside of Oxford, the minister of war production, Lord Beaverbrook, became concerned about production to keep the Spitfires in supply. Not only did they split London's factories and expand to smaller cities across the province, but his office devised a scheme to prevent the loss of a large number of planes in a single blow. Given what's already happening with the RAF battling for the skies over London, the outlying cities have become all the more important to the government's plan."

"We heard of it at the Home Guard. Should an invasion occur, it would come with the Luftwaffe in the skies first. They'd destroy any planes to cripple the RAF. Then send ground forces in by sea and take over."

"Yes. That makes the RAF the most powerful weapon we have. And in the days that followed the height of invasion fears, we received a wire from Mr. David Farrer—personal secretary to Lord Beaverbrook himself. And he posed an opportunity for Holt Manor to be of strategic use in the war effort."

"Let me guess . . . we're not just planting a glasshouse garden for the WLA today?"

"No. And what you are about to see, I must ask that you not reveal to anyone. I've been sworn to secrecy by the ministry."

"Lady Eden doesn't know?"

She shook her head. "Only Mr. Cox, and he's been steering her away from the old outbuildings as often as he can. But I warn you, she believes she's been overlooked in the management of the estate in favor of you. And it would crush her if she knew the manor was in any way at risk. Even if this is something we must do. It is for the safety of all here that I ask for your help."

Charlotte took a deep breath and hauled the doors open.

Sun streamed in, reflecting on the dark-earth camouflage paint and stressed-skin aluminum of three pristine, ready-to-fly Spitfire planes.

"There are three more scattered on the estate, hidden in tenant barns and outbuildings. Mr. Cox helps each time the sirens cry; we unlock the doors in the event the alert is real and the RAF will need the planes. And we lock them up tight again after the sirens have stopped."

Amos shifted his weight and looked over the winged things, like he was calculating the enormity of risks that came with what she'd told him. And no, he didn't seem to fancy it at all, no matter how it might honor king and country.

"With all this, why show the enemy bookseller from across Bayley Lane?"

"Because the sirens cry now both day and night. And with more planes on the way, I need someone I can trust to help keep them hidden so Holt Manor isn't the next target in the Luftwaffe's sights. And I knew that one person would be you."

CHAPTER THIRTEEN

14 October 1940
Brinklow Road
Coventry, England

*T*hree hours had the audacity to fly by without notice.

Yet it cheered Eden as she knelt inside the glasshouse, taking a breather from planting to roll back on her heels and rub a cramp out of her shoulder. She stretched weary limbs, staring out from the central row of tile as she stood to see how much they'd already accomplished.

Jacob and Alec had busied themselves with the tractor, uprooting a stump from the side of the rose garden and chopping the remainder of the felled log for firewood. Mr. Cox and the Land Girls had worked wonders in the glasshouse; it fairly gleamed, with sparkling patina glass and rows of pots at the ready, wire strung from the ceilings for tomatoes and cucumbers in the new year, and row after row ready to begin growing their small army of foodstuffs for winter stores.

At the pace they were working, Eden might tick off the mental list by week's end: Harvesting the last of the hay and potatoes for winter. Trimming hedgerows along the roads overgrown enough to make driving without headlamps during blackouts an extra hazard. Perhaps they could even come to a more regular arrangement with modernizing milk production? And if the Cole money came through . . .

Stop it. Do not go down that road again.

Even if it was a possibility, that was not the same animal as a certainty. And the part that was true—no one but herself and Mama knew the burden of the estate's mounting debts—pinning hope on something that might never come to fruition was risky.

Eden gazed through the glass, just a glance in Jacob's direction as he and Alec muscled the last of the roots' web from the dirt.

Why was he here? Though Jacob had explained himself, if Eden stood to inherit a fortune, it would still cut his in half. Guilt crept in alongside that morsel of speculation. He'd mentioned sisters. And a widowed mother. Then curiosity joined those thoughts. Why was Jacob standing alongside the family that should have been his enemy, laboring with them yet asking nothing in return, as if he wished to be an ally?

It wasn't altogether different from Mr. Darby willingly setting foot on Holt Manor, when the animosity between shops these many years had convinced her that was never likely to happen. Why the change now?

"So, is 'milk rounding' what I think it is?" Dale's question cut into Eden's thoughts.

Eden cleared her throat and tore her glance from Jacob to kneel again, back to shifting the dirt along the edge of the tile. "Probably. It's milking the cows and bottling. And carting butter and milk to tenancies on the estate and in the outlying areas."

"Glamorous indeed."

"Estate management is anything but, I assure you. But milk rounding is also cheering the wives whose husbands have gone to fight. Butter is scarce unless you're on a dairy farm. And if we can share it, it brightens a breakfast table where one of the chairs is empty. Then there's the accounts to keep, but I usually handle the figuring at night, once all the other estate work is sorted."

"Cheering wives with butter? I'd have thought lipstick and silk stockings would do the trick." Dale winked and rubbed shoulders with Eden, glancing in the direction of Jacob as he continued to split wood. "You know we have a Bare Leg Beauty Bar in London.

They'll paint stockings right onto your gams, with a smart line straight down the back. Do you have one of those in Coventry?"

"I'm sure I wouldn't know."

"Don't trouble yourself; we London gals can sniff out a beauty bar double-quick. And I wonder who might appreciate the efforts we ladies go to in order to keep standards high on the home front."

Eden looked away, lest she give the impression she was interested in men in any way other than as co-laborers on the estate. "Well, I'm sure once our new agent helps us get a system in place, we'll get things organized and everything should run like clockwork. And that'll cheer me more than stockings—real or painted."

"You know, you're terribly pretty. Those bright eyes." Dale brushed wisps of wavy hair back from falling across Eden's brow. "But he's never going to see them if you keep them hidden."

Dale was a forward thinker, even by London standards. But to come right out and say it where a man was concerned? Eden couldn't have hidden her shock had she wished to. Love didn't work like that in the countryside—at least not that she'd ever seen.

"Pardon?"

"Listen. That dish Hedy Lamarr has nothing on you. And they say she's got brains and beauty, like you. You could pass for a starlet if you cut your hair. Maybe here?" Dale ran the blade of her palm against Eden's plait at her collar, as if chopping. "At the shoulders. Or a smart bob at the chin? Never hurts to try something new. And it's safer for all the factory girls to keep long locks away from the machinery, so they're starting a nationwide trend with shears. Do that, then put on some lipstick and paint those gams, and that tall dreamboat over there would have to be dead not to notice you."

When Dale tipped her chin to Jacob, Eden backpedaled. Fast. "Oh no. You misunderstand. Mr. Cole is here for a legal matter with the estate. Nothing more."

"My dear, that's not a legal matter chopping firewood over there. You think a clever man like that enjoys muscling through free labor on a farm in the English Midlands?"

It made sense. Too much. And Eden's only way around it was to divert and deflect.

"He is helpful on the estate." She shrugged it off. "I'm surprised to find Jacob skilled with the livestock, including the horses, though he said his family has always had a fondness for them. And his father's family had a stable full of them when he was a boy."

"A fondness for horses, hmm? And chopping firewood. And digging up gardens for Andersons . . . As you like. But there's got to be a reason he keeps showing up. And it's not because he likes wallowing in dirt or spending time with horseflesh in a country stable. And certainly not with a few Land Girls he passes over every time to steal a glance at you instead."

"I . . ." Was that true? Eden's voice fled. And any reply with it.

"When you find a gent looking when he thinks no one will notice? Well, that's when things get . . . interesting."

"Interesting?"

Dale pointed over at their starlet, Flo, elegant even as she planted seeds in pots along the glasshouse wall.

"Take our little Flo over there. She's the most graceful creature that attractive dairy farmer is likely to see in his lifetime." Dale paused, elbowing Eden to look through the palladium doors to Alec, who was chopping alongside Jacob. And now that she mentioned it, Eden could see he was trying not to keep glancing at Flo through the glass. "Now look over there. Alec has only talked to her about putting wax on her hands—bless him for stumbling his way through that—or livestock and the weather. And he's not gone to war because of an injury that gave him that little hitch in his step, yes?"

"That's true. I remember it from when I was a girl." Eden looked over, remembering the day his mother had shown up at the manor asking for help, and they'd sent off to fetch the doctor. "He'd been thrown from a horse and had to have a bad leg break set by the doctor. I suppose it's never healed quite right."

"But does he think she's too posh for him because of it? And does she think him too humble, even with those puppy-dog eyes that could melt stone? It's like positioning chess pieces on a board and watching how the game will play out. Love ticks people off one by one, determining who will win the game next. Agatha Christie herself couldn't have written a better death."

"Agatha Christie makes you think of romance." Eden laughed. And then turned to the glam Land Girl again. "Wait, you read Agatha Christie?"

"Oh, I read everything, doll."

"What? I don't remember seeing an interest in books on your WLA application. I'd have suggested you work in the bookshop straightaway."

"That's because it wasn't on my application." Dale took off her hat and fanned her face as if the sun were from summer rather than late autumn. "Work is work. But it's not living. You do what you must in order to survive. I know—I've been doing it since I was fourteen years old."

"Fourteen?"

"It's all in the stories we tell ourselves, hmm? We play a part. You're the heiress trying to pretend she's not worried about this place falling down around your ears."

Gaping was automatic. Eden thought she'd covered it as only an expert could. But even as she peered around, with a skeleton staff rationed to the hilt, buildings falling into disrepair, livestock managed on a shoestring, and sirens pounding in her eardrums all night, maybe her fantasy of fooling the world could finally be put to rest.

"Is it that obvious?" She sighed. Dale was sharp as a tack. But lucky for them, she appeared just as pragmatic too. "I thought I had everyone fooled."

"I know you did. And I know what people see when they look at me. Sometimes fantasy helps us forget truth. My truth was a home for children until I couldn't stand the leaky roof, the cross headmaster, and twenty girls packed in one freezing room through winter. I used to stay up late with a torch lit under the covers, just so a book could take me out of the world I was in and transport me . . . well, anywhere else. I even fancied myself a writer one day. Imagine that nonsense? But soon as I had my chance, I hightailed it out of there and never looked back."

"It's not nonsense. I've noticed in just the time you've been here, you work without complaint. And the other girls follow your lead. I've had a time keeping up with you three. And that has been the most unexpected, refreshing surprise of this whole arrangement. I couldn't care less about rules or uniforms if we're making real progress. And I'm thrilled that we are."

"Well, it isn't because our county chairwoman's staff demands it of us." Dale let out a hearty chuckle that said Eden had made all the wrong assumptions about her for her youth and beauty. "You live what you're used to."

"And what are you used to?"

"Let's see. I've worked for a milliner and a haberdasher. I was a maid at the Savoy. A dressmaker in Chelsea—that's where I met Ainsley. She really is a genius, you know. I've told her to move to Paris one day and put Coco out of a job. And I met Flo at a theater company, where I was a cigarette girl making all the wrong choices chasing all the wrong men. And she was a chorus girl trying to make it on the London stage. You see? We all have dashed dreams. And we all polish up our personas every now and then, even if just on a WLA application. Except maybe for sweet girls like you. I think you're just about as genuine as they come."

As genuine as they come?

With an estate to save, expectations burdening her shoulders, bombs falling from the sky every other night . . . Eden had thought of little else but herself. And yet, watching others work in the old glasshouse, she realized she'd nearly missed an opportunity. It had been a while since Eden had given a whisker's thought to friendship.

Wearing lipstick or—goodness—painting gams to catch a gent's eye. When had they become young women who talked of dreams like they were dead and buried?

"Dale, had you heard before you left London? Some shelters have begun publishing their own bulletins with Blitz news for their neighborhoods. I have a copy of one in the manor—*The Swiss Cottager*. It's from a Tube station near a pub that fancies itself a chalet. I thought of it because it's not that different than the wattle and daub of our medieval city center. And I wondered if we could do something like that here in Coventry, for the patrons of Bayley Lane."

Dale shrugged it off. "It is an idea."

"What about you trying it out?"

"Me?" She caught her bottom lip with her teeth. "You're having me on."

"No! Not a whit. You're a writer; you've admitted as much. Perhaps you could interview some of the shopkeepers or meet the locals at the tea queue and write about our shelters. I could introduce you to Provost Howard to learn more about the cathedral and the city center. And I could take you to the bookshop. Today even, if you'd like. We have a Remington in the office; you can write all you want while you're there."

"Alright. I'll think on it." Dale beamed and tugged at Eden's plait. "But only if you think on letting me take shears to this and transform you into a modern-day Hedy look-alike—with the brains to match."

The sun shone down on the gravel road from the manor as two figures cut into view. Mr. Darby and her mother walked in tandem. And talked with ease.

"If you don't mind my asking, where are the chess pieces on that board?"

"What? Mama and Mr. Darby?"

Dale nodded, a little sparkle in her eyes. "Do they know each other well?"

"They did once, before the Great War. But I don't think they're even acquaintances now. There's been nothing but indifference between our shops for as long as I can remember."

"Indifference?" Dale said with a knowing laugh, and she put her hat back, square as it should be. "Yes. I'd say that's the exact portrait of it."

The strangest thing, though, as they stood there was that Dale's sarcasm seemed . . . right. The couple walking up the hill looked like a couple.

Mama had her usual guardrails up: perfect posture and standing far enough away from the gentleman to keep propriety in place. But there was also an ease to her that Eden couldn't account for. A softness in her features. A casual, slower air as she strode along with her hands in dungarees pockets. And the sun shone on her face as though she couldn't care less if she freckled or saw more age lines. Mama was . . . happy. And almost strolled, looking up at Mr. Darby from time to time to nod or even laugh when he'd said something amusing.

And then it hit: Mr. Darby was amusing? How was that possible?

Eden stood and brushed her palms on her dungarees as she hopped out to the cobblestone path. "Mama? You're back."

"We are, yes. There was quite a lot of ground to cover." She checked her wristwatch a little too swiftly, like she didn't really catch the time. And was this right? Eden looked closer—Mama was blushing? "Yes, well. Mr. Darby does have to leave us for the day. But I should like to provide dinner for our guests tonight, as a thank-you for all they're doing. I'll just go and tell Cook so she can prepare. And then we'll meet back at the manor for the afternoon shift at the bookshop."

Dale and Flo perked up; the fashion doves seemed owners of an internal radar system ready to pounce on anything posh.

"Did we hear something about a dinner, milady?" Dale snuck up behind and flitted a delighted glance to Eden.

"Of course. And we can dress, if you like, in Six O'Clock Hats and all. Make it a real affair behind blackout curtains." Mama gave Eden a curious, twinkle-eyed glance then. "And the gentlemen are quite welcome to stay on. If you choose to invite them."

"Yes. We'll ask," Eden agreed. "Oh, and Dale will accompany you to the bookshop this afternoon to relieve Ainsley. She's eager to see how things work. And may wish to use the Remington in the reading room."

"Of course. Delighted. Then I will see you out front of the manor after luncheon."

"We thank you, milady." Dale beamed.

Their Land Girls leader gave a little curtsy as Mama smiled and turned back to speak to Mr. Darby again. And Eden couldn't help but notice, as the two talked, that the boorish bookseller from across Bayley Lane wasn't as coarse as he'd once seemed. He still owned the scarred beard and mane of thick dark russet hair given to wildness as the wind caught it, but for the first time, Mr. Darby stood alongside their small party as if he wasn't an outsider. And, in fact, as though he might have always fit amongst them.

"You see? Dinner. That's how the chess match starts," Dale whispered, tossing another wink in Eden's direction as if her every prediction was coming true. "And I suspect milady is far more aware of how the game is played than any of us might give her credit for."

CHAPTER FOURTEEN

15 September 1914
County Northumberland
Newcastle upon Tyne, England

*M*en, mustaches, and marching drills.

It was the view for the last weeks Amos had spent at the Army Riding School. That, and the cricket pitch with endless rows of horse lines set to join the cavalry unit of the British Army's 7th Infantry Division.

Amos still couldn't get used to it, the required mustache for the mounted brigade scratching his lip every time he tried to blow in his palms and warm bitter-cold hands in the early mornings. And though he expected water and clean razors were scarce at the front, he also knew the military ban on shaving might not be the blessed convenience the soldiers seemed to think. A mustache didn't give a tight seal to a gas mask. And while a soldier couldn't question orders from the big brass, it rankled Amos's insides not being able to think for himself as he always had.

Swift and clinical, that was the moving-through process of recruitment he and Tate had undertaken to turn from farmers' stock into soldiers. It took them from a stacked queue at the recruitment depot to passing the basic medicals, reciting the solemn oath to defend the king's country, and then joining a unit that parted them at a train platform. Tate had gone on to a camp outside London— Aldershot, his letter said—with an infantry division soon to see action alongside the British Expeditionary Force.

Amos, a farmer's son from County Warwickshire, oughtn't to have found himself among the distinguished Yorkshire Mounted Brigade. But the experience he had with horseflesh, the ability to care for the animals with a cool head, and the knowledge he'd retained from his reading habit over the years meant he could have rivaled a veterinary surgeon. And that made Amos useful with the first units of the Northumberland Hussars' infantry.

Mere weeks later, he'd been promoted to the new quartermaster sergeant farrier, and no longer recognized the man in the mirror, mustache and all.

That was how he spent his days. Teaching soldiers to ride. Learning the basics of marksmanship and hand-to-hand combat they'd use against the Boche. Reading Dickens and Sir Walter Scott in his bunk—or any books he could find—while the rest of his unit spent their free time on the town. And digging so many ditches that it seemed the whole of England was poised to move belowground.

The nights were longer. Amos lay awake in the barracks most hours, listening to the sounds of an army sleeping around him. Daring not to explore in his mind what might have been with Charlotte. And trying not to think too much on whether there would ever be a tomorrow shared in order to set things right.

"Sergeant Darby?"

A soldier trampled into view, snapping Amos back to the pitch. James, the stable master's son from a Yorkshire manor on his first adventure away from home, skirted up the back of the line of horses. Like a fool.

"There you are."

"You want to be a basket case before we even get to the fighting? I told you—always come round the front." Amos motioned to the rows marked at the horse's head. "You've got to respect them. They could be what keeps us alive out there."

"But I've news. There's a public house—several of 'em, at Lyndhurst. Billiards, brews, and dolls. We'll be dancing tomorrow . . . and that I'd gladly run up this line to share."

Maybe. But moving to a new camp outside Lyndhurst the next day was all the news Amos could see at the moment. They had several horses suffering rain rot. At least two with abscessed hooves. And this one chestnut stallion he was watching kept lifting its hoof off the ground in an ominous sign that he was battling pain from inflammation. If it were more serious, their veterinary officer would have the new quartermaster sergeant farrier do his job, and Amos would have to put the animal down before they began loading the trains the next morning. And Amos couldn't see fit to unless they'd done everything in their power to keep the animal healthy on four hooves the night before.

"A group of us are headed over tomorrow night after we get the horses settled in. You goin' with us?"

"I'm going to pretend you didn't just say that." Amos shook his head, crouching to inspect the hock of the stallion. "And I'd suggest you not be found zigzagging from a pub when you know it's out-of-bounds. And our new captain is shortly to arrive. Don't want to start off on the wrong foot when they're already questioning the quality of the recruit ranks."

"Then you haven't heard? The captain is here. And he's already asked our veterinary officer after you."

Amos snapped his head up. "Why would the captain be asking after me?"

"I don't know. Maybe because the noncommissioned farmer has managed to rise in the ranks to quartermaster sergeant farrier? In a matter of weeks, and without having attended veterinary college? That gets headlines from coast to coast around here." James took the horse's reins. "Seems our captain wants to know the story of the choice soldiers in his ranks, starting with you. If you wanted to pop by the regimental headquarters, you can meet him."

"Now?"

"Yes, sir." James motioned to the sight of officers' uniform hats just visible through the maze of horseflesh between them. "That one out front. He's come to assess the troops."

"Aye." Amos exhaled. Ran his hand over the horse's hock one last time and stood. "Keep an eye on this one. He's tender and shouldn't be. I want a cold compress on that leg until I get back."

"Right, Sergeant." James saluted and knelt to see about the horse.

"And remember what I said. The Boche may not care what you do in the off-hours, but our commanding officers do. So have a care."

Rain misted down as Amos moved toward the front of the pitch.

That was the way of it: Soldiers moving in. Soldiers moving out. Come rain or shine.

With BEF falling at the front, superiors needed to fill gaps in the ranks at the front line. And instead of a veterinary surgeon being placed second in command under their division's major, all Amos knew of their new captain was that he was a gentleman with an education, a fondness for racing horses, and a family name that could be found in the pages of *Burke's Peerage*—as if that lot could forecast a capable leader of men.

The crescent of officers was positioned out front of the recruitment office, surveying horse lines and route-marching drills, with noisy trucks running supplies in the background. And though day had scarcely broken and a heavy mist created patches of fog to drift about the cricket pitch like smoke, that wasn't what caused Amos to tense up.

Will Holt. Standing there, bold as brass, in his freshly minted captain's uniform.

Every last nerve ending in Amos's body charged.

He slowed for a few steps, then marched forward with a clenched jaw, forced a mechanized salute. When it was evident Will wasn't the least bit surprised by their meeting, he was forced to wait for the captain to decide how the scene would play out.

"Quartermaster sergeant farrier Darby reporting, sir."

Will listened, his simper haughty as their veterinary officer explained how Amos had shown great skill with horses as well as wisdom in leading the soldiers and, as such, had been placed in a position of leadership for the small regiment.

"Yes. I'd heard good things from our noncommissioned junior officer. You're a farmer from the Midlands, yes, Darby?"

And you still managed to make it sound like an insult.

"Aye, sir."

Looking to the major standing by, Will explained, "Darby here hails from County Warwickshire—same as I, sir. Just a different side of it." He paused after, surveying Amos, meeting him eye to eye like that last night in his farmhouse kitchen, both knowing the sides of society he spoke of. "The army is adopting a new concept of Pals Battalions—assigning men from the same local recruitment offices to serve together, thinking locally raised battalions would better fight when kinship ties the ranks. It appears that extends here."

Pity Tate was shipped off instead of you.

That burned Amos more than anything, the implication they were anything close to mates.

"What brought you to sign up for this war, Sergeant? Not trouble at home?"

Will crossed his left hand over the other then, showing off the choice to wear not a wedding band but a gold signet ring on his fifth digit that bore the same Harcourt crest that had sent Amos to the county jail not three months before.

Amos tensed his jaw again. Couldn't help it. It was either grind his teeth or deck the captain and spend the rest of the war in an English prison.

"No, sir. I've come to fight for king and country."

"Good. Very good. I'm sure I speak for the entire veterinary staff when I say we're fortunate to have such a dedicated laborer amongst our ranks. And we shall all be waiting to witness your extraordinary talents displayed on the front lines." Will cast his gaze to the place in line where Amos had stood moments before, and where James was administering aid to the stallion. "What's happening there with the roan, Sergeant? Not a wounded horse already?"

"Just a precaution. He's a bit tender in the hock."

"And how do you know it's not a fracture of the tarsal?"

Because he's still standing, you twit. "It's not bad, sir. I'll stay with him tonight, make sure the swelling goes down. We'll see him right come morning."

"I assume you know we move out tomorrow. That means if there's any chance the horse is lame, we must deal with it now."

"With respect, sir, I disagree. The stallion is—"

"Have you a horse killer, Sergeant?" Will lifted his chin, an icy glare slithering down his perfect, privileged nose. Amos nodded, just once. "Then I trust you understand this is the army. And there is no room for emotion when men's lives are at stake. We'll expect you to show no hesitation in doing the tasks assigned your rank from here on out."

"Aye, sir. I'll see to it."

"Good." Will issued an imperious nod. "Dismissed."

Amos saluted, hating that he'd landed right back into subjugation with Will Holt like it was the muscle memory of his life. He gritted his teeth as the officers drifted down the horse lines like he hadn't been ordered to snuff out an animal's life just so an officer could boast his power—even if it was unspoken and only between the two of them.

The front lines of France beckoned; any fool in the barracks knew that. No amount of dancing or billiards in a pub could expunge that fate from a soldier's mind. And though Amos hadn't thought his first order to kill would be a stallion in its prime, he knew this wouldn't be the last time death would cross his path. Nor, he feared, the last time he might go against this captain's order.

The stallion lived, with Amos melding it into the ranks the next morning. But that win was a small consolation when the new game had begun. Would it be the Germans' bombs or Will Holt's slow-burning fury poised to take him out first? The chances were about fifty-fifty either way.

➤┄◄

14 October 1940
Bayley Lane
Coventry, England

It wasn't just dreams and sirens now that would keep Amos from sleep.

The new nightmare would be images of German planes crisscrossing Holt Manor, and Charlotte racing across to unlock stable doors as bombs exploded around her. With outbuildings on three tenant farms that each held one Spitfire, the old stables beyond the gardens of Holt Manor that held three, and a new auto refurbishment shed being built not far off Brinklow Road that would hold two more—at the base of a wide field that could double as an airfield—a host of complications had been triggered where safety was concerned.

And a grisly time of worry for him.

Amos had melted into the chair at his desk in Waverley Novels, stewing behind drawn blackout curtains, the now-worn copy of *Dombey and Son* open upon the desk, and the photograph he kept tucked inside. He swirled amber liquid round the bottom of the tumbler, fighting the temptation to drown out the memories of those first days in the Great War. Even decades later, it was the bloody business of nearly having to put a bullet in that stallion's head that he couldn't expunge. Or all that had come after that first harbinger of death, particularly the cruel dealings of fate that had dared cross Will Holt's path again with his own.

If it hadn't, Will would still be alive.

The pocket watch chimed from his waistcoat pocket, the lilting melody warning time had ticked to the six o'clock hour. They'd be sitting down to dinner in the Holt Manor dining room soon—Charlotte occupying a chair just as she had that night at Christmas Eve so long ago. Lady Eden would be there, with the Land Girls and Jacob. And perhaps even Alec Fitzgibbons, all trying to go on as normal despite an untenable threat of German planes in the sky.

Amos couldn't say why he'd turned down the invitation.

For reasons Charlotte wouldn't understand—despite the past between them—in the end Amos could never accept. That first day, when he and Will had joined at the horse lines on the cricket pitch, became the turn of events that war would use to change everything that came after. And if Charlotte knew why, she'd hate him. At least this way, being alone meant Amos was still in her life somehow. And that would have to be good enough.

If the sirens hadn't sounded by now, they wouldn't. And she wouldn't need her new agent's help on the estate that night any more than she had for the last two decades.

Downing the last of the swill, Amos flicked off the desk lamp and dropped his forehead to the book binding, letting oblivion pull him away again.

→·←

Sirens blasted, rattling the windowpanes.

Amos shot up, rubbing the heel of his palm against his eyes as the sirens' song echoed through the streets. He fumbled with all thumbs against his waistcoat to check his watch: barely an hour gone since his eyes had closed on him.

He pulled the curtains back, peering through the X of splinter-net tape on the glass to the darkness of the alley behind Bayley Lane. Though many slept nights in their shelters now, there were already Coventrians drifting about like ghosts on their way to take shelter, passing by the break where the alley looked from his shop to St. Mary's Street behind.

There wasn't time to check upstairs.

No time for a tin hat or torch, or to fetch mementos from his bedside table. Nor to refill the flask in his boot to see him through the night. This was real; the procedure was for the fire-watchers on the roof of Drapers' Hall to call the alert in to St. Mary's Street Centre, if planes were indeed spotted.

And if they were, the sirens would sing.

Amos tucked the book in his jacket pocket, grabbed his rifle from behind the shop counter, and swept up the keys from their hook as he bolted out the back door. He ran fast as his legs could carry him through to St. Mary's Street to the emergency auto they always kept waiting. Watching the sky for metal birds. Avoiding crashing into prams and citizens traversing the sidewalks to their shelters. And knowing deep in his gut, every time the sirens cried now it became a choice: Would Amos stay and watch over Bayley Lane? Or go, and pray he could get to Holt Manor before it was too late?

He knew the decision before it was made.

CHAPTER FIFTEEN

16 November 1914
Bayley Lane
Coventry, England

Charlotte stood on the front stoop of the physician's office, scanning the missive a second time: "*. . . symptoms consistent with second trimester of pregnancy . . .*"

Those words needn't have confirmed what her body already knew. But it was Charlotte's heart that landed on its own isle of elation. A child had meant everything to Will, and the estate succession meant everything to their parents. But this new life was not a pawn; it was a gift. And Charlotte needed to understand what exactly that meant for their future.

Tucking the paper inside her satchel, she lowered her head and hurried down the physician's office steps, guarding her wine plumed hat against rough autumn wind.

Everywhere was a world at war.

A newsagent shop cried the latest gloom-and-doom headlines from newspaper front pages. People rushed to and fro, some men in uniform toting haversacks to the train depot, and others in civilian dress queued along the sidewalks outside the recruitment office. More queues had formed at the butcher's and fish shops. And still others lined up outside the stationery shop, as if all were poised to write letters and send Christmas boxes to the trenches in France, and they shouldn't dare find themselves without paper and ink supply to do it.

Avoiding the overflow of queues, Charlotte sidestepped the crowds to the doors of the lone bookshop in the city's medieval center—a two-story building of red brick with Georgian windows that seemingly had no business being located where Tudor styling remained the order of the day.

A bell chimed when she entered. And what began as a self-assigned errand to pop in and find a *Farmers' Almanac* turned into a comfort to walk amongst aisles of old friends.

Sir Walter Scott . . . Dickens . . . Austen . . . the Brontës . . . Charlotte traced her fingertips along rows of spines, picking out favorite titles and smiling for the memories of characters who seemed as real as any living in their world. And for the first time, there was a reason to drift to the children's literature and linger over picture books and fairy stories, dreaming of giggles and smiles that would arise from bedtime nursery rhymes. A reason to find hope in stories that created entire worlds for children, those that might exist without the brutality of war.

Charlotte found *Under the Lilacs*, a children's novel by Louisa May Alcott, with a cheery blue cover and the promise of adventure in its pages. What a lovely thought, that the start of something new might be found in an unexpected place. She bought it, then stepped back out to the street. And with one last errand before she must hurry home, Charlotte headed toward the grounds of the St. Michael's churchyard and its bright red postbox positioned against the iron fence line on the corner of Bayley Lane.

She'd written the letter to Will days ago. And now that it was confirmed, all that was left was to drop it in the post. Charlotte kissed the envelope, praying the gift would arrive soon—maybe even by Christmas. Lifting the letter box lever, she sent the news of a new Holt heir to drift down with the rest of the paper-and-ink wishes flying to the front.

➤⋅◆⋅◄

14 October 1940
Brinklow Road
Coventry, England

War meant change in all aspects of life—dinners included.

Gone were the days of the Edwardian ten-course meal, when Will's mother was the lady of the manor and propriety was strictly observed. There was no need for crudités or pudding courses now. Rationed goods and long queues at the butcher's, the fish shop, and the greengrocer were not unlike the way of things during the Great War and ensured dinner at Holt Manor became an unknown affair until it was presented.

On this eve it was Woolton pie of cauliflower crust with steak and kidneys, a new concept of pistachio cakes with carrots and honey instead of sugar, and a dinner schedule that was subject to the mercy of the wireless, set between the BBC's fifteen-minute *Radio Newsreel* at seven o'clock and the nightly news programs broadcast at nine. Guests stayed together instead of sipping pre-dinner cocktails in a drawing room, as per the government's request to compact spaces and thus conserve fuel. The service staff obeyed the same, keeping lights snuffed and fireplaces cold unless a room was in use. And in the event the sirens would cry, coats and torches were lined up alongside Waldybags, like a row of soldiers ready for a quick exit out the door.

A fire on the hearth and port in the glasses made the dining hall seem warmer this night. Charlotte glanced around the table; her heart brightened that despite shuttered windows, blackout curtains drawn tight, and rationing that might cast a cloud, war could not diminish the youthful optimism in the room.

The Land Girls had shined up like a Sunday smile, donning posh London dresses, pin curls and pomps, and the brightest shades of lipstick they'd saved for special occasions. Eden was elegant, too, with her hair pinned at the nape and wearing her ochre opera gown from several seasons ago. And Charlotte had dressed for the occasion, wearing her favorite rose gown with nude velvet flocking at the collar and nipped waist. She'd even plucked silk stockings from the very back of the wardrobe. One never knew what would happen in wartime, so best give them their day.

Charlotte's gaze drifted from the gaiety of their guests to one of the empty chairs at the table. Even now, as her mind wandered to those absent around their table, it landed and stayed on Amos—the man who, unlike her late husband, was living and breathing and still close by. Yet he somehow seemed as far, as untouchable now as Will.

She turned back to her plate. And pushed kidney pie around with her fork, hating to think of what haunted Amos. Why he'd kept himself shut away for so long. And what he might be enduring even that very moment with bottles stacking up in the bookshop stockroom.

"Mama?" Charlotte glanced up, finding Eden's brow creased in concern. "Did you hear me?"

"No, dear. I'm sorry." Charlotte painted a swift smile upon her lips and half rolled her eyes. "I'm afraid my mind was wandering and—"

Sirens cried in the distance, cutting off her words.

All paused, smiles dying around the room. Forks clanged porcelain plates. And the guests pushed chairs back from the table as the party moved to fall into their nightly drill—fetching coats and supplies for a hurried trek to the Andersons in the rose garden.

"Well, that's dinner." Charlotte set her napkin next to her plate and pushed her chair back. She blew out the candles as she rounded the table to join the party moving to the entry.

She caught up to her daughter's side. "Eden, might you fetch the first-aid kit from the bath? I'm trusting you to see our guests safely to the Andersons."

"Of course." Eden took her coat from Dale, pulled mink up over her shoulders, then turned to the rest of the party in the hall doing the same. She seemed to notice Charlotte's coat wasn't among them. "But . . . you are coming too?"

"I'll be along soon." Charlotte hoped her daughter wouldn't notice the fabricated façade, which she nearly always did. "I just want to check the servants' hall is emptied and the manor closed up tight before I go."

Jacob hovered behind Eden—maybe a step closer than Charlotte had noticed before—and sent a cautionary glance to the ceiling, as if planes were poised to take the manor down over their heads at any second. And who knew that they weren't?

"I can do that, milady. You ought to take cover."

"Thank you, Mr. Cole. But no. Your service tonight is to my daughter." She watched the Land Girls file out with Alec. "And to our guests. I trust you both to ensure everyone finds the safety of the rose garden and stays there until the all clear is given." Charlotte reached for Eden's hand, squeezed, then let go. She cleared her throat lest emotion give something away. "Please do look after yourselves? For me."

"We will, Mama."

With one last knowing look, Charlotte hoped Jacob could understand that she was handing him her whole world. He nodded, waiting as Charlotte turned to press a kiss to the shadow of the dimple on Eden's cheek. She held there for a breath as she looked in her daughter's emerald eyes, remembering the first whisper that told her heart she'd become a mother, and relived the day she'd bought their first book at the bookshop and sent the letter to Will, as if no time at all had passed.

"Off with you now. I'll be a few minutes behind."

Charlotte gave a reassuring nod as Jacob and Eden stepped out, her daughter pausing to glance over her shoulder just once as Charlotte closed the doors and bolted them tight.

Rushing through the rooms, she found empty spaces had absorbed an eerie panic as sirens clawed still walls. She rounded to the hall with windows shuttered against the gardens at the back of the manor and sat upon a chaise bench to exchange heels for the pair of wellies she'd tucked behind it.

How ridiculous to be readying for a trek through farm fields in an opera dress, work boots, and nylons that were sure to snag by night's end. Charlotte fought to settle her heart, fumbling as she pulled the boots on and slipped into the deep merlot coat she'd hidden in the hollowed space under the bench seat—the more a dark hue allowed her to slip through night's shadows unnoticed, the better. After checking the pocket to ensure the key to the stable lock was still there, she drew in a last deep breath and made a sign of the cross over her front, then opened the back door and fled into the night.

She flipped her wrist, fighting with the trace of moonlight to check the time.

Twenty past seven . . .

Mr. Cox would have the doors open at two of the outbuildings nearest his cottage, and Charlotte's job was to see to the others. She'd timed it on several occasions before. If she held a steady pace, used the hedgerow along Brinklow Road for direction, and stayed hidden along the tree line, she could have the first set of doors open in as few as eight minutes. Ten at the most. After that, the trek back to the old stables would take another ten at least—maybe longer with how dark it was this night.

If all went to plan.

Charlotte lifted her skirt and sped through the fields best she could, the night air soon burning in her lungs and her hair falling from its pin curls to flap against her jawline with each stomping step.

The first outbuilding was an old shed at a farm that the ministry had approved near some of the outlying factories; the long stretch of fields connected it to a perfect runway should a plane be needed in the sky at a moment's notice. She muscled the old tractor parts and slats of rotting wood she'd leaned against the doors to keep anyone out, tossing them to one side. Faltering through nerves, Charlotte tugged her hair behind her ears so she could see the lock hole. She pushed the key in and turned until she heard a *click*, then dropped it back into place, the lock making a *thud* at the end of the chain.

One down.

Night turned the sky to ink over the fields—too shadowed this far out to see properly through the trees. But there was a faster way back: across the creek and through the grove to the back road behind the old stables, if Charlotte dared chance it. Perhaps the sirens were another false alarm? Every nerve ending in her body protested, but she made a chance decision to flick the torch on. Just for a moment. Just long enough to light her path.

She darted along the stone wall toward the sound of rushing water, her boots thudding against grass and earth, following the torchlight as she rounded the flagstone of the gate. She paused. Gazed up. Flicked off the torch and slowed her breathing enough to listen, finding only the call of sirens in the distance and water tripping over stones in the brook nearby. Until, through the trees . . . a death rattle.

An engine screamed.

Charlotte stopped dead in her tracks a split second before bullets strafed the creek water and peppered the field. She cried out as they pinged stones on the fence and shredded tree limbs along the way. On instinct she dropped to a crouch by the gate with her chin to her chest, hands laced behind her head, and pressed deep into the stones in a desperate attempt for cover.

The guns stopped as quickly as they'd started. The engine faded some. And heaven help her, but did it seem the plane was poised to leave?

Charlotte popped her head up. Looked left. Then right. And tried to calm ragged breathing. Should she flee to the cover of the trees or remain hidden behind the stone wall? If she'd been spotted the first time, the wall could be in a bomber's sights at any moment. But at least if she had tree cover, it might afford enough luck for her to be missed if the plane did circle back . . .

It was seconds only—a heartbeat of time for a fateful decision made—and then the sound of another dive. Plane engines sang on their way toward her again.

Charlotte sprang up, intent to run, only to be pulled back when arms encircled her.

A hand cradled her head as they fell, absorbing the impact against the jagged fence as a hail of bullets pinged stones over their heads. She screamed when a ripping sound cut the sky, followed by the sputtering of a plane's engine as it started its final dive toward earth. It sailed over them, crashing in the field beyond the trees in a hailstorm of fire and exploding bullets.

Charlotte lifted her cheek from the earth, watching through the tines of the gate as plane parts erupted with the heavy scents of smoke and cordite, and an orange-black plume mushroomed from split wing to sky.

"I'm so sorry . . . I shouldn't have . . ." She sobbed against the ground, fear so close that it tangled every emotion to come out as tears instead of coherent words. And left her incredulous that she wasn't alone but, by some miracle, was in Amos's arms.

"Hush, love. It's alright." Amos shushed against her ear, his arms holding firm around her as flames consumed the plane's shell and tiny fires dotted the widespread debris field in front of them. "You're safe."

They lay for long seconds in dirt and dewy grass. Holding. Breathing. Listening to the sound of metal being thrashed by fire as sirens cried in the distance.

"Was it them?" Charlotte whispered, shaking, as the in-out-in of her breaths fogged in the night air.

"Aye. A Me 110—Luftwaffe fighter." Amos pointed toward Brinklow Road, just visible beyond the field. The fire illuminated the outline of an auto abandoned off to the side, its door hanging on a hinge. "Saw it from the road. They don't maneuver terribly well, but they specialize in low-level attacks, like on the factories past the far side of the estate."

"How did you know?"

"I checked in at the St. Mary's Street Centre before I came here. It's why the sirens went off. A fire-watcher spotted a bomber with the searchlights from the roof of Drapers' Hall. Just one, though, which isn't usual. They fly in formation."

Amos swallowed hard; she could feel his neck pulse against the back of her head where he'd rested his chin, as if emotion was trying to overcome him as well and he was fighting to breathe through it.

"You thought it was coming here. To us."

"God help me, I did," he whispered, his voice so rough, it was barely audible this time. "And because I . . ." He shook his head. "I almost didn't make it."

"Because you what?"

It wasn't the words said but the fierce hold he'd kept around her that spoke volumes. Amos refused to let go, despite the immediate danger having passed. And Charlotte let him; there felt no safer place in the world than in his arms.

"You thought there were planes coming to Holt Manor and that seemed the best time to drive on open roads all the way here?"

"I never claimed to be the clever one between we two." Did he smile just then? It felt like it, with how his chin moved against the top of her head and his hold tightened a breath. "We always knew who that was."

"I wasn't clever tonight. It was mad to have used the torch." She felt around in the dark. Where had it fallen to? One tiny decision to use it could have been fatal.

"It's not your fault. That bomber would have been here regardless. He was going for the factory over the hill." His hold slackened after that, and he pushed up from the ground to brace one knee and help her up. "Are you hurt?"

"No." Her limbs were shaking and probably as soiled as a sty, but her arms and legs worked as she stood with him. The silk stockings would be done for, bless them, but at least nothing pained her more than that. "I think I'm alright. You?"

"Listen. No planes . . ." Amos scanned the sky, then the fire, its curtain of smoke roiling to the treetops. "And continuous sirens now."

"What? They can't be giving the all clear, can they?"

Amos turned to her, Charlotte realizing it was the first time they'd actually looked at one another. His chest rose and fell with his breathing. And she might have said something . . . how she was so relieved he'd come to her, or that it must have been a gift of Providence that he'd known where to find her, or a hundred other things she wished her tongue would cooperate and say . . .

Instead, Amos reached for her hand, took it in his, and started them moving on. "We ought to go. *Now.*" He plucked up the torch from the ground on the way. "Keep low. I don't want to take any chances that the fire will draw more planes until we're good and far away from here."

Rushing through the night, he led them along the stone fence, the opposite direction of the field. She glanced over her shoulder, catching a glimpse of the plane as it died, its fire swallowed up by night and the space now growing between them.

"Should we go to the old stables? I still have one lock to let." Charlotte paused to listen—nothing save for the sirens. The night was as still as she'd ever heard it. "If it's the all clear, that means they think this a false alarm. And it's not."

"Aye. And that plane over there would say they're wrong."

"All the more reason." She tried pulling him the opposite direction. "Amos—we have to go to the other door. The RAF may need the planes. And telephone the Home Guard immediately after."

"We're going . . . to the Andersons. I'll let the lock . . . when I know . . . you're safe," Amos answered, still leading, though his breathing was choppy. And then he squeezed her hand—*hard.* In a manner he'd never done before.

"Ow! Amos, you're hurting me."

"I'm sorry," he muttered. "I . . ."

Charlotte tried pulling her hand back, but Amos stumbled in response, like his shoe struck a rock. He hugged his side with his arm and, to her horror, crashed down to his knees.

"Amos!"

As she met him on the ground, it was clear he'd tried to suppress pain with his hand holding on in a lifeline to hers. And though every government pamphlet, cinematic newsreel report, and shred of common sense in her head screamed not to light the torch a second time, she didn't give a fig now.

Balancing Amos's head in her lap, Charlotte reached for the torch from the grass and flicked it on. Her heart sank as light illuminated a wave of crimson that streaked his waistcoat and darkened the tail of his shirt—a sight too threatening to be a mere scratch from an old stone fence.

"Oh no! Amos . . . you're bleeding."

CHAPTER SIXTEEN

14 October 1940
Brinklow Road
Coventry, England

*E*den chewed her thumbnail, then chanced asking again. "What time is it?"

"About two minutes since the last time you asked." Jacob sat on the Anderson shelter bunk across from her, the glow of the torch lantern shining up from the concrete floor between them. He checked his wristwatch. "Five minutes until eight."

"We should go check the other Andersons."

"You know your mother would skin me alive if we did. And the Andersons hold only six apiece. Her Ladyship would know the others are full of the staff and come here first. If she said she'll be here, then she will."

Eden shot to her feet, slipping a little in the dreaded heels that seemed bent on inflicting torturous pain to the wearer. She gave them a sigh of irritation and righted herself. She'd never want to have to dress for dinner again unless the king himself was to sit in their dining room. And even then Eden swore she'd have a pair of gum shoes on retainer just in case they had to hoof it to the shelters. "I'm going out."

"You can't." Jacob stood too, ducking his head so it wouldn't bang the corrugated steel ceiling, and at the same time held his hand out as if he knew she might teeter and fall on those wretched heels.

"You can't stop me."

"No, I can't. What I meant was, your mother would never forgive me if I let you roam the countryside when she believes you're here, and safe. I guarantee she's ducked into one of the other shelters on the estate and she's just been waiting for the all clear to let us know."

"If you *let* me?"

He sighed, shaking his head. And who'd have believed it but Jacob smiled too—a heart-stopping grin that tugged at some cord in Eden's middle and almost made her forget she was supposed to be put off by his bravado. And he didn't even try to hide that he found something terribly humorous about a mad situation.

"What is so amusing?"

"You, Lady Eden. *You* are. In that stunning dress. And shoes you can hardly stand in. And a coat so thin you wouldn't last two minutes before your teeth started chattering outside. Yet you're still demanding to go out and take on Hitler himself if it means you're not held back from whatever it is you've set your mind to. Even if there's not a lick of sense in what you're saying. And even if I wouldn't dream of telling you what to do under normal circumstances. I find all I can do in your presence is smile, whether I want to or not."

Oh. Her heart pounded. *A stunning dress . . .*

Eden ought to be fuming for how he'd dared speak to her, trying to take over as he was. But then, anything being described as "stunning" wasn't exactly the vernacular Eden was used to hearing around the estate. Nor at the bookshop. Nor . . . ever about her. And now, every last word of that speech made her stomach want to flip-flop instead of win the game of wits between them.

"I promise you, Lady Harcourt is fine. You'll see."

"Well then." Eden swallowed hard, never one likely to admit defeat. "I suppose we can't have both of us lost out there in the dark. We'll just wait."

"Good."

"A few more minutes." She parked back on the bench. Crossed her arms over her chest. "Now that the sirens have gone into continuous sound, it should be the all clear. Maybe a false alarm. And we'll be out soon anyway."

He joined her, sitting again in the glow of the torch lamp.

Eden looked down at her hands. Then tapped her heels. And then stared at the bookshelf in the back, loaded with supplies—the first-aid kit, canisters of water, pantry rations, and books—anything so she didn't have to stare into those blue eyes when the space between them had become awkward. And confusing. And why did Eden find her thoughts too often drifting to his easy smile and congenial air when there were so many other concerns to address?

"Tell me something about you." Jacob blew air into his palms to warm them.

"You want to make small talk in an air-raid shelter?"

"Might as well pass the time. And keep warm. Unless you want to dive into that stack of books over there you were staring at like it's about to climb the walls." Something warmed inside her at that. He reached over, swiped a pamphlet from the top of the stack. "'Your Anderson shelter this winter.' Light reading. Let me guess—everything here is to code?"

"We received the government pamphlet in the post, and yes, we took its instruction to heart. Mr. Cox built wire-mesh bunks. We learned how to safely heat it through the night." She pointed to the end-on-end clay flowerpots on the floor, generating scant heat from a candle burning inside. "And should we need to stay for a while, Mama ensures we have books in case of an emergency."

"You carry an emergency book?"

"Doesn't everyone?" She shrugged. "Country life is more often 'hurry up and wait' than you'd expect. And with a mother who owns a certain philosophy when it comes to the world's necessity that is books, let's just say there weren't a lot of gramophones or trips to the cinema in my house growing up. Books were as necessary to us as oxygen."

"What have you then?" Jacob leaned over, lifting titles from the stack to read the spines. "Hmm. Dickens . . . Austen . . . the

Brontës . . . and Sir Walter Scott. Curious company." He tipped his brow in question and held one up. "*Under the Lilacs?*"

"That's right."

"You're interested in children's stories?"

"My favorite when I was young. Remember who my mother is?"

"Touché." He flipped through the pages, skimming. "And what about your father? Was he a reader too?"

"I never knew my father."

"I know that. I'm sorry. I only meant, did Her Ladyship tell you enough about him to know something like that?"

"It was a long time ago. My mother was one of a country of war widows who raised a fatherless child in the years after it. I suppose that's why independence is a virtue she's passed on to me. It's not your typical arrangement for British posterity, but there we are. She wished me to be self-sufficient. And I plan to be. If any estates fall after this war, I don't plan ours to be among them. Holt Manor is the lasting legacy to my father's name, and I won't let him down."

"I saw your father's painting in the gallery. You look like him," he began, then pivoted in the same breath. "What I mean is, he looked like a brave man."

"Really? Most people say I favor my mother, save for the mismatch in hair color. But my father was. Very brave. He signed up as soon as the conflict began and fought as a captain in a cavalry regiment. I'm quite proud to be his daughter. And to work this estate in his memory."

"I think, Lady Eden, he'd be proud to see what you've accomplished here at Holt Manor."

"Would he? I don't know. When my grandfather passed—before I was born—it was revealed the estate was in danger then. Mounting debts that my father hadn't even time to address before he went off to war. It was left to my mother to sort through the lot. And now to me." She tilted her head a shade. Thinking on it. Wishing she knew what was ticking through that head of his. "And what have I accomplished but keeping it a fraction away from death?"

"If any estate deserves to survive this war, it's yours. You have a beautiful life here despite what the enemy is trying to do to it. And I think if anyone can build back from the ground up, you could. And I have no wish to see the manor falter. I have to separate that from why I'm here and remember the responsibilities I have to my own family."

Her heart sank a little; he'd never mentioned a wife or someone waiting for him at home. Perhaps it just hadn't come up?

"Yes. You have a family?"

"My four younger sisters. None of age. And a mother who is mystified to learn her husband left half of our estate to the daughter of a complete stranger. Now I'm afraid she's relying on her only son to fix this so we don't falter ourselves. Investors can be tricky to handle when their backs are against the wall."

Oh, did she ever understand about faltering kingdoms. "I could see how that would be difficult."

"More than difficult, Lady Eden. I . . ." Jacob set the book on the bench at his side. Ran his hand through his hair, then leaned forward into the space between them. "Look. I should have told you from the start that the lawyers back home are—"

The Anderson door slammed on the outside, causing them both to jump. Eden sailed to her feet. Jacob too, with his back blocking her and hand reaching for a rifle as a fist pounded the corrugated steel door.

"Eden? Let us in!"

"*Mama!*" Eden swept around Jacob, charging over the bunk to reach the door. She pulled it open to find her mama standing there with shredded nylons, mussed hair, a stained coat and dress, and a benumbed Mr. Darby leaning heavily into her side with an arm pitched over her shoulders.

"Amos!" Jacob set the rifle down and rushed forward, hoisting the weight of the wounded Amos to ease him down on the cot. "What's happened to him?"

"A German bomber." Mama closed the door. "We were ambushed

in the far field. By the factories. Amos pulled me back. He . . . saved me."

"Mama! You're bleeding."

"No—it's not me." She waved off the crimson streak across her front and knelt at Mr. Darby's side, peeling back his jacket and waistcoat to reveal a hole in a shirt bathed with blood. Then she turned to Jacob with nervous energy, her chin quivering. "He's been shot, I think."

Jacob rushed to kneel with her. "Turn him over so I can see."

"Shot? But how could this happen?" Eden exclaimed as Jacob tore the shirt fabric, Mr. Darby groaned, and her mother let out a muffled cry. "I thought you were only staying to see after the manor. What in the world were you doing out as far as the fields by the factories?"

"The bullet's gone through on the side, lucky devil. If it had been an inch closer to the middle, he wouldn't be here right now." Jacob shouted over his shoulder, "The first-aid kit, Eden! Please. I need gauze. All you've got. And iodine—we have to clean the wound."

"Yes, of course." Eden turned to the bookshelf to the black cardboard box and tore open the lid to rummage through, reading tiny labels to see what was what in the dim light.

"Charlie . . . I . . . ," Mr. Darby whispered.

Eden's hands froze.

She turned back, glancing over her shoulder to the sight of her mama pressing a hand to Mr. Darby's brow and holding his scarred fingers with the other. And with such care as she'd never seen before, save for when Eden had a child's fever and Mama had pressed a cool cloth to her forehead through the night. The same affection was evident now, a softness when Mr. Darby addressed her by the endearment, and the return tenderness Mama offered as his glassy eyes tried to focus on her face.

Jacob seemed to understand that something passed between them and connected glances with Eden because of it.

"Shh, Amos. Don't talk. Not just now," Charlotte cooed, tears misting her eyes as she palmed his scarred cheek. "I'm here. And we're going to help you. Alright?"

Eden stepped forward. "Here." She unstoppered the tiny bottle to hand it to Jacob. The bottle looked so small and the sight of blood and Mr. Darby's near-comatose state so dire, she wasn't sure it could help at all. "Is that enough?"

Jacob poured iodine over the wound, then rolled one of the fresh sheets from the opposing cot and applied pressure. Mr. Darby reared up, his eyes clamped tight as he groaned and balled his hands into fists as Jacob tried to muscle him back down.

"I'm no doctor." Jacob shook his head at the sight of blood all over his hands. "I don't know what to do. But we have to stem the bleeding somehow. He needs to get to a hospital."

He looked up to Eden again. Shook his head. And asked Mama to calm their patient as he rose to meet Eden at the back wall.

"What is it?"

Leaning to her ear, he whispered, "I can get Alec. It's possible he's had experience with injuries on the farm. Or at least he'll know where to go for the nearest doctor. We could try to telephone for an ambulance from the manor, but who knows when they might arrive. If the sirens start up again, I don't know if we can get someone to him in time."

"You think him in real danger then?"

Jacob nodded. "And if we don't—"

A chime sang out then, a singsong melody stopping his thought mid-sentence. Jacob tore his eyes away from her and stepped forward, scanning the tiny space, as if the tune had come from a music box opened in one of its corners. "What is that?" Jacob asked.

Mama heard it, too, and began searching, palming about the cot until she landed on Mr. Darby's open waistcoat and reached into the pocket to retrieve a gold watch.

"Just this." Mama held out her palm to show Jacob the timepiece, its lilting melody louder now as it echoed off steel walls. She popped open the cover, grazing her fingertips over its face. "Eight o'clock."

The chime stopped after a breath, leaving only the sound of Mr. Darby's deep breathing and Mama's sniffling as she turned back to the cot and closed the watch in her hand.

"What's wrong?" Eden touched Jacob's arm, drawing him back from a daze of some sort.

"Nothing. I, uh . . ." Jacob shook his head, then looked down at his hands, the awful sight of smeared crimson still marring them. He reached for a folded blanket from the shelf and wiped them off. "Milady, may we use your auto? It's a risk, but I believe the best chance we have is to take him to the hospital ourselves. We can't wait for an ambulance."

"Right. Yes. That does sound the best option." Mama sniffed again and stood. "May I speak with you outside for a moment, Mr. Cole?" She eased her hand to the door latch. "Eden, will you stay with Mr. Darby, please?"

"Of course."

"Come fetch me if there's any change. Any at all."

They stepped out then, leaving Eden behind.

Sliding down to the cot, she leaned over Mr. Darby and, with gentle hands, applied pressure to the wound. Eden listened to the sounds of his breathing as the gold timepiece winked back from inside his curled, limp fingers. And fought to absorb the roller-coaster revelations of the last few moments whilst surveying the jagged lines of the man's beard, the white rows of gristle climbing his neck, and the crescent above his eye—all scars she'd never seen in detail now illuminated by the torchlight.

The same scars her mama had looked on with such unexpected tenderness.

For all Eden had known growing up, it was the war hero in the perfect portrait hanging alongside the ancestors in the Holt Manor gallery who'd owned the affections of Charlotte Terrington-Holt. But now, within the silence of steel walls . . . doubt crept in.

Who was this bookseller from Bayley Lane? And why had he risked everything to save a woman he'd loathed all this time?

CHAPTER SEVENTEEN

———————————————

25 December 1914
The Western Front
Near Fromelles, France

*A*mos tucked the letter back into his uniform tunic and pulled his collar tighter round the neck, trying to shake off the bitter cold air as he scanned a snowcapped No Man's Land.

Even with established mail routes to the front, the post was oft delayed, like this last letter from home had been. But now he wished it had never arrived, with the news Tate Fitzgibbons had been killed at Marne. Months back. And barely two weeks at the front before a land mine had taken him, leaving a widow and a little boy in Coventry who would grow up never having met his father.

Senseless death.

War was supposed to be over by Christmas; every duty-bound soldier had believed it in the early days. But as weeks passed and the machine of death marched on, trenches were dug as fast as they were blown to bits, and more good men were buried in makeshift graves every day. War became as brutal and bloody as Amos had feared but far more indiscriminate in its choices. Young James from basic training had been killed. Now Tate. And countless others—some soldiers who arrived at the front one day and were killed by breakfast the next, without anyone having time to learn their names.

To survive here meant to hold on to a dream of home.

Whatever it was.

The bomb-blasted landscape had been softened by a blanket of snow and campfires dotting the midday horizon—campfires surrounded by men who weren't on Christmas furlough and should have been choking in their own blood on the battlefield. Instead, Amos watched the unbelievable sight of British and German soldiers engaged in a football match on a manufactured pitch fashioned between zigzag lines of barbed-wire barriers and muddy trenches covered in mounds of white.

"Fröhliche Weihnachten."

Amos spun around, his gas mask slamming down to the snow when he raised his Enfield to the Jerry who'd managed to sneak up behind.

Back off. He held firm, training the rifle square between the soldier's eyes.

"I speak English," the soldier answered from behind a light brown mustache, a square jaw holding a smile he offered with his gloved hands raised in the air. He approached, stepping gingerly to retrieve the gas mask, and held it out to Amos, who didn't dare move to take it back. "I said, Merry Christmas. You heard? There is a truce."

He had, far as anyone could believe it.

Soldiers had been stepping out of the trenches all night. Exchanging cigarettes and food rations with the Germans. Some singing carols. Others sharing a hot brew or Christmas wine over the fire. And even allowing enemy soldiers to cross No Man's Land to collect their dead for burial, before the fighting was to start back up again. It's why the informal match was still going on, with men passing the football around the open-area pitch like they wouldn't have to kill their opponent the next day.

"Aye. There may be a Christmas truce. But not an official one. And don't think I won't break it if you've come to harm even one of my horses."

"You are an officer," the soldier said, more as a statement than a question.

"Does that bode well with you or not?"

"*Nein.* I just came to see them."

Amos lowered the rifle and reached out to take the gas mask, trying to decide whether the soldier was trustworthy enough to stand with his animals. He looked like an officer, too, more senior given the German insignia on cape and collar. And moved with the measured steps of a seasoned soldier. If there truly was a truce, seemed he gave the appearance of abiding by it.

"That one." The soldier pointed to the stallion out front of the pack, the prize of the lot with the gleaming black coat and sleek, muscled lines. He lay his rifle on the ground and then stripped off his gloves, as if asking to approach the animal. "I have seen him on the battlefield. Bombs explode. Bullets fly by. And yet he does not flinch?"

"No." Amos lowered his rifle the rest of the way. "That one doesn't."

"May I?" The soldier hooked a finger around the strap of his helmet and set it in the snow at his feet. Amos could see clearly now as he approached; he was still young, but more mature than Amos's twenty-one years. The soldier made a clicking noise under his tongue and approached the stallion with intentional steps, first patting his mane. Then moving around front and softly blowing breath against its nostrils. The stallion snorted, his breath sending great clouds of fog into the air. And bobbed his head, then stood still.

"How did you know to do that?"

"He must know my scent if I should want him to trust me. Even for five minutes." The soldier cradled the horse's nose in his hands. "What is his name?"

"We don't name them. You get attached that way; it becomes dangerous. He's got an official number with the British Army, but that's all."

"The most beautiful creature I have seen here. Reminds me of one we had when I was a boy. A stable full at home, long before this started. But this one . . . he is special, *ja?*" The soldier ran his hands along the horse's mane, like he was recalling visions of that home even then. He looked up. "Yours?"

"No. But I'm the one who has to shoot them when they're felled by your bullets."

"I am sorry for that." The soldier nodded, then allowed his thick mustache to ease up on a slight smile. "What is his name?"

He smiled back. Of course Amos lied and had named the horse anyway. How could he not? Only a true horseman would recognize that lure. "Toreador."

"Hmm. Not Matador, with his strength?"

"He's a fierce fighter. But not a killer."

"I can see that he is." The soldier looked back. "Like you?"

Amos shook his head. "No. I'm a farmer. Nothing more."

"I would like to ride. With your permission, of course."

Even if the Jerry had claimed to have seen the horse in battle, Amos's first protection was to the officers of his division and the horses that carried them.

Amos looked in the direction of the men across the way, British uniform coats mingling among the Jerries, watching the match unfold. And if Amos allowed the enemy to ride his captain's horse, it could be a severe offense. But Captain Holt wasn't out there to care; he'd been furloughed home to spend Christmas with his wife, warmed by home fires in Holt Manor's palace of rooms. And Amos, having naught to go home to now, had stayed at the front. Watching over their horses. Keeping their battle kin safe.

"Just a short one. Over there and back?" The officer pointed toward the span of open land beyond the trenches, backed by trees and barricades. "I will remain clear of the barbed wire. And you can hold your rifle on me."

"How do you know I won't shoot you in the back?"

"I do not," he admitted, waiting. "I suppose I am willing to risk it."

Amos thought on it, then gave a nod.

If soldiers from different sides could play a game of football and sing "Silent Night" across a battlefield, surely it wouldn't hurt to give the man one glimpse of happiness in their hellish circumstance? Amos watched the soldier swing into the saddle as if it took no effort at all. And within seconds, he was turning the horse and trotting. And smiling. And allowing Toreador to show off a little, rearing up and stamping his hooves in the snow like the restrained athlete he was.

Pointing to the open field, the soldier asked permission. Amos nodded again, allowing him to give it a go and let the stallion fly without the rifle trained on them.

There was striking beauty in it, to behold an animal that could have been at a starting gate for the Coventry Stakes stretch its legs and soar across No Man's Land instead of staring down death every day behind a muddy trench. And the soldier seemed to understand it, too, when he rounded the wide space, then slowed and sat upon Toreador's back to take a good long look at the barren landscape before he swung down again, boots cratering snow.

The soldier whispered something to the horse, talking for long seconds as he pressed its forehead with his. He gave a grateful pat at Toreador's forelock. Then he returned, leading the stallion in a slow gait until he placed the reins back in Amos's hand.

"*Danke schön.* Thank you." The soldier reached into his pocket and pulled out a handkerchief. He unwrapped it and offered the token inside. "A gift. For your kindness."

The soldier dropped a pocket watch into Amos's palm, exquisite gold staring back. Amos turned it over, clicked the knob. The inside cover revealed the engraved initials *FBK*, and a rotating design of sun and moon and gold stars ticking like a Van Gogh starry nightscape mechanized over its face.

This was no mere trinket; it was a priceless work of art.

Amos looked up, stunned, then held it out in return. "I can't take this. It's precious by the looks of it."

"It is, ja. As was that ride to me."

With no intention of taking it back, the soldier reached down, dusting snow off his rifle and the rim of his helmet. A warning tensed through Amos as he noticed the soldier gave particular attention to the Mauser . . . with a scope attached.

Amos tossed a glance over No Man's Land, the span of bomb-blasted earth between the trenches where the German snipers would sneak in, hide all day, and stalk their prey until they found a clean kill. Was that where he'd come from?

"This watch is a gentleman's. Not for a farmer."

"And yet it now belongs to you. Perhaps you shall have to change your profession in the future." He slapped snow from his gloves against the front of his coat. "It is a surprise to find an honorable soldier on this front who would refuse a gift, though he knows its true value. What is your name?"

Amos smiled. "We shouldn't have names either. Makes us harder to kill that way."

"Ja. But we will still try." The soldier chuckled, his breath clouding on air as he offered his hand, no glove between them.

"Amos." He took off his own glove and accepted the gesture, hand to hand. "I suppose we'll see each other out there tomorrow?"

"*Nein.* I will see you. And Toreador. But I fear you will not see me again until it is too late."

Only one type of soldier could claim that; the scope on his rifle had already confirmed it.

"You're a sniper."

He nodded, though not with a sense of pride or accomplishment but rather thinly veiled sorrow. With one last gaze at the steed, he said, "Watch over my friend, ja? And danke schön. Thank you again."

Amos might have asked which one of them the soldier was referring to. But he'd turned and replaced his helmet, swung the rifle strap over his shoulder, and started a slow stroll toward the world of white beyond the German trench line.

"What's your name?" Amos called out. "Toreador here is asking."

"Frank!" he shouted back, tipping an invisible hat. "And I sincerely hope we never meet again."

➤⋅⬥

16 October 1940
Stony Stanton Road
Coventry, England

Amos battled weighty eyelids until he could finally force them open.

He squinted, adjusting to daylight from windows across an aisle and the bright white hospital linens on a row of metal beds down the line. A chair squeaked next to the bed. He glanced up and found the unshaven Yank sitting in a work shirt rolled at the forearms and patched pants instead of expensive suit trousers, wearing glasses and turning pages in a book.

"Amos?" Jacob caught him looking around and started, exchanging the book for a glass tumbler on a table by the iron bed frame. "Here." He leaned forward, offering water.

Trying to swallow proved too much. Amos sputtered when a razor-edged stab from his middle nearly sliced him in two. He waved the glass away and fell back, spent, against the pillow.

"Where am I?" he asked, though the inside of a hospital ward was obvious.

"Coventry and Warwickshire Hospital. City Centre north, I guess? If that means something to you."

"Aye," Amos said, his voice rasping, then rubbed a hand over his face and dared trying to move against the mattress. His abdomen shredded him, forcing him to recoil again. "Feels like I should have expected that much."

"The bullet went through. And you've had surgery and sutures on that side. Doctors say you're going to be sore for a bit."

A bullet. That would make sense. "They say anything else?"

"Yes. That you were either very foolish or very fortunate. Probably both."

Remembrance struck, some of it anyway. The horrific sight of Charlotte crouched in the dirt with her hands over her head, crying out as a German fighter plane zeroed in on the stone fence across the field. And the vision became Amos tearing through the night. Then reaching out. Grasping for her, drawing her back. And falling to the ground over her . . . anything, just so he could get to her side and keep her from harm.

With no memory of what happened after they'd trekked over the fields, he tried to raise himself up, knowing it would hurt like wildfire but not caring. Amos pressed a support palm to taut bandages wrapped around his middle and gritted his teeth as he arched up on an elbow.

"Charlotte—is she . . . ?"

"Lady Harcourt is well. You made sure of that." Jacob placed a hand to Amos's shoulder, coaxing him back down against the pillow. "She and Miss Brewster are running a tight ship of the tea queue at your shop."

Oh no. He leaned back again.

If the tea queue was up and running, that meant more bombs must have fallen. And he wasn't there. Not at the St. Mary's Street Centre or with the fire-watchers on the roof of Drapers' Hall. Or even to prevent a plane from dive-bombing Holt Manor again, though he'd driven like a Mad Hatter through the dark to get there the first time. Guilt washed over Amos that he'd been so overcome by the thought of losing *her* that it had clouded every bit of judgment and all the training he'd had.

A soldier should have known it; emotion complicates duty every time.

"How bad was it last night? I got a good look at the Messerschmitt 110—a Luftwaffe bomber heading for the factories at the edge of the estate. After that, I don't remember much."

"Right. There was a German fighter crash on the estate . . . two days ago."

Jacob took off his glasses and tucked them into his shirt pocket before he leaned forward and rested elbows on his knees. Seemed he wanted their conversation to be just between them by the looks of it.

He lowered his voice. "The Air Raid Wardens' Service and Home Guard investigated. They'd like to hope it was our anti-aircraft guns that took it down, but the plane was too far outside the city for that. More likely the pilot clipped one of the barrage balloons over the factory sector and that's what took him out. Sounds like they're trying to keep it quiet that the factories were a target. Maybe to keep production going without a panic?"

"Could be. Any hurt on the estate?"

"No. But eight killed in the city—authorities said most at the Daimler Works at Radford. Word is HE bombs came down with a whole slew of incendiaries, and the blaze took out a polishing shop and engineering offices. With dozens wounded. Though seems you were the only one to take on a German pilot spraying machine-gun fire in an open field that night."

"That was bad luck."

"I can't say I believe in it myself. But it sure wasn't luck that got you to the hospital. Lady Harcourt saved your life."

"Did she?" Amos breathed out. He'd sort of expected that. "And you? Eden?"

"We're fine." Jacob nodded. "I just drove. Her Ladyship is the one who fought to keep you alive."

The memories of the aftermath remained fuzzy in Amos's mind.

They started as flashes of a plane engulfed in flames . . . fading in and out under the ceiling of an Anderson shelter . . . then the agony in Charlotte's face when he'd opened his eyes in the back of an auto and found her staring down at him . . .

His head throbbed something fierce now, punishing with every heartbeat. And his hands had given to trembling as he lay there—a reminder of the drink he hadn't had in days. The flask. Where was it? It had been on him—always in his boot, and within arm's reach in case he needed it. And now, were two days gone? He'd be clawing the walls soon if he didn't satisfy that ache inside.

"My clothes . . . my, uh, boots?"

"They're here." Jacob pointed to the lower shelf of the bedside table. "Do you need them?"

"No." Amos ran a hand through his hair to stem the shaking, then rested his head back on the pillow. The flask would have to wait.

Jacob was quiet then. Too quiet. Expectant, even, as he paused. And it set Amos to wondering.

Amos looked over. "Don't take this the wrong way, but what are you doing here?"

"We all took shifts. Eden, Her Ladyship, and I. Even young Ginny came. Sat by your bedside through the night. In this very chair." Jacob offered an incredulous smile, but one without any real warmth. "I don't know what to tell you, except that it must mean something when an enemy shows their respect."

"It seems I'm in the Holts' debt whether I want to be or not. Who can keep hating now?"

Amos considered that there was no congeniality in Jacob's features this time. No genuine smile or ease in his eyes; he had something on his mind. Aye, and he looked determined to say it.

"What?"

"Hate. It's a mighty strong emotion for a family you've done your best to ignore." Jacob dropped his voice as he shifted tracks. "Lady Harcourt told me about the Spitfires."

Amos groaned. "She shouldn't have done that."

"She needed help, Amos. And it shouldn't have been a secret in the first place. Not when people on the estate might be put in harm's way because of it. Why didn't you tell me?"

"Lady Harcourt's hands were tied. She'd been sworn to secrecy by the ministry."

Jacob shook his head like he didn't believe a shred of it. "Didn't stop her from telling you. Or Mr. Cox."

"And I barely had time to learn of the planes before the Luft-waffe showed up. Had I more than a handful of hours to decide what to do, I may have let others in. But being with the Home Guard, I can't just . . ."

"Can't what?"

"I don't trust you yet, alright? You're German!" Amos blasted back, shouting it so patients popped heads up from pillows and visitors turned to look their way. He hated that he'd taken his frustration out on the lad, even if his words held a grain of truth.

"And how did you come to that conclusion?"

"I saw you that night, outside the bookshop. Helping the couple from the paint shop. You spoke to the wife. The only way you could have done that is if you're highly educated, German, or both."

Deadpanning, Jacob held firm. "And what do you think?"

"Tell me the truth."

"I have German ancestry, yes. But I'm 100 percent American and have citizenship to prove it. Though I assume you contacted Grosvenor Square, checking in with the consulate as soon as I arrived in Coventry."

"I did. Not long after."

"And? What did you learn?" Jacob fired back. Maybe this was a conversation he'd had too many times before. An American with German roots was therefore suspect, at least in a world at war with Hitler. It put everyone on edge.

"That I can't afford to be wrong about you. Not when I know there's more to your being here. And not when you might hurt the Holts before you leave. I can't take the chance of letting a stranger into our lives."

"Fair enough." Jacob nodded like a man accepting the sting of a punch he'd expected. Maybe even deserved. "But despite that, you can't keep running back and forth between the bookshops and the estate every night. No one can be in two places at once. Not even you. You'll get yourself killed. Almost did. For what?"

For her.

Amos clenched his jaw. Same thing he always did when forced to confront what he didn't want to. It was the same in the trenches all those years ago. You maintain. Clench your jaw when you're forced to pull a trigger. And chew iron when you have to watch machine-gun fire mow down men and horses in front of your eyes, just as you learn to cling to a steely resolve when bombs start falling on those you love.

He clamped his eyes shut on the last thought, the notion of love having set a trip wire inside before he could stop it from happening.

"You don't have to answer. I'll stay at the shop to look after you when you're released from the hospital."

"No, you will not. I've been taking care of myself for some time now, Jacob. And that's how it stays."

Rolling into a deep sigh, Jacob raised his hands, palms out. "Fine. I won't fight you on it. But I'll move my things to Holt Manor and help Lady Eden and the Land Girls, at least for a while. Until you recover. And then we'll decide what to do after that."

"You're staying on then?"

Jacob nodded, resolute. "For now."

"And Lady Eden still doesn't know about the Spitfires?"

"No. And I'm determined she won't. It would only add to her burdens. And that's something Her Ladyship won't abide. So it stays between us as long as it can. I'll work with Lady Harcourt and Mr. Cox to see that the planes are kept hidden. But I can assure you, neither she nor her daughter will be running around an estate throwing open barn doors again when German planes are tearing up the sky. Agreed?"

If it meant keeping Charlotte in a shelter, Amos would have given his good arm for that.

"Agreed."

"Good. I'll get Alec to help if I must. But in the end, we're going to make sure every last soul on that estate is safe. No matter what comes."

It would have been one thing for Amos to say that; his very being seemed entwined with the Holt estate no matter how he'd tried to free himself of it. But for this lad, days into a trip that was only supposed to be to deliver a legal summons, to now say he was staying on? Better than that—he was staying on and willing to stare down German bombers should they come back to the estate, same as Amos was.

That had to mean something.

"Why are you doing this?" Amos pinned him down, staring him square in the eyes.

"Seems I have my reasons. Just like you." Jacob leaned over, stretching to reach the low shelf on the nightstand.

The metal flask glinted, just catching the light as he set it on the nightstand. He reached for the book he'd been reading when Amos had awoken, opened the front cover, and took out the photograph tucked inside. Jacob set it on the tabletop and used one finger to slide the image of a young Charlotte Terrington until it rested on the edge closest to him.

"Get some rest." Jacob stood and slipped his hands in his trouser pockets. "I'll be back. I just want to get news to Lady Harcourt that you're awake. She asked to be kept informed."

Amos lay in the aftermath of Jacob's suspicions, watching as the lad walked away. Then glanced over at the worn book on the nightstand, still not able to decide if it was truly a friend or a foe. The fateful copy of *Dombey and Son* lay there, stamped with the fading Holt crest in the front cover and disguising the secret photo he'd carried with him all these years.

Aye, they each had their reasons for staying.

And now Jacob knew at least one of his.

CHAPTER EIGHTEEN

20 *February 1915*
Bayley Lane
Coventry, England

*I*n war, solace had its own rhythms.

For many, comfort was found in lowering pew kneelers. Some tended war gardens or organized concerts to bolster morale. Others found peace in writing letters to their beloveds at the front. The patriotic went to work with increasing fervor, finding positions in war offices or auxiliary services, and women flocked to factory roles vacated by servicemen, filling them by the hundreds. They drove ambulances and bread trucks. Manned switchboards and tilled farmland. And for Charlotte, who found that the title of Countess of Harcourt offered an unexpected measure of autonomy in social standing, her solace was to remain occupied.

If she was to be queen of the county, one small consolation was that Charlotte could do as she liked. Will wouldn't have agreed, of course, even if it was time spent on charitable endeavors. But her growing middle made it increasingly difficult to engage in any labor on the estate, let alone play the cello. And she'd found a new venture that did not require her to spend the next few months hidden away behind closed doors, knitting and awaiting a visit from the stork.

The British Library Service had come up with a scheme to provide books for wounded soldiers at the nearby British Red Cross auxiliary hospital and convalescent home. There was talk of expanding operations to send books to the front as well, to provide comfort for the soldiers still in action. With the hope to meet increased demand, it was all-hands-on-deck for the ladies of County Warwickshire to answer the call. Whether they were low- or highborn, titled or not, war had a way of diminishing the nonsense of it all. And Charlotte was cheered that as countess, she might appoint whomever she chose to work with her.

The long-abandoned milliner's shop they'd found on the corner of Bayley Lane offered the perfect hub for their efforts. Charlotte leaned over the old shop counter now, her rounded middle just brushing the wood as she slid a crate of books over for inspection.

"The ladies on the board have outdone themselves. We can't possibly house all of these books. And stacks of crates are arriving every day."

"Good. That means the soldiers in the hospital won't have to go a day without at least some entertainment. Or distraction from their worries." Marni stood by the shop doors, her light brown hair made softer by the sunlight streaming in from the shop window and her smile warm as she carried a stack of books over, then stopped to check on the babe sleeping in the pram.

"Asleep, is he?"

"Just," Marni whispered, setting the books on the edge of the counter so she might reach down and brush his little fingers knotted in a tiny fist. "I should like him to dream all the dreams he dares in this world. For as long as they last."

Charlotte watched her friend, knowing it had been a long winter already.

A War Office telegram had arrived at Foxhollow Farm in autumn with news of Tate Fitzgibbons's death. In the months since, Charlotte had witnessed his wife tumble through grief, all whilst keeping up letter writing to her own husband, hoping and praying and lighting candles for his welfare at St. Michael's each week.

She watched Marni try to hide a tear that had escaped from her bottom lashes as she looked on their little boy, Alec—his name chosen by his father before he'd shipped off to war. The action tugged at Charlotte's heartstrings, for even if the letters that came back were few and far between, every wife had to suppress gnawing fear that the bittersweet portrait she watched now could one day be her own.

"We ought to keep going. Whilst he's asleep anyway." Marni drew in a steadying breath and moved on, inspecting a crate of odds and ends in the pile of the latest donations.

"Yes." Charlotte brightened, doing her noble best to banish worry. "These are fiction on the counter. A mixed lot of titles."

"And I've . . . cookbooks? Oh dear. Would it be ungenerous to offer them out now? I should hate to think we're sending people to bed hungry for roast goose and Yorkshire pudding when all they've had for supper is stale tea and bubble and squeak."

"Readers won't take offense. They'll be cheered by whatever we can share from what Dunne Books and Company has sent us."

"Oh yes—the redbrick shop closer to the cathedral? They've taken orders for the *Farmers' Almanac* for years."

"Not anymore." Charlotte sighed. "Closed. Yet another casualty of war. And the owners donated all their stock for the soldiers at the convalescent home."

"Closed? How could that be, with reading materials in such high demand?"

"Used books, perhaps. But with paper shortages and German U-boats blocking anything from coming near our English isles, there's too much risk. And new books are fast falling into diminished supply. Not to mention the extra funds needed to purchase them. Most people don't have it. And if they do, they'd much rather send a care package to the front than spend a shilling on themselves."

"And that's where we come in."

"That is the general idea." Charlotte ran her fingertips over the spines of fiction titles in a nearby stack. Somehow she would find herself pausing to search for Sir Walter Scott on any shelf or in any stack she passed by. "And the hope that someone comes along one day to resurrect a bookshop on Bayley Lane. Until then, we'll provide what service we can."

Charlotte surveyed the derelict space, hoping they indeed had enough to build upon. Leaded glass was cracked in the rounded display window. Cobwebs owned every corner. The floor needed polishing, the shelves ached for dusting, and there were still reams of musty fabric rolled and leaning against the front counter. All in all, it could prove a slow start when they needed to clean it, clear it, and fill it to the brim. And fast. But if the donations pouring in were any indication, the wounded soldiers would soon be swimming in novels and periodicals on virtually every subject under the sun.

"What are these?" Charlotte knelt, inspecting the edge of a paper-covered roll too sturdy for her to move. When she peeled back the wrapping, a sheen of striped peacock blue smiled back from underneath. "It's wallpaper . . ."

"Who would donate wallpaper? Surely they didn't think we'd need it."

Her heart beat faster. "Does it matter?"

The largest space in the building was the back room. Charlotte gazed down the shadowed hallway, picturing it made up with walls of books and cushioned chairs, a tea cabinet perhaps, and shelves teeming with stories. An entire library's worth of comfort or care, entertainment or escape, for whoever might have need of it. Here would be a refuge offered within the pages of a book—the genesis of a temporary peace, and a haven in a world broken down by war. Even if the sojourner found only a few moments of asylum here, it would be worth it.

And the walls would be . . . peacock blue.

"This is brilliant." Charlotte moved to stand, anchored by Marni's outstretched elbow to help her up, and marched down the hall, her friend tracking at her heels. "And I know exactly where we'll hang it."

"Where?"

The stone fireplace was the anchor of the entire space. The rest would build around it. And if anything, the book lover's solace would find another home in Coventry.

"We'll hang it here. In our new reading room."

→ ·←

23 October 1940
Bayley Lane
Coventry, England

It was a miracle Bayley Lane still stood.

Charlotte dropped her bicycle to the sidewalk when she reached Eden Books, the basket coming loose as it clanged to the cobblestone street, and she charged up to the front stoop. She slipped the key in the lock, turned it, and left it to hang as she swept through the open door.

"Amos?"

Flicking on lights, she dashed from the front entry past the counter to the aisles of fiction titles, her oxford heels clicking the hardwoods with each frenzied step to check between shelves.

"Amos? Are you here?"

"What's all the commotion?" He appeared out of the back hall from the reading room, holding an arm to his wounded side and carrying a tin of Twinings in the other hand.

Charlotte braced a hand to the nearest sales table, trying to calm down now that she'd seen him. "You weren't in your shop."

"We were out." Amos held up the tea tin. "So I came over here. But the tea queue's ready to go."

Dawn had scarcely broken. The sirens had just quieted after a fretful night of Blitz bombs. And all the way there from the estate—with every breath and tick of the clock and frantic pedaling of her feet—this was what Charlotte prayed she'd find: Amos, whole and unharmed and setting all the wild fears in her mind to rest though smoke once again filled Coventry's streets.

Palming her middle, she dared to speak. "You didn't answer the telephone at your shop."

"I don't have one."

"Yes, you do. I had one put in whilst you were still in hospital."

"Aye," he said, but shook his head. "And I had it removed soon as they released me."

Of course you did, stubborn man.

"And why would you do that?" Charlotte took a step forward, feeling fire rise in her middle for the terror of hearing the switchboard operator advise it was a broken line when she'd tried telephoning from Holt Manor. "What if there was a problem at the estate? You are the agent, you know."

"Was there a problem?"

She crossed her arms over her chest. "No. But that's beside the point."

"Jacob and Eden would handle it until I could get there. And you can telephone the Home Guard at any time. We'll give you a report on Bayley Lane. Though I'm sure you're sorry to see my shop still stands across the street. Not even a shingle out of place, I'm afraid."

"I don't want a report," she snapped back. "And despite what you may think, I don't wish to see either one of our shops ripped of their rafters. I'd rather force your doors closed the old-fashioned way— because Eden Books matters to the people of this city. Because we truly care about our readers. And we don't push people away."

For the intelligent man Amos was, Charlotte was certain he must have gone completely mad. Or couldn't he remember that night of the plane crash? When she'd held him in the back of the auto on the fretful drive to the hospital. Talking to him. Patting his cheek with her bloodstained hand and fighting like wildfire to keep him alive. And now he had the nerve to remove the one lifeline she had to reach him.

"I was only joking." He paused, adding carefully, "And I knew you'd come to check on your shop. You always do."

She shook her head, defying emotion that choked her voice. For it wasn't the shop she'd fretted over. Not once, as a matter of fact. It was the madness of it all that Amos just couldn't see—walls of brick and shelves of books could be rebuilt. Replaced. Forgotten even, compared to human life. And because of it, every time the all clear was given, Charlotte fled to the telephone only to find out if he was still alive.

"We received news that St. Mary's Street took a direct hit last night. The rest weren't ready to go in the auto, so I cycled here on my own when I couldn't reach you."

"Oh. I see," he breathed out. "But we were in the shelter. Below-ground, remember?"

"How was I to know you were alive when they are still pulling the poor souls from the rubble? What of that?"

Amos nodded, hanging his head a bit. He took slow steps and met her in the center of the shop, setting the tea tin down on a stack of poetry books on the table nearby.

"I'm sorry."

"Amos, I thought . . ." Charlotte shook her head and turned her face down lest he see her tears. And know why she couldn't bear to reveal the truth coursing through her insides. "I cannot do that night of the plane crash again."

"I know, and I am sorry." Amos nodded again, but this time, he appeared to fight for his words too. Those eyes searched for hers, waiting until she looked up again. He furrowed his brow a shade, saying he was every bit as contrite as his tone suggested. "I ought to have thought about you and Eden, and the estate. As agent I should have gone to Holt Manor first thing. But I live my life a certain way. I have rules. Habits of a lifetime of looking after myself. And they are what I can control right now. So if I don't want a telephone, even with everything that's happening . . . then I won't have one."

"I see. And in a world set on fire outside these walls, with bombs falling in the streets every night, you earnestly wish to find something . . . that you can *control?*"

"You don't understand. This is how it has to be."

That's not jolly good enough.

"If that's so, then help me understand."

He shifted his weight, bracing his hands at his hips. Like something was holding him back from answering.

"Say anything to help me understand what you think you can control. Surely not hiding planes on the estate. Nor what will happen in the skies over Coventry every night. Or that our bookshops may not survive to open our doors the next day. Bombs will fall, Amos. We can't predict where they'll land. We can only muster enough strength to survive them, and cling to hope from one day to the next. You must see that. So I am asking you now. Why is this how it has to be?"

Tension crackled between them now that her tirade was out, her accusation hanging in the air.

"Because, Charlie, I can't make any more mistakes," he whispered in a voice raked over gravel, raising a sincere hand to a lock of hair that had drifted down against her cheek and tucking it back behind her ear. "You're all I have left on this blessed earth to care about, and that scares the life out of me."

Amos must have thought he knew her, no doubt as the privileged heiress who'd followed duty all her life. But in the years they'd been apart, Charlotte had grown. She was her own person. An estate owner. And mother. And not afraid to stand on her own two feet in a shop that was her hollow half of their dream together. She stepped forward, closing the distance between them, gave a soft tug to the front of his shirt collar, and rose to her tiptoes to draw his lips down to hers.

And it became as if no time had passed.

Even years later, her lips remembered every contour of his. Her heart hadn't forgotten the overwhelming sense of home that it was just to be near him. And the fear that had tormented her on the way to Bayley Lane abated the instant he wrapped arms around her and allowed his lips to fall into union with hers.

"I've never"—smiling against his mouth, Charlotte paused and reached up to run a fingertip over the scratchy line of his top lip—"kissed you with the beard. I wondered what it would be like."

"Me too." He lifted his chin. Pressed a slow, soft kiss to her forehead, whispering against her skin, "You can't know how much."

And with the world falling down around them, Charlotte couldn't bear to deny the inner workings of her heart. Not this time. Not when it had taken them so long to reach this place.

"But I need to tell you that even if—"

"I've missed you, Amos," she admitted, unable to hold the confession back another breath. Charlotte dared gaze up and allowed her hand to palm his shirt. "It feels as though we've been given a second chance after that night of the plane crash. And now, after all these years . . . I still miss you. And I've never stopped. Not for one moment since that day we said goodbye at the glasshouse and you went off to war."

"I . . . It's not that simple."

"But that's what I'm trying to tell you. I never wanted this shop. I mean, I did. But not without you. Please tell me I'm not alone. That no matter what's happened, this war between us hasn't killed every bit of love there might have been."

The front door creaked—a hollow sound echoing across the open space. And in the bookshop that had begun as a source of comfort for Charlotte during the first war, the illusions of a lifetime were laid bare in this second war.

Charlotte turned in his arms, nothing masked now as she found the stunned visage of her daughter staring back from the doorway.

CHAPTER NINETEEN

23 October 1940
Bayley Lane
Coventry, England

*T*he *click-clack* of typewriter keys hummed in the background as Eden returned to Waverley Novels, nearly turning her heel as she breezed through the open door.

Their tea queue had evolved to a machine-like effort, each person knowing their job and falling into its rhythm. Dale was positioned behind the shop counter, with curls of smoke rising from the cig in her fingertips as she read aloud from the first edition of their soon-to-be-published shelter bulletin. Jacob and Ginny were repositioning the features tables, the legs scraping the hardwood floor as they tried not to unbalance and topple any books.

Eden bumped the door. The brass bell chimed and the room glanced her way.

"Jolly-good timing, Lady Eden! We need your opinion." Dale pulled the paper out of the typewriter roll until it gave a little *ding* and stood up to read. "'Wayfarers and wanderers, and Coventry storytellers of old . . . we bring you *The British Booksellers.*' Like it? It's our new bulletin name—for all of us. We're selling books here, right? And everyone's sheltering together, whether from London or Coventry. Except for Jacob, who we'll make an honorary Brit whilst he's here. We thought we could hand out new editions at the tea queue in the mornings, and people can read them to pass time in the shelters at night. And we can toss in news of Coventry and the WLA as it fits. What do you think?"

"It's fine," she mumbled.

"Did you find Her Ladyship at the bookshop?" Ginny looked to Eden, too, and started edging toward the hall. "And the tea—did Mr. Darby have it? I can start heating the kettles if you wish. We should have Godcakes delivered at the back door anytime."

"What?" How had the air been sucked out of the room? Needing someplace to land or else the world would spin completely off its axis, Eden turned to face Jacob. "What about the bookshop?"

"Eden Books. It's fine, yes? Isn't that why you went over there?" Jacob stilled his hand holding a copy of *South Riding* in mid-transfer. "The bomb blasts were streets behind us. And Flo and Ainsley stayed back with Alec and Mr. Cox to work on the estate, so nothing to worry about."

Ginny turned pale. She flitted her glance to the display windows as if she expected a bomb to fall plumb on the sidewalk and take them all out. "Eden, what is it?"

Jacob exchanged glances with Dale, whose fingers had frozen over the typewriter as she'd been rolling a new sheet of paper in. He set the book back on the table and stalked over, checking the smoky street behind Eden before he eased her farther inside and closed the door.

"Something is wrong." He leaned in, his voice low. "What?"

"I need to speak with you. Alone," Eden whispered, feeling the curious eyes of the room on her and the unavoidable sting of tears forming in her eyes. *"Please?"*

Jacob nodded, shot a glance around the small space occupied at all points. Then took her hand and led her through the shop.

"We'll put the kettles on," he called over his shoulder as the safety of the hall swallowed them up.

It would have been a terrible idea to crumble just then.

Once out of earshot from the rest, however, having marched to the solitude of the back stockroom and because her heart was tossing thoughts in all directions at once . . . it just happened. The dam broke. Eden fell with the tears, clung to the strongest point in the room, and held on for dear life.

Burying her face against Jacob's chest, Eden gave in as she hooked her arms behind his shoulders. He offered no argument. Arms just came around her. Held tight. And he waited without the necessity of words, clasping her for long moments—as long as she needed, it seemed—with his chin pressed against the top of her head.

"I'm sorry." Eden shook her head, mortified, and bobbed his chin as she broke away. What a fortunate circumstance she hadn't worn the wretched cream mascara that day, or he'd have streaks across the front of his shirt instead of just spots from her tears. "I didn't mean to . . . do that."

"It's alright." He scanned the room, spotted a tea towel hanging on the back of a spindle chair in the adjoining kitchen, and moved off to swipe it, then returned and offered it to her. "Here."

"Thank you." She dabbed her eyes with the tea towel, trying her level best not to look like a hopeless frump with a running nose.

Jacob stood by, patient in waiting. "Want to tell me what happened?"

"I saw my mother and Mr. Darby in the shop . . . in an embrace."

"Right. Okay." He sighed, anchoring his hands at his hips. And nodded. And for the life of her, she'd have guessed Jacob wasn't surprised by her revelation. Could that be? "Were they just grateful your mother found Mr. Darby alive, given the Home Guard report we received this morning? News of St. Mary's Street taking a direct hit would have thrown anyone to hear. Maybe if she found him at her shop, it was just a great relief."

"No." Eden shook her head, vehement, and tossed the tea towel on a nearby counter. "That's not what it was. And that's not what they said. Mama declared her affection for him—Mr. Darby. Ardently so. And I didn't say a word. I just stared back at them in utter disbelief. I trusted him. I mean, sort of. I was the one trying to befriend our shops. To stop this supposed war. But . . . I just ran. Like a silly schoolgirl."

"Eden, this isn't tears over your mother finding, uh . . . romance again, is it?" Jacob's pause was indeed awkward. He seemed unable to find the words to talk of love. Certainly not like this. And not with her.

"Never. I'd have supported her remarrying had she wished it."

He raised an eyebrow. "Even to Mr. Darby?"

"Well, that never crossed my mind. Until . . ."

"Until what?"

"I've suspected for some time that there may be more happening here. Something they're not saying. There have always been whispers in town—I just ignored them as idle gossip." Eden caught her bottom lip with her teeth as she thought it through. "But since the night of the plane crash . . . Do you remember what Mr. Darby said, what he called her when in a bemused state of pain and loss of blood? He whispered something, no doubt thinking they were alone. But we were there. And I know you heard it too."

He nodded. "Charlie."

"Yes. And that blindsided me. When I was a little girl, Mama and I used to read books and play endless games in the rose garden. We'd visit the old glasshouse, and she told stories of what it used to look like, long ago, when they'd had a gardener who grew beautiful things within its walls. Even though both of my grandmamas heartily disagreed and believed I ought to have a nanny, Mama insisted I grow up under her wing. And we were inseparable. She gave me a pet name, after one of my favorite toys: Eddy Bear. It's silly to think of now. But I laughed. And said if she hadn't one of her own, we should give her a pet name too."

"But she already had one?"

Eden nodded, her heart heavy. Not understanding.

"She told me someone very dear had once given her a pet name: Charlie. She'd loved that person very much and said that she'd kept the name close to her heart, always. I just assumed she spoke of my father. But all this time, all these years later . . . *he* uttered that name. When no one else could have known, except the one who'd given it."

Jacob stood there just watching her as something washed over his face akin to . . . guilt? Eden blinked, wary now, and stepped back from him in the same instant a sickly wave took hold of her middle.

He was far too pragmatic not to face facts, nor to refuse to ask questions about them. Why was the solicitor presenting a more detached front now?

"But you . . . already knew."

"Maybe," he admitted. "Or I suspected anyway."

"What? What did you suspect?"

"When I was at the hospital with Amos, one of the things found on his person when we brought him in was a book, tucked in the inside pocket of his jacket. Inside its front cover I found the Holt family crest and a photograph of a young woman." Jacob sighed, his shoulders weighted with it. "Your mother."

"And you didn't tell me?" She stared back, incredulous.

"It wasn't my place."

"It's not your place to be honest? How very cosmopolitan of you."

"What I mean is, it's not my place to judge a man, or a woman, for a past I know nothing of. This isn't a court case to them; it's their lives. And I've no right to step into it."

"But you have no qualms about stepping in and threatening our estate?" Another thought blasted her as quickly as the last. "Did you say anything to Mr. Darby about this?"

"Of a sort."

"And?"

Jacob shook his head. "He didn't deny it."

There was a grain of truth in what he'd said. It had been as if Eden were standing in the doorway of her mother's shop, watching a photoplay of some stranger. Not the countess of County Warwickshire who fought for causes and stood up for the tenants on their estate. The image of the woman embracing Mr. Darby in the center of the bookshop exuded a long-standing and deep devotion. And in a blink, the woman who'd professed that love became someone Eden didn't know.

"My mother claimed to love Mr. Darby for all the years they've known each other. And said she's never stopped missing him. I know them to have been childhood friends. And close before the Great War. But if what she said is true . . . then where is my father in all of this? Did she ever love him at all?"

Jacob held firm, standing steps away from her. He slipped his hands in his pockets, as if sorry to confront what he, too, must have had ticking through his mind.

"Please tell me you're not wondering if Amos Darby could be your real father."

"You blame me? Anyone can make mistakes. Perhaps they did. I could be that mistake."

"Is it the truth you seek, or something else?"

Jacob had mentioned that night in the Anderson shelter that Eden looked like her father from his portrait in the great hall. The ebony locks. Strong jaw. Slender build and high cheekbones could all be his. But something puzzled her that night and had been relentless in pricking her mind after.

Eden swept the long plait over her shoulder in front, holding it out before him. Demanding he consider what had been a private torment in her mind. "What do you see?"

Jacob looked as though he understood but refused to answer. He pulled his hands free from his pockets and answered simply, "Your braid."

"Not the plait." She stepped closer and stopped inches away. Then she flashed the ends of her hair beneath the glow from the kitchen, a gentle sheen of russet hidden in the strands just catching the light. "See it? The copper is buried. Just like Mr. Darby's. But nevertheless, it's there. I've seen it in him and it's right here. With me."

"Eden . . ." Jacob reached out, tentatively, and ran his fingers over the silk strands at the end of her plait, his fingertips brushing hers. "You're angry. And hurt. And you're reaching out for something that's not there."

"Am I? My mother says she wishes me to have the life I want—to save my father's estate. But am I not to wonder when puzzle pieces fall into place? Mama didn't even consult me when she brought Mr. Darby on as estate agent. Now I know why. War does not change everything; it cannot change secrets of the past."

"No. But it can change *us*. For our future. For who we might become. I think you should speak with Her Ladyship about this. You don't want to—" He paused again, as if searching for words, and allowed the plait to fall from his fingertips back down over her shoulder. "You don't have to go down this road. What you know to be true is already in your heart, Lady Eden Holt. These questions—or these rumors about the booksellers—have no merit if you already know who you are."

But did Eden know who she was? If everything she'd believed up to this point was thrown into question, was there anything sure upon which to stand? Perhaps Mama really did wish her to conform. To marry. To carry on the family name and eschew love in favor of a profitable match, if that was what meant the Holt legacy was assured.

A desk sat in a lonely corner, its roll top open. She glanced from Jacob to it, then stalked over. She yanked open the top drawer, rifling through until she found what she'd sought. "You're right, Jacob. Doubts ought to have no power over us."

"What does that mean?" He watched, crestfallen, as she swiped up the spindle chair from the kitchen. "Where are you going?"

"If I'm to be like my mother, then I ought to shed anything that keeps me from moving forward. If she wants a society-approved heiress, that's exactly what she's going to get."

Ginny and Dale lingered by the shop counter, heads together, chatting in quiet voices and waiting for goodness knew what to come out of that stockroom. They hushed at Eden's approach down the hall.

"Hedy Lamarr, please." Eden set the chair down in front of Dale.

She doused her cig in an ashtray and stepped up. "What's that, doll?"

"You said it—if I cut my hair, I'd look like a starlet. I could be someone entirely new. Well? That's what I want. To be someone else." Eden handed a pair of shears to their Land Girls leader and drew in a steadying breath as she tossed her plait behind her shoulder and sat down. "Go ahead. Take it all."

CHAPTER TWENTY

12 June 1915
The Western Front
Near Artois, France

*A*ll Amos could think about now was keeping his feet dry.
Leaning against a felled tree in the dark, he sat on his tin hat and propped his feet on a pallet of old fence wood gathered from a pasture to keep boots and puttees from the mud. He'd seen some other chaps suffering trench foot—wasn't going to dare endure that, not if there was a scrap of something he could use to prevent it.

Seemed even if they won these days, they lost.

The British Army battled for a victory at Neuve Chapelle village in March. Had suffered a bloody loss to the Germans at a place called Aubers Ridge a month later. And triumphed at Festubert several grueling days after that, in support of a brutal French offensive at Vimy Ridge. Even then, barren villages became dots on a map. Days and nights ran together like the sea of mud in the trenches. Gas masks were kept close as bombs shook the earth with maddening rhythm, leaving behind busted rifles and bits of men and bomb craters to mar empty fields. Snipers fired at any blessed thing that moved, with bullets that whizzed by to pierce flesh right through the parapets. And in the midst of the grit and blood, when you finally did get a few precious moments to breathe, you didn't waste time thinking about tomorrow. Not when sitting through the night again, waiting for the next bombs to fall come morning. It was only about keeping dry today.

Nursing a cup of tepid brew, Amos kept his eyes trained in the dark, watching for any movement behind the horses and along the treed ridge at the edge of the British Expeditionary Force flank. A shipment of books had come to the front—some new undertaking by the Blue Cross Fund that, once Amos had learned of it and volunteered to organize books for the men, served as a lifeline of distraction to pass the drudgery in between battles. He turned the copy of *Dombey and Son* over in one hand now. Wondering, with canvas bags full of books to distribute nearby, if he'd ever open this one and finally read it again. Now it was more of a habit just to hold something from home as time ticked on.

A twig snapped behind him. Amos tossed the cup and flew into position over the felled log with the Enfield slung taut around his arm, the bolt cocked and sight trained in a single breath.

"Care to lower that SMLE before I take a bullet in the wrong place?"

Seeing it was a known face and not a Jerry ambush, Amos lowered his Short Magazine Lee-Enfield rifle. "Captain Holt."

"At ease." Will waved him off when Amos moved to salute—as he must—and instead dropped down with his back pressed in line with Amos's against the felled tree. He flipped a pocket manual into Amos's lap. "Brought you something new for those books you're always peddling."

Whether or not he'd seen the copy of *Dombey and Son* was another matter Amos didn't want to confirm. He swept it under his gas mask and angled the manual up to the moonlight. It did little good without a campfire or bright moon, and he couldn't make out the title on the pale blue cover.

"It's *The Drivers' and Gunners' Handbook to Management and Care of Horses and Harness*. Quite a mouthful, even for the blessed Blue Cross Fund. I doubt you'll find anything there you don't already know. But the officers all get one anyway. I've stacks more in the mailbags that just arrived."

"Thank you. I'll see to distribute them first thing." Amos tucked it in his haversack and leaned back again, thinking that'd be it. And he'd be back to minding the state of his socks for the rest of the night.

Until it wasn't.

Their captain wasn't one to socialize. Not with junior officers who were scraping by on the bottom rung. And certainly not with Amos Darby, given their history. It had been fight alongside. Issue and take orders. Care for the horses. And steer clear of each other in all else. But the fact Will was cupping his hand to light a cigarette in the dark, then lingering on to smoke it, said more than all the words ever exchanged between them.

"We're not supposed to use lighters out here. But if we're going to die tomorrow anyway . . ." Will drew in a long drag, then blew out a slow tunnel of smoke that drifted up to the trees. "We need to talk."

"Sir?"

"You should know, Charlotte and I have a daughter. The last letter said born in April. So she'd be a couple of months old by now."

"Congratulations." And he meant it. Though Amos still gripped his Enfield tight, just for something to hold as a thousand thoughts awakened and started a brutal careening through his mind.

Charlotte has a child.

"I didn't come for congratulations. Though they are heartily accepted." Will flicked ash from his cig. And rested his elbows on his knees, staring with Amos through the maze of forest in front of them. "Even if I know you're still in love with my wife."

Amos swallowed hard. But kept his eyes fixed, staring at the line of horses along the trees. And chose to keep his silence, no matter how Will tried to goad him.

"Not that I blame you. Most mortal men would be." Will took another drag of his cig, leaned his head back, and stared up at the starry sky through the trees. "I'm in love with her too. In my own way. She just doesn't know it. And hasn't, even since we were all kids."

"It has nowt to do with me."

"Oh, but it does." Will raised a palm, stopping him from interjecting. "I'm not here to rake it over. Nor to warn you to watch your back. Britain needs every one of her soldiers in this fight, and I'm not about to kill another over it. But in the end, the daughter Charlotte and I have is flesh and blood. *My* flesh and blood. And my heiress. And I won't let anything come in the way of protecting my family, whether in France or back at home. Do you understand me?"

Aye, Amos understood.

And had to appreciate Will had the guts to say it. He wouldn't have thought the sod had it in him. But then, almost a year of continual battles could manage to beat valor into even the most toffee-nosed of soldiers. And though Amos never would have admitted it to anyone but himself—and even then with gritted teeth—the man sitting next to him really was a captain. Will had proven courageous enough times when the bombs fell, even if he was misguided in everything else.

"I would never hurt Charlotte. Nor her family," Amos answered in truth.

"I know that." Will looked over, his features dark behind the tiny glint of ash glowing at the end of his cig. "And that's why my wife can never know about that day at Gretna Green."

"You're asking me to lie?"

"No. Just offering friendly advice. When this is all over, you stay away from Holt Manor. Stay away from my family, and there will be no need to ever speak of it again. Adhering to it ought to keep you from a repeat visit to the county gaol. Or prison—whichever you choose next time."

Weak threats. Amos knew better than to take the bait.

A marriage couldn't sustain a false foundation, and certainly not with Charlotte's inquisitive nature in the mix. Will knew it, too, or he wouldn't be sitting here shaking in his boots as he nursed his cig. At some point Charlotte would figure it out. She'd demand the truth about what Will had to do with Amos's failure to appear at the altar. And when that day of reckoning came, Will would have nowhere to hide. And Amos sure wasn't going to prop the fool up to do it.

"And if Charlotte asks me for the truth?"

"You're so confident she will?"

Amos wasn't about to answer that. "She's cleverer than you think. And I covered for you the first time. I won't be doing it again."

"Then that would pose a problem between us." Will paused after the veiled threat. Even chuckled under his breath when Amos didn't reply. And kicked at something in the dirt by his boot. "I see. You want recompense. Is that it?"

"No, sir."

"Too principled, Darby? Come now. Every man has his price. What's yours?"

Amos shook his head. "I want for nothing."

"Surely there's something. Farmland away from Coventry? A fine cottage for your mother and sister? Whatever you want, it's within my ability to gift."

"Just an end to the fighting is all."

"You're weary of fighting. Here?" Will snapped back, standing to stomp his cig in the dirt under his boot. "And if some provision were made to come your way when this is all over, would you fight that too?"

"With respect, I could not accept."

"Then we have nothing more to say. And I'll bid you good night so we might both prepare for what lies ahead."

They might have left it there.

Probably should have, for the noxious truth aired. If it was just Will and his pretense, Amos might have let the earl stew in his own pudding. But a baby changed everything. A man's life meant more when he was a father, because he wasn't just living for himself any longer. And that meant something to Amos.

"Will?"

"What is it, Sergeant?"

Amos had made an earnest attempt at candor, using Will's childhood name. It didn't work. He kept the walls up, wearing the air of captain like a crown, and stared down with a cool haughtiness in his glare.

"Toreador, sir." Amos watched the stallion mingling in front of the horse line before them. "I have to ask again to consider changing your mount."

"And why is that? Not that sniper business."

"Aye. The snipers have been picking off officers left and right. I don't tell you now out of a grudge. But it's a fact you're at a greater risk than your men. Sergeant Lockey was killed last week—on the one day he rode your mount. That says something."

"Officers are always a target. That's not news in this war. Every man here puts his life on the line; if he loses it, so be it."

Amos shook his head. "Something's changed. That sniper out there—he's an officer who's noticed Toreador in the field before. That means the horse is both an asset and a threat." He paused, pointing to where night clung to the stallion lingering at the end of the line. "Toreador is strong and stable in battle, aye. But he also stands out. Especially for a scope that's searching for him. And that means he'll be looking for you too."

"Of course Toreador stands out; he's the best."

Fool. Amos sighed under his breath. Will just wouldn't listen. And wouldn't bend an inch beneath what he supposed he was due—for his birthright, his pride, or both.

"I only mean to say, sir . . . I believe he's biding his time."

"You think a sniper is hunting me?" Will scoffed, a light laugh that said Amos ought to leave military strategy to the leaders in rank. "That is a story. Even for you."

"It's just advice, sir. I thought if it means your life, you ought to know—for your family's sake if not your own."

"I'll take that into account then, Sergeant. And I recommend you get some rest. We move out tomorrow. Here." Will tossed Amos a brass cartridge case, a lighter made from a spent .303 round that landed in his lap with an extra hand-rolled cig. "A truce, for old time's sake. Let's declare the past dead and buried, hmm? You know what they say, 'The enemy of my enemy is my friend'? Well, let's chuck everything we've got at those Jerries to prove it's true."

Will started to walk away, his boots clipping the forest floor behind the fallen log.

"What's her name, sir? If I'm allowed to ask."

"Eden." Will laughed behind Amos, his voice uneven. "How do you like that? The first piece of heaven on earth. And I find out it's my daughter's name when we're here, in hell's answer."

Amos turned the lighter over in his hand as Will walked away. Thinking. Listening to horse whinnies and cicadas trilling through the trees, and the occasional warning shot fired from one side to the other.

Starting a fire would have been a risk, even in their semi-secure position away from the trenches. But Amos made the decision then; the next time he was camped in front of one, *Dombey and Son* was going in. No more would he live for yesterday. And never would he bust up a family over what might have been. He'd made the decision for both of them at Gretna Green. Now he had to live with it.

Enough.

Flipping the gas mask out of the way, Amos thought to shove the book in his haversack. Out of sight, and sure as anything, Charlotte would be out of his mind. But the cover fell open, butterflying to the ground. With it, a tiny scrap of something that had been tucked in the binding came away. Amos lifted it from the dirt, his heart racing as he flicked on the tiny stream from the trench lighter in front of the image . . . a flame just bright enough to illuminate Charlotte's sweet face smiling back.

He flicked the lighter off and leaned back, hand shaking as he curled his fist around the photo.

Will knew Amos still loved her. But to find the photo concealed where Charlotte had left it confirmed one truth: They'd said goodbye.

And with both of them honor bound, it would stick. But for every single battle in which Amos had unknowingly carried her next to his heart . . . she was saying a part of her would always carry him too.

➵ ⬻

6 November 1940
Brinklow Road
Coventry, England

You don't feel the deepest cuts when you're riled.

Amos couldn't, balancing atop a garden ladder whilst thrashing about the hedgerow bordering Brinklow Road, tearing through twists of bramble and cutting back prickly vines like the overgrowth itself had stoked his ire. Instead of what had really caused it—a moment in the bookshop with Charlotte days ago, which ought to have brought them closer together instead of splitting them further apart.

Days had flipped by in an odd monotony of bombs and blood and normal country routine. The numbing sound of sirens cried out every blessed night. Schedules were kept to the letter, whether for blackouts, fire-watchers or air-raid wardens, or antiaircraft crews keeping post on Coventry's rooftops through the night. And their trio of Land Girls, the Holts, Alec, Amos, and Jacob kept splitting duties between the bookshops, the tea queue, and the farming, milk rounding, and livestock care on the estate. It was a host of needs. A scattered existence of where to be and when. And in the whole lot of it, he still hadn't spoken to Charlotte about the baring of her heart that morning before Eden interrupted them in the bookshop.

Now Charlotte avoided him.

Or Amos avoided her. Or the practicality of their schedules kept them from meeting at all, at least in a place where they could speak to what in the world they were fixing to do. In any case, it made for a testy battle between man and hedge, with the blackthorn bearing the brunt of his frustration.

"Amos?"

At Jacob's shout Amos halted in his forceful rhythm of the hedge trimmers' chopping and yanked at a dense knot of overgrowth that had been giving him fits. "Aye?"

"You just going to let that go?" The lad paused in tying off a span of twine for the line of growth to follow along the ground and motioned up to Amos. "Your arm."

Looking down, Amos found a stream of crimson running from his forearm, smudging down his wrist to darken the edge of his leather work gloves.

Must have taken a thorn. He didn't even feel it. Just kept going. But now that Amos was aware of it, his nerve endings came alive and decided to annoy with a right good sting that felt like his skin had been seared with a flaming poker. He ripped off his glove, holding it with his teeth whilst trying to stem the flow of the cut against the tail of his work shirt.

"Hold on. We've got better than that." Jacob set his secateurs on a ladder rung, heading for the open truck bed by the side of the road. He found the first-aid kit, rooted around, and tossed a roll of gauze across the way.

Amos caught it and descended his ladder. "Thanks."

"We ought to take a break anyway." Jacob eased over to a great flat stone between them. He carried a cider jug, set it by his ankles as he sat, and stretched long legs out in front of him. Leaning over, Jacob offered a tiny bottle of iodine. "Might need this."

"It's just a scratch." Amos waved off the fussing, though he thought better of it in a flash. He'd seen infections at the front. It was usually the little scratches or bullet grazes plus time and dirt that opened the door for gangrene to finish a man. Maybe he could set stubbornness aside for once and just be sensible.

He sure didn't want to be making another trip to hospital any-time soon. "On second thought, hand it over."

"You certain you should be out here? It isn't that long since the hospital."

Amos issued a sharp look that said he wouldn't be answering that. Not even close. And to let it be or he would have something to say then.

"Alright." Jacob raised his palms, arrested. "I'm not your father."

It was a cool, crisp autumn day. But sweating in the sun and soil always seemed to make it feel like high summer, no matter what the temperature gauge or calendar read. Jacob uncorked the cider jug. Took a swig. And sighed, as Amos field-dressed his arm in a roller bandage and fallen poplar leaves drifted by on the breeze.

"We're never volunteering to trim the hedgerows again." Jacob's shoulders drooped. "This is absolute murder."

Amos smiled. *That's why we volunteered.*

Not that the Land Girls couldn't have handled the task. They each held their posts with dedication, with the surprise of Flo especially proving herself a hearty green thumb on the land. Point was, Amos didn't want them to have to fight the hedges, knowing what the Holt Manor blackthorn was like all those years ago when he'd worked Foxhollow Farm—tempestuous, unforgiving, and wild to a fault.

Let the Germans invade; this hedgerow would stop them dead in their tracks.

"What time is it?" Jacob bladed a hand at his brow to block out the sun.

Amos tied off his bandage. Then reached into his pocket, pulled out his watch, and flipped the cover open. "Quarter to four."

Jacob glanced over, watching, a little spark of something curious about his profile. "Where'd you get the watch?"

"From someone I knew once." Amos returned the watch to his pocket, looking over the span of Holt Manor spread out in front of them. "Doesn't matter."

"Something you carry around every day doesn't matter?"

"We've little more than an hour before the blackouts." Amos shut down talk with any hint of familiarity, no matter how mundane.

"And an hour after that, they'll need you at St. Mary's Street?"

"Aye."

In the distance the manor house stood quiet, the late-afternoon shadows already collecting around the windows. An autumn breeze rustled the pruned hedges in the manicured garden beyond.

"Have you talked to her?"

Not you too. Amos sighed at the inquisition.

These people liked to talk. And for a stranger among them, Jacob seemed to fit right in. Why couldn't he see what everyone else did? Amos was scarred. A brooder. A loner who liked it that way. This blessed war was shaking too many things at their foundation, starting with folks expecting Amos to have heart-to-heart chats, and now a Yank who wasn't old enough to know the first thing about life or love but seemed bent on instructing his elders in the finer points of it.

"Which one are you referring to?"

The lad laughed at that. "Either. I'd say start with Her Ladyship. Then get her to help sway you out of the daughter's bad books. If, that is, you can talk long enough without one of them making you swallow your own tongue. I've tried reasoning with Eden before."

"No luck?"

Jacob shook his head. "None at all. Wicked smart, that one." He did smile, though, as if caught up in an amusing memory that it seemed he could have tried harder to hide. "She always wins, even against a lawyer."

"The Holt women are a force to be reckoned with, aye."

Like mother, like daughter. Amos couldn't help but chuckle too. But the fact the lad opened up about it and didn't mind that they seemed to be in the same lot with mother and daughter said something. "What is it you're really asking?"

"I know you're not keen to this . . . but suppose I was making small talk about what happened at Eden Books?" Jacob gave a half smile—guilty on all counts. "Eden told me. Sorry."

"Then I suppose it wasn't a surprise, given you saw the photo that day at the hospital. And the book. You know the Holt Manor crest is in the front cover."

"I do." Jacob paused, as if treading with careful steps.

"Why keep quiet?"

Jacob shrugged and stared out at the rolling hills, same direction as Amos. "Whatever it's about is none of my affair. Who you loved before. Who you love now. Makes no difference to me."

"Pump the brakes. Who said anything about love?"

"Isn't it?"

The way Jacob was leading the questions said he knew exactly what he was doing and was aiming to trap Amos in revealing more than he wanted. But Amos wasn't about to let anyone in. Not now. Probably not ever. The encounter with Will that night in the darkness when he'd first learned about Eden had left enough of a bitter taste in his mouth to think better of trusting so easily again.

"As I suspected. Look, Amos—it's nothing to be ashamed of. Love has snared better men than us. I must say, though, I was cheered to find you're a member of the human race. I doubted it for a good minute or two."

Amos ignored the quip. "This all may not matter to you, but it does matter to Lady Eden, doesn't it?"

"It does. Where this estate and the legacy of her father's name are concerned, very much so." Jacob picked up the jug, started a gentle swing between his knees. "But if it means anything, I believe you and Lady Harcourt are a . . . fine pairing. Her Ladyship needs someone here. Not to take over. Not because she's a woman. She needs a partner, someone who cares about this place and the people fighting for it. We could all see fair to find an arrangement like that in life. Even if it's a bit later than we'd imagined, it's still rare and welcome when it comes."

"Maybe."

"So what's the problem?" And when Amos shot Jacob a glare that said *You've gone too far*, he pivoted. "Begging your pardon, of course. What did you say when milady shared her wishes that day in the bookshop?"

For the love of . . .

What was Amos supposed to do now? It felt like he'd been thrown into the plot of an Austen novel—a prospect that gave him considerable pause in opening any of his hidden corners to Jacob. Even if he was something of the closest thing he had to an actual mate.

"It's complicated, Jacob."

"Well, at least you can admit that much. I'd say that's a Grand Canyon–sized leap for you." Jacob smiled and slapped Amos on the shoulder.

Amos nodded. Gave the lad a little vinegar with a one-word answer of "Ja," his sarcasm not even a shade veiled.

"Alright. How about one last go? I'll come over to your side." Jacob stretched out his limbs as he stood. "At least we can finish that bit of the hedge before we have to hoof it to get behind blackout curtains."

He followed Amos, ladder in tow, until one of the wooden steps caught on a gangly root and nearly sent him into the hedge face-first.

"Oy!" The ladder clanged to the ground, and Jacob pushed off where his hands had broken his fall, thorns jabbing red puncture marks into his palms. "Where'd that come from?"

Amos marched over, stooped to pick up the secateurs the jostling had sent to the ground, and inspected the root. If it wasn't too thick, they could nip it so it didn't trip up anyone else.

In the twists of leaves and bunches of purple damson-like fruits, something glinted—a sharp reflection of sunlight that could only come from metal or glass. Looking deeper, Amos pulled the greenery back, his stomach sinking like a stone when he saw what was concealed there.

Splittermuster. The German armed forces camouflage fabric pattern was unmistakable, with a metal ring attached to a strip of leather folded against a ream of it.

"Did you get it?" Jacob knelt with him, still holding a fingertip in his mouth to stop the bleeding from a thorn prick. "Whoa . . . what do we have here?"

Amos tugged on the canvas and the lot came spilling onto the ground at their feet—a sight he'd seen in photos from the Home Guard in the event they ever came across the getup: a jumpsuit jacket and helmet and M37 trousers. The bits and bobs of a canteen, a food ration—torn open and eaten?—an empty gas-mask cover, a leather harness, and magazine cases . . . all empty. And the long, wet, and soiled silk of what had to be a German parachute.

"This isn't from some flyboy on French leave, as they say?"

"No. It's not a soldier gone AWOL." Amos scanned the worn path along the hedgerow, looking for fresh footprints. "Not a British soldier at least."

"Then . . . is this what I think it is?" Jacob pulled reams of fabric out like the chute had no end. He sent a warning look over to Amos, the pulse in his neck all of a sudden pounding.

"Aye." Amos shot to his feet and headed for the truck bed, forgetting the ladder as he grabbed up his rifle and started scanning the length of the field for any figure who oughtn't be there. "Pack that up and let's make tracks!"

"I got it," Jacob called back, gathering up the paratrooper gear in his arms. "We need this, right? To report to the Home Guard."

"You bet we do."

Amos stood on the truck's running board, eyeing the long span of hedgerow in front of them that curved with the road . . . leading all the way to the factories that backed up to the far fields. That grass was still black from the crash weeks ago, and the stone fence bore divots where bullets had flayed its top like Swiss cheese. Somewhere out there now was a new foe, one who'd ducked out of sight without their even knowing it. And who could be on the grounds that very minute.

"Hop to it!" Amos called, as Jacob fled from the hedgerow and dumped the wares in the bed. He slammed the back shut and hopped in the cab.

"What was all that?" He grabbed the side of the open window for leverage as Amos avoided running over the ladder and sent the truck tearing down the hill.

"German paratrooper gear."

"Right. That's what I was afraid of."

"Aye. And I'll tell you this: the 'green devils' are elite. If they've dropped one, they've dropped many. And it's for one reason: they're scouting the land before more trouble comes. That means Holt Manor has a whole heap of trouble, too, because that gear is missing two critical things."

Breathless, Jacob cocked the bolt-action on his Enfield and held tight, just in case. "What's that?"

"A nine-millimeter submachine gun and the devil who's planning to use it."

CHAPTER TWENTY-ONE

17 September 1915
Brinklow Road
Coventry, England

A chill pricked Charlotte's spine as she peered down from the upper-floor nursery window to the official-looking auto that rolled in a sleek wave down the drive.

They'd had a pleasant morning together, she holding Eden as they watched the flight of starlings outside the windows and followed squirrels leaping in their agile dance from limbs to dreys high in the poplar trees. And as having a night nursery suite far from her own chamber was quite out of the question, they occupied rooms with a connected door from Eden's to her own. That meant Charlotte was there to be a part of every nap or smile or giggle. And their rooms on the gallery closest to the stairs gave the best view of the great lawn, the front gates, and the long gravel drive that rounded to the front doors.

Shallow breaths escaped Charlotte's lips as she kept pressing a soft kiss to Eden's brow.

One of the footmen rushed out of the manor down below and opened the auto door. Charlotte leaned a knee to the buttercup-yellow window seat cushion and pressed a palm to the glass, tapping a rogue index finger as she waited to see who'd come calling. Just one gentleman emerged—not in military uniform but a trim charcoal suit with maroon tie and white hair tucked under a smart trilby, and a massive leather briefcase that looked as if it ought to be carrying him, instead of the other way around.

It's not the War Department . . .

You can stop racing now, heart.

"Did you see that, darling?" Charlotte peppered relief in soft kisses against the ebony curls at Eden's temple. Her daughter wiggled and squirmed and gave a little slap to the edge of the drapery tassels by their heads. "Your papa is . . ." Charlotte exhaled. *Calm down.* "Fine. He is quite well. And that means Mama ought to see to our guest, whoever he is."

Charlotte pulled the cord for the service staff, only to meet with Mrs. Mills knocking and stepping through the open door with barely a moment between the two.

"Pardon, milady, but a Mr. Evansbrook is requesting an audience." Charlotte started at the name. *Whatever could he want?* "I was on my way up to tell you we've put him in the downstairs library."

The solicitor for the Holt family's affairs? Charlotte had heard his name in passing. But never would Will have allowed her to take audience with the man for Holt family business. She couldn't even say whether they'd ever spoken except for once when the gentlemen's meeting had overstepped the dinner hour and he'd stayed on. But even then Charlotte had been positioned on the other side of the dining table with a slew of guests, with service staff slipping silver trays into the spaces between them.

Her stomach churned with butterflies anew. What could he possibly want now?

Charlotte planted one last kiss to Eden's head and set her in the nearby cot. "If you'll just stay here with Eden, Mrs. Mills, I shall see to it. And I'll request that Harriet or one of the other maids be sent up to spell you just as soon as it can be arranged."

"Very good, milady."

Flustered, though trying to project a countess's aura of assured calm, Charlotte moved from the gallery to the stairs—refusing to allow her heels to take them two at a time. Twisting her hands at the gathered waist of her muted pistachio frock, Charlotte hurried across the marble entry for . . . goodness knew what.

The butler announced Charlotte and she drew in a calming breath a scant second before she stepped into the library.

"Lady Harcourt." Evansbrook stood and greeted her, his head hiding a bushy white mustache as he bowed it. "My apologies for calling unannounced."

"Not at all, Mr. Evansbrook." Charlotte looked to their butler. "Tea, please, Andrews. And fetch Harriet to report to the nursery."

"Very good, milady."

Charlotte joined the gentleman at the settees before the hearth, sat, and waited until she was certain she heard the door click closed before she began.

"I can't say that I expected you today, Mr. Evansbrook. But as my husband's solicitor, know that you are quite welcome in this house. No matter what news it is you've come to relay."

"Thank you, milady. But if I may . . . I should like to put your mind at ease. I bring no ill news with me."

Whether proper or not to release the frightened breath that had been locked in her stomach, she did. Breathed out an "oh" and palmed her stomach for a second before dropping her hand in her lap again. "Thank you. That is quite good news indeed. But to what then do we owe this visit?"

"Your husband, milady. I've lately received a letter that gave me explicit instructions: if he had not returned home within six months of any child born of your union, then I was to set things in motion. Merely as a precaution, mind."

"I see." Oh, that palm wanted to rise up to her middle again. But Charlotte straightened her spine in a no-nonsense fashion, prepared to take whatever "things" they were like the Countess of Harcourt ought. "Go on."

"The Earl of Harcourt has sent me to you with two requests—matters that will require your signature to put forth, milady. In proxy."

"And what are these matters?"

"The first." He pulled a folder and swath of papers from his satchel, then turned to the last page of what looked like a contract of some sort. He handed them over. "The earl wishes to make it official: Lady Eden Holt is to be his heiress, to inherit Holt Manor and all of the Holt family principal holdings. Minus allowances for the dowager countess and yourself, of course."

Shock was not a friend, it seemed.

Charlotte's heart had just rebounded from the prospect of ill news, and now it fairly stopped dead in her chest with this. It had been the ardent expectation of their parents—and she thought Will as well—that Charlotte would provide sons to settle the succession. And whilst not unheard of to declare a girl the successor of the estate, to do so with both parents living and seemingly able to produce more heirs was highly irregular. Abrupt. Yet . . . wonderful.

"And this is indeed what the earl wishes?"

"I assure you, it is. He was quite clear. And though your daughter may not receive the title—that will go to the next male heir—the earl has asked you to sign in his stead, so the estate is in a tenable position should anything . . ." He cleared his throat, adjusted his seat, and leaned forward, holding out a fountain pen. "Well, as I said, it is merely a precaution. But nonetheless, a precaution the earl has gone to considerable effort to ensure is in a locked position. He wishes you both to be . . . looked after." He pointed to a line on the last page. "Just there, milady. Sign at the bottom."

Charlotte stood, crossed the short distance to the gleaming black Chappell occupying the corner in front of the shelves, and set the papers on the piano top. Her hands shook and she scrawled her name.

She stared down at the glistening ink of her own penmanship— one signature that had opened a Pandora's box to a thousand questions. Why had Will made this seismic alteration? Why now? Though tremendous, it was in no way what they'd discussed. Or rather, what Will had ordered her would mark their future. He expected sons. And her duty was to provide them. But if Eden was to inherit Holt Manor and all of their holdings, what then?

Charlotte glanced to the coffered ceiling.

An heiress, just six months old, sat cooing in a cot upstairs. How could that precious babe possibly understand what this meant? How everything might be changed with one signature on a page?

She turned back. "Is that it?"

Mr. Evansbrook nodded, taking ownership of the papers Charlotte handed back, and reached in his satchel for another folder. "Yes, milady. For this first matter. And your signature settles it."

"Alright." She wished for the tea to arrive so she might have something—anything—to distract nervous hands. "And the next?"

"A smaller matter, milady. A trust to be set in the name of one of His Lordship's acquaintances. It is a sizable amount, though— two thousand pounds. This requires a signature to allow me to see the transaction through. As His Lordship is unable to provide it, you may serve as proxy in this matter as well."

"Is that so?" That was an absolute fortune for a gift, wasn't it? She stood, crossed the few steps to the piano again, and turned to the last page, skimming the notary.

Everything appeared in order, much as she could see. "Very well then," Charlotte said as she scrawled her name and offered the papers back. Evansbrook gave her copies of both contractual agreements. And that, it seemed, was that.

He stood to make his leave.

"Oh—you don't wish to stay for tea, Mr. Evansbrook?"

"I'll beg your pardon, milady. If you'll allow me to take my leave, I have other engagements to attend. I can see myself out."

"Nonsense. I shall walk with you." She smiled as they moved toward the library doors. "One more question, sir? I didn't see the name of the beneficiary listed. Is it a charity? Perhaps the British Red Cross Auxiliary Hospital and Convalescent Home by chance?" Something sparked inside, a glimmer of hope that Will had read her last letters talking about their makeshift lending library out of the shop on Bayley Lane. Perhaps he'd taken it to heart and wished to show Charlotte affection, in his own way?

"I've lately been working with them for the benefit of wounded veterans from County Warwickshire," she continued, "and I should love it if we could provide more assistance for their needs. You have no idea how a gift of that amount might be useful in our efforts."

"No, milady." He replaced his hat, obviously eager to leave. And that made her eager to press the issue. "It is not a charity. Not the hospital either, I'm afraid."

"Oh. I see. Then who is the beneficiary?"

"No one of consequence. But . . ." He paused in the entry, riffled through his satchel for the folder, and at a quick look added, "A business acquaintance, apparently. By name of Mr. Amos Darby."

She blinked. "Pardon?"

He packed the papers away again. "A Mr. Amos Darby. I know nothing of the circumstance, save for the earl bade me to arrange the trust with said funds. He was quite clear on this matter too. I've a letter stating so."

"I see," Charlotte whispered, her sedate smile back in place. "Well, thank you, Mr. Evansbrook. I appreciate the swiftness in seeing to my husband's requests."

Never had Charlotte entertained such a visit.

By and large, the fact the solicitor came and went within a span of ten minutes was a distinct mercy. She couldn't have absorbed the waves of such bombshell news had he obtained her signatures and then stayed on for tea. What would they talk about—how impetuous her husband had proven to be? And whilst it was a godsend that a baby had been gifted ownership of her own future by a papa she'd never met, the fact that Will had made some provision for a man he surely hated made not a shred of sense.

Thank heaven the War Office hadn't sent a telegram that day. The revelations surely would have finished her. Charlotte could only pray now for Will's safe homecoming. And in due time, an answer as to what in heaven's name her husband was playing at now.

->··<-

11 November 1940
Brinklow Road
Coventry, England

Holt Manor was crawling with autos, suits, and speculation.

From the moment the German paratrooper gear had been reported discovered on the estate, Charlotte had entertained a round-the-clock circus that descended upon their doorstep. Officials had trickled in and out a revolving door for days so that by the time the last suit left, the unfortunate blackthorn hedge had been clipped down to its roots, the staff questioned in triplicate, and poor Jacob nearly carted off for his presence alone. Yet no connection to the "green devil" had been found. They were left with the knowledge that an enemy combatant could be wandering the estate with a 9mm in tow, inspiring little confidence on their nightly treks to the rose garden.

More than that, Eden was crushed.

After the plane crash, knowledge of the Spitfires had remained lock-lipped so only those with duties when the sirens cried should be burdened with the risk. But when the investigators arrived, the truth had come spilling out all over the mat. And the rift between mother and daughter ballooned to a behemoth degree when all Eden could see was that her mother didn't trust her to manage the estate.

Now, days later—and too long since the unfortunate incident with Amos at Eden Books—her daughter had withdrawn into work with the Land Girls. Chopped her lovely hair that had always been the hallmark Holt shade, and for goodness knew what reason. And mother and daughter were hardly speaking save for "good morning" and "good night" and "stay safe" before heading off to their next post.

Charlotte stood at the window in the downstairs library, watching the last of the autos fade into the bleeding afternoon sun, and wiped a tear from her cheek as the weariness of the day finally caught up with her.

A *knock-knock* rapped on the open library door, drawing her back. She gave a hasty wipe to her bottom lashes and turned. Amos stood in the doorway with a business card in hand.

"They left another one." Amos held the card up.

She flipped her wrist, checking the time. Four o'clock.

That's right. It's later than I thought.

Charlotte found a smile and pointed to the brass charger on the piano top. "They go in the tray. I'll file them in my diary later."

Amos walked in and set the card on the stack, then lingered for a breath, sorting through what was there. "The Air Raid and Control Centre . . . Foreign Office . . . Home Office . . . Women's Land Army . . . Air Ministry Intelligence . . ." He sighed and braced his hands at his waist. "I'm sorry. One afternoon at the hedgerows, and it seems we've brought the whole of London down upon you."

"It's not your doing. Though I haven't a clue why every 'office' that could spare a uniform seems to have sent one to County Warwickshire in the last few days. And I'm fairly certain a field agent from MI5 accompanied an investigator from Lord Beaverbrook's Ministry of War Production, as both spent considerable time shoring up the Spitfires. They've taken that over completely now. Though I'm encouraged by the added security, I cannot think why our estate is any different than hundreds of others across the country."

"I'd say your instincts serve you well, milady."

"Tell that to the county chairwoman for the WLA. Her secretary paid a call to see that their Land Girls were in a 'secure post,' as she put it. Which is laughable given the fact bombs continue to rain down on the lot of us every night." Charlotte clasped her hands together in front of her waist—or else she'd start wringing them again—for the truth was, they hadn't any place in England that was truly secure now. "But hearing the Home Guard will now run patrols across the estate proved a tonic to the woman's sensibilities, and she's consented to leave our post alone."

"That's good to hear," Amos said, though something held him to stand firm before her as if another matter was keen on his mind.

"Was there something else?"

Commotion in the hall burst forth then, as the Land Girls filtered into the entry in a wave of khaki and green and sun-kissed skin after a long day of labor. Charlotte peered past his shoulders at the sound of voices filtering through the entry hall. Dale met up with Flo and Ainsley, the group passing the library doors on their way to the stairs.

Charlotte eased away from the window. "Eden? Is she . . . ?"

Amos shook his head. "Lady Eden and Jacob are out seeing to the glasshouse work. With all this, seems we've managed to get behind on the gardening."

"I can't imagine how," she offered with a slight smile, sarcasm proving easy at this juncture when they were up to their cravats in troubles. Then, almost as an afterthought, she whispered, "We haven't spoken much these last days, so I didn't know."

"Jacob assured me they'll be in before the blackouts. And Ginny and Dale just arrived back from the bookshop, so all are accounted for."

"Of course. Thank you." Charlotte noticed the girls lingering on the steps, giving coy glances down in the direction of the open library doors. What must they think? What had Eden told them? It helped that Charlotte needn't have to ask; Amos slipped over as if he'd read her thoughts, discreetly closed the doors, then joined her back in the center of the room.

Amos had proven to be an oak on the estate the last few days, doing far more than required as agent. He'd supported her. Sitting beside her through each meeting. As the autos came and went and the stack of cards grew. He'd even gone so far as to carry an Enfield anytime the Land Girls were out on the estate. Yet for all that solidarity, he held an air of unease now as silence clung to the air between them.

"There is something else."

"Aye. There is."

"Well, this isn't 1914. I suppose I can be alone in a library with the estate agent in my own home." Though that was the best of lies. Charlotte played aloof and in control as she stood before him, yet her insides were dangerously devolving into mush. Amos had no idea what he looked like, even now. Even in trousers and a worn work shirt rolled to tanned forearms, years behind a bookshop counter hadn't hurt his rugged build, though the time had altered his spirit. She awkwardly offered him a seat on one of the brocade settees by the hearth and walked over to sit opposite. "Come. Sit. I could use the warmth of the fire."

He waited for her, then took a seat. "I'll have to go before too long." Amos hooked a thumb toward the gravel drive beyond the windows. "Fire-watch duty tonight for Provost Howard."

"Yes, of course."

"I don't wish to alarm you." He leaned in, lowering his voice though no one was close enough to hear. "But what do you make of all this?"

"What do you mean? The whole officialdom of England having invaded our doorstep these last days?"

"Aye."

A one-word reply: typical Amos. He didn't waste and rarely minced words. But it must have meant something that neither did he hide his scars from her. Even now, as firelight glowed against his profile, those hazels stared back with such intention and did not turn away as he awaited her opinion.

"It doesn't sit well, Amos. None of it."

"Not for me either. I've taken enough reports from County Warwickshire in the last year to fill a dozen books for the Home Guard. We found the German paraphernalia in the hedge. That is serious. But not so out of line with what London has seen thus far, with German bombers in the sky every blessed night. And we had a fighter plane crash right here on the estate, which caused a heap of telephone calls and mounds of paperwork to wade through."

Is that what it did? Charlotte remembered it quite differently, seeing the horror of Amos's blood on her hands every time she closed her eyes now, and she had to suppress the memory of an auto ride where she was certain he was slipping away in her arms.

She cleared her throat. "I've given numerous accounts of that night over the last days."

"As have I. But even then, I've never seen a response like this." He braced his elbows on his knees and laced his hands together, like he was trying to make sense of it all. "I have to wonder why every outfit in London would descend upon us now."

"What do you think it is then? You must have an idea or you wouldn't have stayed to speak with me."

"I don't have anything sure, but rumors are out there."

"The rumors being . . . ?" She swallowed hard. Her breath locked. *Please, no.* "Invasion?"

He shook his head. "A targeted attack."

"What—here? In Coventry?"

"We can't rule it out. Those uniforms were a mite concerned about the factories on the edge of the estate. And keen to know every last detail about them, down to how many buttercups grow in the meadow behind. It makes sense now, with rumors we've heard from the Home Guard."

"What rumors?"

"There was an RAF attack on Munich just days ago. It didn't do much compared to the Luftwaffe's raids over London, but enough to shake German confidence. And some think Hitler's not likely to let England get away with it. Some in the Home Guard believe we have more factories in Coventry than those known in the manufacturing hub—*shadow factories*, they're called—positioned outside the city and producing Spitfire parts for near the whole of the RAF. If the enemy became aware of that and could take them out in reprisal, we wouldn't be able to keep our planes in the sky. At least not for long."

A heavy exhale escaped her lips as the ramifications set in. "If that's true, and we have clear evidence of German presence on this estate, then . . ."

"Coventry could be in their sights. But it's all just a guessing game. It could just as easily be London or Birmingham. Edinburgh, possibly. Or a hundred other places."

Heaven help them if the Germans had gleaned information on the Spitfires or production at the factories. Bombs falling on innocent citizens and decimating whole neighborhoods was brutal enough. But for Coventry to be in the Luftwaffe's crosshairs for their critical support of the RAF . . . The consequences could be disastrous for Britain, and the world.

"What do we do? Surely one of the names on those cards can give assurance that London is doing all it can to protect us."

"Do you not think if they could give assurance, they'd have shored up London against Blitz bombs by now too?"

Right. That did make sense.

The battle had raged over London for as many weeks, with Britain holding on by a thread as citizens slept in the Underground and the RAF backfilled devastating losses to keep pilots in the skies. And between all the moving parts for them—with Land Girls, the tea queue, and bookshops tossed in the mix—there was much to fret over. Though Charlotte's inclination was usually to act first and apologize later, that strategy couldn't be properly employed now. Not when this had the power to change everything.

"We'll telephone Whitehall then. The prime minister wouldn't know my name, nor be likely to give a fig about the countess title. But surely someone in Churchill's cabinet would take our report in favor of credibility to these rumors? They'd have to listen then."

"These are the cleverest thinking heads in all of England. I'd say they already know." Silence ensued for long seconds between them as his words sank in. "Look, we'll do all we can. But we ought to have everyone stay close to the estate for now."

"Agreed."

"And I've asked Jacob to check in at Waverley Novels and the

St. Mary's Street Centre several times each day. I'd feel better knowing all is well when I cannot be here myself."

Charlotte stared back then, meeting his gaze eye to eye. And found not the animosity of the past or uncertainty of their present plaguing them but a softness that said Amos had been at her side for days—and was still here, sitting across from her now—because he genuinely cared.

"How will you manage without a telephone?"

"I don't mind accepting defeat, *sometimes*." Amos's reluctant grin confirmed it, though he added, "It wasn't difficult to have one put back in."

"You did?" She brightened.

"Aye," he whispered. "Someone once reminded me you don't have to win every battle to triumph in the bigger war."

Oh, fortune; could you please favor the brave now? Charlotte swallowed hard but kept her posture composed, pleading with her nerves to back her up. If this was a door opening, may she be strong enough to step through.

"Should we . . . talk about that day at the bookshop? I meant every word I said about the telephone. And all that came after."

Her heart sank a measure with his silence. Was it Gretna Green all over again? Had fear played her a fool again?

"You have no reply?"

"I wish I could, but . . . no. I can't. And if you knew everything, you wouldn't want me to. You'd never want to speak to me again." Discomfort gave way to some odd sense of anguish washing over his features. Amos shook his head and, as if he'd just remembered his scars, gave a sharp turn to angle his profile away. Then half rose, intent to leave. "The blackouts. I ought to go."

Leaning forward, Charlotte reached out, taking the liberty to brush her fingertips against his hand enough to hold him still.

"You don't have to," she whispered entreatingly. "Please? *Stay*."

Amos settled back again, though he hung on the edge of the

settee as if ready to spring. But even then, he refused to look her in the eye.

The night Charlotte had kept vigil at the hospital, she'd seen the hip flask on the bedside table. And Jacob had relayed, out of genuine care, a secret: he believed Amos was taking to drink in his chamber—every night, and sometimes during the days too—since he'd been released from the hospital. Even now, her glance drifted down to Amos's boot. Was the slight rise against his calf evidence he still carried the silver-plated lifeline on his person?

"Amos?" Charlotte breathed out his name, soft and tender as she could, and brushed her thumb against the thick white scars on his hand. "I know about the bottles."

He snapped his attention back. "Bottles?"

"I found them by accident, mind you, that first day of the tea queue. But I've wanted to help—to say something about them since then. It never seemed the right moment. Especially not in front of the others."

"So you scold me in private? Because you think that's why I was late the night of the plane crash—because of drink? And you blame me for what happened."

The line of his jaw hardened as he clenched it. He stood, abrupt in breaking away from where her hands had tried to comfort his. And then he turned like he'd bust right through the library doors if he could.

"No! You misunderstand. I don't fight you on it. Nor do I judge. It is the opposite." She followed on his heels, catching up with a hold to his elbow from behind. "I simply say that whatever it is . . . you can tell me. You can trust me, Amos."

"You have no right!" he blasted back. "And you can't understand. You can never understand."

"Then help me to." Charlotte coaxed him with the truth, holding on, giving him a gentle turn at the shoulders. "Look around you, Amos! All of the people who have stood in the way—they are gone.

This library is empty. Save for us. *You* and *me*. I made a promise once that every year on the day Will died, I'd go to St. Michael's and light a candle in my husband's memory. And I have honored that. For his daughter. For the brave sacrifice he made. And for all that we lost in that war. But that is the past. And I'm standing before you now with a new promise, telling you that we needn't run from having a future anymore."

"No? You think I'm the one who's running?"

"Whatever do you mean?"

"Why don't you play the cello?" Amos stared down, almost looking straight through her with the intensity of the accusation. It was a deflection, of course, an attack made from his own wounds. Though Charlotte knew he was right. And hated that the arrow he'd sent from the quiver hit the dead-center bull's-eye of her heart.

"I don't have to explain myself to you."

"No. You don't. Because when we were kids, that day I sold your trunk in the secondhand shop, I saw it even then. You loved that instrument as I loved the written word. And you were willing to give up everything for that love. And yet I saw your cello that day I was in Eden Books—stuffed in a corner. Hidden away and covered in dust like it never mattered to you at all. When it used to be what you lived and breathed for. Yet no one's here to stop you from playing now. I am not the only one hiding pain, am I?"

"That is different, and you know it."

"It is the same."

"Then surely you must see whatever plagues us cannot be so bad to lock us away from each other forever. I would play again . . . if my heart had a reason. And I believe if you were to share what tortures yours, then we might meet in the center of this messy, broken world we live in. And find solace in that place. To be known—isn't that all anyone truly wants?"

"And you can look beyond all of the past between us?"

"I'm saying that I can. And I believe you can do the same."

He shook, voice rough as he uttered, "You ask too much of me."

"I ask nothing, save for you to know you don't have to do this alone. Don't you see?" Charlotte searched his face—that beautiful, scarred visage she knew so well—and stared back into the anguish in his eyes. She raised her palms, ever gentle, and placed them to hold either side of his face, drawing his gaze down to look at her. "You were not alone. Not when you earned these scars and not when you brought them home from war. Not when the plane crashed in the field that night. Just as you are not alone now."

"I *must* be, milady." Amos seemed to battle with something, then peeled her hands from him with acute pain etched in his face. "In order to protect you and Lady Eden . . . I must go. And next time, I won't be coming back."

CHAPTER TWENTY-TWO

14 November 1940
Bayley Lane
Coventry, England

6:15 p.m.

*T*his is how we thumb our noses at Hitler," Dale declared, tidying the stack of the latest edition of *The British Book-sellers* bulletin on their table tucked in the snug. "We hand out as many of these as we can here at the pub, then dance the jitterbug behind blackout curtains all night."

"It's that easy?" Eden asked.

"Not easy at all." Dale slid a sheet across the table so Eden could take a look. "But the bookshops are the spirit of Bayley Lane. And no amount of bombs can diminish that."

The brand of moxie their Land Girls leader possessed was well timed. They'd dolled up, headed to the city, and slipped through the doors of the Lion's Gate just as the blackouts took serious effect. Whilst Drapers' Hall had canceled the official dance, and night set in as another in which Coventry would be hanging on tenterhooks, the pub next door offered the overflow of guests music and craic—at least until ordered to close at nine o'clock.

At a glance Eden could see every barstool occupied. A bench by the door was piled with a miscellany of gas masks, satchels, and torches. And musicians circled the piano at a stone hearth, playing mandolins, guitars, and fiddles, giving a folksy vibe to the impromptu dance scene. The Land Girls had fallen into the mix of it all, joining factory workers and shopkeepers alike to blow off steam after the last grueling days of work and waiting out the long nights in shelters.

"What do you think?"

"It's marvelous, Dale. Truly." Eden beamed for how the bulletin had come together. And in a blink, too, showing Dale's obvious prowess for her writing ambitions. "I heard Mama say that when the WLA chairwoman's secretary looked in at Holt Manor this week, she took a copy when she left."

"She didn't."

"Yes. And mentioned something about the WLA in development of an official handbook and a magazine for volunteers, *The Land Girl*. The Ministry of Agriculture is said to begin publishing the first editions out of Sussex in the spring. I'd say they'll be impressed enough with your bulletin that you could expect to hear from them. Who knows what might happen?"

"Well, that colors me speechless for the first time. I wonder— how many new doors might open for women once we survive all this?" Dale tapped her palm to the tabletop in time with the music. "It feels rather wild, seeing the owners chuck the rule book to allow women in the pub tonight. I'm quite impressed with how far Coventry's come."

"Not so fast. See the old guard lined up by the bar?" Eden felt frustration that whilst war affected many things, it still had not managed to reach its tendrils into the ancient traditions of the old English pub. The line of gents stretched from one end of the bar to the other, their eyes peeled to guard barstools from any female interlopers. "They may have let women in, but they've relegated us to two spaces allowed: hidden away in snugs or in a gentleman's arms on the dance floor. And even then, they're watching like hawks."

"Then I admire their dedication. I may have to go abscond with a barstool just to see their faces." Dale laughed, a little impetuous gleam in her eyes. "Will Her Ladyship be joining us? Surely they would show your mother respect."

"They would, but no." Eden could answer that in truth. A countess in a public house? Even Mama wasn't that progressive. "This is not exactly Mama's cup of tea, even if she does champion a woman's place alongside the men. I think she'd have much preferred we stay close to the estate just now, times being what they are."

"But you're of age. And able to make your own decisions. You *should* dance whilst you're young. None of us knows how long this war will last; we have to live despite uncertainty. Surely Her Ladyship understands that."

"She does, if anyone."

Dale's countenance softened as she leaned in, tapping a manicured fingernail against her pint glass. "Have you spoken with her since learning of the Spitfires?"

"No." Eden toyed with the edge of the bulletin in her hand. "Not as much."

So went the understatement of the world.

Between the secrets swirling around Mama and Mr. Darby and her discovery that Jacob, too, had known of the Spitfires and that information was kept from her until the day the paratrooper gear was found . . . it was a dominoes' fall of little betrayals on all fronts.

Eden fiddled with the dangling cherries of one of her earrings as she looked over the bulletin, trying to be ever so clever so as not to let her gaze wander around the scene over the top of the paper.

"I'd wager a guess at what you're thinking. That terribly handsome Yank of yours is late." Dale blew out smoke from her cig and flipped her wrist, checking her watch. "And here I thought that man had more gumption than not to show at all."

Eden snapped her attention back to their snug. "Jacob is not *my* Yank."

"No? Why are you looking for him then?" Dale grinned and downed the last swig of liquid in her glass. "Remember that day I cut your hair? We all saw the look on that chap's face when he came out of the back room. Jacob nearly dumped two steaming kettles of water all over himself when he saw you and jaw-dropped it to the floor. That was a checkmate if ever I've seen one, doll—for him if not for you."

Eden's cheeks burned. A little flutter had shown up in her middle when he'd held her in the bookshop's back room, and the memory of it had lingered in secret, quite past its expiration date.

Dale lit a cig and pointed in the direction of Alec and Flo in the corner of the room.

"Those two have been locked in a dance since we arrived; I'd expect to hear wedding bells within a fortnight. Ainsley managed to snag the only RAF uniform to walk through the door tonight. And I've been up and down from this seat so many times, the heels on my dancing shoes are thin as paper. But you?" Dale gave a little *tsk-tsk* of the tongue. "Not one dance. And in that jolly new frock, no less. I could cry for the tragedy of it all."

"It does fit like a glove." Eden breathed out, atingle as she scanned the pub and palmed the row of tiny red buttons at the nip-waist of her new ivory and red pin-dot frock.

"I told you—our Ainsley is a bona fide genius."

Certainly seemed to be.

The Ainsley rush job was a wonder considering the limited time they'd had that week; their expert seamstress had taken older-season dresses and a few basic measurements and used her time in the Andersons to render magic with a needle and spool of thread. By the time the sun had come up the first day, Flo had a kicky navy number with gold trim. On the next, Dale had a wine number with scallop sleeves and a daring square neckline—perfect for dancing. And for that evening, Eden wore a dress with enough chic that it could have fallen right off a Paris runway. Partnered with freshly docked ebony waves and the deep cherry pop of borrowed lipstick on her pout, Eden could finally see a sisterly resemblance to the Land Girls' cherished screen siren.

"She's a Land Girl's secret weapon. And just in time too." Dale doused her cig, then gave a fluff to the riot of pin curls at her nape for good measure. "Mayday, mayday. Stormy seas ahead," she whispered, nudging Eden's shoulder before she smiled at two uniforms staked at the end of the bar.

"What does that mean?"

Too late. The uniforms stepped over, and she was about to find out.

"We noticed you ladies looking lonely over here," the first chap piped up, leaning into the snug doorway. He had the dark and handsome look down. With a little risk in the eyes. And far too much arrogance to be masked. "Care to dance?"

"Madly," Dale chimed and shot up, tugging Eden to her feet alongside. She wrapped her arm around the trim of Eden's waist, gave a little squeeze. "Go on." She nudged Eden toward a uniform with soft brown hair and too much pomade. "Take that sweet skirt for a spin. See how she flies."

Eden placed her hand in the uniform's to lead her to the dance floor, only to find her breath was stolen when she nearly bumped into the interceptor waiting there.

Jacob stood in his posh suit at the center of the dance floor, looking every bit the Mr. Detroit who'd walked into Eden Books that first day. Gold cuff links winked at his wrists. Heaven help her, but he'd shaved, too, and the scent was like something out of a Cary Grant cologne ad from *Vogue* magazine . . . and suddenly the handsome face she'd come to know so well and ice-blue eyes she had been looking for all night were upon her, and prepared to vie for a dance with the farmer-heiress playing the part of Hedy Lamarr.

"I'm cutting in." Jacob ignored the chap, instead offering his palm to her.

With a lift of the brow, the uniform bit back, "The lady's promised me."

"Oh, Lady Eden would have to be dancing first for you to cut in, Mr. Cole," Dale remarked, nosing in on the dance floor like the sight of two suitors locking horns was the greatest thing she'd beheld since her first pair of silk stockings. "That's etiquette."

She tossed a wink in Eden's direction with enough mischief that said not only had she seen the instant Jacob stepped through the pub door, she'd orchestrated a dance with the uniform simply to goad the Yank into making a move.

Marvelous. No help there. Eden would have to handle this first . . . and quite possibly kill Dale later.

Jacob kept his glare locked on her and repeated, softer, but with firm intention, "May I cut in, Lady Eden?"

"She heard you the first time. And still says no." The uniform spat a slur and pulled on Eden's hand, edging her behind his shoulder. "We know who you are—the Yank. There are rumors about you at the Home Guard. Enough that she doesn't want to be seen with you."

"Take your hands off her." Jacob took a step forward, hands curling into the message of fists at his sides.

"I won't dance with either of you if you don't stop this nonsense." Eden sidestepped between the men to face the uniform. "You are misinformed somehow. Whatever you allude to, this gentleman is a friend of the Home Guard. You can check with Amos Darby at the St. Mary's Street Centre if you question it."

"You mean you'd dance with this dirty—"

"That'll be enough of that." She held her palm out before the gent's uniform shirt at the shoulder to ease him off. "Thank you for the offer, sir. But we're finished."

The men exchanged steel glares, but blessed be a new war didn't start in the pub. The uniform took his pint to brood in another corner. Dancers dispersed. Dale bubbled with a delighted smile that her plan had worked. And the two were left standing in the center of the floor as the pianist and fiddler began a softer-toned version of "If I Didn't Care" to lilt in the background.

"Delicately done, Mr. Cole."

"I'm sorry." He shook his head like he truly was sorry, even if he had a little bluster left over. "Will you still honor me?"

"Lovely. And the old guard at the bar will never allow women in here again," Eden whispered under her breath, trying not to laugh as she allowed Jacob to take her in his arms and ease them into swaying.

"I should have shoved that pompous—"

"Are you going to threaten every man in Coventry, or are we going to dance?" Eden gave a playful slap to his shoulder to shut him up. "What did he mean, though? What rumors?"

"I don't particularly care what anyone thinks. Least of all that sod stewing in his pint over there. I needed to speak with you," he answered, totally unromantic. And then in the same breath, he recouped his losses by adding, "Then I saw you, and . . . I needed a dance more."

"Oh," she breathed out, the little speech redeeming him enough for the moment. "Why the suit?"

"Why the dress?" he punched back.

She tipped her shoulders in a dainty shrug. "I don't know. A girl should fancy putting on a pretty new frock every once in a while. Though I didn't think you were joining us tonight."

"Her Ladyship was concerned when she returned from the bookshop and found the manor empty. I changed quick as I could after Mr. Cox and I finished up for the day, and she sent me after you ladies."

"She didn't receive my note?"

He shook his head, his brow furrowing with it. "What note?"

"I left it in the mail tray in the entry hall. To say where we'd gone."

"I don't know about any note. Alec mentioned earlier that you ladies were going out dancing tonight at Drapers' Hall. Thought it a good idea to try there soon as I could make it. And then I found out people came to the pub instead. But I'll need to telephone Her Ladyship that I've found you, lest she worry."

"No. I should do it."

Foolish. The ramifications washed over her. For a night of dancing, she'd sent Jacob out on the roads into the city and Mama into a frenzy. All because Eden was cross about the Spitfires and felt she'd been slighted on her own estate. And had no answers about what was truly bothering her: the long-brewing storm between Coventry's booksellers.

"Jacob, I'm sorry. You'll be stuck in the city all night now."

"As are you."

"Yes, but it was impetuous. We should have thought better than to—"

Between the music and dimmed lights and unavoidable flustering in her middle anytime he was this near, Eden turned a heel, nearly careening into a couple dancing at their side. Until Jacob righted her. Drew her closer, like he had once before. But this time, he didn't let go. Like he didn't *want* to let go.

"Those shoes again?" he whispered, his fingertips giving a tender brush against the curve at the small of her back. "Don't worry, Lady Eden. I won't let you fall."

Jacob smiled, just a hint, and looked down, his eyes piercing hers from mere inches away as their gentle sway brushed her skirt in a caress against bare legs.

"You may look like a screen siren in this pub, and I might have to fight off every chap in Coventry for just one dance, but I know you too. You've got a beating heart under that beautiful, tough exterior. You'd give up anything you might want for yourself if it meant upholding your father's legacy and saving the livelihood of everyone on the estate. And that sod over there isn't nearly good enough for you. Not if he tried for a million years. Not even for one dance of your time."

"And who is?" Breathless, she waited for him to answer. And fell deeper into doubt as the seconds ticked by with his silence.

Remember how infuriating this man is. Yes, and Eden had to remember he was the only thing standing in the way of Holt Manor's security. Jacob was dashing in a suit. Dangerous when he smiled. And far too comfortable a fixture in Coventry in the too little time he'd been among them. She was, under no circumstances, to fall for this man.

Or perhaps she was to fall no farther?

"Um . . . you said you needed to speak with me?"

"I do."

"What is it then? We're not hiding something else on the estate, are we?"

"No. I mean, I'd tell you if we were . . ." Jacob fumbled through the reply. A little too fast. And sighed. Like the next words out of his mouth wouldn't be nearly as sweet as the previous ones were. "The inheritance case is moving forward."

"Oh. I see. And what does that mean?" Silly question. Of course it meant a lot. It could mean nearly everything to them both. Eden half teased, half hoped, masking apprehension by adding a light, "I won't have to see you across a courtroom in the near future, will I?"

"Not exactly. But it does mean . . ." Jacob shook his head, a shade of indecision entering his gaze as he looked down on her. "I have to leave. I'm on the six o'clock back to London tomorrow."

CHAPTER TWENTY-THREE

3 November 1915
The Western Front
Near Artois, France

*G*erman sniper fire worked with surgical precision.

It had taken too many men to count over the last weeks, leaving Amos no illusions when every square inch of their unit was covered in grit and blood and the stench of smoke from burning flesh after the battle for the coal-mining village called Loos. And though their fighting men in the BEF had finally busted the German line—and the fighting between sides was rumored to be reaching a stalemate—enemy snipers had rooted in the area. And were choosing when and where to pick off British Army officers, one by one.

Where are you hiding?

Tapping his index finger against the bolt of his Enfield, Amos eyed the BEF flank from horseback and scanned the backdrop of the coal mines' "Tower Bridge"—the pithead lift named by British soldiers for its likeness to London's own Tower Bridge. The thing did look like a bridge, standing alone, not hauling crater-sized mounds of coal as it used to. Now it was the only structure still untouched by bombs, looming high enough behind the village to be seen from the British trenches.

His job? Keep track of their British Army officers positioned along the tree line whilst watching for hints of movement in the hollows leading to town. Amos eyed the stretch from the bridge they'd taken to the mountains of debris shoved on either side, keeping the road clear so the trickle of British supply trucks could get in and red cross–bearing trucks could roll the steady stream of casualties out.

Will was out front, the captain leading their mounted unit with sergeants flanking just behind. A bomb shook the earth nearby— ordinary now but still jarring each time. And enough that Amos flipped his view from the bridge to zero in on the officers as blackened tree trunks splintered and cracked behind them, and debris busted apart like a fireworks display.

It was a perfect split-second diversion.

A whistle cut through the trees—*zing*—and one sergeant was picked off. The bullet hit with such a ruthless sting, the officer was blown off behind his steed, the horse rearing back when the sergeant yanked the reins as he fell.

"No, don't cluster together," Amos breathed out, keeping eyes peeled through drifting smoke as Will gave the order to halt his men from their charge. And stopping them in what he couldn't know was the worst possible spot—before one of the few buildings left standing against the flank.

"Spread out . . . Spread out . . ."

Once a sniper gave away his location with his first shot, it was customary for him to flee and find another den in which to hide. But the manners of this marksman proved disparate. Odd in the way he didn't seem inclined to follow protocol for his own safety. And everything in Amos's gut said the Germans' retreat from the bridge left little for them to care about now. If they were poised to lose ground, they'd take out as many of the enemy as they could before being pushed back.

Amos tore his gaze away from the trees, searching, scanning the side of the building with a wounded façade and the eerie sight of shredded fabric drifting on a breeze from the third floor.

You could have made it from that vantage point.

And now you've got nothing to lose . . .

Checking the windows, sweeping the view floor to floor from the south side that was completely gone . . . Amos calculated the just-right angle for the bullet to have made its way to the unfortunate sergeant, whose body now lay heaped in a spreading crimson pool beside his horse's hooves. Amos slid down from his mount, needing stable footing to search the sniper's hideaway, whilst watching out of the corner of his eye as Will moved up and his sergeant held back at his left side.

Another blast. A whistle cut through the trees before Amos could do anything but watch.

Another officer down.

Certain now, Amos slapped his mount's hindquarters and threw himself to the ground, lying low against a debris pile as the second officer crumpled off his mount. The riderless horse fled over the bridge like a ghost animal, charging through smoke that had gathered in a haze over the water.

The sniper had played his hand. Taken the shot. And, uncaring, revealed the certainty of where he hid.

That's two . . . Will's next.

This time, Amos had him—the third-floor window overlooking the bridge and the road that cut through, where a tiny glint of sun to metal flashed from the curve of a windowsill meeting a broken wall of stone. But without the critical aid of a scope on his own Enfield, nor the skill of a marksman to back up the shot, all Amos could do now was hope to get Toreador and his captain out of the line of fire.

The unit retreated. Another bomb blast crumbled the edge of the bridge, a great *crack* of stone searing the air and spreading the horses that were already on the jittery side. Amos took the fortuitous seconds as the cloud of smoke drifted over to bolt into the fray. With his rifle trained, he moved along the bank of the stream, keeping low and out of sight until he reached Will's side.

From behind, Amos lurched, yanking Will off his mount, plunging their captain into boot-deep water just as a bullet sang through the trees.

"Have you gone mad, Darby?" Will screamed, fighting with the reins Amos snapped out of his grip. "My men!"

"Your men are dead, sir," Amos bit back, pulling Will with a rough hand to the shoulder to stop him from angling his boot in the stirrup. He shoved Will back, keeping them low behind the rubble piled at Toreador's flank.

"Get behind the horse."

"If I don't get back up, we'll lose this entire unit!"

"And if you don't stay behind this horse, that sniper will kill you next!" Amos pointed to Will's ear, the flesh at the top of his earlobe and a line of blood rolling down the side of his neck.

Will ran a fingertip over the nick, crimson marring his hand.

"I will not leave my men," Will gritted out, looking to the tree line beyond the bridge. The view proved too murky to see through the smoke, but both of them could hear the guttural screams of wounded men and mounts suffering as more bombs blasted down.

"Are you mad? Think of Charlotte. And Eden. Those sergeants lying dead over there . . . He only shot them when they moved away from your horse." Amos shook his head. Then pointed the end of his rifle to the crag of rock on the building's side and the busted window on the third floor. "There. Third floor. It's him. And he's willing to wait for a clean kill. He'll amend his shot if he thinks the animal can be saved."

"How do you know this?"

"Doesn't matter," Amos blasted back, entreating with every bit of sway he owned to convince Will to listen. "At least once in your life, allow yourself to find an ounce of value in a lowborn man's judgment. I'm telling you this is true enough to save your life."

The rattling *pop-pop-pop* of the devil's piano followed another blast, and the bridge became a horrifying shooting gallery. They watched the road from the bank below, and the sight of their cavalry unit scattering under the Germans' last-ditch effort to hold the flank, machine-gun fire punishing through the trees.

The agony of watching men and horses riddled with bullets

proved too much to bear. Will shoved Amos off-center and tried climbing back up.

"If you go, you're good as dead," Amos warned, righting himself to yank Will down by the seat of his trousers and adding, "This unit is *gone.*"

And it was true, God help them.

The flank had fallen. The bridge was blasted in two. Barbed-wire barriers became traps through smoke, and nests of Jerries peppered the road with machine-gun fire as men fled and horses bled to carry them . . . There'd be nothing left in a matter of minutes.

"I won't be a coward! I'll die with honor alongside my men."

"No—you're going home to her!" Amos screamed, hauling Will up by the lapels until they crashed together, nose to nose. "Do you hear me? You are going to survive this war. Even if I have to shoot every Jerry out here to make sure you do!"

Will stared back, stunned it seemed, as blood ran a track from his ear through the mud and ash smeared across his face. And didn't move until Amos set him down, shoved a rifle in his hands, and yanked on his collar to get them moving the direction of the BEF uniforms retreating from the bridge.

"See? The unit must have the order to fall back. Now come on or I swear I'll shoot you myself!"

Amos reached out for Toreador's reins, the stallion holding firm where they'd left him on the side of the road.

Thank you, old friend. For the animal's fearlessness provided a shield when they needed it, and Amos knew there wasn't enough that could be said for a steed to stand like steel when the world was blasted to bits around them. If they lived through this . . . that soldier on four legs would have made it so.

Bullets ratcheted in a deafening chorus through the trees.

They ran, Amos not thinking about the threat of mines or death or the unit that was being decimated all around. He just kept Toreador at Will's side and his shoulders as an obstacle between the building and Will's back, in lockstep with the captain's ankles until they could once again see a British trench to dive in.

Whether he was dead or not, Amos wouldn't have had the time to judge.

All he knew was the world stopped. A whistle sang. Toreador reared. And Amos fell behind a curtain of black, never having heard the bullet that took him down.

→·←

14 November 1940
St. Mary's Street
Coventry, England

6:17 p.m.

Amos had seen the Air Raid and Report Control Centre in battle mode before.

Just never like this.

RAF reports had increased warnings since the afternoon. They'd picked up to a steady pace toward evening blackouts. And by the time Amos's pocket watch chimed through the six o'clock hour, reports were burning up the ticker tape into St. Mary's Street Centre with as many alerts as it seemed stars in the sky, and command center telephones that nearly rang off the tabletops in response.

A clock ticked on the wall, unheard through the cacophony of men's voices. Rifles and tin hats were readied at each man's station, should they have to burst aboveground at a moment's notice. And in the midst of it all Amos sat, feeling his hands tied as the news turned dire.

"Moon's full tonight, Amos. So bright, it's a spotlight in the streets."

"Aye," Amos muttered to Patrick—the middle-aged butcher by

day, Home Guard member by night, who was manning the telephone station next to him. "It's what we keep hearing."

"Provost Howard's on my line now." Patrick paused from speaking into his headset, then looked down, scanning notes on the desk. "That's it, Dick. Too many to count. We've all sorts coming in . . . An estate sixty kilometers outside the city reported a downed Junker on the east side." He flipped to the next sheet. "A host of stations on the coast reporting birds in the air. Nothing confirmed by ARP or RAF officials as yet. But looks as though signal trajectory isn't London this time, so everyone's scrambling."

An eerie pause later, he looked to Amos, nodding as he repeated, "Right. Fire-watchers to the nave roof. We'll make sure they get to you." Another pause, then, "If you need to make that decision, then do it. We don't expect you to come back down and call in. We'll all know if it's real."

"What was that Provost Howard said?" Amos asked as soon as Patrick hung up the line.

"He's calling fire-watchers to the nave roof. Was asking whether we ought to ring the cathedral bells twelve times if we have to alert everyone within hearing distance . . . to take up arms."

"The signal the air invasion's begun. We know what to do if that happens," Amos muttered, getting ready to make the call and alert the AFS closest to Bayley Lane. "But I wouldn't chase shadows just yet. Not until we've something real to fret over. We're still waiting on the RAF to give us the facts."

"Right." Patrick faded back into his desk, headset taking the next call that rang in.

No. Something's different tonight . . .

They're headed here.

Amos's mind dreaded it. His heart defied it. And even now, as experience said he ought to listen to his gut—for it had saved him once before—Amos wished more than anything he could say that it wasn't telling him to pay heed now.

"God help us wherever they go," he said, only to himself.

Charlotte. Amos swept his headset back on with the thought of her, his hand shaking as he dialed out to connect with Holt Manor. Breathless until the line clicked, he exhaled relief.

"Mr. Cole on the line, please? This is Mr. Darby."

"He is not here, sir," a female voice squeaked. "Mr. Cole has gone out."

"Mrs. Mills? You say Jacob's gone out? At this hour, after the blackouts?"

"Yes. He's gone after the girls, sir . . ."

The usually sage housekeeper had an edge to her voice that was too urgent, too laced with something that hinged on those last words. A thousand thoughts attacked at once, from the proximity of the factories to the paratrooper who'd vanished into thin air, to any number of scenarios that could render a man powerless to intervene.

"What's happened?"

"A right mess. The Land Girls and Lady Eden—they've gone to Drapers' Hall for the dance tonight. They were all aflutter over their new frocks after working all day."

His mind shifted tracks as the woman droned on. This wasn't ill news—yet. Drapers' Hall had a sure shelter beneath that could fit two hundred souls if needed.

They were still alright.

"Aye. But they've a sound shelter at Drapers' Hall. The girls will be fine. May I speak with Her Ladyship, please?"

"No, sir," she said after a delay, her voice wavering as meek as a mouse on the edge of tears. "Her Ladyship is not here either."

Amos shot to his feet, the force spilling a cup of coffee off the side of the desk. "What?"

"She returned late from the bookshop for dropping some of the wives back at their farms, after the late shifts at the factories. When she realized the manor was empty, she requested Mr. Cole go after the girls. I informed Her Ladyship she'd received a note in the mail tray from Lady Eden. But seems a telegram had come in for Mr. Cole as well. She found it in the tray after he'd gone and read it by mistake."

"What was this telegram?" Men were beginning to look at him. Thinking he'd best get control, Amos mopped up the mess with a towel and eased back into his chair.

"I don't know, sir. But milady went pale as a ghost right before my eyes and called for the chauffeur to bring her auto around. She left after Mr. Cole without another word."

"For Drapers' Hall?"

"She did not say. But I'd venture a yes. And I could not keep her," she sniffed through the line. "Though I tried."

"Aye. Of course you tried." Amos bade the woman to let go of any guilt, no matter what the night would bring. This was all his doing. Since the afternoon in the library. And he knew it. "Go on to the Andersons now, Mrs. Mills. And take the whole staff with you, please. And the first-aid kits, Waldybags, and torches too. I beg of you, don't wait for the sirens tonight."

"We will, sir. Godspeed."

The line clicked.

Right. Drapers' Hall. He checked the clock on the wall. Charlotte could be there in twenty or so minutes. Fewer, maybe, with the moon shining bright as it was. And when she arrived, the shelter at Drapers' Hall would be sound. Safer than the Andersons in the Holt Manor rose garden, especially if planes were signaled toward the factories by the far fields . . . Or was it worse to be in the city center just now, knowing what could come?

Amos tore off his headset and threw it against the wall.

He raked a hand through his hair, then braced the angry palm at his neck, wishing more than anything that he had any measure of control in what was shaping up to be a hopeless situation. If Amos hadn't failed Will all those years ago . . . if he'd owned even a shred of faith that things would work in their favor . . . he'd have known what to do now.

"Blimey." Patrick breathed out and reached over with a firm grip to Amos's shoulder.

Amos turned, found the man scrawling notes like his pencil was afire. Patrick gave a stern "ta" through the phone, then pulled his headset back off his ears and wheeled his chair over, slapping the paper down on the desk in front of Amos.

"Dorset sighting: Kampfgruppe 100. Thirteen pathfinders counted, all headed due north. Signal beam points to Coventry, but they're not following direct—yet."

A hush fell over the room.

Seemed all were thinking the same. All seeing the same dread in each other's eyes. The truth washed over, silencing the chatter so the only sounds left were the ticking clock and hearts beating in everyone's throats.

"Pathfinders carry flares, Amos."

"And the Luftwaffe won't wait for sunrise to do their damage tonight," he admitted, feeling sick to his stomach and wanting to punch a fist through the wall at the same time. "They'll drop incendiaries as beacons for the next planes to come. And so it will go."

"What do we do?" Patrick shuddered.

Helplessness coursed through Amos as he thought of the people he cared about most, all in an unpredictable line of fire. And he could do nothing on this earth to stop it. He felt the flask in his boot, sinking like a stone against his leg. Wanting to curse the burning liquid that had owned him for so long and was trying to own him still. Even in that moment. Even as the worst was yet to come.

"Back to the phones, lads," Amos muttered, picking up his own headset. "Someone get some fresh brew. It's going to be a long night."

That morning from St. Michael's weeks ago came back to mind, when Provost Howard had summoned Amos to the cathedral. He'd walked out of those doors into the sunlight daring to hope, despite what was to come—hope for the first time in all the years since that day at Artois. But what would a man do now? Stand his ground on the nave roof though the enemy charged straight for him, dropping fire from the sky? Amos had nothing left but rage and blinding fear that threatened to upend his senses so he almost didn't know which way was up.

"Patrick?" Amos kept his voice low, all whilst wishing he didn't have to say what he knew he must.

"Aye, Amos?"

"When Dorset is confirmed, it's enough to put us at Air Raid Message Yellow." Resolved, Amos knew—but still dreaded—what they were headed into next. "Once we know the attack is to be Coventry, ready the sirens for an Air Raid Message Red. And might be a fair idea to start praying for cloud cover now, before it's too late."

CHAPTER TWENTY-FOUR

14 November 1940
Bayley Lane
Coventry, England

6:48 p.m.

*R*esentment alone couldn't have pushed Charlotte through the pub door.

Neither could anger. Nor disappointment, though she was greatly unsettled that her initial doubts about Jacob Cole had proven valid. As she hung at the edge of the dance floor for long moments, having spotted Eden in Jacob's arms—so close their foreheads brushed with each sway of dance steps—it was the gut punch of what Charlotte must say that weighed upon her.

This would break her girl's heart.

"Eden?"

The couple stopped. Turned. And Jacob released his hold as Eden brightened to see her mother standing alongside.

"Mama! You've joined us." Eden clutched Charlotte at the elbows and let out a soft laugh when it seemed she remembered where they stood. "Oh no—what have we done? You're a countess in a public house, stuck now in the city for the blackouts."

"I apologize for the timing, dear. But I must speak with you." Charlotte looked over Eden's shoulder to Jacob, standing by with a brow that tipped over to concerned in a blink.

"What's happened? If it's the estate—"

"It is not the estate, Mr. Cole. But I should need a moment alone with my daughter," Charlotte bade, sharp and direct. "Now, if you please."

"Of course, milady." Jacob gave a soft bow of the head as he eased back. Until Eden reached for his wrist and slid her hand down to catch his with a little tug, asking him to stay.

"Whatever it is, Mama, you may say to us both. Jacob has earned a place among our number. And if this is about the legal case, I already know it is moving forward. He's just told me the worst of it, that he has to leave tomorrow."

"Has he indeed?" Charlotte directed them to the protection of the wood-paneled snug, then reached in her pocket. She offered the missive, the folded paper trembling ever so softly. "I am sorry, my dear. But perhaps Mr. Cole should part our company tonight."

Eden took the telegram. With careful hands, she unfolded it. And the shades of disillusionment painted her features as she read aloud.

"'To Jakob Kole, Esquire . . . convincing evidence of doubt in claimant's parentage . . . confirm derivation not from William Holt III, Earl of Harcourt, as referenced in newspaper articles dated August 1914 . . .'" Eden's glance darted to Jacob, questioning. And Charlotte's heart bled for the honesty in her daughter's eyes. "Jacob? What is this?"

He took a step forward. "I've been trying to tell you."

"Tell me what? Because . . . this looks as though you've been playing at both sides." Eden fought to fold the telegram back in its creases, her shaking hands all thumbs. She gave up, tossing it on the table instead. "Your name is Jakob? Jakob Kole—with a *K*?"

"It shouldn't matter. But does. In England anyway." He sighed into the revelation instead of denying it.

Eden glanced in the direction of the uniform she'd sent from the dance floor, still swirling a half-pint glass of amber liquid in his hand as he glared daggers from the end of the bar.

"That's what he meant by rumors? The Home Guard must have

looked into it. Because if you spell your name with a K, no matter the country, then it's a dead giveaway."

"Come, dear. Perhaps we should—" Charlotte reached out to her daughter with a graze to the elbow. Eden rebuffed the coaxing, keeping her eyes fixed on Jacob.

"You're German?" Eden demanded. "I want the truth."

"My family was—or is. But I'm 100 percent American. It was simply a change my father made to the company name once anti-German sentiment grew after the Great War. And we kept up with it as this war grew as well."

"And how are any of us to believe you now? The newspaper articles—what does that mean?"

"Eden, it's not why I came here. And as for what the lawyers found out at home with digging into the Holts' past . . . I didn't believe it. And I won't let them take their suspicions any further. That's why I have to go back, to convince them they're baseless."

"Suspicions? That was your mission all along, wasn't it? To come to England, plant seeds of doubt in my mind in order to strengthen your case and prevent a stranger from inheriting your millions? Or did you not want to tell me . . . because you know it's true?"

Pub goers noticed a storm brewing next to the dance floor as Eden shook her head, tears forming in her eyes. She backed up, wrapping her arms around her waist when he reached for her. And instead of what ought to have happened—her daughter stepping back and blasting Jacob for his serious breach of integrity—Eden turned to *her*.

"Well? The newspapers must have had some right to print Holt family gossip. Is it true? Is Amos Darby my father?"

"Eden!" Charlotte breathed out. "You cannot think to question this?"

"In all honesty, Mama, I have for some time. I know about the book Mr. Darby had with him the night he was injured. And the photo in its front cover. Just as I know what I saw between you two that day in the bookshop. Please do not do us both the dishonor of trying to deny it."

"What you saw was innocent. And certainly not enough for you to speak to me this way."

Jacob shifted his stance, to his credit looking oh so sorry he'd tossed paraffin on the flames of such a private affair. With Charlotte's virtue on trial before him and anyone else within hearing distance in a packed pub, the rumors of both a German and an illegitimate daughter in their midst could feed the gossips for a good long stretch.

"Eden? You stay. I'll go." He reached for her hand again, trying to ease her into the safety of the snug. "Just take this inside, you and Her Ladyship. Please? We'll close the door and you can be alone to talk this through."

"I deserve an answer now, don't I?" Eden swung her hand free, stepping back from both of them. Wiping fresh tears from her eyes. And sending a pain-stricken gaze to rest not on Jacob but on Charlotte. "This telegram reveals the truth—that Jakob Kole cannot be trusted. But it reveals a deeper betrayal that has existed from my birth. From the one who has been there for me. Always. Feeding false dreams of a fairy-tale romance between my parents and of the legacy of this dilapidated estate we've been fighting so hard to save. And that, Mama, is what I find so difficult to understand."

"Please. Allow me to explain." Charlotte drew in a steadying breath. "There is a history here that you do not know."

"Because you've never shared it with me!"

"Every woman's heart bears hidden corners, Eden."

"But this throws everything into doubt, and because of those secrets my whole world is falling apart. And now?" Eden shook her head, a pitiful action that didn't show malice but acute pain. "I look at you—both of you—and realize I don't know you at all."

"This is what you think of me?" Charlotte's voice shook. "To question the very virtue upon which we have built our entire lives?"

"He called you *Charlie*."

"And?"

"And that is a name I know cannot be from your husband but rather the man you have loved in secret—keeping the truth even from your very own daughter—all these years. And I can find only one reason a respectable woman would ever do that."

"Yes. I suppose there is only one reason." *I did it for you.*

For the love of a mother to her child. But how did Charlotte explain it now, that the greatest love she'd ever known was standing before her, wearing a darling new dancing frock, looking back with her father's trademark dimple in her cheek and emerald eyes that now showed only pain and accusation? How could Charlotte explain that every decision then, and every decision now, had been and always would be . . . for her?

"How do I know William Holt is my real father?"

Charlotte raised her chin. "Because I am telling you so. You know who your father is and always has been."

"That's just it," Eden whispered, her chin losing the battle against trembling. "*I don't.*"

War chose its timing in the cruelest of measures.

The sirens cried out then, their shrill warning penetrating the ancient pub walls. Dancers scattered and music screeched to a halt as bodies swarmed the bench for their belongings at the front of the pub and bottlenecked their way through the doors.

"Go to Drapers' Hall with the others. You will be safe there." Charlotte slipped the telegram back into her pocket and edged back from the snug. And the last shred of hope within her pressed a soft hand to the trail of tears upon her daughter's cheek. "To experience the deepest of loves for what it is, my darling daughter . . . I pray one day you will understand. I made a promise to someone, and that is why I must go to keep it."

Charlotte slipped out to where a spotlight moon created shadows the length of Bayley Lane and fled into the night.

CHAPTER TWENTY-FIVE

14 November 1940
Bayley Lane
Coventry, England

7:16 p.m.

$\mathcal{A}$ curtain of moonglow outlined craggy stone and wattle and daub where the back side of the Bayley Lane shops met the alley.

Eden fled through the gate. Her heels clicked on cobblestones as she darted past stacks of crates behind the bakery and a tarp-covered cart by the flower shop, following the path to its end at the blacked-out windows at the rear of Eden Books. Silvery moonlight illuminated the bookshop's back door, dressed in French blue paneling like the front and bearing a hanging *Closed* sign with blackout fabric drawn tight against splinternet-taped glass.

"The sirens, Eden!" Jacob called out from behind.

"She must have come here." Eden cursed her hands for shaking as she tried—and fumbled—to fit and turn the shop key in its lock. "We've a bogey hole shelter beneath the stairs. Where else would she go?"

"Her Ladyship would go to Drapers' Hall, where we should be. Or the street shelters. Anywhere but packed up in an alley underneath the open sky."

"But she said she had a promise to keep. What promise is here but her beloved shop?"

Jacob caught up to her just as the door creaked open, the bookshop's back hall darker inside than the silvery sheen spotlighting them in the alley.

"Mama?" Eden stepped in to be greeted by the barren stillness.

"She's not here." Jacob took her hand, edging back toward the path that led to the shop fronts on Bayley Lane. "Come. You can be as angry at me as you want tomorrow. Just as long as I know you're safe tonight."

"I'm not cross . . ." She shook her head and eased her fingertips from his. The uncontrollable humiliation of tears stinging. Confusion mounting. And the sirens' call they were so used to, sounding shrill and desperate now that they were not underground or behind walls of corrugated steel.

"Then what?"

"I cared for you!" Eden blasted him, stepping up with the challenge so the tips of her shoes bumped his. "Is that what you want to hear? The whole truth of that telegram? Fine, Mr. Kole with a K. I fell for every last word you said. Like a poor lovelorn sap. Between the rose garden and dancing and this ridiculous dress. And for the promise of saving my home . . . I believed you. And I ardently wanted to trust you when every instinct within my body said not to. Much the fool me."

A rumbling drew near, with an eerie overhead hum that echoed off the buildings in the closed space. Jacob shot a glance up to the span of starry sky between rooftops, then hauled her inside the shop and slammed the door behind. He pulled her with him down the hall and past the row of windows, pausing in the safety of the arch in the reading room's doorway.

It could be the RAF, couldn't it?

They listened in the dark, breaths hitching their bodies against one another, the wide doorway pressing against the small of her back as the humming of engines passed over.

Slivers of moonlight shone around the rim of blackout curtains as Jacob stared down, as if he only just realized he'd hauled her up against him and was holding so tight, one wrong move and their noses could touch. And in the terrifying stillness, he looked on her with a mixture of genuine fear and affection, followed by desperation in lips that couldn't help but graze hers. In a flash they became the pursuer in a kiss that was not a graze at all but as much a confession from him as her words had been.

"You care?" Jacob whispered, mouth still against hers. When she didn't reply, he gave a little squeeze against her waist to nudge her. "Please tell me I didn't imagine all that, or I'm going to have to insist you kiss me again."

"Oh, what does it matter now? When you're intent upon sinking us."

"No. It means . . . everything." Jacob swallowed hard, then brushed a wisp of hair back from her eyes with the curl of his fingertips to her skin. "I'm connected to this family. To Coventry. And to you, in those estate hills you fight so hard for. I didn't know how exactly, and I still don't know why. All I know is, I don't want to leave. Not before I explain. I'll send a telegram back, saying we can't move forward. Despite what my family wants, I will do everything in my power to fix this."

"What do you mean, you're connected to my family? For the court case?"

"Not just that, Eden. It's . . . something else. I haven't untangled what it means myself." Jacob shook his head, arms keeping her close enough to see the pain etched in his face even through the shadows. "It's Amos's pocket watch."

Eden stepped back. "Mr. Darby's watch?"

"Remember the chime we heard in the Anderson shelter?"

She nodded. "That little melody? I suppose so."

"It's '*Schlaf, Kindlein, schlaf*'—one of Brahms's lullabies. The lyrics match the face with the rotating sun, moon, and stars. The design is unique. Priceless, in fact. And unmistakable. I know. Because I've seen that watch and heard its melody before. So many times, in fact, it's forever etched in my mind."

"But how could that be, when you only just found us because of your father's will?"

"Only two of the timepieces were made—prototypes for a jewelry company started by two brothers in Berlin in 1905. I own one, inherited from my late father. I don't know how it's even possible, but the one my family thought lost years ago is in Amos's possession. And if this case moves forward, no matter the outcome for my family, I still need to know the truth about him."

"What are you saying?" Eden's heart thundered in her ears. "You think Mr. Darby is in some way connected to—"

A whistle suspended time.

A falling bomb cut the split-second world between Eden's words and its blast. Pressure snapped. Glass shattered. And Jacob's hold was torn from her own as the explosion ripped them apart and left the storied bookshop on Bayley Lane under a cloak of darkness.

➔∙◆

14 November 1940
Bayley Lane
Coventry, England

7:25 p.m.

Singed bits of typeset paper floated on air, giving the impression of a grim falling snow.

Eden lay with her cheek pressed against the hardwood floor, her ears ringing and heart beating a crescendo as she fought to gather her wits. The terrifying hum of planes crisscrossed overhead as the building groaned, settling into its wounded state. She raised a palm to a bookshelf the blast had wedged over her, the action stirring a layer of grit from ebony curls at her shoulders and inducing a coughing fit when plaster dust clouded the air.

If this was the direct hit they'd long feared in Coventry, citizens had been schooled in the basics: *gas mask on.* Eden grasped about the dark in a desperate hunt for her Waldybag, but her satchel had been lost in the chaos. The search netted nothing sure, save for a stinging spot at the tender skin of her temple.

She reached up—fingertips blotted crimson. Even in the scant light left over from the electric having blown, Eden could see that much. The wound mustn't be too terribly bad, though, for the blood flow was already waning. She pulled the cuff of her ivory and red pin-dot frock over her palm, winced as she pressed soft knit to the scratch, and looked around, her eyes adjusting to the darkness.

A faint glow shone down overhead, leaving the bookshop covered in shadows that stretched across the floor like cruel taunting specters. Books paved the hardwoods. Bricks lay in piles coated with dust. And ivory stuffing lay strewn from a gutted wingback nearby.

With wainscoting and the old brass knob of the shelter door pressing at her back, that meant the blast must have thrown Eden against the back stairs. Just that quick. And a wave of remembrance washed over her then. It hadn't been just her in the bookshop.

This time, it had been *them.*

"Jacob?" Eden's voice cracked in a feeble effort.

Maddening seconds of silence followed. Then . . . eerie sounds invaded the shop where his voice ought to have been.

A series of explosions ripped the streets, not too far down Bayley Lane judging by the shaking beneath her body. Match that with air-raid sirens, the distant wail of fire-brigade pumps that warned the local AFS had been deployed, and the strange popping of something that could very well be the much afeared broken gas lines . . .

Hitler's planes had come to punish Coventry.

And this time, punish well.

"Jacob?" Eden cried out again, stronger this time, and rammed her shoulder against the bookshelf in a desperate bid to shift its weight. "Jacob Cole—answer me right this moment!"

Dig. Eden's mind spoke nothing but *dig.*

The nearest book in a debris pile turned out to be *Death on the Nile*—an Agatha Christie title that was still selling. Eden tossed it out of the way, followed by works by Orwell . . . Tolkien . . . Faulkner . . . and the celery- and red-hued rural landscape of Winifred Holtby's *South Riding* that could barely be made out with its shredded jacket.

The hodgepodge of names meant the features section of bestselling fiction at the front of the shop must have been damaged. And a shattered frame bearing a smiling photo of her mother at the Coventry Stakes from years back meant the mosaic of photos on the reading room wall must have been damaged too, as plaster pieces with its peacock-blue wallpaper lay strewn in the mix.

Eden rolled to all fours, thinking to crawl her way out. But she crumpled down again, crying out as rubble cut into her palms and punished bare knees below the hem of her frock.

"Charlotte!"

A bellow echoed from the street, the voice from a blessed brave soul who'd come to help. The man called "Charlotte!" again, stronger this time, followed by the sounds of tumbling debris.

"I'm here!" Eden called back.

"Lady Eden . . . ?" A pause, and then, "Is that you?"

"Yes! I'm here." Eden tossed a book out from under the shelf, hoping it would signal the rescuer where to tunnel in. "By the back stairs!"

"Stay put. I'll come fetch you out."

A series of crashes followed, like glass shattering upon the black-and-white deco tile in the entry. Eden rose up again—this time avoiding the rubble trap—and stretched to peer out, hoping to confirm her location as the man tucked into the darkness. But her rescuer was forgotten in the instant her eyes adjusted to the full weight of the reality around her.

Half of Eden Books was . . . *gone.*

Instead of the entry's grand vault of a timbered roof above her head, the bones of the upper floors had collapsed into her mother's beloved bookshop, so only a starry sky winked back overhead. Neighboring buildings appeared wounded too, with silvery moonlight outlining walls of medieval-era timber now exposed to the street front. Fires flickered orange in the distance. And searchlight beams cut tracks through the sky, their eerie movements watched over by a brilliant full moon that on this fair night had surely guided German planes straight to them.

"It's alright, Lady Eden." An outstretched arm appeared, and a hand reached into the haven under the bookshelf.

That voice . . .

When Eden didn't move to take hold, he shimmied his palm. "Hurry now—before the next planes come."

Eden slipped her hand in his, leaning into the man's strength as he pulled her free. If the shop's state was a shock, her savior issued another when moonlight was cast upon not a stranger's face but the deep-russet-and-pepper beard and scarred visage of their longtime enemy—the very man who'd made her mother's life a torrent of competition and bitter strife these last many years.

The man whom she now looked on with every question in her heart: Was this her father?

Mr. Darby stood before her, his hair wild and windblown, breathing hard, like he'd sprinted all the way down Bayley Lane and was only just able to process that someone was alive beneath these collapsed walls. It had been rumored he never smiled. Though Eden remembered that day at the estate when he'd walked with Mama and could now see laugh lines tendering the corners of his eyes that betrayed something of an affable past. And even more rare for the man who'd shut himself away so the world could not gape and gossip about the scars the Great War had marked upon him, those same eyes now looked on Eden with genuine concern.

"Are you keen to stand?"

The voice was so clear now. How hadn't she realized it was Mr. Darby from his very first shout?

"I believe so." She tried. Held on. And waited for her oxford heels to steady beneath her.

He nodded but kept a hand braced at her elbow as she balanced over the uneven beds of rubble, then turned his attention to the sky. With gaze fixed, he led her to the cutout where their street-front windows had once been, and where blackout curtains had been laid as a carpet over the trail of broken glass.

"Come now." He urged her on as the sirens wailed through the empty street. "We ought to go."

Only just realizing where he was taking her, Eden curled her fist in the corduroy of his lapel and yanked hard, begging him to turn back. "I can't! Not without—"

"Is Her Ladyship inside then?" Mr. Darby stopped, staring back with an intense glare, as if the answer might terrify him.

"No." Eden shook her head. "But Jacob is."

"You mean your young man is in there?"

Eden stared at him, not correcting the presumption that Jacob belonged to her. He didn't. But all that mattered now was finding him and finding him alive.

"Wait—you're hurt?" Mr. Darby must have just noticed the blood because he turned her chin to the moonlight so he might inspect her profile. Then on an exhale, he issued, "It's not bad. But let me see you out now. Lady Harcourt would want her daughter looked after by a doctor. I promise you, I'll come right back for Jacob."

"No. I can't leave him. And I need to tell him that what happened between us . . . It doesn't matter. Please, Mr. Darby? Help me?"

For the hard case the man was, there was no argument. No questions. Just a nod.

"Aye. Let's get him out then." Amos took a kerchief from his jacket pocket, tapped the side of his head, and handed it to her. "Where did you say?"

Eden pressed the kerchief to her temple and pointed where the wall opened at the back of the shop. "There. At the back door. By the reading room."

"Jacob lad?" Mr. Darby cupped a hand to his mouth and shouted as they moved deeper in. "Stay where you are. We're coming in to fetch you."

"Jacob!" Eden shouted, scanning the remnants for movement.

Shoulder to shoulder, they angled steps over displaced layers of wattle and daub that had rained down from the buildings nearby. Searched under timber and around felled bookshelves. And the farther back they went, the state of what remained caused the blow to deepen.

"Watch that." Amos pointed out a hazard in their path. "What about the Land Girls? And Alec?"

Eden moved around it, grateful the jagged shard of metal hadn't the opportunity to slice her ankle. "They aren't here."

"You're certain?"

"Yes. They'd have seen citizens to the shelter at Drapers' Hall. Helping others is what Land Girls are trained to do. And ours do their jobs well."

"That saves looking for four then." Mr. Darby paused, then looked back at her, that haunting intensity in his eyes again as he asked, "And Lady Harcourt?"

"I . . ." Eden shook her head. "I don't know where Mama is."

"What do you mean you don't know? I telephoned Holt Manor. They told me she'd gone to Drapers' Hall. Wasn't she with you there?"

"No. They canceled the dance tonight."

"Here then?" Amos tensed his fist against the bookshelf he'd been muscling out of the way. "Your mother is always in her shop after closing. *Always.*"

"She was. But came to find us at the pub instead." Eden braced her hand to her temple, trying to sort out the jumble of thoughts muddled there. Not easy when bombs had just upended their world. "And then . . . I don't know."

"Try! You must think. She must've said something."

To piece together fragments of the evening at the Lion's Gate pub was to remember how everything had gone so spectacularly sideways. As the telegram spelled out its painful truth and the sirens cried, the admonitions from an overwrought mother had escalated to the long-overdue row that combusted between mother and daughter.

How could Eden tell him that in the chaos, they'd parted?

Badly.

It was why she stood here now. Dazed. Her head pounding and punishing through every frenzied heartbeat as they looked for Jacob. And as she tried to untangle the lot in her mind with Mr. Darby's stare pinning her down.

"Mama would not come back to the shop. Not after tonight."

Allayed for the moment, he went back to muscling debris out of the way, adding over his shoulder, "What happened tonight?"

"Nothing. Or something. She was cross. I was too. We said things . . ." *Things we can't take back.* Eden half hid behind the kerchief as she turned away, willing herself not to cry in front of the man who had inadvertently caused her tears. "I know about Jacob. His family. His past . . . She came to warn me. And I'm ashamed of what I did. And said."

Amos nodded. Seeming sorrowful but not surprised.

"All I know is she said she had a promise to keep and left."

"A promise?" He looked up and down the street, and the shudder of bombs shook in the distance. "Whilst under an Air Raid Message Red?"

"Yes. Just as the sirens went off. She could be anywhere right now."

"Right." Mr. Darby accepted the explanation, though something sparked anew in his profile, and he shrugged out of his jacket and flung it aside. Yanking linen shirtsleeves up on his forearms, he cut through the debris faster, like a long-dormant creature had been loosed from within and he'd defy Hitler's entire Luftwaffe if that's what it took to feed it.

They moved through the rounded arch doorway to the reading room, its back wall, too, cut in a jagged line against the sky. Behind it, the roof of Drapers' Hall was outlined by the horrific sight of flames licking high in the distance, an orange glow consuming points around Coventry's beloved cathedral.

"*Oh no . . .*" Eden looked on as the blaze raged in the medieval city center. "St. Michael's has been hit?"

"With incendiaries. Word came in at St. Mary's Street that Provost Howard called fire-watchers to douse the nave roof. A squadron of pathfinders hit Radford Road. And another tore up Bayley Lane to hit here. It's how I knew to come."

Of course. The Air Raid Report and Control Centre at St. Mary's Street would have known the locations of bomb blasts before anyone else, and they'd have immediately coordinated an emergency response. Mr. Darby must have learned of it, then run a street over when he heard their bookshops had been in the line of fire.

"This is a full-scale attack then."

"Aye. None like we've seen before. And if the winds shift . . ." Mr. Darby leaned in and pointed to floating lights Eden hadn't noticed until then—odd chandeliers drifting like ghosts through the sky. "Look. There."

"What . . . ? Those lights?"

"Flares."

She exhaled on a low, shaky breath. "Heaven preserve us."

"Between the fires and those parachute mines, what's left of these rooftops won't be long in coming down. And as soon as the incendiaries hit, they'll start fires. The Luftwaffe will follow those beacons to know where to hit us next."

Eden nodded her understanding. They'd have but minutes to get survivors to safety before the next wave of bombs would fall smack on their heads.

"Wait—" She stilled him with a palm to his forearm. "Did you hear that?"

A stirring caused fireplace stones to tumble from a debris pile first. And then in the midst of the chaos, a moan rattled from beneath.

"There!" Eden charged forward to a broken section of the reading room wall that had tipped over the stone hearth, and a bloodied shirt cuff extended from under the collapsed wall. "Jacob!"

Terror and bliss crashed together within her, and Eden dropped to her knees under their weight. The kerchief was forgotten; it drifted to the ground as she clawed at the debris. She was joined by Mr. Darby, who'd soon unearthed the hand with the familiar wink of gold from the Cole family crest on his cuff links.

"We found you . . ." she cried, gripping his hand and digging with the other. "It's going to be alright."

Mr. Darby relieved the pressure of bricks from Jacob's shoulder and neck. Both pulled back when a stream of crimson darkened his collar. Mr. Darby shot a warning glance to Eden. She understood, and as he took a flask from his boot and poured liquid over the wound, she tore a strip of fabric from her skirt to add pressure on top.

"Here, lads!" Mr. Darby shouted, waving to direct St. John Ambulance Brigade stretcher-bearers who'd begun moving up the street. "Over here. We've another."

A terrifying slow-motion reel played before Eden as strangers worked in tandem, muscling debris and shouting as fire brigades rushed down the street, all tossing cautionary glances to the sky as bombs shook the ground. She joined them, not even realizing she'd been holding her breath until the workers unearthed the limp, plaster-dusted body of the German jewelry maker's son.

"On three—" Amos slipped his arms under Jacob's shoulders and on the count, the men heaved him to the bed of canvas. "Look smart! Best make tracks before the planes return."

Eden stayed close as the men raised it, the litter balanced in strong hands as Jacob was lifted into the waiting ambulance.

Before she climbed in after him, a refusal to leave stirred within her. Eden turned back to Mr. Darby, finding him dusting off his jacket in the bookshop doorway. She wanted to ask what he'd do . . . where he'd go . . . whether he'd move on to the cathedral or seek out where Mama had gone. Or if they had all the blessed time in the world, to get an answer to her one burning question before it was too late and she risked losing another father.

He seemed to understand that she couldn't go without some assurance and approached the tailgate.

"Here." He slipped his jacket over her shoulders. Eden only then realized she'd been trembling. From cold or fear? "Go. It'll be safer to shelter at the hospital. I'll get word to Lady Harcourt where you've gone, soon as I can."

Emotion bade her chin to quiver as she asked, "You know where Mama is?"

"Aye. I believe I do. And I will find her. You've my word on that."

Eden swallowed hard and surprised even herself to offer the longtime enemy her hand. Mr. Darby hesitated only for a breath, staring at her palm as it hovered on air between them, as if deciding something. And then with care, he extended his right hand to meet hers.

"Mr. Darby. I don't know how to . . . ," Eden whispered, enclosing the scarred fingers of his right hand into the softness of her own. "Thank you. We're in your debt this night. Again."

He nodded. Just once.

In a knowing way—a very *human* way. And with an authenticity that in one instant buried the strife of long-wrought bookshop wars and too many questions of the past. How Mr. Darby could understand her, being the troubled soul that he was, Eden couldn't know. But somehow, standing before the remnants of her mother's beloved shop, he seemed to. And if anything of the past weeks had taught her to look beyond the surface of a soul to what lay beneath, Eden now knew why.

"Miss? We must hurry!"

With the ambulance driver's urgency, Eden climbed up to the metal bench, tucked her scraped knees in next to the cot, and took

Jacob's hand in hers. She offered a last hopeful smile to Mr. Darby as men moved to close the doors.

"Wait! Please?" Mr. Darby stopped the metal door mid-swing, his grip too fierce for the men to ignore. Then, turning to her, he offered desperately, "Today is 14 November."

Eden flinched. And her heart lurched because—*that date.*

How could she have missed it entirely? It was the date both bitter and beloved to her family. And it was the very same etched on the gravestone of the father Eden had never met—his grave by the glasshouse in the far rose garden, tucked away on their private property.

"Yes. With all this, I'd forgotten."

"It's the day your father died."

Arrested, she exhaled low. Almost terrified to ask the gentleman to explain further. "And how do you know that, sir?"

"I know because . . . I was with him." Mr. Darby anchored his hands at his hips with a heaved sigh and turned his gaze to his boots, as if surrendering to a hidden torment. "Lady Harcourt promised she'd always light a candle at St. Michael's on the day her husband died. To keep his memory alive."

Eden stared back at the enemy from across Bayley Lane, finding no more words needed to be spoken.

Lady Charlotte Holt, Countess of Harcourt, was likely dead. And unless Providence had intervened, it meant both of Eden's parents would have been killed on the very same day.

CHAPTER TWENTY-SIX

4 November 1915
The Western Front
Near Artois, France

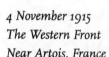f Amos was dead, he couldn't make sense of why a jackhammer was rattling in the afterlife, splitting his skull from the inside out. He groaned and raised a hand to the pain point at the back of his head, his eyelids cracking open as soon as it registered that someone stopped him.

"Don't touch it," the voice bade, deadly quiet. "Shrapnel wound."

Amos looked over through the shadows, recognizing Will lying next to him and both their faces pressed on a hardwood floor like they'd been tossed in a heap upon it.

"I thought it was a bullet that hit me—"

"Shh." Will pressed a finger to his lips, cutting him off, then gestured to the far side of the room. The silhouettes of two coat-clad figures stood, backs to them, looking out from their positions on either side of a window cutout.

There ought to have been solace that he and Will hadn't been killed—yet. But by the distinct rounded shape of the *Stahlhelms* on their heads and the shadowed outlines of scopes attached to their rifles, it was clear they'd awoken in a German sniper's den. And if they were captured by the enemy, it could be a fate worse than a clean death. No soldier wanted status as a prisoner of war when it meant a camp with deplorable conditions, starving through your days with the dreaded tension of whether some Jerry would put a bullet in your skull.

"They don't know we're awake." Will's breath fogged on air, stirring a tiny cloud of plaster dust from his lips against the floor. "Stay still as the grave."

Amos gave a tiny nod of understanding.

Doing his level best not to move, Amos made a quick survey of their situation. Darkness had fallen, with enough night air coming through the broken window that it could freeze a man's bones. There was no indication of whether they were on a ground floor or not; Amos couldn't see stairs. Only a closed door and wallpaper peeling from the walls. There was no furniture or additional men that he could see. Just two Jerry snipers, a shell of an abandoned building, and goodness knew what happening outside now that the bombs and machine guns seemed to have quieted.

The sound of conversation crossed the room, German words hushed but stark.

The two snipers were at odds about something. Amos's lack of education plagued him, but he could understand that much. And just as sure that he had no clue what the soldiers were saying, he could look over and know that Will did. His attention darted from the men to Amos and back—listening he was, and interpreting every word.

"You know what they're saying?"

Will gave a tiny nod. "They're arguing about which one of us to kill."

"Fancy that. Shouldn't have asked."

Amos guessed he and Will were back to telling the truth between them.

If fate or Providence had thrown them together, it wouldn't help to sugarcoat the details. At the very least Amos could appreciate that. Even though it meant as captain, Will was the senior officer and, therefore, more valuable. And it would be the quartermaster sergeant farrier between them who'd face a firing squad if anyone would.

"Why wouldn't they just kill us by the bridge?"

"Save us for a prisoner exchange?" Will shook his head, a tiny movement of his jaw against the floor. "But no one is dying today. Not if I can help it. So you will keep your mouth shut. No matter what happens. No matter what I say. Do you understand me, Sergeant?" He paused, then added an iron "That is an order."

"Aye," Amos gritted back.

Without warning Will shouted something in German, drawing their captors' attention. Amos flitted his glance from Will to the snipers, incredulous when one marched over with his rifle raised.

"Have you gone mad?" Amos pleaded with Will, backing up in an awkward crawl against the floor as the rifle bore down on them. "What are you doing?"

Will shouted something else to the sniper—a scathing tirade of German so fierce that spit ran off his bottom lip on the only word Amos could recognize: "*Holt.*"

Without warning the Jerry sent a boot into Will's face, the kick causing him to groan and spit a mouthful of blood on the hardwood. Amos rolled on his side, grateful his limbs worked considering he had no idea the state of his body. He tried covering Will with his torso, taking a boot to the abdomen that made his eyes water and spine recoil. And before Amos could rebound from the blow, he was yanked up by his uniform collar, boots dragging on the floor from disorientation.

The sniper spat German that he expected Amos to answer, whilst Will continued coughing blood behind them.

"I don't understand what you—" Amos shook his head in a wild denial. He'd floundered reading his way through the German poets and could barely grasp the basics of the language. "I don't speak German."

The Jerry yanked off Amos's army-issue belt, sending it to clatter on the floor. Then ripped his tunic open, buttons *pinging* to the hardwood as Amos's pockets were emptied. Amos was shoved to his knees after, same time as Will was hoisted up on his—both of them made to kneel before the pile of Amos's wares strewn on the floor: ammo, canteen cover, first-aid kit, the pocket watch, Will's .303 shell casing lighter, and a worn book they'd both seen too many times before.

Amos glanced over. In his peripheral vision, it looked like Will's head was swimming something fierce, making him sway enough he might fall flat on his face.

Poor fool. Blood ran like a faucet down the front of Will's chin from what surely had to be a broken nose, and he was fighting to focus his eyes like he couldn't see straight from the pain. Amos edged over so the front of Will's shoulder could lean against the back of his, should he pass out and chuck forward.

The Jerry shouted an order. Raised his rifle on them both. And Will gave a ginger raise of his hands behind his head.

"Hands up," Will mumbled to Amos, his hair flopping over his forehead as he rose up, giving the Jerries a defiant glare. "Seems they're a mite irritated with us."

"You don't say." Amos followed suit, palms cradling the back of his head. "What did you do—insult their mothers or something? I might have convinced you otherwise if what you said caused this."

The Jerry stooped in front of them, using the tip of his rifle to sort through the wares. He snapped something in German to the sniper posted over his shoulder, tapped the pocket watch with the rifle barrel, then stopped at the Dickens novel. He rested the rifle over his thighs as he lifted the book and opened the front cover.

The photo fell out, drifting to the hardwood in front of their knees.

That, Will had to see. Plain as day before the Jerry picked it up and moved back to the other sniper positioned in a thin slice of moonlight by the window.

"What are they saying now?" Amos mumbled.

"The one with the overactive boot is . . . making lewd comments"—Will sniffed, blood dripping off his chin as he struggled to breathe—"about . . . my pretty wife."

"Will—"

"I said shut it."

This can't be it. Not the way they were going to die, with Will's busted face and shattered heart when he saw the photo of Charlotte. And knowing there was only one reason it would have been there. Amos should have taken that boot. Should have received every bit of the snipers' ire. Should have burned that book long ago and left every last memory of Coventry behind before more lives were ruined.

Amos swallowed hard, listening to the snipers debating over the open cover of the book. "What's the other saying?"

"He's telling the soldier with the boot . . . we're officers." Will paused. Spit blood. And wiped his chin on his shoulder. "And to show some . . . respect."

Amos looked back, finding Will staring straight ahead through the dark. Like they weren't in war-torn France but back in the Holt Manor dining hall, and a vision of Charlotte could be standing across the room in front of them. And for every blessed thing that had ever combusted between them, Will Holt did the one thing Amos never expected: he smiled.

"If they have to kill us . . ." He sniffed and coughed. "Then I'd like it to be that one who pulls the trigger."

"Aye." Amos nodded, not understanding why his eyes were trying to burn with the sting of emotion as he gave a stalwart soldier's grin back. "Me too."

The tiny singsong of a watch chime cut the air.

The snipers looked up. Eyed them and the watch.

From the dark corner behind them, footsteps approached—heavy. Measured. And slow. And a voice gave a single command snapped in German so sharp that it shut the mouths of the snipers positioned at the window.

"I told you, Amos. I did not want to see you again in this war."

Amos watched as the figure stepped around Will, stopped in front of them, and knelt—another sniper. The familiar face stared back at him, eyes colder this time than they had been at Christmas.

"I am very disappointed that you chose not to listen to me."

"Aye, Frank," Amos bit back, ignoring Will's stunned glance as he looked back and forth between them, questioning what on earth was happening. "I didn't recognize the other two. But expected you could be lurking around somewhere."

"It's *Hauptmann*—Captain—to you now." He gathered the watch and chain in his palm. "You've taken good care of this, I see."

"And it's Sergeant. You looking for Toreador then?"

"Nein. He is safe outside." Frank gazed down at the watch, took his time popping the cover and looking at its face before continuing. "But since you and I are old friends, I'd like to think we can be honest with one another."

If Will was shocked, he didn't let it show. Just kept his eyes fixed forward as Amos answered, "About?"

"Perhaps you can tell me why the captain is trying to convince my comrades you are the senior officer instead of him. And was trying to use the name in the front cover of that book as evidence to do it."

Amos shot a glance back at Will, whose steely glare didn't deny it.

"I am curious, Sergeant, why Captain Holt here would seek to save your life instead of his own."

➻⋅❮

15 November 1940
Bayley Lane
Coventry, England

10:44 a.m.

The citizens of Coventry drifted through curtains of smoke like ghosts in the mist.

The shell of St. Michael's still smoldered some four hours

after the all clear had been given. Amos trudged down Bayley Lane with his Enfield slung across his back, navigating debris piles and smoking rubble and the remains of dismembered buildings, using every last bit of energy to shoulder the cello case he carried at his side. Rescuers loaded blanket-covered bodies onto canvas stretchers as he passed Drapers' Hall—a blessed miracle the guildhall had survived at all—and AFS teams worked fires in the skeletal remains of shops along the street.

All melted together. The battered and bruised. The stunned still digging out of their shelters and basements to find that their city of Coventry . . . was decimated.

With every step Amos had prayed he would find Charlotte among them.

As the fires raged at St. Michael's through the night, they'd battled flames that burned so fiercely that sandstone bricks glowed lava-red. Amos had joined the search of bombed-out shells of buildings. Carried the wounded. Unearthed the grisly sight of the dead—friends and neighbors, shopkeepers and strangers, and even poor souls he recognized from their tea queue. And dug through every inch of the rubble at Eden Books, twice over, finding that nothing but piles of books and a beloved cello had been left behind.

Relief came in small measure when he'd found Flo and Alec, shaken but alive at the Drapers' Hall shelter. Even as he'd checked shelters up and down the streets, and names of the killed began to be posted on the Council House wall, Amos had held out hope. And prayed. And defied the clawing unease of his insides, telling him there was nowhere to go but home if he'd found no word of Charlotte alive anywhere on the street.

Waverley Novels looked to have taken some damage, but the roof still stood—Amos could see its redbrick façade in the distance. And in its shadow, able citizens had set the wooden features tables from the shop for the tea queue outside.

He drifted along the back of the queue now, with dazed and soot-covered citizens who'd gathered at the end. It moved as quickly as always, with hands accepting mismatched teacups and saucers, and bowls of high-heelers with curls of steam rising against the crisp morning air.

Little Ginny Brewster, her woven jumper sporting a large hole at the elbow and apron smudged with ash, carried a kettle to refill the teacups of those sitting on nearby rubble piles. And then, in the midst of it all, his sleep-deprived mind playing the cruelest of tricks . . . Amos caught a glimpse of a crown of gold flitting by one of the tables.

Heart thumping, he stretched to look above the chaos of the street.

And there she was.

Alive. Beautiful as could be, like the image in the photo she'd given so long ago.

Charlotte moved about the sidewalk in front of Waverley Novels, holding something out. A photo? Asking anyone who would listen. With a bloodstain on the sleeve of her delicate ivory blouse, hair mussed with waves she tugged behind her ears, and ash smudged over her powder-blue skirt and the side of her cheek, she swept through the crowd, stopping to comfort a woman with a cup of tea and a patchwork quilt draped over her shoulders. And stooping before a young boy in short pants and knee socks and a plaid jumper buttoned against the cold. She gave a little shimmy to a stuffed bear he'd dropped and offered it in an outstretched hand. He took it and hugged the gift as he followed his mother's lead to walk on.

Amos reveled in the pure sight of her, only able to stare . . . to breathe . . . to allow tears to cloud his eyes a few blessed seconds before finding his voice. And before she left his sight again.

"*Charlie!*" he roared from the back of the line.

Some turned back. Stared in his direction—the people quick to startle after the trauma of the last hours.

"Charlie!" Amos called again, not caring, and stepped out of line into the bomb-blasted street.

Setting the cello on the pile of bricks strewn across the sidewalk,

Amos waited. Watching as she searched the crowd for the source of the voice. And when she'd found him, she locked in on his gaze.

Tears overtook her, too, just like when Amos realized this was not a mirage but they truly had found each other in the chaos. Charlotte abandoned the queue. Skirted the table. And took to a run in his direction, restricted only by her pencil skirt and the need to angle oxford heels around obstacles strewn in their path.

Only this time, there was no past to stop them. Or regret to hold them apart. And neither slowed until they blasted into each other's arms.

Are you real? his insides begged as Charlotte fell hard against him, holding tight as he lifted her shoes from the sidewalk.

Amos buried his face in her hair, crying against her neck. Gripped a scarred palm to cup the back of her head. And thanked Providence with every last breath in his body that she was alive and whole and once again in his arms.

"I looked for you. All night. All morning."

"Me too," she cried. "I found a photo of you in your shop. I've been down the street a hundred times, asking if anyone had seen you . . ."

Amos wasn't ashamed to whisper crying words against her ear. To shudder and shake as he held her. To wrap his arms around her waist and press a desperate kiss to her tearstained lips, for as long as he needed to before he could find the words to speak again. "I'd almost given up—God forgive me."

"Me too. I thought . . ." Charlotte shook her head, hiding her forehead against his scarred neck. "Never mind what I thought."

He leaned back, just remembering. "Eden? And Jacob?"

"They're alright. Both fine." She calmed, looking at him and catching emotion with her bottom lip in her teeth. "Jacob was taken to the same hospital you were after the plane crash. It's where I found them. I checked the hospitals first, right after the all clear this morning. Eden told me you saved them. You pulled them out and went to St. Michael's. And it burned all night . . . and I couldn't get to you. I had to watch the clock and feel the shake of bombs blasting the street, knowing you were out there somewhere. Helping others all that time."

Praise was foreign, undeserved. Amos shook his head.

"Look at me." She paused, eyes misty before him. "All that was left of my bookshop was part of the reading room. But you saved my daughter's life. Both of their lives. And I cannot forget that."

"How did you know to come back here when the whole side of the street—when even your own shop—is gone?" Amos wanted like wildfire to kiss her again. To make her his. To be hers. To not have a war between them for one more second of this precious life they'd been gifted. "You said you made a promise to light a candle at St. Michael's for Will every 14 November."

"I did."

He squeezed her tighter, the fear so raw it wouldn't allow him to let go just yet. "But I looked everywhere around the cathedral. I couldn't find you. Not in any shelter."

"I lit the candle yesterday morning." Charlotte looked up at him with those eyes, so honest in how they'd always greeted him. "And I made a promise to someone else, remember? In the Holt Manor library just days ago. That someone was *you*. And I knew then the only place I could go last night was to be wherever you were."

"We might have passed in the street." Amos shook his head. Felt a wave of pain in his chest at the mere thought and squeezed her tighter. One fraction of a second difference in any direction and they might not have been holding each other now.

"You shouldn't have been out. Not for me. You could have been . . ."

"But I wasn't. I knew I'd be safe if I could get to you. And I waited at the St. Mary's Street Centre all night. Because that was the one place, my love, you did not think to go back and check."

He dotted a kiss to her soft, knowing smile. "So you came here? To search at the tea queue?"

"Of course I did."

"But how did you know I would come back?"

"The cello," she whispered, looking to the dusty friend on the sidewalk over his shoulder. "It was the one thing missing from the reading room. And I knew if I was patient, and waited long enough, eventually you would carry my heart back home to me. Just like you did once before."

CHAPTER TWENTY-SEVEN

4 November 1915
The Western Front
Near Artois, France

I know where we are," Amos whispered to Will, keeping his arms folded across his chest as they sat in the shadows, their backs pinned against the peeling wallpaper of an industrial office.

"And?"

Amos tilted his chin to the window. "Look."

Just beyond the lip of the windowsill, sunlight illuminated BEF trenches and the razed village of Loos in the distance—a telling view that said they were on an upper floor. And to the ever-mounting anxiety of their captors, shelling had begun again, the battle outside drawing near enough to shake dust from the walls each time a blast got too close.

"You see the shadow? Sun's at a forty-five-degree angle."

With eyes only, Will gazed past the heads-down exchange of the two under-rank snipers seated in the foreground. They muttered with rifles in their hands, drawing imaginary maps in the dust on the floor and only glancing up every now and then to check that their captives were still seated in the shadows with the appearance of silence between them.

"So it is . . ."

"That means it's three o'clock, give or take. We don't have long before the sun goes down." Amos shut it for a breath when the Jerries glanced up. "They'll be forced to make a decision—hold us or put a bullet in our heads and make a run for it when darkness falls."

Will turned a bloody and bruised face to him, always offering that pompous bewilderment when someone of Amos's station showed the least sign of intelligence beyond a pair of laboring hands and cobwebbed mind. Amos would have rolled his eyes if they weren't all each other had at the moment.

"So that shadow cutting across the ruins—"

"I know. It means we're at the Tower Bridge." Will groaned and cursed under his breath. "Not good news for us."

"Nor for them." Amos couldn't help but add the spike of a rebuttal. "You look terrible, by the way. *Sir.*"

"Annoyed, Sergeant? That someone rearranged the nose you always wanted to get your fists on first? Get in line."

Amos eyed the snipers, the window—which might be their only escape route—and the things he'd take with him when they ran. A glint of sunlight winked off his gold watch, lying with the book and other wares in a precarious position by one of the sniper's boots.

If the French had taken back Vimy Ridge and the BEF secured the busted points in the German line leading up to it, the Tower Bridge was the one structure left that could make a shadow that large. Based on the shadow out the window, they were at least one floor up and directly under the head lift's high tower . . . in the center of a hornet's nest of advancing British troops.

The snipers were surrounded. Trouble was, they knew it.

"Those chaps are running scared without their leader. Their captain's been gone a good while now, leaving their trigger fingers to itch."

Will paused, as if thinking on it. "How did that captain know who you are? Last night."

"It's nothing. The truce, at Christmas. You were on furlough. He has a particular fondness for horseflesh—your mount being a rare bit of perfection of it. I could tell when I mentioned the horse: he didn't flinch. He said Toreador's still alive. And I'd venture to guess he's keeping him somewhere close. If we can get out of here, that horse may be our ticket back."

"So that's why . . ." Will clamped his eyes shut and tapped the back of his head against the plaster. "You tried to warn me."

"And why did you try to convince them I was the captain?"

"They might seek a trade for a more senior officer." Will shook his head, looking down at his boots. "It's my duty. An officer protects his men."

"Aye. But we're both officers. That's why we've got but one chance at this before the captain comes back. On the next blast—"

"Den Mund halten!"

The sniper with the fondness for kicking faces jumped to his feet, shouting with his Mauser in a dead point as he stalked over. Amos lowered his head. Will too. Both of them trying not to shake as the sniper shouted out a tirade, floating the tip of his rifle barrel back and forth in front of their heads, whilst the other sniper stood behind, eyes wide and complexion washed.

Gritting his teeth, Amos looked in his peripheral vision for any clue as to what Will might be thinking. Whether he'd back him up if Amos dared make a move. Or whether Will would even believe he had the guts to do any such thing. The other sniper had weapon in hand, but not raised. And certainly not ready.

Without warning, another bomb blast hit and Amos made the choice for them—*now or never.*

In the split second the blast shook the wall, the snipers' instincts curled their shoulders down in protection, and Amos sprang, hurling his weight forward to crash into the sniper closest. He grabbed the rifle and twisted so the Jerry was thrown off-balance, the Mauser torn from his grip to clatter across the floor as they locked arms and tumbled down.

"Will!" he cried, as the other raised his Mauser and Will sprang forward, dodging a bullet fired just shy of his head to pierce the plaster where they'd sat.

In a wrestling match of arms and legs and white-knuckled fists vying for the Mauser, Amos slammed a hook into the Jerry's jaw, dazing the soldier enough that he could rise, load the bolt action on the rifle, turn, and fire.

Twice.

A split-second series of explosions shook the room—the door crashing open behind them as Amos fired two shots in rapid succession, picking off both snipers in fluid motion, and then the *thump* when Will went lax and fell against Amos's shoulder, having taken an S round that pierced his upper back.

"*Stop!*" the captain shouted, his rifle trained firmly between Amos's eyes as Will tumbled to the floor. "Don't move!"

They held, both breathing heavy—Amos with rifle raised on the stunned Frank, the Hauptmann, who stood frozen in the doorway with an ice-cold glare.

"You killed them, ja?"

"Aye! And if you shoot, *then you shoot!*" Amos bellowed back and, uncaring what happened next, lowered his rifle. He held his hands out, arrested. And as the enemy looked on, he tossed the rifle away. "But I'm going to help him."

He knelt at the labored-breathing Will, whose collar was bleeding like a sieve.

Ripping off his own tunic, Amos applied pressure to the wound, Will writhing with guttural cries as he pressed down. Without warning a second pair of hands appeared, Frank's strength helping hold Will down against the hardwood.

"Let me see." Frank pulled the tunic back enough to inspect the wound.

Amos shuddered at the sight of a gaping hole at Will's collarbone that said the bullet had gone through, but not before doing a heap of damage. He needed medical attention.

Fast.

"I told them not to shoot. I told them the British officers were our only way out . . . The fools," Frank blasted at the dead snipers on the floor as he retrieved the brown leather first-aid field kit from the side of one of the bodies. "They have killed us all."

"I started it," Amos spat back. The sight of so much blood was nothing he hadn't seen before, but his hands shook nonetheless to see Will's blood flowing out as he rummaged through the kit. "But it doesn't matter now, does it? When he's bleeding all over the floor?"

"I saw what he did—stepping in front, taking the bullet meant for you."

"I know that!" Amos shouted as Will fought the hands that helped him, moaning in pain. "But the captain has a family. I don't. Help me? Please!"

"Give me that." Frank pointed at the packet of Boracic lint. "There."

Amos tore into it with his teeth, then handed it over, the captain pressing it and a gauze bandage to Will's chest. Watching the wound turn the white gauze blood-red, he shook his head.

"We are surrounded by your BEF troops." Frank sighed. "But if you go now, you can make it to the British line. There is a Regimental Aid Post behind the coal pit. South side. We gave the ground yesterday. You can see it from the window—three hundred yards out, dead straight at twelve o'clock."

Popping up then, Frank rushed back to the pile of Amos's wares on the floor by one of the bodies. He scooped up the book and watch, returned, and offered them.

"You can make it if you run. There is no one to stop you now."

"You mean you won't shoot me in the back as I ride Toreador away?"

The memory of Frank riding across No Man's Land that Christmas bounded back into his mind. Must have for the German, too, as he shook his head.

Compassion was so scarce in war; Amos almost couldn't recognize it for staring back at him. They weren't enemies then, not as

Frank looked down on Will's agony and promised that the one job he'd been given in this war, he would not do. Seemed they were willing to save a life, enemy for enemy and man to man, no matter the cost.

Or maybe to kill was the greater cost.

"Give him . . . my uniform . . ." Will's gritted entreaty silenced the room.

"He's right." Amos knew it was true. "The BEF troops will protect one of their own. And they'll recognize Toreador. My tunic means nothing, but they won't shoot you if you ride out in the captain's uniform—bloodstained or not. Down the road that cuts the village. Over the bridge to the last place our unit was. It may not work, but it's a chance at least."

Without time, Amos stripped Will of his uniform tunic—carefully, avoiding jostling in hopes of not tearing the wound further—then stood, offering the bloodstained garment to the enemy.

"Here, Hauptmann." Amos held it out. "*Go.* It's what Captain Holt wants or he wouldn't have said it. And I follow my captain's orders."

Frank tore off his German uniform tunic, took the bloodied one, and slipped it on. Then held for a breath, looking from Will's body on the floor, now going dangerously slack, then back to Amos. He took the Luger from his belt, turned it so the butt faced Amos's palm, and offered it.

Amos took it, adrenaline charging every muscle as he gripped the sidearm.

"I will not forget this, Sergeant," Frank vowed, slipping the strap of his Mauser over his head. He looked to the floor. "Nor you, Captain Holt." One nod and, disappearing into the shadows of the hall, he was gone.

Seconds passed by, long and terrifying ticks of the clock as another blast shook the windowsill. It sent Amos back to his knees and rained plaster dust over Will's place on the floor.

With no more time, Amos shoved the watch in his pocket, tucked the book in his waistband, and hauled Will in a fireman's carry over his shoulders, following the sniper's path through the door. Down two sets of rickety stairs, he ran. Keeping his back to the wall. Following the length of a smoke-filled hallway as bombs blasted broken windows and shook the structure like it was a house of cards. And defying the darkness in the corridor until he finally saw the bright light of an open door at the far end.

"God go with us." Amos adjusted Will over his shoulders into a surer hold. And with one steadying breath, he charged over the threshold into the hellish sunshine beyond. "Let's go."

CHAPTER TWENTY-EIGHT

15 November 1940
Bayley Lane
Coventry, England

12:02 p.m.

*T*he room lay still; a stark emptiness compared to the tumult of Coventry's streets outside.

Charlotte left Amos leaning his weary body in the doorway of his bedchamber to cross the room and pull back the blackout curtains. Light burst in, highlighting specks of dust floating through the air as her eyes adjusted. Sun cast a bright stream upon the humble space: a mussed quilt and divot in the pillow on his bed. A side table with a single lamp. The mantel lined with stacks of books. A bureau with a mirror and porcelain basin on its top. And two Glenlivet bottles with nearly all their amber liquid drained.

She'd seen it as they tried to help at the tea queue: Amos's hands shaking. His body about to fall over from exhaustion. And his nerves so rattled, Charlotte had insisted he take a few moments of privacy, to calm himself away from the rest.

Ignoring the bottles for now, Charlotte looked to the corner. She picked up a spindle chair tucked in its shadows and carried it to the light in the center of the room.

"Come." Charlotte patted the chair back. "Sit."

He obeyed, given the sound of his weary footsteps, and the settling of the chair followed as Charlotte turned to the bureau.

Opening the top drawer, she searched through the wares until she found them: razor, comb, shears, and a linen tea towel hanging on an iron rod screwed into the wall. She carried them over, laid them out on the bed, and, without the necessity of words, walked down the hall to the bath, filled a porcelain basin with warm water, and returned to his side.

Charlotte draped the tea towel over his shoulders.

And began.

Amos stared up, she knew, taking in every line and contour the years had tracked upon her face. His hazel eyes tender as they looked upon her, open and earnest, as she raised the shears to his skin and began trimming along his hairline. She gave attention to his hair and beard, combing and cutting and shedding the mask he'd worn for so many years.

Charlotte wet her palms in the basin and brushed warmth to his skin. Smoothed shaving cream over his jaw. And held her breath as she slid the blade down the first time, then over and again in a soft cadence of razor to skin. And stirred the razor in water to begin the intimate melody again.

"The bottles, Charlotte."

"Hush now," she whispered, dipping a cloth in warm water to sponge away the trails of blood and ash from his scars. "They do not matter today."

"I want to explain." Amos caught her hand as she swept the cloth along his smooth jawline. "Please. I need to tell you why."

"I know why. It's why I brought you up here now—no one else needs to know."

"But you don't know this." Amos drew her hand down with his and laid the cloth in the basin so she might sit on the edge of the bed before him. "I see death every time I close my eyes."

"Oh, Amos . . ." She bit her bottom lip.

Coventry was dying outside, and yet he saw that same tortured view every day of his life? She couldn't bear the thought.

"What do you mean?"

"I see it right in this room. Just as sure as you're sitting here. When the curtains are drawn and the clock ticks loud as a cannon through the night. When I'm alone, blood and bombs return. They wound down to my bones, again and again. It's as real to me inside these four walls as it was all those years ago on a battlefield. I cannot escape it. I can't breathe. And I can't rest . . . save for those."

Amos tipped his brow to the bottles on the bureau, the streams of sunlight cutting sharp lines to pierce the glass.

"I didn't want to need them. But I did. And I still do."

"I know that. And we'll see what we can do about it. But not today. Now you need to rest."

"No. I need to tell you that Will . . ." Pained, Amos clamped his eyes shut. Shook his head, a bit of leftover shaving cream just dusting the underside of his jaw. "He . . ."

Charlotte swallowed hard, a tear going rogue to slide down in a track to her chin. "He what, Amos?"

"In the end, Will knew you loved me. Even before he saw the photo I had of you. From the book? I didn't even know myself you'd given it to me until almost a year later. And by then it was too late. I think it's why he gave up at the front. When he had you and Eden and I had nothing left worth living for. Will was trying to send me back to you, instead of himself."

"Amos," she cried, or else she'd not get through what she knew he needed to say. "It's not your fault."

"I tried. I swear to you, I tried to get him out."

"Get him out of where?"

"We were nearly to the British trench line. I could see it. Could reach out and almost touch it. But a bomb caught us, and I didn't learn until I woke in a hospital days later that I looked like this . . . and he'd died in the bed right next to me. The morning of 14 November," he cried. Shaking. Hands gripping hers in a white-knuckled hold. "And I couldn't hurt Will after that. Not the memory you had of him, nor the image Eden has grown up knowing and is so proud of. I may not be her father, but I am the reason her father died. And it's unforgivable. I've had to live with that—God help me—every day since the war.

"When I came home, I had to have something of you left, so I opened this shop. On my own, after you opened Eden Books. When all I wanted was to ask your forgiveness. I don't want this anymore—the bottles. I'd have already poured them out if I was strong enough. But I'm not. I'm weak, Charlie. And wounded. And afraid . . . I'll never be whole."

Charlotte lifted her hand, slow, in an intentional skin-to-pain touch of her palm to the side of his face.

"There you are." She lifted his chin, looking in his eyes, tears streaming free as she brushed her fingertips over his scars. "You have been here all along, haven't you? Shut away in this shop, right across the street from me? Brave and true and stronger than you know. You've been trying to carry this alone. When you needn't. We all bear scars, Amos. Yet you think yours so bad, they cannot be redeemed?"

"No." Amos lowered his eyes, shaking his head as if guilt was an all-too-frequent visitor. "Will gave his life to save mine when I didn't deserve it."

"I need you to understand something. After Will's death, I received a letter. He'd already sent it to his man of business, and in the event the worst happened, it was to be delivered to me. And in it, he asked my forgiveness . . . for preventing you from meeting me at Gretna Green that day."

Amos's brow flinched in bewilderment. "He told you?"

"Will bore responsibility for convincing you that if you persisted and married me, and if you were killed in the war . . . any family we had would be left destitute. And I would be branded a woman of ruin. You see? Will used your love for me against us. And he asked me to right that wrong if I were ever to receive the letter."

"Why would he do that?"

"There was an amount of money for a trust Will arranged in your name—"

"And I told him I wouldn't take any money," he blasted back and tried to stand, as if pride had triggered springs in the soles of his boots. "I still won't."

"I know that. I'm not asking you to." She paused, letting that sink in. Imagining what kind of ugly exchange must have passed between them in France all those years ago. "But if you offer a confession, I have one as well. I knew you would never accept the money, and that is why it has remained untouched all these years. Until you were able to free yourself of this burden."

Allaying him with her hands reaching for and holding his, she exhaled.

"I never wanted this war with you," Amos said.

"And neither did I with you. Even when I fired the first shot by opening Eden Books across the street." She laughed a little, the weight of truth feeling less of a burden and more of a soft kindness to be able to share in jest now. "But I wonder, after all this time, might we change our tactics? As you shared the scars of those bottles with me, and if I were to share the burden of my own scars with you . . . might we stop warring and instead choose to walk through life at each other's side? Alone is a place the human heart was never meant to dwell."

"Am I a fool, then, to think a man can change now at my age?"

"Not at all. If there is a woman willing to aid the task." She smiled back, feeling hopeful through the tears.

"I can't say this is over . . ." He looked to the bottles on the bureau. "I'll pour them out. Today. But it won't be gone overnight, the wanting of it. Maybe never. I don't know if the hold can be broken. I've been alone with it for so long that I might disappoint you. I'm not a perfect man, Charlie. And I never will be."

"That is a relief. Then I suppose we should marry as soon as it can be arranged, Mr. Darby, so you'll never have to claim a day alone again. I hope another journey to Gretna Green is not too great a favor to ask of you, once all is healed here in our home. And as for the trust I know you'll refuse with every fiber of your being, perhaps we offer that back to Will's generosity and use it to heal his family land? We tell Eden together this time, both about the money and about us. And if you'd be agreeable, perhaps you could see fit to love me for the rest of our lives? If that's not too much to ask."

"Not too much at all, for an old friend." Amos leaned in, forehead brushing hers as he shook his head, and his lips inches away when he affirmed, "Because I already do."

CHAPTER TWENTY-NINE

15 November 1940
Stony Stanton Road
Coventry, England

7:12 p.m.

A fingertip dotted the end of Eden's nose, startling her awake. Opening her eyes, she realized she'd fallen asleep in the chair by the hospital bed, with her head on the pillow next to Jacob's. When she looked up, ice-blue eyes blinked back and he brushed a fingertip to the apple of her cheek.

"Eden."

"Y-you're awake . . . ," she stammered, rising up to inspect the face she'd worried might never look on hers again.

"Looks like it. I felt for Amos when he was in one of these beds. Feeling a little worse for myself now to have followed his lead."

Tears filled her eyes as Eden brushed the hair back off his brow and pressed a featherlight kiss to the bruise at the corner of his mouth. He turned his face toward her, unshaven skin prickling her cheek. Then kissed her back and raised an arm to curl her in a hug to his chest.

They lay for a long, quiet moment.

"Don't you ever do that again," Eden whispered without wit or guile, just the desperate need to feel his warmth. "Do you hear me? Not ever."

"I suppose I don't need to ask what happened. Judging by how this feels, I'd say I tried to make friends with a brick wall," Jacob mumbled through a return smile, then grimaced when he shifted his body.

"Something like that." Eden backed up, not wanting to injure him further.

The terrible sight of bandages covered sutures at his neck. A deep gash was stitched and swollen at his brow. Bruises colored nearly every span of skin. And even scuffs on his wrists and knuckles appeared red and raw, or else she'd have tried to hold his hand.

"They said you've a mild concussion and a fractured ankle." She tugged at her hair, an absentminded action to sweep it over her shoulder like she used to when it trailed down her back. "And the wound at your neck was . . ."

As if able to read the distress in her thoughts, Jacob reached out, opening his palm on the coverlet. Eden filled it with her own, careful as she laced her fingers with his.

"Still angry with me?"

"Yes. Always." She shook her head at his ability to jest even then. "But for an entirely different reason now, scaring me like that."

Jacob looked her over, trying to reach a finger to the scratch at her temple. Then glanced at her dress, his brow softening to notice it was the same from the dance, now covered in dust and blood under Mr. Darby's jacket that swam over the top. "Are you alright?"

No. Not alright at all. She forced a weak nod. "It's nothing. Just a scratch."

"You stayed."

"Of course I stayed. And now I fear this will forever have to be a one-dance dress. I couldn't possibly wear it again."

"Pity," he said, a coltish little glimmer at the corners of his eyes. "I wanted to remember the first time you wore it. At least the better parts of the night."

Noise bustled in from the hall—the only true disturbance now as the wounded kept flooding in. They sat quietly for a moment, Jacob looking around the ward with its high ceilings and crowd of beds, and nurses hurrying down the aisle to meet a patient wheeled in. There was some activity outside in the city streets, mostly the AFS teams working on the last fires. But rain had helped with that; a calm mist settled over their smoking city, and for all they'd been through, a subdued silence followed for the first time in ages.

"What day is it?"

"Friday." Eden didn't know why she looked to the blackout curtains covering the window over his hospital bed. Habit, maybe. Though they couldn't show her anything now. "Late, I think. Evening."

He paused, listening. "No sirens?"

"Not so far tonight. But they don't think the Luftwaffe is coming back after yesterday. At least not to Coventry."

"Why is that?"

"Because . . . nothing is left."

Jacob's features grew serious, his eyes pained and questioning. Eden could see he was trying to find a place to land, having woken at the doorstep of their utter devastation. Or perhaps anger coursed through him, knowing it must have meant an enormous loss of life if what she'd said was true, and Jacob had, in some measure, the same German blood that had caused it. Or maybe he even succumbed to fear, for if he dared ask, she'd have to tell him the attack had not left their small number from the bookshop unscathed.

"Tell me." He brushed his thumb over hers. And for the tiny gesture it was, it did give a measure of courage to break the news.

"Ainsley is . . . gone." Emotion muted her words on a pitiful sob. "We found out this afternoon when we couldn't find her with the rest. And then casualty lists were posted. Mr. Darby took it quite hard, feeling as though he'd let her down. Being the estate agent, he took all of the responsibility upon his shoulders."

"And that's why you said about the dress—"

"Yes. She made this for me. Made one for all the girls. It feels almost precious now, dirt and soot covered as it is."

Jacob gritted his teeth like blood boiled in his veins and he wished nothing more than to pick up his fists and start flinging frustration at the nearest wall. "How?"

"A bomb blast near Drapers' Hall. They said she'd been trying to help people to the street shelters when . . ." Eden paused. Drew in a steadying breath. "We were hit at Eden Books, too, in the first wave. Mr. Darby found us at the shop and dug us out—you and I both. With his bare hands."

"Did he? I'll have to thank him for that. And what about Her Ladyship? Alec, Flo, and Dale? And young Ginny? Did he find them too?"

"They're safe. All safe." Eden nodded, feeling both fortunate and yet racked with guilt that she still had the people she cared about whilst so many were desperate in poring over names of the missing posted on the St. Mary's Street Council House wall.

This was the desolation that had settled upon their shell of a city in the last day, with craters marring the streets, whole blocks wiped from the face of the earth, and bodies mounting with not enough graves to hold them. They were forced to accept a city left to ruin, yet none seemed able to.

"They've run the tea queue round the clock since the all clear. But the city center took a devastating hit—including Eden Books and nearly all the shops down Bayley Lane. St. Michael's has burned to cinders. Most all the factories and homes are damaged or destroyed. Hundreds are dead, Jacob. *Hundreds.* So many that this very hospital has been unable to identify them all. And they fear more are to come the deeper we dig." Her chin quivered. "Mama has sent telegrams to the WLA and Ainsley's family in London. An aunt and uncle, I think. She's invited them to stay with us at Holt Manor as long as they need."

He exhaled low, bracing a wrist over his forehead as he stared at the ceiling. "What of the estate? Were we hit?"

"Ginny came into the city with her mother, bearing news as well. Holt Manor survived. But part of the rose garden took a nasty blow. The staff were saved, praise be. But not the Andersons at the other end of the garden. And the glasshouse is gone."

"You mean if we'd been there?" He sat up, elbows against the pillow behind him.

She shook her head. "The shelters could not have saved us."

"Amos might call that luck."

"But you don't?"

"I couldn't. Not after this." Settling back against the pillow, Jacob reached for her hand again and raised it to his lips, pressing a kiss to her fingers. "Not now when I woke to see your angel face sharing my pillow."

"Jacob, I owe you an apology. For what I said—what I thought about your family? I feel terrible." Calculating the risk of what had occurred when he was in absentia, Eden scooted her chair closer. "Mr. Darby did too. And came to check on you."

"What did he say?"

"You won't remember, but when he saved us from Eden Books, he offered me his jacket when I was in the ambulance with you. Later, when you were in the trauma theater and I was in the shelter here to wait out the bombs, I found the book you spoke of, with my mother's photo. But I also found this." Eden paused, reached in the jacket pocket and, opening his palm, pressed the watch in. "It chimed in the pocket and I remembered what you'd said in the shop, about the tune? I told Mr. Darby and he said to leave it with you. That when you woke you'd know what it meant. And when you're able, he says he has a story to tell us about the man who gave it to him, and why. Someone named Frank. Do you know who that might be?"

Jacob ran his fingertips over the watch, staring at its gold face. He gave a soft nod and popped the cover, and she watched the shades of knowing pass over his face when he pointed to the engraving on the inside. "Here," he whispered, pointing to the initials *FBK* engraved in gold script. "*Franklin Beckton Kole*—my uncle."

"Kole. Yes, with a *K*."

"My jacket?" Jacob glanced around them, patting the side of the bed. "Is it—?"

"Here." Eden reached under the bed frame, then pulled his once pristine but now disheveled and bloodstained suit jacket from the shelf. "It's here. They gave me your things to hold."

He groaned, having moved too fast. "The inside pocket, please."

Eden found the weight of a watch in his own jacket and pulled it out, holding a perfect match in her hand. "How is this possible?"

Pointing to the inside cover, he continued, "*CEK*. Charl Eduard Kole—my father. He was to come to America first in 1912, to lay the foundation for a family jewelry company in Detroit. In seeing there were some tempers that boiled over with anti-German sentiment, he changed the company name to Cole with a *C*, thinking it might bar some prejudice. My uncle, being the eldest, would stay behind in Berlin to manage the family's holdings. They had quite a stable of horses and assets he felt he could not leave. And then tensions rose. Emigration became impossible as war turned probable. And my uncle was pressed into service for the kaiser while my father served his new country."

"What? You mean they fought against each other in the Great War?"

"They never met in the field. But yes. They knew each gun was pointed at the other. And the strongest bond between them had been who they were as young men—as both business partners and brothers—before the war. And I understood an absent father more than you knew, though mine was due to the demands of business. And the all-encompassing grief of losing his brother. You saw my suit waltz into Coventry and thought straightaway that I could know nothing of your situation. Or loss. Or hardship. But maybe for the first time, having a reason to get my hands dirty gave me pride in an honest day's work. And helped me understand a father I couldn't talk to before his death." Jacob turned the watch over in his hand, slowly wrapping the chain around his palm. "My uncle was killed at the Somme in 1916."

"Oh, Jacob . . . I'm so sorry."

"We thought the watch was gone with him. My father received

a letter from his brother, delivered sometime after his death. Uncle Frank spoke of a British officer who'd shown a great amount of courage in battle, and who saved his life by giving up his horse. Though my uncle's fate was sealed a year later at the Somme, he said the horse survived to be delivered back to the British. Upon reading the letter, my father stopped winding his own watch— never spoke of it again. But now here they are, together all these years later. I just wish he was alive to see it. It would have meant a great deal to him."

Eden set Jacob's watch on the coverlet, and he brought his hand down to meet it, setting Mr. Darby's alongside so the covers touched. And reached for her hand again, this time as if he would never let go even for treasures of the past.

"I'd often wondered what else that letter said. But my father took the rest of its contents to his grave."

"You think now your uncle is the connection to my father, or to Mr. Darby, given he has the watch?" Jacob nodded at her question. And given the path of the timepiece, it certainly was a possibility. "Do you remember what you told me, Jacob? That war may not change the past, but it could change who we become in the future?"

"I said that?" He frowned at some pain in his side, closed his eyes for a breath, and groaned as he hugged his free arm around it. "Sounds a little elegant for a busted-up lawyer."

"It's true, though, isn't it? Is that what you were trying to tell me at Waverley Novels when I first questioned Mama and Mr. Darby? You didn't want me to doubt my mother or who my father is. You seemed to be steering me away from the very questions that might arm your court case against us. I'd like to know why."

"It started out as just doing my job. I was only supposed to stay in Coventry long enough to deliver the papers. Just one day. But that first night when Amos and I were directing people to the shelters . . . something shifted."

"What was that?"

"That maybe there is more to life—more to fight for—than

wealth and privilege and shoring up our kingdoms. You showed me that by allowing me to work at Holt Manor. You taught me there's value in doing for others, in caring for others, and in fighting for what we know to be true, core deep. And I couldn't see that until now. The case may be moving forward, but it'll have to move on without me. The moment I'm out of this bed, I'm going to wire back. I won't contest the will. And I won't believe the lies in those newspapers. Not now. Not ever."

"But what about your mother? Your sisters?" The thought sank deep then, that Jacob would be giving up his own future too. His birthright for some connection they didn't yet understand. "What about you? And your future?"

"My family will be fine. Maybe they only have one summer palace in Newport from now on. And funny thing about lawyers—we've been able to find work as long as humans have had disagreements. I shouldn't think that's about to change anytime soon."

Breathless, she dared ask, "You'd give up a million pounds for this? *For me?*"

He gave a little brush of the hair at the side of her face, smoothing it to graze at her shoulder. "The man who isn't willing to give up everything for you is a fool."

"And if I should win but refuse the money in the end?"

"What do you mean?"

"Your family's legacy belongs to you, just as mine does to me. We'll find a way to make the estate thrive again. Mama says it often: 'Making do is what we Holts do best.' Well, I ask you: Am I a Holt or aren't I?"

"I think you are." He paused, answering with a soft, "Eden." Leaving off the title. Giving them both the intimacy of just being themselves. "But maybe you'll consider changing that name one day."

For the pain of the last weeks and the sheer trauma of the preceding twenty-four hours, Eden might have thought she'd never smile again. But looking at Jacob now, with his bruised face the most handsome she'd seen in all her life, there was no recourse but to lean in close. And kiss him. And show him every bit of a hopeful smile that just bubbled up from her heart to her lips.

"Could you stay a bit longer, Mr. Cole?"

"I think I'll have to." He looked down at the wrapped ankle propped up on hospital linens. "I'm not ready to walk away from you. Not now. Not ever, if I'm a clever man at all."

CHAPTER THIRTY

16 November 1940
St. Michael's Avenue
Coventry, England

What defines the human capacity to love?

It had always seemed to Charlotte the ability to find the inherent goodness in another, overlooking the failings and flaws in order to let light overshadow our darkest corners. But as she gazed over the piles of brick and twisted girders in the fallen sanctuary of St. Michael's, it seemed the opposite. To love meant to accept all—the grit and grief alongside the beauty. To endure the harshness of life not with despair but with hope. For if they could forgive the sheer volume of pain that left Coventry in ruins, what right had hate to remain in their hearts at all?

Will's sacrifice was made even more selfless and beautiful in Charlotte's eyes once Amos shared what her husband had done. Frank Kole's gratitude to a man he hardly knew, and his own brother's willingness to mark that atonement as a dying wish, had become a cord of communion drawing them all to heal, so many years later.

"You ready, Charlie?" Amos asked at Charlotte's side, helping stabilize her chair over the pile of stones near where the cathedral altar used to stand. "You don't have to do this if it doesn't feel right. Just say the word and I'll take you back home."

"Yes, I do. But I love you for saying it anyway."

Charlotte settled in the wooden chair as the crowds continued gathering, her flowing ivory skirt brushing against her legs in the cool breeze. Amos flipped the clasps on the cello case and opened it, gazed up at her, and handed over her old friend. She reached out for the bow and positioned the cello, seeing a gentleman unloading wares just as they were. Though his tools were an easel and brushes and a snow-white canvas that shone pristine against piles of rubble all around.

"Who's that?"

"I don't know much," Amos qualified. "An artist, I'm told. Goes by name of John Piper? They said he's come to capture Coventry on canvas, as it is now. Soon as he heard the news reports, he loaded up an auto and drove straight through. I should think he'll want to paint you in the scene, too, with the rest of the crowd."

"Well, that is some relief then. That I won't be alone up here."

"You won't be alone; I'll be off to the side in case you need a friendly face. Just look my way. And then Provost Howard will lead the king in, just there." Amos pointed out a doorway still standing in the southwest corner of the cathedral ruins. "He'll greet the citizens along both sides of the ruins. And then stop near here to listen as he's moved through."

"And I'll just play . . ." She breathed out, willing her hands to stop their infernal shaking. "Oh my. For the king of England."

"Aye, beautiful. You'll play. Just as you always said you would," he whispered, reaching out to squeeze her hands, knowing her well enough to realize there might be a tremble or two that needed to be allayed in them. "Just on a different kind of stage today."

"You don't think I should have chosen another selection?"

"Could you have? We both know the answer to that. Just pretend you're at our glasshouse. Playing Bach only for us. And the music will come back."

Amos pecked a kiss to her pout and moved off, leaving her to the spotlight of a humble chair and cello surrounded by ruins, and a dusty path that in a few moments would be walked by a king.

Golden sun streamed through the holes in the nave wall, the

tiny flecks of color fracturing through what remained of the wartime "cathedral glass" broken in its cutouts. A starling wove through the sky, diving against the clouds in a tiny blip behind the bell tower. Charlotte could hear the riotous cheers of citizens who lined the streets, chanting, "God save the king!" and the growing murmur of the crowd of officials who were straightening ties and dusting off suit jackets in standing room around the edges of the rubble.

Closing her eyes, Charlotte exhaled and welcomed the coming home.

The music flowed with her heartbeat as she drew the long lines of the polished body against her own . . . as she guided the bow to fly . . . and allowed her hand to fade into fluid movement on the fingerboard, the first deep-chested notes of the cello crying out to the vault of a brilliant blue sky.

Charlotte played as long as she needed to before opening her eyes again. And when she did, she saw Amos first, pride covering his face as he looked from her to the hushed crowd. Flashbulbs burst in a chorus of *clicks*, capturing the moment their sovereign had paused and was so moved by the devastation that he could not hold back open tears. King George VI stood solemnly, state uniform and polished shoes covered in ash, as he surveyed the great destruction and wept in communal grief.

For all the time that had passed since Charlotte had last performed, Bach's Cello Suite no. 1 returned from soul-memory. She'd not chosen it as an affront to play a German composition on such an occasion. But instead, she longed to echo without words Provost Howard's call for forgiveness over retribution—that love was needed by, and freely offered to, all who stopped in to partake.

EPILOGUE

21 May 1948
Bayley Lane
Coventry, England

*T*he sign is crooked. Isn't it?"

Charlotte fixed the blade of her hand to her brow, blocking the sun reflecting off the rounded glass windows of the shop front, trying to judge that *The British Booksellers & Co.* sign was indeed level.

"Aye," Amos echoed. "A bit more to the . . . left, perhaps?"

She stared up at her husband's profile. How in the world could a man as handsome and intelligent as Amos Darby be so unequivocally blind—and *wrong*—about what was right in front of his nose?

"You mean to the right."

Amos tilted his head a bit, then nodded. "It's exactly what I meant, love. Down and to the right."

"Now is not the time to placate me, Amos. It needs to go up and to the right. Princess Elizabeth's auto will drive right by here on her tour to reopen Broadgate tomorrow. And everything must be just so. It's for the pride of Bayley Lane—and for Coventry to rise again before the world. We must be in our best looks."

"Then let's make it right." He pressed a beardless kiss to her cheek and stepped toward the ladders straddled over the sidewalk, the workers hanging their new sign over the brick and French blue–paneled façade. "I'll just go tell them that Her Ladyship wants this bookshop opening to be a grand occasion. And if the sign is unbalanced, then . . . I can't account for how many Austen books we may not sell. And that would be a great tragedy, aye?"

"*Aye*. It really would." She laughed as she slid glasses over her nose to head back to work in the shop. Then called out, "And I'll put every last Sir Walter Scott novel on the lowest shelf if you're not careful. And flood your side of the office!"

The heartbeat of Coventry had always survived, even if the sound of laughter, the smell of fresh paint, and splashes of color on new signs took years to return.

Rebuilt shop fronts were starting to pop up along Bayley Lane. The bakery, with its wafting scents of fresh-baked bread and Godcakes—if ongoing rationing held the supply of pastry a little thin. The flower shop had reopened, too, boasting buckets of May blooms on either side of the front door, its lavender hue crowned by a lily of the valley bower, which was rumored to be the visiting princess's favorite. And the Darbys' bookshop was built up from the ashes of the city center, the final design combining what they'd lost of both shops into one singular dream that brightened the corner of Bayley Lane once again.

"See?" Amos returned to her side, slipping an arm around her waist to hug her close so she couldn't sneak off to work but was held to gaze up at the sign. "I told you. To the left."

"If Eden were here, she'd have agreed with me. She's always been a proper judge of what a bookshop needs."

"And an estate too. Our agent at Holt Manor does have her wits about her. Like her mother, Lady Eden is." He took his watch from his waistcoat, popped the cover. "But I'm sorry to say they're running late. So you'll have to make do with your husband's opinion, milady. If that holds any weight with you."

"Of course it does. But Jacob said they are coming?"

"He telephoned. Said he and Alec had a time with the glasshouse—some of the panes arrived broken and the work crew didn't finish as early as they wanted today. And Eden and Flo are still working at the rose garden, so it'll be their husbands to see the children are ready. I'd gather our grandsons are creating a bit of a bother in the background, with Flo and Alec's girls as well. It sounded like another war brewing when Jacob telephoned from the manor."

"I knew you should have stayed to make certain everything went off properly. Seeing the Spitfires out of the estate was one thing. But the glasshouse is such a big job to burden them with."

"You think anything having to do with the estate is too big a job for Eden and her husband to look after? You realize they'll be looking after Holt Manor long after we're gone."

"Of course I know that. I didn't mean to suggest anything less. It's just . . ."

The shades of indecision passed over her profile, as Amos turned to her, slipped his hands into his trouser pockets, and, with his clean-shaven face boasting a knowing smile, tipped a brow in question at the wringing hands in front of her waist.

"I know that look every time it lands on your pretty face. But no more work for you today." He waited as she picked up on his meaning and took her glasses off to fold and stow back in her skirt pocket. "This is a special occasion. Eden and Flo will have their families here for the opening. They wouldn't miss Ainsley's dedication for the world. I can promise you that."

"But there's so much to think of. Princess Elizabeth herself is decorating you for your work with veterans at the convalescent home. And how you've lobbied for more support of veterans and their families after the war, especially for those burdened as you were. We can't miss an honor like this. But then we've had a wire from Dale that she's arriving on the late train—some publishing soirée in London has run over time. And Ginny's university schedule is such that I don't even know if she can catch the bus to—"

"Charlie? Hush." Amos pulled his hands from his pockets and opened them palms up in front of her. He waited until she accepted before drawing her in close enough to whisper away from the workers. "We've waited long enough for this, haven't we? We'll all be here to see the shop open. As it should be. With the original booksellers to christen it, and Ainsley and all of Coventry remembered. You did a good thing here, bringing our lot together."

"*We* did it. Remember? Partners, fifty-fifty. That's what you said."

"Aye. But it was your thought to stop this battle across Bayley Lane and come together to see us through the larger war on our doorstep. There's not another woman on earth I could be prouder of than I am of you right now. And that's something considering a princess is going to pin the front of my coat."

Scars of the past—she wouldn't have changed them.

Not now, when Charlotte could return his smile. Or look up at Amos and see the sun brighten the scars on his face and find him all the more exquisite for having endured them. Some pain would never go away. Some choices could never be altered. But if they'd learned anything from the beauty and brokenness of this world together, it was that light always overshadowed the darkness. And home would always be the place she had with him.

~ The End ~

AUTHOR'S NOTE

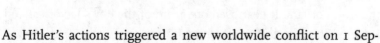

As Hitler's actions triggered a new worldwide conflict on 1 September 1939, the people of Coventry had already been planning for what was to come by late summer the year before.

Trench digging had begun in public parks, and concrete-lined shelters would follow soon after. Coventry's many factories shifted to increased production of wartime goods—such as gas masks and gum shoes. And as England had been readying its industries to switch to airplane parts production (should it be needed) as early as 1935, it was Coventry's booming automobile manufacturing sectors that would soon become integral to the war effort, producing parts for bombers named Whitley, Mosquito, Lancaster, Manchester, and the RAF's famed Spitfire.

All signaled for Coventry, too, war loomed quite close to home.

Air-raid sirens first rang out across Coventry on 25 June 1940. Hitler's Luftwaffe (a.k.a. the German Air Force) would target the West Midlands over the following weeks, with bombing raids that resulted in loss of civilian life at sites throughout the city and villages beyond—but nothing like the devastating attack on the night of 14–15 November 1940, in the horrific events of the Germans' Operation Moonlight Sonata, which would become known as the Coventry Blitz.

The first bombs fell at 7:20 p.m. local time on a crisp autumn evening with a remarkable full moon. Within four minutes, reports of fires and broken gas lines flooded the office of the chief fire operator of Coventry. And in a raid that would span some eleven hours and involve an estimated five hundred Luftwaffe planes, the city would endure a devastating barrage of incendiaries, five hundred tons of HEs (high-explosive bombs), oil bombs, flares, and parachute mines, as well as the testing of the Germans' new destructive weapon: the explosive incendiary bomb.

Though estimates vary, in the end this lethal combination saw thirty thousand incendiary bombs pummel the city's manufacturing hub, killing some six hundred civilians and injuring nearly a thousand others. It destroyed one-third of the city's factories (and inflicted damage to the other two-thirds), damaged or destroyed an estimated thirty-seven thousand homes, and burned entire city blocks with fire so intense, it was reported that buildings' sandstone bricks glowed red—including those around Coventry's famed medieval cathedral, St. Michael's. The fiery glow in the sky over Coventry was said to have been so violent that it was reported by German bombers as they flew over the English Channel some 266 kilometers away.

In its aftermath, the Coventry Blitz raid was dubbed a complete success by the Nazi regime, who would coin a new term in modern warfare: *Coventrieren*, meaning "to devastate, or raze a city to the ground." Coventry is still referenced as one of the sites of "the Forgotten Blitz"—the devastation that stretched beyond London, but in less reported Blitz bombings of cities across England (such as Norwich, Liverpool, Leicester, and Coventry) and Scotland (Clydebank, Greenock, Glasgow, Aberdeen, and Peterhead—the last being the second-most bombed location across Great Britain, enduring some twenty-eight raids).

In the decades since the Coventry Blitz, it has been theorized that Prime Minister Winston Churchill's cabinet had not only received intelligence reports that an attack over Coventry was imminent but, once having strong evidence for that impending disaster, failed to act to prevent it. One belief is that though Whitehall had reports attacks were to occur, they did not have definitive proof Coventry was the chosen site. Another belief is that Britain's highest levels of government chose not to warn authorities in Coventry, as it would have alerted the enemy that

Bletchley Park had cracked the German armed forces' "Enigma Code" of encrypted messages—a potentially disastrous move that could have serious ramifications in the larger worldwide conflict.

While still debated, the stories of Churchill's inaction to prevent the Coventry Blitz are generally discredited by historians, though the people of Coventry did endure devastation that was largely buried by the British press during the war years—hence coining the term "the Forgotten Blitz." The decision to quell reports of the Luftwaffe's bombing in areas outside of London (principally the graphic ruin and loss of life seen in Coventry) was believed to have been made in order to keep overall morale boosted across England's battered shores—a critical factor in a yearslong battle to defeat Hitler and the Axis powers.

Part of the necessary component for England to triumph in the World War II effort was to bolster the contribution and resilience of those fighting at home—such as those in the Women's Land Army (WLA). First established during the latter part of the Great War, the WLA had seen some twenty-three thousand enrollees placed into active service from 1917 through the end of the war. By 1939 a second worldwide conflict meant the WLA was called upon once more, this time with food production becoming an urgent need and rationing instituted early in the first year of the war.

London girls were plucked from the bustle of the cities and sent to farms and open land across the United Kingdom by the thousands, to do their duty for king and country—many living in group hostels that served only basic needs. By 1944 the WLA is estimated to have housed some twenty thousand women in seven hundred hostels across the Commonwealth with assignments in fields and farms, encompassing work such as tractor driving, planting and harvesting, dairy production and milk rounding, livestock care, timber and forestry work, poultry and sheep farming, gardening, and the lesser desired tasks of ditch digging and assignment to "anti-vermin squads," or official rat-catcher roles. All of this was managed under sometimes harsh weather conditions in isolated posts far from the luxuries of city life—a shock to the systems of many metropolitan Land Girls assigned to rugged locations across northern England and Scotland.

Even with paper shortages and production disruptions during the war, stories became a refuge to many, like the found family in the bookshops on Bayley Lane. From books written and published during the war years to official publications for the WLA workers across the United Kingdom (such as *The Land Girl Magazine* or *Land Girl*, the official manual published for WLA volunteers in 1941) and shelter communities who crafted their own neighborhood bulletins in London Tube stations and beyond, wartime publications read like a diary of those who bravely endured the nightly barrage of Blitz bombings in 1940 and 1941.

As with the many stories to come out of Britain during the war, keen students of history will recognize real historical figures in this novel, such as Lord Beaverbrook, Britain's minister of aircraft production; Beaverbrook's secretary, David Farrer; official World War II artist John Piper (who famously painted the destruction of St. Michael's Cathedral on-site after rushing to Coventry the day after the attack); King George VI (England's sovereign, who visited Coventry on 16 November 1940 to tour the devastation firsthand and raise the spirits of the people); and the Very Reverend Richard "Dick" Howard (provost of Coventry Cathedral from 1933 to 1958)—who is credited with calling for forgiveness in a mass funeral service at London Road Cemetery on 20 November 1940, with his famed words, "Let us vow before God to be better friends and neighbors in the future, because we have suffered this together and have stood here today."

Included in this novel are accounts of more irregular incidents leading up to the Coventry Blitz bombings—some with no seeming connection to each other (and which were included for the fictional purposes of this novel). On 24 May 1940, a plane clipped a barrage balloon's steel cable and crashed in a cricket pitch on Binley Road, but the incident involved a British Hampden bomber with engine trouble—a crash that unfortunately killed the crew on board. "Robin's Nests" were indeed employed across England's countryside to hide Spitfires on farms—in barns and outbuildings—with the British government seeking to keep them from bunching on RAF airfields from July 1940 onward. And it was recorded on 3 November 1940 that on an estate some sixty miles from Coventry was found German paratrooper gear, folded and concealed in a hedgerow, including a parachute and food parcel that had been opened and eaten. All of this before the Coventry Blitz might have been simply incidents indicative of events during wartime. But after the events of that fateful night, a string of such happenings might paint a portrait of the landscape of dire events that were to come.

In this novel, the Coventry Blitz serves as the backdrop for a story that could have been mirrored in a host of other cities across Europe and the world. In the face of the tremendous loss of life, the resolve of a people determined not to bend—and certainly never to break—and the resilience of a generation to rise up with remarkable courage, faith, and fortitude . . . this is the legacy of the Coventry Blitz that we research and write about today.

May history teach us to steward these lessons well.

ACKNOWLEDGMENTS

"When you read a book as a child, it becomes a part of your identity in a way that no other reading in your whole life does . . ."

A bookseller deals in magic; they understand what it means to share the art of the human experience and do so as their life's work. Ask a bookseller about the stories that have changed them—like Kathleen Kelly's quote in the 1998 film *You've Got Mail*—and they have an endless stream of answers. And as the beloved film remains an ode to the enchantment that is books, bookshops, and the journeys of our own life stories, the second-chance romance of warring bookshop owners in this novel evolved as this author's vintage-inspired nod to it. (As is Eden Books: *"Patricia Eden, Eden Books . . ."*) And it is to the generations of booksellers who have been and who will be—the readers, writers, waymakers, and friends—that this novel is so lovingly dedicated.

Appreciation goes to the archives team at the Coventry History Centre of the Herbert Art Gallery and Museum in Coventry, England. Their generosity in providing researchers with virtual access to maps and photos, newspaper articles, building plans, and other historical data on the city of Coventry proved invaluable to the crafting of this story.

The heart of this novel is about the stories we live.

To the entire publishing family at Thomas Nelson, and especially to dear friend and editor Becky Monds, who has forever changed the story I've lived: Your heart speaks for itself. I'm humbled to have spent over a decade of storytelling together (*What!*)—the best years of my life so far. To Julee Schwarzburg: We did this again! And I've loved every minute of laughing with and learning from you. For friends who remained encouraging dream-defenders during the writing of this book, I can't thank you enough: Sarah Ladd, Katherine Reay, Beth Vogt, Maggie Walker, Marti Jackson, and Jodi Seevers—the last of whom, with wisdom, reminded me to always look inward to find what is true. To Rachelle Gardner: You know you've always been more than an agent. For the leader, mentor, peer, and dear friend you are who's changed my life . . . thank you for believing in me.

The debt I owe to the faithful in life cannot be put into words. To Jeremy, Brady, Carson, and Colt: It is the privilege of my life to share every day with you. I love you more than words can say. To my dad, Rick; my momma, Lindy; and sis, Jen: We'll always be the family we were once upon a time. I'm so thankful for you. And to the Savior who's never left: You're still here, in every word. In my heart. And in every thank-you I'll ever write.

FURTHER READING

Aslet, Clive. *The Story of the Country House*. New Haven, CT: Yale University Press, 2021.

Bell, Amy Helen. *London Was Ours: Diaries and Memoirs of the London Blitz*. London: I. B. Tauris & Co. Ltd., 2021. First edition published 2008.

Heffer, Simon. *The Age of Decadence: The History of Britain: 1880–1914*. New York: Pegasus Books, 2021.

Larson, Erik. *The Splendid and the Vile: A Saga of Churchill, Family, and Defiance During the Blitz*. New York: Crown, 2020.

McGrory, David. *Coventry's Blitz*. Gloucestershire: Amberley Publishing, 2015.

Nicholson, Virginia. *Millions Like Us: Women's Lives During the Second World War*. London: Penguin Books, 2011.

Shewell-Cooper, W. E. *Land Girl: A Manual for Volunteers in the Women's Land Army 1941*. Gloucestershire: Amberley Publishing, 2011 (reprint).

Tyrer, Nicola. *They Fought in the Fields: The Women's Land Army*. Gloucestershire: History Press, 2008.

DISCUSSION QUESTIONS

1. From Dickens to Austen, or Sir Walter Scott to the contemporary authors of 1940s England, an undercurrent of the characters' beloved books is carried throughout this novel. What are your favorite books? Why have they endured the test of time to remain on your list?

2. Though the heroines in this novel are unorthodox in battling propriety in order to fight for their dreams, Charlotte, Eden, Ginny, and the Land Girls are all bound by societal expectations of the day. What friction existed for women in both the Great War and World War II as business owners, wives and mothers, and defenders of the home front? What were they able to achieve despite the obstacles in their paths?

3. From deep friendship in their youth to an abiding love through adulthood, Charlotte and Amos's relationship changes through the decades. Had Charlotte married Amos instead of Will in 1914, how would their relationship have differed from their second-chance romance in 1940? Was theirs a deeper affection because of the stories they lived in order to find each other again?

4. When Charlotte discovers the empty Scotch bottles in Amos's bookshop, she realizes physical scars may be a tangible portrait of the pain Amos endured in the Great War, but it is the hidden scars of past trauma, alcoholism, and guilt and shame that he's battled with most of his adult life. How does our private pain differ from the scars the world can see? What changes when we allow others to walk with us in our pain?

5. When Jacob first arrives at Holt Manor, the circumstances of his life and Eden's are not dissimilar. But in witnessing Eden's dedication to the land and her father's legacy and to those working on the estate, Jacob finds his view of wealth and privilege is forever altered. How does finding a new purpose change Jacob's view of his life? How does Jacob change Eden's view of what's important and what she's willing to fight for?

6. Amos and Will are put together in the same unit during the Great War—called Pals Battalions—and must confront their mutual dislike at several turns during the course of the conflict. Why do these men ultimately show each other compassion and courage, each one even risking his life for the other? When Amos finally asks Charlotte for forgiveness after Will's death, how does her view of her late husband change?

7. The November 1940 bombing of Coventry remains one of the most disastrous Blitz bombings of World War II, coined "the Forgotten Blitz" for many of the areas devastated outside of London. How did Coventrians band together before, during, and after the Coventry Blitz? Where have you seen communities come together in the wake of devastation or extraordinary circumstances?

8. From rationing to blackouts, doused headlamps for road travel, and the hiding of Spitfire planes in "Robin's Nests" across the countryside, how did England prepare for an expected invasion at the start of World War II? What risks were involved and bravely endured by the citizens during both wars?

9. Throughout the generations, booksellers have been harbingers of the stories we love. Which bookshops are your favorites, and why have they made lasting impressions?

From the Publisher

GREAT BOOKS

ARE EVEN BETTER WHEN THEY'RE SHARED!

Help other readers find this one:

- Post a review at your favorite online bookseller

- Post a picture on a social media account and share why you enjoyed it

- Send a note to a friend who would also love it—or better yet, give them a copy

Thanks for reading!

LOOKING FOR MORE GREAT READS? LOOK NO FURTHER!

THOMAS NELSON
Since 1798

Visit us online to learn more:
tnzfiction.com

Or scan the below code and sign up to receive email updates
on new releases, giveaways, book deals, and more:

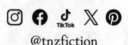

@tnzfiction

ABOUT THE AUTHOR

Author photo © Whitney Neal Studios

KRISTY CAMBRON is an award-winning author of historical fiction, including her bestselling debut, *The Butterfly and the Violin*, and an author of nonfiction, including the Verse Mapping Series Bibles and Bible studies. Kristy's work has been named to *Publishers Weekly* Religion & Spirituality Top 10, *Library Journal's* Best Books, and *RT Reviewers'* Choice Awards; received 2015 and 2017 INSPY Award nominations; and has been featured by CBN, Lifeway Women, Jesus Calling, *Country Woman* magazine, *MICI Magazine*, Faithwire, Declare, (in)Courage, and Bible Gateway. She holds a degree in art history / research writing and lives in Indiana with her husband and three sons, where she can probably be bribed with a peppermint mocha latte and a good read.

→··←

Connect with Kristy at:
kristycambron.com and
versemapping.com.
Instagram: @kristycambron
Twitter: @KCambronAuthor
Facebook: @KCambronAuthor
Pinterest: @kcambronauthor